Love to

Book Three
of
The Absence of Pity Trilogy

Also by Richard A. McDonald

The Absence of Pity Trilogy
Moral Chains - Book One
The Flattery of Knaves - Book Two
Love to Justice - Book Three

The Presence of Hope Trilogy
The Counsels of the Wise and Good – Book One
Vanity and Presumption – Book Two
Sobriety of Understanding – Book Three

Coming in 2024
The Chronicles of Insuldom
The Bond - Volume One
The Rend - Volume Two
The Cusp - Volume Three

Exclusively available for sale on Amazon

Copyright © 2016 Richard A. McDonald

All rights reserved.

This book is a work of fiction, and, except in the case of historical fact and character, any resemblance to actual persons living or dead, is purely coincidental.

(Second Edition 2024)
ISBN: 9781537429205

Cover Design.
Last Resting Place?
By RichDesignsLtd. Image by AdobeStock.

"There were cries to the sky; the cries in the bunker, in the crematoria, in the gas chamber were horrible, horrible.
I still wonder today how God didn't hear these cries."

Dov Paisikowic - born 1924 –Velky Rakovec – Czechoslovakia
Prisoner number A-3076 – Slave Labourer - Auschwitz-Birkenau Crematoria no.1 – 1944

Died 1988.

Chapter One

Thursday 10th September 1942 – Morning - Bletchley Park

Captain Archie Travers sat alone on the hard wooden bench outside his intelligence team's building at Bletchley Park. The building was unmarked and unnumbered; strictly speaking, it should have been named Building Thirteen, but there was no Building Thirteen. Thirteen being deemed an unlucky number.

He didn't believe in luck, as such, good or bad. He believed in planning, practice, and hard work, then accepting the luck that brought you. He stared straight ahead at the well-kept grass and mature Oak trees, took a slow deep breath of fresh English air and tried to recall what had given his life such purpose and clarity.

The Battle of Calais, the invading German Army and World War Two, he tried to find more, but he could only see closed boxes in his mind. The straightforward simplicity of that particular war reassured him.

He concentrated on what he'd gained since Calais. He couldn't; there was too much, things he'd never dared to hope for. He had money, status, friends, and family, love even. More love than he could cope with but hardly cause for complaint. He'd been nobody before the Battle of Calais; he'd become an animal in Calais and survived, now he was somebody. Good people regarded him as somebody, good people, not the flattery of knaves.

He was almost mortally tired and sore; the short walk from his hospital bed to the bench had drained him. He'd left his hospital bedroom once in the weeks following the fight at his cottage and then in a wheelchair for twenty minutes. The rib, broken by the impact of a close-range rifle bullet, half piercing his body armour, would take the longest to heal properly, and it still stung if he didn't keep his breathing shallow.

The short conversation he'd had with his friends

Conner and Alan, only seconds before, drained his mind as well as his body. He needed rest, and he needed…

"I'm here now," Una, his wife, said as she sat next to him and held the fingers showing below the cast and sling that still held his broken right arm.

It had only been seconds since he'd asked for her soothing presence. She'd been in his building, waiting for the talking to end, he thought. He smiled half a smile and breathed in her scent.

"I'm sorry, Archie, I stayed away, I knew I couldn't stop them, and I knew you'd stop if they asked. I couldn't watch them break you."

"They're right," he said, "I know they're right, admitting it's the difficult part, it's a loss of face, there's a shame to it; it's done now, it's in its box. I am broken, though; look at me, for fuck's sake."

Una looked at the scars and stitches above his eyes; the deep yellow around his left eye still made him look jaundiced and sick, even with the swelling nearly gone.

"We're going away for a bit," she said, "two weeks complete rest, just you and me. We'll go to Hevlyn first and take it from there. I've sorted it out, I've packed your bags, the car's only round the corner, I'm driving. No arguments."

"None… can we go now? I don't want anyone seeing me this… weak."

Una wanted to argue with him; he wasn't weak; he was the strongest person she'd ever met or even heard of; he set impossibly high standards for himself. She said yes, then guided him carefully to the car. He'd be back; she knew it. In the corner of her eye, she saw Rebecca inside Building Thirteen. Without words, she called her over to them.

Rebecca reached Archie as he arrived at the car door, tried to think of something positive to say and couldn't. She gave him a peck on the cheek and squeezed his hand; he nodded and smiled at her.

Rebecca knew she'd find the right words eventually,

but not yet; the breaking was still too raw. She'd already told Conner and Alan she'd still help him with his private war if he refused to stop, as had Una.

Conner had let both teams know Archie was taking leave, and they all wanted to say goodbye and perhaps give him a hug too, but Mary Murphy said a firm no.

"What he needs is for us to leave him alone. I want to give him a hug because I need it; it isn't necessarily what he needs. He needs his wife, time alone with her, and nobody else needing anything from him. Oh hell, I don't even know if that makes sense. Rebecca, you give him one big hug from everybody."

*

Una and Archie reached Hevlyn Mansions by mid-afternoon. The journey was quiet; she'd talked a little, and he'd been monosyllabic in reply. She remained patient, letting him think.

Once inside the flat, he'd suggested dinner at the Savoy, and he managed a full smile when she told him she'd already booked the table for seven o'clock.

He said they'd need to do food shopping, as he only had powdered milk and tea in the flat. He smiled even wider when she said she'd already ordered enough for a week and Billy's contacts would deliver it tomorrow morning.

Dinner at the Savoy was perfect; sitting opposite Una and looking into her eyes for two hours was bliss. He'd worn civvies for the dinner, his best suit and Una wore the evening dress Rebecca had worn for Churchill. She cut up his food for him, fussed over him, and he loved her for it. Around him, he saw all he'd gained since Calais.

The staff all knew his name and called him Mr Travers; other patrons nodded hellos in his direction. He belonged there; he was somebody, and so was Una. Maybe he'd done enough already. Perhaps he should go to America; he'd think about that later. He'd certainly earned some rest and decided spoiling Una and treating her like a princess was the worthiest deed he could do.

Yes, to Hell with the war, to Hell with the world, I'll be

with Una, nothing else matters, and that thought gave him a measure of relief.

That night, they tried to have sex, but his lack of fully working parts made that too difficult, so they made each other come with mouths and tongues. They fell asleep as closely as they could manage, fully relaxed, knowing for certain that none of their friends would die the next day.

In the moments before sleep, Archie knew he wasn't going to kill anyone the next day; he was going to do nothing. Then he began to wonder whether anyone would die precisely *because* he did nothing. The thought went straight into a box, and he slept.

*

Friday 11th September 1942 – Morning – Hevlyn Mansions

The following morning, Friday the 11th of September 1942, they rose very late, around ten. She wore one of his best white army shirts while he wore some boxer shorts she'd bought him in America. There seemed no point in dressing, it was warm, and his wounds still felt better unclothed. He asked Una to replace the soft crepe bandage tightly around his ribs. He'd slept awkwardly, but he did it to stay closer to Una, and she was worth the pain.

The phone rang, and he picked up the receiver, cut off the call and left it off the hook.

"It's you and me today, nothing else," he said.

Around 1030, there was a knock at the door.

"That'll be the shopping," Una said and went to answer it.

"Oh my goodness," he heard her say, "General. Oh, I'm not dressed. You'd better come in. Archie, it's General Eisenhower."

They'd spoken to him at the President's Mansion, Hyde Park, on their trip to America, and his presence was unmistakable.

"I think it's easier if you both call me Ike; everyone else does."

"Sir?" said Archie.

"Good God, you look terrible; they told me you weren't in Dieppe?"

"This?" Archie said, conscious of the cast, scars, and bandages around his chest. "Let's call it a live fire training exercise that went badly wrong."

"Trouble does seem to find you, son."

"You're not the first to say so. A cup of tea?"

"Hell no! Have you got any coffee? Strong and black?"

"Sorry, we don't drink it."

"Yes, we do," Una said, "we have the stuff Winters gave us; he did say we'd need it. I'll make it; you make the General at home."

Archie sat down at the dining table with Eisenhower.

"Sorry to disturb you, Archie; I tried to call you. I'm only in England for seven days, so I need to see you while I can."

"What can I do for you, sir?" said Archie, trying to get his brain into working gear.

"Don't worry; I've ordered Winters not to kidnap you; *Harsh* and I were at WestPoint together."

"Okay."

"We don't need to now; we're coming here to join you. I'll shortly be announced as the Supreme Commander of Allied Forces in North Africa; they'll probably change the title again before it's announced, you get the basic idea.

"I need some British liaison attached to my team permanently, they offered me some Sirs and minor royalty, and I'll probably have to take a couple of them to keep the peace. What I really need is a tough sonofabitch who's seen action, old Harsh tells me that's you."

"Could be; I'm not dead yet, anyway."

"When I asked for you, your top brass nearly died; Churchill said you'd do very well and told me later they were afraid you'd tell me the truth, not a version of it. I need someone who knows hokum when he sees it and ain't afraid to say so. Is that you?"

"Well, it sounds like me; why didn't Churchill order me to do it?"

"It's a big commitment, years, it's not front line action,

and I prefer to ask, not tell a man if I'm able to."

"And Churchill said he would order me to do it if I did say no."

"You're as sharp as I expected, Archie."

"He knew your asking would be good enough for me, a few things are falling into place now, and I do owe him rather a large favour."

"That's what he said too. How does Major Travers sound?"

"I'm more interested in the task than the title, but if it makes people listen to me, I'll take it.

"Good answer."

"Do I get to meet Patton?"

"He's asked to meet *you*, he read your paper on Guderian, and you already know we need all the help we can get."

"Coffee for two," Una said as the doorbell rang; it was the groceries. "Bacon sandwich, anyone?"

"Listen," Ike continued while Una cooked, "I've got a few hours this morning, there's a car waiting for me outside, and there're some words to be said when we're alone. I've learned some hard lessons in the last few weeks. Four weeks ago, I had twenty senior officers ready to take the credit for Operation Jubilee, now I can't find one who's responsible for the failure.

"The strange thing is, four weeks ago, I asked what your role was. Your Brass told me it was minor, and you'd not been actively engaged in the planning process. What the heck does that mean?"

Archie took a deep breath and let it go.

"It means I thought it was complete… hokum, but I didn't have the nerve to say that to the top brass. I should have spoken up, but it's difficult when you come in half way through an operation. I didn't know how to argue my corner, at least not there and then.

"My usual practice in conflict is to shoot or knife the enemy, which wasn't a practical proposition… I still need to learn how to operate at that level. I need full involvement from the beginning and as much control as I can possibly get. Dieppe was like the Emperor's new clothes."

"Okay, so you tell me exactly what went wrong with Dieppe?" said Ike.

While apparently busy in the kitchen area, Una listened intently to every word they said. The problems with Dieppe Archie had been reluctant to detail how to do a beach landing properly, where to do it in North Africa, France, maybe Sicily and Italy as well. How to fight fire with fire, to fight Rommel with Patton, and the importance of continuing to crack Enigma. Detail, detail, detail, planning, practice, resources, logistics, organisation.

"I need to ask specifically about Northern France, too," Archie added as the sandwiches arrived.

"Ask away."

"When do we go back there? It's unfinished business; I need to go back there, if nowhere else."

"Next Summer or the summer after."

"Next Summer's too soon, we haven't got enough ships or landing craft, and I'm sorry, we haven't got enough good men yet."

"Okay, when would you go?"

"May or June 44. That gives Jerry plenty of time to prepare his defences, so we have to go where he least expects."

"Which is?"

"Normandy, but we have to make him believe it'll be Calais or nearby, with a short Channel crossing time. We need a real plan and a couple of dummy plans; a dummy army would be another good idea. Me and three mates took out two tanks because we weren't hiding where they expected us to."

"The Church Tower?"

"Yes?"

"I saw the movie; Winston showed it to me."

Archie smiled at the good memory, simpler times if only he'd known that then. He continued.

"The other significant fact is... you're not allowed to say this, so I will. The longer we delay, the more Germans and Russians kill one another. The fewer Germans there are, the fewer we have to fight to win this war. The fewer Russians there are, the fewer we have to face off against for the next war."

"You're right, of course, Archie... I'm definitely not allowed to say that," Ike replied with a warm smile that told a story of its own.

"We can afford to be patient on that one, Archie; there's another landing I need to talk about first, Operation Torch. I do *not* want another Dieppe."

"First, I can get you three scouting parties; if you can get me submarines, we can scout your landing beaches in three nights; the tides in the Med are easier to handle. A quick reconnaissance, and we can do some smash and grab diversions as well if you need."

"I'll do that; I'll do just that."

"There's another thing, sir."

"There always is...."

"If you're planning Torch within weeks, we'll need to know exactly what's happening in the Desert; there must be a full-scale set-piece battle lined up before Torch can start to work properly. Una, you saw all the German comms in the desert recently; where did you say we were attacking from?"

They knew there were ten times the usual number of decrypts coming from Ultra, and the team could barely cope; once the fightback started in earnest, they had no chance.

Una stepped towards them.

"Yes," Una said, "we're obviously feeding false information to them, and they're expecting an attack in the south, but the army they're worried about, doesn't exist. We'll be using dummy tanks and the like, and no-one will tell us any details because we *'don't need to know.'* Dummy tanks were your idea; they're happy to steal the idea and take the credit. The point is, if I can sit in Bletchley Park and see what we're doing from German message intercepts, then so might the Germans. If they told us what they're doing, we'd be able to help with the cover story. My best guess is we'll attack along the coast, El Alamein, at the end of October. It's like trying to walk with a stone in your shoe."

"My mother told me it was a waste of time telling a woman a lie," Ike said.

"She's right," Una smiled.

"The battle of El Alamein will be the last week in October and Torch the first week in November, once we know how it's gone."

"That Montgomery fella," Una said, "likes people to think he can read Rommel's mind; he's reading his mail more like. We've got twice Rommel's men and armour, and he's still scared of him."

Ike smiled, "There's one more task I need you for; I don't think you'll guess."

"Try me."

"We need your diplomacy for the Vichy French in North Africa."

"You're right; I wouldn't have guessed that. I do like a challenge, though."

"When I meet them, I want an Englishmen beside me who was ordered to fight to the death in their country and did it. You fought harder than most Englishmen and most Frenchmen too. There's an outside chance they might respect that and display some humility when I ask for their help."

Archie managed not to laugh.

Una giggled inappropriately and discreetly. Then heard Ike telling Archie he'd repeated word for word what Archie had told him about the principles of multiple redundancy to Roosevelt and Churchill when they'd offered him the leadership role he now had.

"I like to think I had the thoughts in my head already, I'd never heard them so well expressed before, so I stole them, sorry."

"That's okay, I stole them from Caesar!" said Archie.

"That's why I don't trust anyone else not to give me any hokum."

Una saw the purpose, determination and passion in her husband's voice as he spoke and saw the man she loved returning to life. She saw the weariness leave his limbs and mind and the spark returning to his eyes. She knew that spark could be deadly, but not to him or his friends, and she relaxed. She knew she wasn't getting two weeks' leave, so she relaxed and served more strong coffee; Jesus, the smell of it would keep her awake for a week.

"Are you up for the job then?" Ike asked.

"Yes, sir."

"When can you start?" he said, looking at the state of his body.

"Straight away."

"Sure?"

"Never more so."

Una heard that and went into the bedroom to make herself decent.

"Good. I'll send a car for you at 0800 Monday morning, you'll meet the rest of the team. Bring both your ladies with you, I cannot imagine where you find two women that strong, but we'll surely find good work for them. I understand they've seen more action than me and most of my Generals. We know you think well on your own, and we know you think better when they're with you. A man fights twice as hard when he knows what he's fighting for."

After three hours, as Ike left, having arranged more meetings for Monday morning, he asked Una if she'd heard everything okay, and she said she had. She kissed him on the cheek.

"Thank you, more than I can say."

"I can't promise you'll never find a stone in your shoe. If you do, you can always tell me. You've already earned that," he said, smiling, as he left.

Una joined Archie, where he stood staring out of the window. She could almost hear his mind working

10

overtime, cogs and gears winding excitedly like a child with a dozen new toys on Christmas Day.

"You have a purpose, then?"

"Yes."

"Wasn't it good when he said Rebecca and I should be part of the team?"

"You weren't here when he said that; you were in the bedroom."

"Are you sure? I'm certain I heard him say that."

"Either way, we need to let Rebecca know. Where will she be?"

"She's next door in Conner's flat, waiting for us to finish with Ike."

*

"Sorry," Rebecca smiled at Archie, "we honestly didn't know he was coming today; we thought there would be a meeting set up next week or sometime soon. I heard him knock and Una answer, so I waited and hoped for the best."

"We had to give you as much choice as possible," Una said, "we couldn't try and bribe you into giving up. You've stopped because your friends asked you to, and you've joined Ike because you wanted to and because he wanted you. You've made the right decisions for the right reasons."

"And whose idea was all this?"

"It was all..." Una started.

"It was Una, all of it," Rebecca interrupted, "she knows you better than you know yourself."

*

The next day, Saturday, Archie went by taxi to his private doctors; he wasn't surprised to find out that Una had arranged the appointment for him. His doctor removed the cast on his arm; unusually, for an adult, it had been a greenstick fracture and had healed more quickly than was expected. The stitches in his palm, leg, shoulder and head had been removed by the medics at Bletchley. The scars left were still pink and fresh, and with care, they wouldn't break. He was doing it all a little too early. He was young, and the skin and outer flesh were healing quickly.

He flexed his right leg and knew he'd never run as well again, the wound had been deep, and there was muscle damage that would never fully repair.

His right arm had grown pale and weak from its plaster imprisonment. He sensed the weak point where the bone had bent and knitted together; he'd never be as strong again. Worse than that, he'd expect to be weak and, therefore, would be.

The hand wound still felt tender, he knew that would never heal entirely, and it would stay as a permanent reminder of his vulnerability… his Achilles' palm, his stigmata.

The scars above his eyes didn't bother him; they made him look older, stronger… a survivor, one of the fittest.

The other bits of damage would each knock a few per cent off his best performance, taking fifteen to twenty per cent off in total. That lost percentage would get him, or the man beside him, killed; he'd be a liability. Killing his friends when he was at his best was bad enough; he couldn't let them down by being slow or weak. He was finished with frontline action; he'd have to become the best planner and leader he could. He wasn't sure he had the stomach to lead from the back. Alongside the liars, cowards, talkers and cripples. What else was there? A desk? A pile of papers?

The doctor offered him a crutch or a cane, and he refused. The strain of using it with his weaker right arm prevented him from favouring the leg as much as he needed to. He dismissed the idea and took a taxi to the flat where Una and Rebecca waited for him.

Una was making dinner for three and told Archie to have a proper bath to ease his muscles. He'd had bed baths for nearly a fortnight. She told Rebecca to help him get in and out and make sure she washed his back properly for him.

In another marriage that would have seemed unusual to the three of them, it seemed natural. Archie knew Rebecca and Una had no secrets, and he trusted them with his life, so his naked back was fair game, and it proved very relaxing.

When they sat down to dinner, Archie spoke as casually as he could.

"I've seen my last action; the leg and arm aren't up to it any longer."

"We know that," Una smiled at him, "we've decided we'll stop too and keep you company. We'll help you do some thinking instead. We have an exercise regime planned that'll restore as much of the muscle wastage as possible."

"She did ask the Doctor, especially about pelvic muscles!" Rebecca added, giggling.

"Purely in the interests of exercise, of course," Una kicked her under the table, then giggled too.

"Anything else I should know?"

"There's a Major's uniform for my husband in the spare room."

"And a Lieutenant's for Una and me, I'm reverting to Lieutenant, my Captaincy was a field commission only, and I'm happy with that," Rebecca added.

Archie suspected she didn't want to be a higher rank than her friend and sister. Rank barely mattered to him, although he knew he needed the influence it carried if he was to get his way. He needed to get his own way; he needed as much mental control as possible, especially if the physical act was beyond him.

*

Friday 18th September 1942

Major Archie Travers and his two Lieutenants spent all the next week at meetings, conferences, and introductions. If there was a medal for listening to bollocks, he deserved it, first class.

Ike's meetings were sharply focused, with the right degree of detail and clear decisions followed. *'Action this day, make sure this is given extreme priority, and report to me that this has been done.'* Archie knew he'd stolen that line from Churchill, so he felt able to steal it too.

Other meetings were dire, sleep inducing, and without decision other than thinking about something manifestly unwise for an undefined timescale. Archie's mind drifted many times, and while seemingly taking detailed notes of proceedings, he compiled lists of what not to do and what to do instead.

He didn't get it all straight away. Una and Rebecca told him he saw solutions too quickly and needed to explain his reasoning a little more, to carry people with him rather than drag them.

"You need to tailor your speech to the audience," Una told him.

They arranged for Una to take notes of his meetings, sit next to him and kick him under the table when he needed to do that.

Rebecca said she'd watch the body language for him. He said he didn't know what she meant, and she slapped him on the shoulder.

"I learned that from you, you idiot."

By the end of that week, he'd secured vital roles for himself and his teams, worthy tasks they could do now and for the next two years. Tasks they would accomplish better than any. It would take patience and planning, but he had time and the best help. He needed to prove that soon, though, any early failure, and some were hoping for precisely that, would be hard to overcome.

After a few meetings, Archie could recognise the adversarial quality of the verbal engagements. Some of these armchair warriors wouldn't last a minute in a real battle, so they'd developed their charlatanry to a level he'd not seen before. This was all simply another fight, another battle, another struggle, another survival of the fittest, the verbally fittest. He needed allies around the table rather than behind a pile of sandbags.

Others sat around the table complaining how difficult it was; he was simply working out how he would make it happen in practice.

He also decided that this softer, less deadly battle

needed neither quarter nor pity. Feckle had killed a hundred men with his cowardice and incompetence. Some of these idiots were capable of killing a thousand or ten times that with the same effort. Not this time, he told himself, not *my* men, not *my* war. He secretly resolved to destroy any man who threatened the truth of that promise. Words and truth might do the trick; perhaps one or two untimely deaths, or accidents, might go unremarked. Real war weeded out the real weak; he knew that and intended to make sure it continued.

Apart from untimely accidents, Conner had agreed to all of it, as had Gubbins, and it was what Ike had asked for too.

Archie had what he needed.

Chapter Two

Friday 18th September 1942 – Bletchley Park

Una and Rebecca drove Archie back to Bletchley on Friday evening, satisfied with themselves. Archie had a new purpose, and they shared it with him. A newly rented house awaited them; it felt cold and unlike a home. The original cottage was beyond repair at the time, the three of them were there, so the house would be home for that reason alone.

*

Saturday 19th September 1942 – The Manor

On Saturday morning, Archie called an urgent meeting at the Manor for both teams to discuss their new roles.

Everyone was pleased to see the real Archie return. He received the hugs and back slaps he'd forfeited a week earlier, and that warmed him more than he expected. The approval of those he respected meant infinitely more than the false platitudes of the serial meeting attendees and sycophants he'd seen in the last week.

"Ladies and Gentlemen, I'm so happy to be here in better health, you need to know what's been decided, and I'm certain you'll be pleased.

"Everything I say is most secret. It must not be discussed outside this group. However, you absolutely must discuss it among yourselves, we must get this right, and each individual here will have an active role in making sure we do.

"I am British Auxiliary Liaison to the American Forces in Europe and North Africa, working with General Eisenhower, Rebecca and Una are assisting me.

"The operational team will undertake urgent reconnaissance missions in the Mediterranean and Atlantic for the Americans. You'll ensure safer landings for the biggest allied operation of the war so far. We're finally attacking properly, and you'll be first ashore, a piece of cake, I told them.

"The non-operational team will become Intelligence Team DELTA. Our usual task of overall intelligence analysis and coordination is so well tuned we can safely pass it to a new team. Conner and Mary will train them. Mary, be quick please because we can't do without you for more than a week. Take whoever you need to help you, we'll have a chat afterwards.

"Intel Team Delta's task will be to gather and analyse every single piece of information and intelligence we already have on potential invasion sites in a particular part of Northern France.

"After we've done that, we'll start gathering everything we don't know. We'll spend at least eighteen months doing that, non-stop, until we land in France.

"I've written an Intelligence Requirement for the operation. That's a list of every detail I think we need to know. The top commanders have read it, and they're content. I need you all to look at it and see what we've missed, there will be things missing, and I know you'll find them for me.

"The ops team will be parachute and glider trained as soon as I can organise it. We plan to drop Gabe over Berlin and see what happens."

Laughter interrupted the serious nature of the message.

"That was a joke, by the way," Archie added.

"That's a shame; I was gonna ask if I could go with him," said Freddie to even more laughter.

Una and Rebecca had sat at the rear of the team while Archie spoke.

"He's Conner now, isn't he?" Una whispered to Rebecca.

"Better," she replied.

When the meeting ended, Archie spoke briefly to Freddie and squeezed his shoulder; Freddie nodded and went to talk to Marion Hill.

Archie told Mary he'd be back in ten minutes, then nodded discreetly to Billy and left the Manor House, heading towards the workshop.

Billy followed, watching closely, seeing him favour using his left leg slightly; he was catching him up more easily than he should have. Archie still reached the door before he did.

As Archie entered the workshop, Billy watched him fall to the ground like a dead man.

Billy looked briefly over his right shoulder for any witnesses, then jogged the last few feet to the door, closing and latching it behind him.

"Billy, it's this leg, I'm all right when I'm sitting, but if I stand too long like now, it's agony. The foot's always cold, and sometimes I can't feel it."

"I'll get the Doc."

"No, Billy, I lied to the Docs to leave that hospital bed. It'll be alright; I've just got up a bit too early, the wound's healing slowly, and I really need some painkillers."

"I'll get some for you."

"No, Billy, they're no good; I need more than tablets; I need your morphine."

"My morphine?"

"Yes, the stuff you've got stashed here. I need one of your syrettes, Billy."

"… Okay… only once; it's bad stuff, you know that."

Billy climbed a ladder to a high shelf and removed a small syringe and ampoule from an old kit bag.

"Now listen! Only once, Archie, after this, you see the Doc, I take it maybe once a month when my back's real bad; I shouldn't even do that. Don't ask me again, don't make me say no, and don't you dare make me say yes either."

Billy slid the needle gently, from the perfect angle, into his thigh and squeezed. Archie felt the ice cool flow of the liquid ease into his leg and then his mind. He passed out for a moment, euphoric at the relief it gave him. The narcotic drug did its work within twenty seconds, and a minute later, he was on his feet.

"Look at me," Billy said, grabbing him by the lapels, "look at me! I know you, look me in the eye and say, I promise never again."

"Billy, I promise never again."

"What else?"

"All right, I was going to try and lie to you, and I won't waste my time trying."

"Right, I believe you now, and don't think I won't fucking watch you anyway."

"Okay, okay, could you make me a walking stick? If I build up my right arm muscles and wrist, that'll take the pressure off the foot. I need to work out what my new limits are. I stood up for too long inside the Manor. I needed to stand up in front of them today. There're some things a man has to stand up for; I'll work them into the ground, you know."

"They know that. That's my boy. Here take this," Billy said, handing him an old tennis ball.

"Carry it with you and squeeze it regularly when you get a chance. It'll work, I promise you."

"Thanks, Billy."

"Now, is that girl of ours pregnant yet?"

"Don't *you* fucking start!"

*

Friday 7th November 1942 – SOE HQ - Baker Street, London

Two months later, Russell Lescott sat at his desk in SOE Headquarters in Baker Street.

Russell had no direct involvement in the small SOE raid scheduled to take place that night. He knew nothing about how difficult it was but saw it in the faces of his new English friends and comrades. He was tired, and it was late, seven o'clock, yet he felt the need to do more. He picked up two more documents for translation. Good men would die tonight even if it went well, so he boiled the kettle in the nearly empty premises.

His daughter, Aria, would be home from school; she'd make her own tea and do her homework. She knew hard work; a farm in the Upper Volga region of Russia was a hard place at the best of times. In the famine of 1932, it became a deadly place. He took a big risk leaving; the state forbade any travel and took other risks in finding somewhere that gave them refuge. To be welcomed in England was to win life's lottery. He had no doubt Aria had a good future, and that single thought sustained him.

They'd worked hard here, especially when his wife, Malvina, had died of pneumonia, contracted on the journey and never fully cured. Aria had learned English quickly and taught him well, too, including the local accent. Those two skills and his honesty had secured his job with the British when war broke out.

He'd wanted to fight for the British. As a stateless person, he couldn't do that without Russian Government approval. So he stopped being Ruslan Leshchyov, became Russell Lescott and settled for his desk job. He was good at his job, his translation was perfect, and he always conveyed the feelings behind the words. Aria had taught him that. He took satisfaction from working with the best of men; merely shaking the hand of a man like Gubbins and hearing him say well done was an honour. Being trusted, not treated as a Kulak, a peasant who owned a little land, seemed a small desire. Ruslan only wanted some small thanks for his worth, and he wanted to be English.

He picked up the small tin of the extra strong tea leaves he preferred and went to the kettle. How the English killed good tea with milk and sugar was one of the few traits he didn't understand about them. He sipped his tea regularly as he wrote; it helped his concentration.

He worked quickly and, fifteen minutes later, started on the second document. Feeling unusually tired now, he yawned wide and long, the kind of yawn that filled your whole head. He decided to go home after all, then felt dizzy as he tried to stand, then slumped forward onto his desk and papers as if asleep. He didn't wake up, and when they found his body the following morning at 0500, he'd been dead for nearly ten hours. The blood that seeped from his nostrils onto his desk and his pale blue lips told some of his story to those who tried to investigate his death.

*

7th November 1942 - 2300 - The Atlantic Coast of Morocco.

Captain Asgeir Thorson sat impatiently in the cramped, noisy and stifling atmosphere of HMS Triton, which, for the purposes of Operation Torch, was an American submarine.

It was 2300 on the 7th of November 1942, and in two hours, Archie's Chosen Men, his men now, would start their mission which would precede the main landing operation by General Patton's Western Taskforce. United States Forces, comprising thirty thousand men in over one hundred ships, were to land in three areas on the Atlantic coast of French Vichy-controlled Morocco. Two other sets of landings would take place on the Mediterranean coast of Algeria to target Vichy forces there.

Following the Battle of El-Alamein, as accurately foreseen by Una, British troops were now pressing the German Afrika Korps back along a broad front in Egypt, from east to west. American forces would now land in the west and push eastwards to catch Field Marshall Rommel and his men from two sides. The next few weeks would secure the whole of the Southern Mediterranean under allied control, enabling an invasion of southern then northern Europe. Operation Torch was the biggest invasion by sea in modern history. Quite simply, it must work.

*

Patton had personally asked for a demonstration of Archie's team's abilities to take place for two of his three landings, and he'd see how his action fared when compared to the two other task forces. It was a test, and Archie had asked for perfection, no less; the conversation was burned into Asgeir's mind.

"I've told Patton we can scout the waters leading to the invasion beaches in advance, take detailed notes of currents, sea depths, unseen rock hazards, and sandbanks," Archie had said. "We're landing on beaches next to ports; there are historical reasons why those safe harbours are somewhere else, we need to know why. When you've found safe passages on the three landing areas, you'll split into two teams and act as pathfinders for the landing craft and get them beached right on target. Begley and Billy will make signalling torches with green lights and a hollow tube to shield their glare from the landside. In darkness, a green light shows further and clearer for the human eye. You'll be pathfinders for landing craft like the RAF have for bombers, we'll be more accurate, and we'll save more lives."

"Are you sure you want me to lead this mission? The first time we met, I crashed my own boat into a rock, remember?" Asgeir asked.

"You took a calculated risk to save my men, and you succeeded; I'm sure I want you, no one else, end of story, don't doubt that for one second. When you asked me to be best man at your wedding, I thought you should ask Baldr because he was your best friend. You told me the job description was best man, not best friend, so I said yes. I wouldn't have done that if you hadn't been the best groom. Now, let's get this job done, and we can get you and Briony married.

"When we get this right, they'll ask us to do it again, then they'll ask us to train other people to do it. Every Dieppe we avoid saves a lot of lives; maybe we can save some lives instead of taking them; let's see how that feels."

*

The first part of the mission went perfectly. Over three nights, the sub had dropped them off in their usual craft, three semi-rigid dinghies. The sea was calm enough for accurate depth measurements, and the beaches were stable enough for tanks and heavy vehicles. The tide marks showed the beaches were wide enough for a landing in force. They'd used a handheld drill to silently test the depth of sand and bring back samples. You couldn't possibly undertake adequate reconnaissance of a coastline from a periscope the best part of a mile offshore, but they'd done exactly that on other landing beaches.

On their southernmost invasion point, near the port of Safi, Operation Blackstone, they identified a hidden sandbar you could easily avoid once you knew it was there.

Further north, Fedala, outside Casablanca, Operation Brushwood, they identified offshore rocks and a strong current. That meant a slightly more northerly drop off for the landing craft would make an accurate landing easier and quicker.

At Mehdiya, further north, Operation Goalpost, they found the passage to be clear and easy.

Having something adverse to report, and having it taken into account, made Asgeir feel more confident. He still muttered a short meaningless prayer to his legendary Gods that he'd missed nothing and the wind and water would favour the Norsemen that night.

Asgeir had said that prayer before when sailing and rowing in the countless fjords and even narrower inlets near Stavanger. He didn't believe in the Gods, and the prayer would do no good if you didn't keep your eyes open for the spray, rise, and swell of the waters. The best Mariners swore they could smell the wrongness in the wind's direction and see a rock through the slightest swelling of water.

'May Odin give you knowledge on your path.'

*

8th November 1942 - Pre-Dawn – USS New York – the Atlantic Ocean

Archie stood four or five paces behind General George Smith Patton, the American General commanding the Seventh United States Army. He was on the command deck of a United States Navy Destroyer, the USS New York, the headquarters vessel for the Western Taskforce of Operation Torch. The operation was to start imminently, at dawn on the 8th of November 1942.

Major Archie Travers was quiet, content to remain behind the group of older, more senior officers. He had concerns about his eleven men and their small task; the others worried about a hundred ships and thirty-three thousand men. They also worried about standing next to George Patton. He was an intimidating man who said exactly what he wanted to say whenever he wanted, usually accompanied by the worst language Archie had ever heard from someone that senior.

*

Archie had first met Patton three weeks earlier in New York on board the same ship while last minute preparations for Operation Torch were taking place.

He'd been nervous before he'd first met Patton. Archie didn't have heroes; he had a few role models, people whose traits and example he'd like to follow, in part at least. He admired Churchill and Gubbins but couldn't be them. He admired Caesar and Heinz Guderian but would never meet them. Patton was the American version of Guderian; he'd fought bravely in the first war, he led his men from the front, fought alongside them, and he was going to meet him as an ally.

Patton met Archie alone in his quarters.

"Travers, come in, sit down, you've got half an hour, and I'll talk first."

He fired question after question at Archie for twenty minutes, asking secondary and tertiary questions, probing, brisk and intimidating in tone. Archie knew Patton was testing him and had run this conversation in his head a dozen times, sometimes awake, sometimes in dreams. Patton asked the right questions, listened carefully to the answers and never missed the point.

"Okay, I'll give your reconnaissance teams a try on the Western Task Force, directly under my command, and you'll be next to me when it's happening. Okay?"

"Yes, sir."

"Now, you've been in action, haven't you, Travers? Tell me about it."

Archie spoke for an hour and a half; Patton showed no sign of disinterest and asked more questions, gently now, his passion mixed with empathy. Patton had taken wounds when leading his men in the First World War. He soaked up everything Archie said like a sponge, like a man reading an excellent book he simply can't put down. He saw Archie look at the clock and told him to carry on. Archie omitted the more murderous aspects of his military career, describing them as 'most secret'.

Patton pressed him hard on Major Feckle's fate as if he knew Archie wasn't telling him the whole truth.

Archie tried to draw a line under the subject.

"The best thing about war is," said Archie, "it truly becomes survival of the fittest, so those weak links that happily progress as complete charlatans in peacetime come to notice and don't survive."

"If it came right to the crunch, would you take down a dangerously bad officer?" Patton still pressed.

"You ask hard questions, General, so I'll give you a hard answer. Yes. My job is to kill as many of the enemy and as few of my men as possible. If it needed doing, and I was certain I'd get away with it, I'd do it in a heartbeat. I'd also make damn sure I never told another soul, ever," and he returned Patton's smile at the answer he gave.

"Archie, I like you, but if your team lets me down, you're gone."

"I knew that before I walked in, sir."

"Will that leg ever get better?" Patton asked, eyeing the sturdy wooden cane Billy had made for Archie.

"I don't know, it's all right if I can sit down regularly; I can't stand for too long. There's muscle missing, I can't replace."

"Tell me, Archie, I believe I was made for war, this war; what about you?"

"I don't know; I sometimes think this war was made for me."

"God damn, that's a good answer. I'll steal that and use it. Now you get outta here and back to Ike. Two of my Majors are waiting outside, they've been there an hour, and I'm going to tell them their plans have changed again. Spend the rest of the day with Danbury outside; tell him what you need for your teams, and he'll start on it."

Archie decided he liked Patton, and he was still nervous when he left. He liked the Patton he'd talked to but saw another one, hidden, barely under the surface, he wouldn't like; a ruthless one.

Archie knew he could be ruthless when a few people were involved, a countable number, a number you could see in front of you. Patton would be ruthless with tens of thousands, far too many for Archie; maybe he wasn't such a big fish.

*

The journey from America to re-join Patton on board the ship was long and eventful for Archie. Air, sea, air and finally, submarine near the island of Madeira. He hadn't seen Una and Rebecca for two and a half weeks, and that seemed like forever.

Eisenhower and Churchill had wanted Archie to be with Ike when he met a senior French General known only by the codename *Kingpin*. They hoped he would encourage the Vichy French Forces in North Africa not to resist the American landings. The meeting would take place in Gibraltar, and *Kingpin* had made his anti-English feelings apparent, so he would likely refuse to meet at all if any Englishmen were present. Churchill agreed to not be personally involved, given his history of sinking French vessels at Mers-el-Kebir. However, he insisted a British officer be present during the Gibraltar talks; Archie Travers.

Archie had already worked out who *Kingpin* was, General Henri Giraud, a bitter enemy of the English, the Germans, and the Free French Leader, General De Gaulle, and kept that knowledge quietly to himself.

Giraud had been a Prisoner of War, held by the Germans for two years, following his capture on the 19th May 1940, only a few days before Archie's life defining moments in Calais. He'd successfully escaped from captivity and sheltered in Vichy France, since.

Giraud chose to remain in Vichy France, however, and appointed an old army colleague and fellow former POW,

Brigadier Charles Mast, to meet General Eisenhower and other Americans. Ike designated the meeting as Top Secret and held it at Cherchell in Algeria on October 23rd, 1942, to discuss American action in the Vichy Colonies.

A large number of people were present, Ike, his deputy General Mark Clark, Vichy French, and Resistance leaders; Ike introduced everyone with great respect. Archie was self-conscious, being the only Englishman present, although Ike had given him an American Major's uniform to wear.

An attractive young French girl aged about twenty-two instantly translated the English and then French words spoken. She had what Archie could only describe as Gallic poise, or in plain English, was a stuck up, little madam.

Eisenhower introduced Archie last, uncomfortably and obviously so.

"This is Major Archie Travers, he used to be British, but he's an American citizen now. President Roosevelt gave him citizenship four weeks ago when he agreed to join my team and be part of my liaison with the British."

There was a pause and a few unfriendly glances before Ike added.

"You were in France in 1940, weren't you, Travers?"

"Yes, Oui,"

"What was that battle called again?"

"The battle of Calais, Le Battaille de Calais," Archie said.

"How many were in your company?"

"More than a hundred, plus d'une centaine." Archie realised he was answering in French, and the interpreter was still translating his French into English for the benefit of the Americans. He stopped looking at Ike and looked straight at Brigadier Mast, meeting his stare head on and continued in French only. Holding himself upright with his walking stick.

"How many got out alive?" Ike asked.

"Five," Archie answered, "but I left at least thirty-two Germans and most of my soul there on the ground beside them."

"How many of the five are left alive now?"

"Three."

"And you've been back to France since then?"

"Yes, only twice, Wissant and Bordeaux; we didn't stay long. My new men have returned, St. Nazaire and Dieppe. I'd love to return, but I don't move as fast as I used to, and we're not exactly welcome."

Mast looked at him and then said in excellent English.

"You will be welcome next time… perhaps, sit down please, you may stay."

The talking lasted hours, and the verbal jousting was riveting. Archie watched and learned. Ike was a master, held most of the good cards and played them perfectly.

There would be token fighting in Algeria and Morocco, though less than Archie feared. A small and tenuous attempt to engage Vichy with the English was partially successful, one per cent only, a start nonetheless. Ike was a masterful manager and leader; he'd brought Archie thousands of miles just for that short conversation and maybe another one later. He was beginning to build an alliance he'd need later, and Archie didn't mind being used one bit.

As Archie left the meeting, the lovely young interpreter approached him, her walk itself was an arousing invitation, and as she approached him, he could smell her perfume more clearly.

Oh no, he thought, here we go, imminent danger.

She reached him and looked from side to side, ensuring no one could overhear, then whispered in perfect English.

"Your accent is terrible. I would have made you stand, Cochon," then turned and walked sharply away from him.

And that expensive perfume smells cheap on you; Archie laughed inwardly and made a mental note never to visit France socially, only with an army and taking no prisoners.

As events unfolded, Kingpin's arrival in Gibraltar was delayed until a few hours before Torch began, so Archie never met him. He had met one of his nieces in Cherchell, though.

*

Sunday 8th November 1943 – Dawn – USS New York

"Archie, where's Archie?" Patton shouted from his position on the bridge. "Get up here, where I can see you."

Archie's reflection on some wasted effort ended, and he returned to the present and the command deck of the USS New York.

"Sir," Archie said as he hobbled forward; he'd been standing up a little too long and was stiff; the stiffness turned to pain as he began walking the few strides.

"Get up here, man. Safi, landing craft on the button, thanks to your lights. Mehdiya, without your lights, we're on the wrong goddamn beach. Fedala, despite bad weather, we are on the button, thanks only to your lights, firing reported on that beach before we landed; we don't know any details."

Archie couldn't ask for more information. The fate of a few men was unimportant, while others focused on thousands in tens of different places; his men were nothing; at least he knew they'd done their jobs.

He waited for another hour in the command room; still no news of his men, and it still seemed trivial to ask. Asking wouldn't change anything, and stoicism seemed the proper pose to adopt. He stayed silent, listened, waited and learned.

The pain in his leg steadily worsened. He couldn't ask to sit down. Not while everyone was standing, nor while some of his men might lie dead on a beach.

He concentrated on his pain to distract him, he knew it started in his thigh, and he felt it most in his foot and ankle. He tried to imagine the muscle that was no longer there and traced its path to his brain, then pushed it to his foot and ankle. He couldn't feel his foot at all, yet it moved when he told it to; he saw it flexing. He couldn't understand why he couldn't feel his foot and still knew that was where the pain was. So, he drew the pain slowly up his body and into his brain; it hurt even more in his brain.

He took his pain and tried to put it into a box. The pain was too great, and the box couldn't close. Changing tack, he looked at the box and made it bigger until the box itself pursued the pain and caught it. He slammed the lid shut quickly and as tightly as he could muster, and the pain was gone.

Only the box remained, alongside other boxes, marked and labelled clearly, and he pushed them all to the back of his consciousness.

He felt clumsy and confused; he wasn't sure what he'd done or how he'd made it work. People could block out pain sometimes.

Whatever it was, he hadn't known he could do that.

"Right, let's get on that beach and show those Vichy bastards some American guts," Patton said. It was 0730 on the 8th of November 1942; Archie had stood up for the last five and a half hours and now felt no pain.

There had been no preliminary bombardment on any of the landing areas; the Americans naively hoped the French wouldn't resist. Archie told them categorically that they would, but the risk was theirs to take.

"They'll fight for a while, then surrender when the going gets tough and call it honour," was what he'd said, and he was right.

Chapter Three

Sunday 8th November 1942 0400 - Operation Torch

Shortage of submarine resources meant the Chosen Men would only act as pathfinders for two of the three landing beaches. Asgeir led one larger team of seven, and Brad the second team of five.

Brad's team, Baldr, Mickey, George and Henry, landed exactly on their planned target, in good weather, near the port of Safi. They soon found and secured two well-hidden positions from which to signal and guided the first landing crafts ashore under no immediate fire. They watched as the Americans secured the beach and landing zone, reinforced it, then made their move on the port. They received no more thanks than a back slap from the first men ashore. If you did your job properly, no one noticed; if you fucked up, everyone noticed, even the other fuck ups.

Asgeir led his two dinghies with Freddie, Gabe, Doc Ward, Lightfoot, Roebuck and Brayden towards the landing zone north of Fedala.

*

Both sets of men discussed whether to wear their armour, as they had done on the recce missions. They didn't feel right wearing them when so many others would fight without armour.

"I'm ordering you to wear yours," Archie had said earlier to Asgeir, "you have to get used to being too important to take too many risks. It's not easy, I know, but it's an order, and I'll tell your men it is."

"What should the men do?" Asgeir asked.

"That's up to you; they're your men now, I'll back whatever decisions you make, and that includes any dead Frenchmen who fall at your feet. We have no alternative other than to accept the 'must not shoot first' policy, but I know the Vichy French will fire at us whatever uniform we're wearing. My second order is, do not hesitate to shoot second. I know why there won't be a bombardment first, and that shouldn't affect what we do quietly; it didn't do much good in Dieppe anyway."

Archie hadn't said a word about Freddie; he didn't need to. Asgeir knew it was his job to watch over him and do it without anyone noticing, especially Freddie. They all knew Archie had over a hundred men in his company in France. Only three were left; Conner, safe in a new role upstairs; Archie, in Patton's Command ship; only Freddie left at the sharp end, as he wanted. Asgeir knew Freddie was the one man Archie hadn't killed… yet; that's definitely how Archie saw it.

*

Asgeir's two dinghies landed with their usual quiet precision, and the men dragged them up the beach into a hollow between sand dunes they'd scouted earlier.

'May Thor grant you strength and courage on your way.'

They took up their planned positions, a hundred good paces apart and facing the sea. Three men on the right, four on the left, including Asgeir. They waited until the precise time and signalled with their lamps to the distantly approaching landing craft, giving them ample room to land, five at a time.

Asgeir heard the Frenchmen approaching from their left when they were still a hundred yards away. They were noisy, talking and laughing, expecting nothing amiss in the warm night air.

He knew they'd see the green lights soon, and the dawning light and air would carry the sight and sound of the landing craft well before they were ashore.

If they were Germans, he'd kill them, silently or noisily, in that order.

He wasn't allowed to fire first and knew he needed to. He could only watch as they got closer; five of them, he thought.

"Be ready to fire second," he whispered to his men and waited until the French were twenty-five yards away.

He stood up, held his empty hands high in the air and shouted.

"Bonjour, je suis Norge," his only four words in French.

No one would ever know why one of the French soldiers fired straight at Asgeir. It could have been malice, stupidity, fear or general trigger happiness. He did fire, and he did miss by a distance. Asgeir had flung himself to the ground, wearing his armour anyway.

The sharp and instant response from Freddie and Gabe's Thompson Machine Guns was enough to kill all five unfortunate Frenchmen. Lightfoot continued to signal; Doc watched his back; Roebuck and Brayden had already moved to outflank the advancing guards then checked they were dead.

"They definitely fired first, sir," said Gabe, "we made damn sure we fired second, third, fourth and well... you get my point, I'm sure."

"Why'd you jump up like that, Boss?" added Freddie.

"Well, it was such a fucking stupid idea, so I thought I better do it before someone else did."

"Well, it worked, Boss; that's what matters."

When Roebuck and Brayden returned, Asgeir asked them all why they'd moved the way they had; how did they know to do exactly the right thing, even without orders?

There was a short, puzzled silence before Gabe finally opened his mouth.

"Could be the way, Archie, then you made us practice and practice non-stop at all times, in all weathers, until we hated your guts and wanted to kill you, but we did it anyway. It's that one per cent he talks about all the goddamn time, only right now, it feels like fifty. We did it without thinking because you already did our thinking for us."

"Besides, we was gonna shoot them anyway, Boss; you made sure it was legal like," Freddie half-joked.

"Okay, boys, well done; let's get these Americans safely on shore," he said. Those short sentences were the most he'd ever heard Gabe say in one go, and Freddie had called him Boss!

The Americans came ashore, slightly behind schedule,

in numbers and secured the beachhead under some distant sniper fire from the French. That cowardly gunfire was unwelcome and deadly for a few GIs, at least the kid gloves could come off now. The sooner the fight began properly, the sooner it would end.

The sea was choppy, and the wind had tried to take the landing craft too far south. The clarity of the two green lights ensured they landed in the right place, if a little slower than first planned.

Asgeir and his team accepted some on the spot thanks from the landing troops and beach masters. They didn't know yet how the other two Western Task Force landings had gone. Asgeir's team had made a significant difference at Fedala, and they hoped it had gone well at Safi too.

*

At 0800, Archie landed on the beach; he was seasick and had discreetly put that in a bag rather than a box. The flat-bottomed landing craft rammed right up on the wet sandy beach to avoid getting the senior officers' feet wet. Archie knew engineers would have to drag it off later; it took up valuable room where they might have unloaded a useful tank or ammunition instead. He said nothing; he scanned the beach for any sign of his men. It was under intermittent and poorly aimed shellfire; frantic activity was underway along its length. He could hear distant sounds of gunfire inland and the rumble and blasting of tanks moving towards those sounds.

He saw Gabe first, then the others, counting them quickly, seven, yes, seven. He walked hesitantly towards them, stick in hand; you were never worried, remember that, he thought, don't let them see any doubt in your eyes.

Archie shook each man's hand in turn, firmly and looking into each man's eyes. The hands were clean, and so were his; he shook Asgeir's first, then spoke to him afterwards.

"What was the shooting about?" he asked.

"They shot first, we shot second, just really quickly."

"You didn't take any chances?"

"No, none at all."

"You can tell me later privately, probably something I'd have done myself," Archie laughed.

"Probably," Asgeir laughed too.

'And may Loki give you laughter as you go.'

*

Patton approached Archie around 1000 and gave him a brief update, no casualties from his team at Safi. The two Auxiliary assisted landings went well; Safi had worked perfectly. Under fire and adverse weather, Fedala went safely and efficiently. The unassisted landings at Mehdiya were problematic, some craft having landed troops on the wrong beaches in fair weather.

Archie hid his pleasure at the failures that highlighted his team's success. Patton quietly gloated at the problems encountered in the Mediterranean. Ships had run aground in unexpected shallows and sandbars in the absence of scouting the channels, depth, and currents.

"Goddamn, well done, Travers," he said, "I'll get my command team to write up the success of your work. They'll run that past you first, then I'll recommend to Ike that what you do becomes standard procedure. You sure you haven't got any American blood in you?"

"You sure you haven't got any English in you?"

"Get the fuck outta here. Go and see those murdering Vichy bastards Ike wants you to see."

"I cannot understand the French, God knows, I've tried. I know we didn't part on the best of terms; some love us, and some hate us more than the bloody Germans. If we went there and surrendered, they'd still find some way to be offended. I promise I'll be on my best behaviour."

"Why do you think they don't let me anywhere near the bastards?"

*

Tuesday 10th November 1942 – Gibraltar

Archie left North Africa and reached Gibraltar by sea, slowly but in relative comfort and safety. Asgeir's team was returning to England by freighter. The inactivity and lack of communication were frustrating and downright boring, so Archie spent two days asking questions of officers and ratings. What would they want if a seaborne invasion involved them? It was a big list, strategic and tactical. He might need a Royal Navy man on his team, and if he had a couple of big ideas, Caesar would be proud.

When he reached Gibraltar, the battles in the sea off Africa were fully underway, as well as those on land. Frenchmen were effectively fighting alongside Germans against the Americans, and Archie found that inexcusable. It would stop quickly, and the Americans would win; it was still plain wrong, 'honour' and pity were absent.

Ike had already left for North Africa and meetings with the Vichy French leaders. On arrival, Archie received sealed orders that he was no longer required for Vichy liaison and should remain in Gibraltar for seven days until Ike returned. A handwritten note at the bottom said, "Speak to Rebecca. Ike."

That disappointed him, but he was tired and needed rest on dry land anyway. When he saw Una and Rebecca after the best part of a month apart from them, he asked if he could go to their quarters. They shared a small room with two bunk beds in no more than a cellar; there was no homely cottage or small rented house in Gibraltar. He told them how tired he was, how much he'd missed them, and hugged them both warmly. The hug gradually and gently changed into an urgent, beguiling desire to fuck them as hard as he possibly could, then lie peacefully asleep next to them for all eternity. The scent of them in his arms at the same time overwhelmed him.

He knew for certain they both had exactly the same fragrance. He knew they would both taste exactly right everywhere; their saliva would mix with his effortlessly. He knew their skin and flesh would taste perfectly on his tongue wherever it went. He knew if he closed his eyes, he wouldn't be able to tell the difference between them. He knew he belonged to both of them and would do anything, everything for them.

Not here, not yet; there would come a time, there had to be.

Una was his wife, his lover, his best lover, forever, his best friend, his saviour. He would never betray her, but he yearned for Rebecca's happiness and fulfilment too. She should feel what Una felt, what Una enjoyed, what fulfilled Una; she deserved it. He knew he would kill any man who laid a finger on her. He'd kill any man who even thought about hurting her, and he'd kill any man who dared to love her.

With a supreme effort, he broke the hug and asked them to tell him what they'd done while he was away.

Rebecca told him what Ike had tried to do earlier.

'Kingpin' General Henri Giraud arrived in Gibraltar on the 7th of November, only hours before the start of Operation Torch and met with Eisenhower personally. Ike asked Rebecca to act as interpreter, to wear a British uniform and to follow his lead.

Giraud insisted his entourage, including one of his sons, should attend the meeting. Ike had reluctantly agreed. Giraud questioned the presence of an English Officer at a meeting with Americans. Ike explained she was his best interpreter, a member of his team, this was a British base, and Rebecca was half French. Giraud said the French half could stay; Rebecca told him the English half was the brain, heart, and mouth.

Ike, with determined diplomacy, asked Rebecca to recount the details of her recent visits to France, which she did. Like the news of Giraud's audacious escape from POW captivity had spread in France, the news of Rebecca's escape from St. Nazaire and disembowelling of Germans had also spread. Giraud would know her betrayal must have come from Vichy.

Giraud reluctantly agreed she could stay, then proceeded to demand of Eisenhower that he would only support the Americans if Ike gave him overall command of the American forces involved. A suggestion that was preposterous and impossible, logistically and legally.

When Ike declined, Giraud then refused to be involved.

"I'm sorry, Rebecca, the French are beyond my comprehension; I do love you dearly, both the French and English parts, but it can't change that," Archie said, taking her hand and holding it.

"That's about what Ike said when they'd gone. He was so glad circumstances meant you weren't present; he said he wanted to strangle the pompous little shit himself, so God alone knows what you'd have done. That's why he's asking us to return to London. He said his strategy of showing us to the French would have impressed any country on earth, even the Germans or Japanese."

Archie Travers, a man who'd broken every rule of civilised behaviour in his struggle for survival and justice, could only shake his head and fail to fathom the French psyche.

Following his escape, Giraud had achieved nothing but arguments and strong words with his fellow Frenchmen in Vichy, although the Vichy regime had refused to hand him to the Germans. That refusal had led to Heinrich Himmler ordering the arrest of any known relatives of Giraud as hostages, transporting them to Germany and almost certain death. Giraud himself remained free, yet still unwilling to accept the help offered to his country rather than to him personally. Archie couldn't see where the man found honour in that.

Rebecca then told Archie that after the meeting, Giraud had said her French was good, but her accent was common.

"Oh, for fuck's sake," he said, "get me back to London soon; I'll kill the bastard if I ever see him. Mind you, I might not have to; Frenchman will kill Frenchman before this is finished. There are certain uncivilised countries where only the common hatred of the perceived or actual oppressor prevents them from killing each other. I didn't expect the French to arrive there so soon. They killed their aristocracy and state-sponsored mind control by means of religion, then reinvented it with added arrogance and entitlement disguised as honour. Giraud's *honour* has killed many Frenchmen and Americans alike; it's unforgivable."

"All that is necessary for the forces of evil to triumph is for enough good men to remain silent," Una said.

"I think I'll go for some fresh air," Rebecca said, "for about an hour?"

"Two," said Una with a twinkle in her eye and looked at Archie expectantly; it had been more than three weeks.

*

Monday 16th November 1942 - Gibraltar

Ike delayed his return to Gibraltar from North Africa until over the seven days he'd expected and scheduled a meeting of all his senior staff for immediately after his return by air. There were a huge number of issues arising, complicated beyond Archie's reckoning; he knew the campaign was going well overall, though.

Ike flew in with Patton and Clark, who were in animated conversation even as they left the plane. Archie, as usual, watched carefully from an unobtrusive distance and half listened, half watched the body language.

It had been ten days since Operation Torch started; Ike looked exhausted and walked straight past Archie without even seeing him. For the first time, Archie realised Ike was on trial too; one medium sized mistake and he was gone. Clark broke away from the group going straight into the meeting, and came towards Archie.

"It's frantic, Archie; you're needed for the first half hour of the meeting; say yes to everything he says, then leave for London as soon as possible. Then you're needed even more, okay?"

"Yes, sir."

"Good man. He has a lot of time for you, you know, but not today."

Ike opened the meeting with no preamble, no introductions, no agenda, only orders.

"The following is Top Secret, and I will not repeat it, so listen with great care. You'll be aware of the service record of Major Travers," he said, looking briefly at Archie.

"Travers, I want you in London assisting with the planning for the next operation in the Mediterranean. I want every single lesson learned from this operation and no repetition of the mistakes. That's your job; you don't have to do all the planning; lessons learned is your job. Shout, swear, say what you like but make sure we're better next time.

"Gentlemen, I make no apology for the blunt nature of this order; we made mistakes on this one… acceptable errors; the cost of those mistakes in terms of lives lost was… acceptable. If we repeat those mistakes against the Germans in Northern France, our losses will be at least one hundredfold higher… if… we… are… lucky!

"Major Travers will read your reports on the landings and conduct personal interviews with *all* of you; you will tell him everything you did, right and wrong. His subsequent report will be for my eyes only. Do not attempt to bullshit him; he'll see it, then so will I. I quite like him, but he has a tendency to shoot people who upset him. He has personally killed more men than anyone I know; I am ordering you to ensure his aim remains on the Germans.

"Archie, I want you to carry on working simultaneously on the landing after next. Has your team started working on the intelligence requirement yet?"

"Yes, sir, three weeks ago."

"Well done, and the beaches."

"Two trial missions yesterday, sir."

Ike already knew the answers to those questions; he was giving Archie a chance to look good in the best company.

"George," he said, turning to Patton, "do you have any observations on the subject?"

"Well, I was hoping you'd let me keep the sonofabitch and his men in my team for the duration, but I'm content with your proposals; I'm sure we'll keep in touch, Archie," he nodded to him.

Something was definitely going on here. Archie thought.

"Mark?" he asked Major General Mark Clark

"Fine with me, Ike."

"Travers has my full confidence and that of the President and Prime Minister," Ike concluded.

Archie nodded firmly and quarter smiled, keeping his peripheral vision on the men in the room. Apparently, they'd expected Patton to explode at having to explain his actions to someone other than Ike. Then they could all join in with numbers to make their point. Instead, there was silence and the occasional nod in his direction from those present.

The event astonished Archie; he didn't show it for one second, though. Fortunately, he'd decided to practice nonchalance years ago. The assembled men looked at him and his youth; he couldn't be more than thirty, they thought. They'd seen him enter the room using his stick to walk better and the still-fresh scar above his left eye socket and the older one over his right eye. They saw the American Uniform Ike had insisted he wear for this meeting. They all promptly reasoned that a man bearing those marks and holding the confidence of Eisenhower, Clark and especially Patton was a man they should respect.

Ike watched the same faces and their reaction and knew he'd played it right. He'd ensured Archie would successfully achieve all he needed from any debriefs that followed. If Archie did some of his thinking for him, it would save him so much time and effort; the war was so young, and he was so tired already.

These senior men were old comrades and friends of his. Each one would trade on that in their dealings with him. Archie had no history with them; he'd have a clear mind and be impartial yet uncompromising in his analysis. They'd be wary of Archie, and that would do some of his dirty work for him. He'd keep them sharp in the early part of the war; some wouldn't be up to the job in real combat; Archie would find out who and tell him. He knew it wouldn't be Mark or George; he also knew Archie would see how he was using him and hoped he wouldn't mind.

Archie was such a useful tool, he'd fallen into Ike's lap, and he had to use him.

Ike knew he would use others less and kill them more readily; he'd decided he shouldn't kill Archie or any of his team if he could possibly avoid it. He made himself no promises and hoped for the best; having introduced Archie and his purpose to his senior officers, he asked him to leave and start his work immediately. He had other messages for his men he couldn't deliver in front of him. Although he knew George Patton well enough to know he'd talk frankly to Archie later. He would readily tell Archie where the others went wrong, and the others would take it better from anyone but George. He hoped Archie could do the same for George. Hindsight was a wonderful thing. He removed that thought from his mind and concentrated on North Africa, the battle and war not yet won.

*

Thursday 19th November 1942 - Bletchley Park

Archie, Rebecca, and Una arrived in Plymouth two days later and in Bletchley the same day. Conner was waiting for them, and tired as they were, he briefed them on the transfer of old tasks to the new team. Precisely how to use and not use, the intelligence coming in from Ultra was the new crucial issue, and Conner was the Officer in Charge. Too much action on the incoming messages would betray the code breaker's success; the right amount, released in the right way, was required, a tightrope walk without a safety net.

Conner had actively sought the leadership role for the sifting, grading, and dissemination of the Ultra Intelligence. He'd partly done that so he could spend more time with Alan, but he'd also decided to do it precisely because he didn't want to do it. The actual desire to undertake some very onerous tasks actually disqualified you from being the best person to do them. Anyone wanting to decide who lived and died was the wrong person for Ultra dissemination.

In practice, the task was already making him

withdrawn from others, and his relationship with Alan had to be as secret as Ultra. They couldn't be seen socialising too much, so much of their contact remained clandestine.

He'd been much more gregarious when he'd first teamed up with Archie. This wasn't how he'd envisaged himself then, he had intended to be what Archie was now, and he'd thought that was his purpose. He'd believed that all his upbringing had been so he could be Archie.

Now, Conner thought his purpose had been simply to find Archie and help him become what he was destined to be. He felt no jealousy or disappointment; he knew this was the foreordination he'd felt in Calais. It remained one more puzzle, and he was patiently waiting for Archie to solve it.

*

Archie took Conner aside, alone, to the bench by the rose bushes and sighed deeply.

"Are we no longer a team then?" Archie asked.

"We're two teams now, Archie old boy, mine and yours."

"Can I still come to you for help when I need it?"

"Oh no, Archie," he said. "You really haven't been paying attention, have you? I come to you for help now; you haven't caught me up; you've overtaken me, outgrown me now."

"Fuck off!"

"How would you like me to fuck off, sir?"

"Oh shit, I'm in it now."

"Yes, you are."

Chapter Four

Monday 9th November 1942 - Paris

Dolf Von Rundstedt laughed out loud.

It was the 9th of November 1942, one day after he found out about Operation Torch, the American invasion of the Vichy French controlled territories in North Africa along the Mediterranean and Atlantic coast. The French, ludicrously, were resisting the Americans; some had already surrendered, and more would certainly follow. In the meantime, as Dolf's jackboot ruled their capital city, the French Navy was attacking the American fleet.

Dolf's men were throwing Mr Thierry Lagardine out of his office, none too gently, but nothing undeserved. Lagardine was the French civilian Head of Public Transport in Paris. The meeting was nothing more than a courtesy; the man invariably did as he was told. The coward was without any backbone, balls or cock, and he'd talked of Vichy France fighting the Americans in North Africa for honour.

What a fucking imbecile; you died for honour; you didn't kill for it. Killing was for something else, for yourself, an extreme form of selfishness perhaps, maybe you enjoyed it, maybe someone paid you to do it.

The Americans were going to free France from German occupation. They were going to do that because the English refused to capitulate or sue for peace even when they knew they couldn't possibly win. So the Vichy French declined to speak to the English and shot at the Americans.

Dolf couldn't understand the French people. He had infinitely more respect for the French Resistance fighters he tortured and killed. They'd died with honour, alone and in agony; most still had balls, metaphorically speaking anyway.

His mind drifted towards his own escape plan, and he considered carefully what and when his next move should be.

His personal phone line rang. What now, he thought.

"Hallo, Von Rundstedt," he said.

"Dolf, it's Johannes; I need you now for Operation Fall Anton; bring your combat uniforms, be here by midday; that's an order, by the way."

"Yes, sir."

*

General Johannes Blaskowitz was in charge of the German First and Seventh Armies in Northern France. He was an old family friend of Dolf's and a true gentleman; he'd helped Dolf earlier in his career, so a debt was owed to him. Awkwardly, Johannes was not in the Fuhrer's favour; the SS and Himmler hated him, regarding his manner as far too soft.

He'd criticised SS tactics in the East to his superiors and to Hitler. That was an honourable act, fucking stupid, but with a measure of honour, somehow he'd survived and remained a General. His good family name was still useful, even under the Nazis.

Blaskowitz was leading Operation Anton; both his armies were to enter and take over Vichy-controlled parts of Southern France to the Mediterranean coastline. After the American landings in North Africa, the Vichy area in Southern France was no longer trusted, and German troops were to take over the whole area immediately. Future landings there by the Americans and British were highly probable. Sicily, Sardinia or Corsica were possible. A Vichy-controlled coast in Southern France was their easiest target, and he needed to negate that threat first.

They also needed to seize a large number of Vichy French Naval vessels based in the southern French ports before any Allied action could capture them. Seized then used by German personnel instead was another aim.

Hitler and Himmler wanted one SS man as Head of Security in Vichy when any fighting ended. Johannes had insisted on choosing who and chose Dolf. Johannes knew him, and the SS respected Dolf because of his work in Paris and public support for Major Oskar Alber instead of his softer superior. Oskar was also moving to Vichy and said he had no problem working for Dolf. Oskar was highly regarded in the SS. However, no Wehrmacht man would touch Oskar except Dolf.

Dolf had been offered a commission in the SS before the war; his bloodline and physical attributes made him an ideal candidate. He had politely declined; he wanted the fruits of war, not a never ending war.

Now, Hitler himself was effectively ordering Dolf to transfer to the SS and to exercise brutal control of the no longer neutral and now treacherous Vichy regime; no element of choice was involved.

As for the expected battle, well, it never materialised. The honourable Vichy resistance to the German occupation amounted to hostile radio broadcasts. The 50,000 men in the Vichy French Army surrendered with barely a shot being fired in anger. The Navy scuttled ships without firing a shot rather than allowing itself to fall into German hands. In North Africa, the French Navy had fired on American vessels; they resisted them more than they had the Germans. It ended, militarily, by the evening of the 11th of November 1942, but that was only the beginning of Dolf's troubles.

*

Dolf found his new quarters comfortable, and the absolute power he now held should have been attractive to him.

His new SS charges were, as he expected, difficult to control. A semi-civilised status quo existed in Paris that was absent in Vichy. The desire for fresh vengeance by his troops grew, albeit there was nothing much to avenge. His men treated the locals badly as a matter of routine rather than for any practical reason. He didn't fully trust his new men or the French, an uncomfortable position, even for a man with Dolf's Machiavellian nature. He could manipulate Oskar; he knew that from previous experience, it would take time and effort, though. What other choice did he have?

*
Monday 16th November – Vichy

Seven days later, after briefly sampling some of the local whores, none of whom made it past the door of his quarters, he sent to Paris for his friends. Two of his staff officers and ten of his most loyal guards, people whose trust he'd bought several times over, and they brought Annette with them.

Principally, the army chose Dolf for Head of Security as the only man acceptable to the SS and Wehrmacht. Having a joint team underneath him was unusual and acceptable only because of the high regard in which Dolf was held. Dolf and all his people adopted the SS uniform and had the obligatory tattoo showing their blood group under their left arm, the Blutgruppentätowierung. Not all SS men had the tattoo, but all of Oskar's men did, so Dolf made his men do the same. Dolf did it too, and he showed it proudly to his new men. They cheered and applauded.

Dolf's tattoo had worn off by each day's end, and Annette would redo it each morning, using the particular brand of ink and pen Johannes had procured for him. That tattoo might lead to summary execution or trial and a noose when the war ended. Definitely not what Dolf had spent years planning and working for.

Dolf knew when he judged Von Brander to be too soft in Paris, he was murdered by his more enthusiastic juniors. He didn't think Oskar would do that to him, though some of his new men might. He needed to be entirely ruthless, without mercy or pity, and to be clearly seen as such. He wouldn't have to do the dirty work himself, of course. Oskar was born for that gruesome task, but Dolf's full name and signature were on every set of orders issued.

If Gerolf and Gottlieb had been in Vichy, he would have had to let them stay.

*

The most inconvenient issues were his priorities; fortifying the southern coast of France against invasion wasn't a priority, but identifying and tracking down any resistance movement was. His top priority, which would consume most of his resources, was the deportation of Jews. They'd die on the journey, be gassed to death on arrival or worked to death while there. The lucky ones would be shot resisting arrest.

Now, Dolf didn't like Jews. Your upbringing defined what you liked, which was usually people who were similar to you. Some Jewish people looked fucking stupid, with their hair and funny hats, their false God with his stupid rules, and some taped a book to their foreheads! So Dolf looked down on them. He looked down on all of them, wouldn't want to live among them and felt that was a fair choice for him to make.

The industrial scale of their slaughter was beyond his reckoning. He had committed crimes, many crimes, killing and murder, all for his immediate survival and long-term benefit. Herding human beings like animals to a slaughterhouse was more than conventional crime, worse than evil, yet here he was, doing it. He was in charge of it, he was responsible, he also knew he'd continue to do it until he could effectively put his overall plan into practice.

Dolf was changing; he recognised that change without understanding it fully. He knew he'd carry on doing what he needed to for his own survival. It was how he felt about it that was different. Regrets and reflection were for after the war when he would be someone else. He might try to do some good; perhaps he'd pay someone else to do it for him. That would be easier, one step at a time, he thought.

Dolf's road to redemption would be a long journey; for the moment, he needed to concentrate on the cul-de-sac he was facing.

*

Monday 16th November 1942 - Vichy

Annette spoke to Dolf the evening she arrived in Vichy after they'd made love and lay on the bed.

"Sorry, Dolf, I didn't feel safe when you weren't there. Can I stay here with you? I know from what your men said on the journey… what you have to do now; I don't care.

"Your men like you, you know that. They'd rather be working for you than stay in Paris, they don't care what colour the uniform is, black or grey.

"I think they know the war is lost; they won't say it to me; they want to lose it as well as they can, get back to their families or to survive. They treated me well, with respect, more respect than the French. One of them, Dickon, the one with the best French, he said they liked me because I made you happy. He said no girl had ever made you happy, he was going to say whore, not girl, I know, but he didn't, and he smiled at me."

"Dickon is a good man, as good a German as you'll find in France, anyway. We should have stayed at home; what were we doing? What were we thinking? The victory felt good; it felt like revenge. We felt entitled to do it because we were the better men and because we could do it. It came too easily; we were never going to keep what we'd taken, never… but…."

"But what?"

"If we'd never done that, all that evil, all that murder, I'd never have met you. So I cannot wish it undone, the loss of my soul, for you is a price I'll pay."

She hugged him and saw a tear forming in his eye.

"Oh, Dolf, Dolf, what are we? What are we?"

"We are lovers. Star-crossed, foolish, damned even, but we have become lovers, whatever the world would call us. Annette, I am sorry; you must know this of me before we go on; you've never asked. Your family, I tried to find them after the café and the gendarme, they were already dead before you even saw the café. The SS are extremely efficient, and now I am the SS."

"I knew it, Dolf, so I never asked; I also have to survive with you. Do I… make you happy?"

"Yes, of course, you do, and I promise you, we will survive together," he took her face in his hands and moved her eyes up to his.

"I promise you, we will survive."

*

Tuesday 1st December 1942 – Bletchley

The marriage of Asgeir Thorson and Briony Samms took place at the local register office in Bletchley two weeks after the team returned from Operation Torch. It was a small functional ceremony, only Archie, Una and Rebecca as guests, no suits or dresses, only best uniforms. They did remember a camera this time and had to ask the Registrar's Clerk to take the photographs. Afterwards, they rushed to the Manor, where both teams were waiting.

It was bitterly cold, and a strong wind made it colder still that afternoon.

"Good Viking weather for a good Viking marriage," Asgeir said.

The legal ritual was essential to both of them, permanent and official. They still wanted to do something personal, not lavish but something with more meaning.

Asgeir had discussed doing something Norwegian or Viking, but goat slaughtering and an axe throwing contest seemed inappropriate. Archie had said he would arrange a surprise for them.

He asked Billy to track down two Viking style knives; there must be some in England. It was challenging and expensive, especially when Archie insisted Billy purchased them legally and needed documented provenance as well. Billy tracked down a matching pair at Sotheby's Auction House, not Viking, Norwegian and about two hundred years old. Billy had to pull a few favours and pay well over the reserve price to secure them without public auction. Archie didn't care about the cost; he never did.

The knives were beautiful, slim, pointed, silver blades with intricately woven gold threads around the handle. Each thread formed what looked like an old rune letter. They were impractical for any functional use except maybe a letter opener. They looked beautiful and classy, which was essential for the gift. The couple could exchange them as gifts from one another. Archie swore Billy to secrecy on their exact value.

Briony cried when she saw them, and Asgeir almost

cried too.

"How did you do that? How did you find them? You couldn't have made them?" he said, "Briony, I give you this knife marked with the Viking Rune B, and I accept from you this knife marked with an A. May our enemies see them and withdraw from battle."

Billy and Archie exchanged looks and shrugs; they hadn't known what the Runes signified; they'd thought they looked good. Una and Rebecca gave Archie a hug, then moved to Billy, who got a bigger one.

The men, while slightly tipsy, decided to have a knife throwing contest in the garden regardless. Lightfoot won.

Freddie was spending time talking to Marion Hill, not together yet, but closer. Una would know what was happening; he'd ask her later.

Begley was exchanging glances with Celia Cordingley, who, as far as Archie knew, came from the landed gentry; he wasn't expecting that.

Billy helped Mary Murphy with baby Molly as usual. Uncle Billy, she called him now, somehow Archie didn't think Billy was content with that; Billy was a big boy, and Mary was his problem.

Today was a good day, so little care, only happiness and rest with a few pleasant future possibilities. Archie enjoyed the day; Una insisted he have a glass of wine too, which he did and suddenly felt tired, so Rebecca and Una took him back to their new rented house. They put him to bed, then stayed downstairs and talked for hours. Archie slept soundly for twelve hours, secure in the certain knowledge they were safe and only a few feet away from him.

*

Monday 7th December 1942 - London

Archie went to his first meeting of the advance planning committee for the invasion of Northern France. Twenty men sat around a perfectly polished set of tables and chairs, strictly organised according to rank, except for Archie, placed as far as possible from the Chairman.

They reluctantly allowed Rebecca, Una and Mary Murphy into the meeting; they had a higher security clearance than most at the table. The chairman told them to sit behind Archie and told them not to talk. Idiots, Archie decided; the three of them knew more about the war than many of those present.

Ike had already given Archie his tasks in two specialist areas: the scouting of the beaches and the Intelligence gathering. He wanted the freedom to do that, to his own high standards and to attend as few meetings as possible.

Brigadier Francis Kesler introduced himself and went around the table as each person identified themselves.

"Gentlemen, we are privileged to be present at the beginning of the boldest plan. You will already have seen the original ideas, and the top brass tell me we have a blank sheet of paper."

Or blank minds, Archie thought. They'd drafted the original plan nearly two years previously when there was no American involvement, no Atlantic Wall and before Dieppe! It was a joke now.

"Sir, I have a large number of sheets of paper, each full of writing; I'll pass them around," Archie said, determined to be listened to as early as possible.

Archie handed out copies of the invasion's strategic aims, the tactics necessary to deliver that strategy, the intelligence requirements resulting from those documents and an early draft of what was already known. Then finally, a list of specialist needs, a deflection strategy designed to conceal the invasion site and finally, a list of flaws in the planning and execution of the Dieppe raid.

"The review paper on Operation Torch remains with General Eisenhower," he added to emphasise his point.

None of it was perfect, he couldn't do it all himself, but none of it was wrong, none of it would cost lives, most of it would save them, and all of it was practical. An idiot could understand it. An idiot would have to.

"Right, thank you for this, Travers; I'll get one of my team to look at it later. We will now proceed to discuss what the standing agenda for these meetings will be; any ideas, anyone?"

Yes, I sent it to you last week, and you haven't looked at it, you old fool.

And you'll do more than look at it; you'll do it. Ike's already seen and approved it, but he wants to see unguarded rather than sycophantic responses to it.

Ike was good at this game.

This was still going to be a long, tedious meeting; at least four people from the disastrous Dieppe planning were present. None of them were pleased to receive his unofficial verdict on Dieppe, which, of course, was a complete success. If you told a lie often enough, it became the truth; all good liars knew that. Only the very best liars told themselves the truth.

One of the Dieppe Planners particularly annoyed Archie, a handsome, immaculately dressed young man, a nice chap, he was sure. He was there, in that rank, on that day and others, only because of his ancestry, nothing else.

One American queried incredulously the option of using a floating harbour to avoid the danger of capturing a port intact, and a few uninformed sniggers echoed around the table.

"There's some background to that idea," said Archie, interrupting the awkward silence.

"The report doesn't mention this, but when I originally wrote down the idea in 1939, it was from the German's perspective, using them to invade Southern England. The Germans do have a working model. It's just too small for the Channel depth and tides. If you can make a pontoon bridge, you can make a pontoon harbour, and before we quibble about credit for the idea, Julius Caesar reportedly used one in Egypt in about 50 BC. So, unless we're saying Hitler and Caesar can make one and we can't, we should tell the engineers what we want and let them build it."

*

"What a bunch of cunts!" said Rebecca angrily, thankfully once they were safely in Archie's car.

"That's not fair," Una added, "some of them were just wankers."

Mary giggled.

"No, some of them are okay, honestly," said Archie, "it's when you get them all together they adopt an unspoken collective herd instinct. Self-protection, a conspiracy of incompetence, one cannot criticise another, or you admit your part in the historical deception.

"I think Moses started it, the Ten Commandments; I ask you, you only need a couple, one being don't be a cunt and pretend you've met God up a mountain with no witnesses.

"Ike'll sort it out; he's already got my reports. I've said my piece early enough this time. I'll get to say I told you so, at least, keep an eye out for idea theft, renamed and credited to some lordly toff."

"So you don't want to kill any of them then?" asked Rebecca.

"Oh yeah, I'm bringing a fucking bomb in my briefcase next time… and that's a joke, by the way, Mary."

Mary giggled so much he feared she might wet herself.

*

Saturday 12th December 1942 – The Manor

A few days later, Archie arranged to meet Conner privately at the Manor, it was dry, so they sat in the garden under the Pergola.

"Conner, these meetings I go to, even the ones I chair and control, there's something there I can't define. Una and Rebecca see it; there's a barrier I'm up against; there's a club I'm not in and don't want to fucking join anyway. They merely tolerate me. I have ten times the fighting experience of any of them, and the bastards look down on me. Yes, there's maybe three in ten I can stand; the rest are insufferable half-wits. Is it just paranoia?"

"It's partly routine paranoia; it's also the establishment; we've talked about it before. They know you didn't go to the right school and don't have a family name. They're frightened of you, too; you say what you think now. You're dangerous in your own right; you've killed personally, they'd get someone else to do it, or they'd kill metaphorically by ostracising, refusal of club membership and the like. I'm tolerated because I went to the right schools and am independently wealthy; they like that."

"What about you, long term?"

"Oh, yes, I'm tainted by association with you, I'm afraid. When the war's over, we're gone, I'm sure, no longer needed. SOE and the American OSS, full of rich landed gentry and country gentlemen. In the States, it's family, like Vanderbilt, Astor, Roosevelt even."

"So what about those names I got from Winters, loose tongues, divided loyalties, high birth, usually a mountain in Germany. What happened to the names I gave you and Gubbins?

"Country Gentleman, I'm afraid, club members discreetly moved to less sensitive areas of Government, and a promotion thrown in as a comfort."

"For fuck's sake, will it change after the war? What if the socialists get to power?"

"Oh God no, they're worse than the toffs, treat their staff like dirt, and they need the money, most of them. Their grip on power is even more desperate."

"And Gubbins, what club is he in?"

"He's Churchill's man; no one can touch him while Winston's in power. After that, who knows?"

"You're not cheering me up at all."

"This might, they're transferring Duke Disaster of Dieppe, another promotion actually. You won't have to suffer his unwanted attention at meetings; he does like you ever so much," Conner laughed. "At least we can do our jobs while it matters; after the war, we'll do whatever the hell we like."

"And how are things?"

"Things?"

"Yes, things, relationship things."

"Good, very good, thank you, we do need another country to be in or another planet."

"Good. One day we'll be exactly what we want without

fear of convention or law, approval or otherwise. We could buy our own country, a small island maybe? There's definitely an idea there."

*

Christmas 1942 – The Cottage

Archie didn't like the new house the four of them shared; it didn't feel at all like home. He called in favours and paid excessive rates of pay, and he had the cottage restored and ready for occupation by the 20th of December 1942. They worked doubly hard before the holiday so the five of them, Alan included, could enjoy Christmas Eve and Day in peace and lock out the rest of the world.

Conner and Alan could relax and be themselves safely. They had a tree, decorations, small presents, food, and drink. Alan did ask what they were actually celebrating since none of them believed in the Immaculate Conception, and St. Nicholas was a Greek.

"We are celebrating family," Archie said, "the fact that none of us are related by blood is irrelevant. This is my family right here; we'll toast one absent friend, Billy Perry."

He raised the small glass of wine he shared with Una.

It was such a simple, uncomplicated time, a log fire seemed the height of luxury, and they played Monopoly on the floor in front of it. Alan won; he'd already established the mathematically best strategy to win, even if the dice were "an almost random factor", as only he could put it.

Archie and Una won at Snakes and Ladders.

Conner and Alan went to bed early.

Archie kept an eye and an ear open and four Thompson submachine guns and a sniper rifle in the corner of the living room. Archie and his two girls slept together on the sofa under a couple of blankets, still fully clothed. Una said Rebecca shouldn't be on her own that night, and Archie agreed. It was pleasant, and their proximity did give him a relaxing erection, and he did nothing about it.

*

Dolf and Annette spent all Christmas Day and night

alone in his quarters. His trusted guards worked hard shifts to keep them safe; they needed to; Dolf was not a popular man in the south of occupied France.

He drank rather too much, as did Annette; Heinrich Himmler had sent him a dozen bottles of Champagne as a present on Christmas Eve. The drink came with a note thanking Dolf for achieving his monthly target number of deportations. It was a high number he didn't want to think about; thousands, so he drank more. Perhaps if the reward disappeared, maybe the sin would too; he'd give some bottles to his men, he thought. Yes, that would work.

There were ten executions on Christmas Eve to teach the French a lesson. Oskar wanted twenty, and Dolf could hardly go walking around the city, explaining it could have been worse.

Dolf had useful connections and plans. He labelled each of the execution victims as Jewish and sent them on his next deportation train. The ten Jews saved by that action wouldn't escape; they'd die a little later than scheduled. Was that good or only less evil?

He needed a better plan; he needed clerks, yes, clerks here and at the destination. It wouldn't work forever; it wouldn't need to; it might work for long enough to make a small difference, two minutes fewer in the fires of Hell perhaps.

*

The following day, Dolf was alone with Dickon in his office, trying to work out how to artificially inflate the number of Jewish deportations from Vichy. When they'd drafted a rough plan they could manoeuvre into place, Dolf was silent for a few minutes, lost in thought.

"Dickon, what am I?" he asked.

"You are Rodolf Von Rundstedt, and I follow you; that's all I know."

"Why do you follow me?"

"I like the direction you take."

"Thank you, Dickon, that's a good thing for me to know."

Chapter Five

Summer 1943 - England

Archie felt he spent most of 1943 in meetings and planning. A piece of paper with words typed on it stood as his measure of success. Attending a meeting that wasn't pointless became his goal. He was with his friends and his lover, although real action, physical jeopardy, was missing. There was plenty occurring across the entire world, but none belonged to him.

His intelligence team became relentlessly efficient, and an enormous sharp picture of the Normandy coastline was taking shape. Mary Murphy had turned into Spud, Archie would ask if she could do something, and she'd say she'd done it the previous day. She managed and led her team; some could do one, but most couldn't do both. He made her a Lieutenant; she was doing his job for him and deserved the recognition. An additional tinkering with the ranks in the team rewarded merit; he let her take charge of that and take the credit for it too.

His operational team undertook a long series of reconnaissance visits to the Normandy coast and trained others for that task. Archie knew what Gabe had said to Asgeir on the beach at Fedala and made sure they continued to practice exactly that way. The men who'd complained about the hard work they'd had to do were imposing the same strict discipline on the men they trained.

Begley was doing some work with Percy Hobart on his 'Funnies', Specialised Armour Development for use on D-Day. Begley had no shortage of novel ideas for blowing things up; Archie gave him a couple of ideas and asked him to consider ways of protecting his men from being blown up.

Billy also accompanied some recce flights in a converted two-seater Spitfire; Archie knew Billy would see what no one else could.

*

Billy marvelled at the feeling of flight; he'd never flown before. Why would he? Where would he go?

This was a new world for him. Flying was glamorous, Billy wasn't.

He'd done with school aged twelve, too big for a chimney, too small for a hard man; he'd been a runner. A delivery boy for a neighbour, Nathaniel Cairney, who worked on the Royal Albert Docks. Nothing legitimate and nothing deadly, some cream off the top, breakages and the like. Billy grew up tough; most did, could manage a fight if necessary, and knew when to make a joke or plain run away from trouble. He knew right from wrong, his parents had been good people, but he couldn't follow the rules and make a living, so he did a little of both.

He'd done that till the First War started, and like a million other mugs he'd joined up, it felt like the righteous choice at the time. Old Nat Cairney knew people in the local regiment and pulled a few favours to get Billy, a decent assignment as a machine gunner. He got proper training and better rations. Some running and delivery duties earned that for him.

As a machine gunner, Billy was relatively safe, apart from the cold, damp, rats, fleas, poison gas attacks and shelling. He could hide when the shelling started, come out when it stopped, and then man his gun with his mates.

Billy never went over the top, never walked, crawled or stumbled towards a German trench facing certain death from someone just like he was.

Billy was the triggerman on his gun, and he was good at it; *Billy Steady,* they called him. He could fire a series of short blasts across a wide area, maximising the firing on the biggest concentration of targets while not letting his gun overheat. He had nerve and could hold it; his squad mates liked him, and he was lucky.

The first few times he'd fired the gun, it had been good fun, a few stupid slow Jerrys moving in his general direction from a good distance away. They came at him, he fired, and they stopped coming.

As time went on, the attacks lasted longer and involved more men, who got closer.

It came to hand to hand fighting once, only once, and Billy had killed without hesitation with his bayonet.

This was a different war; he was a different Billy.

*

Gabe said Archie had cabin fever, "that boy needs to kill something or be in danger somehow. If this was the States, I'd take him hunting; there's no game worth the name in England."

Conner suggested Archie learn to pilot a plane, and he took enough lessons to take off and land in a Spitfire; he flew for ten hours in total. He felt he knew nothing and was shocked that many who'd fought in the Battle of Britain had fewer hours and still been thrust into combat.

*

Summer 1943 – Vichy

For Dolf Von Rundstedt, the summer of 1943 was an uncertain and busy time.

Dickon was driving him and Annette back to his Headquarters near Vichy. The summer's day had been unusually warm, and he'd taken Annette for a picnic next to the nearby river. It seemed a ridiculously indulgent thing to do, but Annette could rarely leave his quarters. She'd become known as his mistress and couldn't blend into a small city as well as she could into Paris.

So he'd taken her for a picnic, warmth, and fresh air, to pretend to be normal for a few hours. Ten armed guards in an armoured personnel carrier nearby were as normal as it could be for Dolf. Dickon selected fifty guards for Dolf, fanatics to a man, battle hardened, competent, diligent and absolutely necessary. He had been most discerning in his choices; he had chosen the best killers but no rapists.

Dolf knew there wouldn't be any Allied invasion of Northern France this year, and yet the ease of the Allied landings in Sicily still surprised him. The war in the east was going badly, and the High Command were diverting excellent German troops to deal with the new threat in Italy. The Italians wouldn't be much help. Dolf did need the war to end quickly but needed the Americans and British to beat the Russians to Berlin. The Americans and British might display some pity, but the Russians wouldn't, especially given the treatment his comrades had meted out to them.

His current role required an absolute absence of pity, obliging him to sign papers each day that committed mass murder, and there was nothing he could do to avoid that. So he did it, and he always met his target numbers.

However, as with much of what Dolf did, what he wrote down was not the whole truth.

From his local holding camp, he sent two trains each week containing nine hundred Jews to the Treblinka extermination camp, where the vast majority were killed immediately. One of those two trains also 'went' to Buchenwald, where Gerolf, Gottlieb, and key personnel were heavily bribed to record false details of arrival and death. That train should have held another nine hundred but only held four hundred and fifty.

Oberfuhrer Hermann Pister was the Commandant of Buchenwald. He'd been a mere car salesman before the war and was keenly profiting from his temporary power. His profit was trivial and unimaginative; Admiral Canaris had told Dolf he was open to approach, lacking in scruples as well as competence. He was an easy target for Dolf's spare Deutschmarks and false promises of wealth securely salted away in Switzerland.

Records at Buchenwald were already notoriously poor, partly to disguise the number of Prisoner of War executions, partly due to lack of competence, partly, nobody cared. It was an easy task for Pister's clerks to show another few hundred extra deaths each week; it helped the lazy bastard with his targets too.

Dolf tried to work out whether he was saving four hundred and fifty lives per week or taking nine hundred. Was delaying their round up and killing, saving anyone or killing them more slowly? By saving four hundred and fifty, was he only responsible for killing four hundred and fifty on that train?

The certainty of his privileged upbringing hadn't prepared him to reflect on his actions, and he'd picked a bad place and time to develop scruples. He had to use the skills he possessed.

He knew they'd catch him out eventually and reasoned he could weasel his way out of it. He was a valuable asset, had a deserved reputation as a killer and had financial resources sufficient to purchase a blind eye if he needed one.

By not wasting all his resources on the pointless killing of Jews, he'd ruthlessly repressed the French Resistance in Vichy. Oskar was a good comrade in many respects; when well directed, he'd foiled two attempts to assassinate Dolf. In practice, many Vichy French collaborators had assisted their German hosts far too readily to earn any prospect of forgiveness from their own countrymen. They were as good as dead already; Dolf would use them without hesitation or pity until then. Their information was always good.

*

Dolf half relaxed on the return journey from the picnic and held Annette's hand in the back seat of his staff car. It was a pleasant illusion.

Dickon slowed the car down as they approached the small side country road that would take them to his headquarters, a mansion in its own secure grounds.

"Down!" he shouted, speeding up and swerving to the left. Dolf heard a thud on his car door, followed by the noise of a grenade exploding to their rear.

Dolf had thrown himself over Annette and couldn't see what had happened. Then he heard three rapid bursts of gunfire, then silence.

"Wait, stay down, stay down," Dickon shouted, "it's quiet now; yes, they have them; it looks like only two of them."

"Take Annette straight home now," Dolf said, then calmly climbed out of his car; he knew what role the situation required him to play.

He walked casually back towards his men about twenty yards away, straightening his uniform and tie, smoothing his hair away from his forehead. His men continued checking nearby hedges for others and were confident they had both men involved. One man lay on the ground, riddled with bullets which would kill him soon. One guard was searching his pockets and finding nothing, his identity papers discarded earlier. The second attacker was a boy, perhaps 14 years old, not shaving yet, small and pathetic, trying to look brave with a poorly faked look of defiance.

Dolf shook his head without physically moving it; the stupid fools had brought a child to a man's war. He toyed with his Luger, which he'd taken from his holster, then looked closely at the boy, considering briefly whether to shoot him in the head on the spot. He had that within him, it would be a mercy, but this was the third recent attempt on his life, and Annette had been at risk this time.

He looked at his men, smiled and nodded.

"Take him, torture him, find out everything he knows; I want all his contacts and family arrested by ten o'clock tonight. Tell him If he talks quickly, then we might let his family live; make sure he knows that, make sure he doesn't know we'll kill them, anyway."

*

At nine o'clock that night, Dolf was still in his office with Dickon. He had no real friends; only Dickon came close; he liked and trusted him more than anyone. Dickon was forty-one years old with a wife and three children. Dickon should have been a school teacher or an office manager. Dickon had never seen real action, and Dolf was glad he'd never made him kill anyone. Not yet, anyway. He wished he hadn't made him have the tattoo, but it was too late for that now.

His phone rang, and he answered it himself. His men had arrested all the boy's family and contacts. The boy was no longer available for questioning, he hadn't survived his interrogation, and he hadn't talked quickly. There was one unexpected success, they'd found an English girl hidden behind a false wall in the cellar of the family farm. They'd told the Gestapo, who wanted to take her to Paris immediately.

"No, not immediately; it's me she's tried to kill, I'll speak to her now, and the Gestapo will wait their turn."

*

The girl's cell was clean and well lit, the small bucket was still empty, there was nothing else in the room and no window.

The girl was young, around twenty-five and naked, crouched in the corner; she had a cut on her mouth where they'd searched her for a poison tablet in a false tooth. She wasn't a beauty, slim and full breasted, long haired, and a man could certainly enjoy that body.

"They have searched you everywhere?" Dolf asked in English and received no answer, so he motioned his men outside, shutting the door.

He sat on the floor opposite her, cross-legged and relaxed.

"My name is Rodolf Von Rundstedt," he said confidently, "Head of Security in Vichy. I can see from your expression you know that fact already."

The cell door opened, and a guard offered the girl a blanket and a tin mug of water. She didn't accept them, and he left them next to her.

"You have the base of a false tooth to hold the poison capsule firmly. I expect the English made it poorly, it kept coming loose, and you had to ditch it instead of risking death if you sneezed."

The girl looked sideways at him briefly, enough to show him it was true.

"Please, use the blanket; it's cold," he said, but she still stayed motionless, avoiding further eye contact.

"I have another poison capsule, British issue; I can give it to you if you wish, I can say it was deep in your arse, so we didn't find it. You could attack me, and I could shoot you. You could insult me loudly; I could shoot you on a whim. I'm known to be capable of that."

Nothing.

"The choices I give you are better than you face in Avenue Foch. The Gestapo will take your fingernails first, then the toenails, then any part they take a liking to. Your breasts will appeal to them, I assure you."

Still nothing.

"Let's talk about common friends then, my friend Archie Travers Austin and your colleague Maria Secondigny, Rebecca Rochford. I hear my sources are excellent, you know."

A glance and an open mouth.

"Good, we are making progress."

"Can I have the capsule then?" she said, holding out her cupped hand.

"Well, I said you could, so I must give it to you. Please don't break it yet."

"Thank you," she said, holding it between her finger and thumb, then pulling the blanket around her.

"There is one small detail I wish to know. Why me? This is the third attempt on my life in two months. I'm not a good person, but I'm not a good target either; it won't help win the war if I'm dead; I'm not a great General. Why me? Does Archie hate me so much?"

He paused at the puzzled look he received.

"Good, it's not Archie, that would have been a great pity, and Rebecca Rochford deserved to escape. Wait, I see it in your face, the person who sent you doesn't like Archie, and you're thinking what that means. I'm a target because it will hurt Archie, that's it. It still doesn't quite make sense, does it?"

She shook her head slightly.

"The people who sent you," he said, watching her face change when he got something wrong.

"No, the man who sent you, he fucking hates Archie. You're realising he knew about my connection with Archie, didn't tell you, and he should have. He's killed you by sending you here for nothing. There are nearly fifty people who'll die for this act today, they must die, and I cannot save them."

He took a small hip flask from his pocket.

"Please have a sip; look, I'll go first," he had a sip, passed it to her, and she took it. "Do you need a cigarette? I don't smoke, but I can get you some."

The girl shook her head, "No, thank you."

"This is bad, very bad," said Dolf

"No, it's a very good Brandy."

"No, not the… sorry, the English humour still sometimes escapes me. Your presence and your mood are very bad news for me indeed. I am the worst SS bastard in France; an Englishman has sent you to kill me because it will hurt another Englishman who I met for twenty minutes three years ago. Now, I have to fucking save you. Look at me, woman. Do you want to be saved? Yes or No?"

"Yes, of course, I want to be saved."

"Right, I need your real name, date, and place of birth, where you went to school, where we met in 1936, how we met in England when I first fucked you. Then what you've done since, in the service of the Reich."

Twenty minutes later, Dolf and the girl emerged from the cell; she wearing his uniform jacket and nothing else; he doing up his flies as she embraced and kissed him, laughing.

"Gentlemen, let me introduce an old friend of mine, Judith Cunningham; she has worked for me since 1936; as you can see, we had some catching up to do. We can shoot the rest tomorrow; we have everyone we need."

"And find the idiot who failed to find this capsule inside me and give him a slap. The dolt thinks a woman's vagina only extends as far as his pinkie; he must have a small prick, unlike Dolf," said Judith in excellent German.

*

Dolf made one quick call to his old and reliable friend that night, called in one favour and promised two others in return. Canaris was a good man who had trained and briefed Dolf before his studies in England in 1936. He was also Admiral Wilhelm Franz Canaris, Chief of the Abwehr, German Military Intelligence. If he agreed that Dolf had a secret English contact, then it was true beyond doubt. Canaris was playing a hard game, though, and Dolf would be taking great risks when his old friend called those favours in.

*

Annette didn't like Judith even when Dolf assured her he hadn't fucked her in the cell, as everyone said, and she definitely wouldn't share their bed. She did have to stay in his quarters; nowhere else was remotely safe. The Gestapo were angry but dare not challenge him directly. He had the others executed immediately; he couldn't take a risk on them saying anything to throw doubt on his story. It was merely one more atrocity bearing his name; he hardly gave it any thought; he planned to change his name later.

All his attention remained on why someone that high in British intelligence would target him; why would they want to ensure he never met Archie again? That was all he could guess.

He remembered that first instant he'd seen Archie and recognised him; he'd seen him somewhere before. It must be the British Library; he knew now they'd both spent time there. The timings were wrong; they were there at different times, different ages. It wasn't logical.

It had to be his dreams, but you couldn't dream a face and then see it again years later. It couldn't happen; it was a trick of the mind, coincidence, and confusion. In the dreams, he'd been older than Archie, fifteen years at least, and Archie was his pupil; the reality was the other way round, Archie bested him.

He took Judith out onto the balcony of his quarters; she was calm and watchful, still wary of telling him too much, still making him guess.

"You still won't name your handler?"

"Not yet. I can't just tell you who the highest ranking

people in British Military Intelligence are."

"Especially MI6."

She said nothing.

"Describe him to me."

"No," she said in a protective and defensive tone that caused a leap in Dolf's thinking process.

"Shall I describe him to you?"

"Go on then."

He described his short wavy hair, the lines across his forehead, the full arched eyebrows, wide eyes, round face, a little overweight and a strong, prominent chin, long nose, bulbous even, with matching lips. A face that looked weary of whatever world he inhabited, whatever dream.

"Your family name includes a noble title; he was fucking you before he sent you here and said he'd marry you when you came back. He may even have meant it."

"Fucking Hell, you can't know that, you can't, you can't."

"You're right, it's not possible, I cannot know his names, and he cannot be using them. I am sorry, Judith, you can never go back to England and hope to live; you are safer here. When you tell me the name he's using now, I'll tell you who he really is."

*

Two days later, Judith Cunningham had gone without a trace and without telling him more. Dolf couldn't be sure if the Gestapo had taken her and created an excellent cover story. It was unlikely; they weren't that inventive or subtle, maybe she'd done it all herself, or it could involve a third party. Whatever, he had other pressing matters to attend to, his survival.

The same day Dickon drove him and Annette to Abwehr headquarters in Berlin, where he scoured every single photograph they held of British Military Intelligence Personnel.

Eventually, he found a picture of Brendan Bracken and Churchill leaving a building in Whitehall with Colin Gubbins. A smaller sturdy man descended some steps in the background, his face circled in red ink with a question mark next to it. It was the face he expected, beyond doubt and beyond any reasonable explanation. It was the forty-five-year-old face of Gnaeus Pompeius Magnus. Pompey the Great a man who had died on the 29th of September 48 BC.

He'd seen that face in dreams; he'd seen it in books, too; you could dream of a face you'd seen, especially as a young man with lofty aims.

He took the photograph to Canaris in his private office.

"Yes, I know the man's name now," Canaris said, "it's only in my head, nowhere else. He has many followers, and yet he works entirely for himself. One of his followers is also mine, so I know a little about him. It's strange to relate this, Dolf; I know he has asked about you and Travers, Calais and St. Nazaire. His bloodline is noble, but it isn't German or truly English. I'll tell you all I know, but the favours you owe me are increasing in number."

Dolf said nothing of this to Dickon or Annette, who sensed that no questions were welcome anyway; they would think he'd lost his mind, and perhaps he had.

They made the long drive to Paris with an overnight stop and went to the Musee du Louvre. Dolf's face was influence enough to be granted sight of a bust he knew was carefully stored in the Museum cellars. Not valued enough to have been stolen, not interesting enough to be displayed.

It was a white marble bust of Marcus Licinius Crassus, Consul of the Roman Republic, in 55 BC, and it was Dolf's face.

He'd seen a grainy photo of the bust in a textbook at school and thought nothing of it when he'd seen the two-dimensional image aged 12. Crassus had longer hair, perhaps twenty years older than Dolf was now, a fuller face through decadence, yet still his face, beyond all reason.

He shook his head and considered all he'd planned so carefully for so long and felt doubt. Were they even his plans? Was he the player he'd supposed, or was he part of the game?

"No," he said aloud, "I am not without power; I am one of three; if I choose the right partner, I can win this time. I won't be anyone else's quarry."

He returned to his car.

"Get me out of this place, Dickon; anywhere else will do, home," he said, then closed his mind to everything outside of him and thought.

'Wherever home is? Another city, another town or country, another world, another time. I need time to think.

I have reason, and I can still doubt.

Two people could share the same looks, that could happen, family resemblances, identical twins. The odds were long, but it could be so.

Maybe Archie looked a little like Gaius of the Julii, but what of it?

Three people looked like three other people; that could happen. There was no divine purpose in this, no meaning; there were no Gods.

He'd read books and had dreams; the mind could play tricks on a man in those moments between waking and sleeping.

He knew Archie had read the same subjects as he; many young boys read of the Romans and Greeks and played at soldiers, kings, and empires.

This was the biggest war the world had ever seen; war made enemies of friends. Archie had made friends and enemies, and so had he; jealousy and rivalry were constant themes throughout all ages.

He could explain it all as highly unlikely but still possible.

All of it except one detail.

Why would a man, who looked like Pompey, want to kill a man who looked like Crassus in order to hurt a man who looked like Caesar? Perhaps Canaris could find out more.

I do have other bigger problems to worry about.'

*
September 1943 – Bletchley Park

Later in September 1943, Gubbins and Conner

intriguingly requested a hush-hush meeting with Archie in the Mansion at Bletchley Park.

"We need someone to go to Denmark and bring someone back," Gubbins said.

"Piece of cake, shall I swim?" Archie answered.

"It has to be you."

"I'll need a boat then. So, why is Bohr in such danger now?"

"The Germans have decided he's Jewish, and you're not supposed to know who it is."

"What about all the other Jews there? The intercepts show they're planning a purge there."

"We can't rescue them all."

"We could get a bigger boat."

"Be serious, man."

"Dynamo, what about lots of small boats going to Sweden? It's only a tenth of an inch away on my map. There're a million beaches and inlets on both sides."

"We need Bohr, we don't need… you're right, we've spent too much time not doing anything because the problem's too big and too far away."

"This is a workable option," Archie said, "a few thousand, a few small boats, a few short miles. We know the Swedes give shelter to pilots, POWs, and refugees; they don't shout about it for fear of the Germans. Well, they don't have to fear them so much now; they're not going to invade Sweden, they can't defend what they've already got. We can make them promises of protection; the Americans can anyway. We can quietly put the word out to the Danes that they're welcome, so it's worth the risk. Then we get one of our own Royals, preferably one that's not too German, to speak to their King Whatsisname."

"Will you help when needed?"

"Glad to, as long as I don't have to swim."

*

Wednesday 6th October 1943 - Sweden

Gubbins and Churchill were real players of the game Archie only dabbled in, and they developed a plan.

On the 6th of October 1943, Archie found himself in the co-pilot's seat of a de Havilland DH.98 Mosquito Night Fighter that bore the colours and livery of the civilian British Overseas Airways Corporation. A forgivable falsehood as it landed anonymously in neutral Sweden. The pilot remained sitting in the aircraft while the Swedish ground staff refuelled it for an immediate return.

Archie stepped outside and saw a huge pair of Swedish Naval Personnel; they looked like even bigger versions of Asgeir and Baldr; he could use a couple of those back home.

"Good morning, Mr Travers."

"Good morning."

"We have your passenger; there will be no conversation," the taller one said.

"Okay," Archie said

Archie took the arm of the nervous Nils Bohr, ushering him into the plane's bomb bay, where a mattress, helmet, and oxygen mask were laid out for him. Archie reached down to lift the boarding ladder and shut the door; the taller Swedish Naval man approached the aircraft, crouching next to him.

"Major Travers, please know, there are many of the old blood who regret that we sit and watch other men fight our battles for us in this lifetime. I hope to do better in the next one. Give my regards to my distant cousins who fight alongside you, to your wife and your skjaldmaer. Good Luck."

Archie smiled and nodded.

The return journey was incident free and dull, so Archie decided to check on Bohr. Archie's ten hours of training that year technically qualified him as a co-pilot, or so Gubbins told him when stressing again that the pilot mustn't see Bohr's face.

The boredom proved useful; he discovered Bohr was unconscious, having taken his oxygen mask off. Archie replaced it for him and waited until he was compos mentis, showed him again how to use the radio and mask properly, spoke to him briefly, then resumed his seat by the pilot. He checked him twice more on the journey.

The Mosquito wasn't pressurised and flew at high altitude to evade any enemy aircraft over Norway.

They landed near Glasgow, Abbotsinch Airport. Representatives of the 'Alloys' team whisked Bohr immediately away with a couple of shady looking types in civvies, MI6 Archie concluded, they didn't look stupid enough for Special Branch.

Conner was there waiting to drive him south. "Everything go okay?" he asked.

"We nearly killed him; he took his mask and helmet off halfway back, said it was too tight. Did you see his forehead? It's twice normal size, there he is, brain the size of a fucking building, common sense of a house brick. Fucking idiot, are you sure we've got the right bloke."

"Typical boffin."

"Who's that round-faced cunt with the Alloys chaps?"

"MI6, I think. Never said a word, kept his distance."

"Looks vaguely familiar, and he gave me a funny look like he knew me too. Kind of… that he knew me but was shocked to see me. Ugly bastard, though; I wouldn't forget a face like that."

*

On the 2nd of October 1943, Swedish Radio had already announced publicly that Jewish refugees would be offered asylum there. The Germans did little, but the Danish resistance movement was very active and brave; thousands of Danish Jews escaped with their help. Archie would never know how many were rescued, but he knew from intercepts the Germans expected to deport and kill 7,800.

*

The drive to Bletchley was a good chance for two friends to catch up; they rarely spent a full day together.

"They've stolen another of your ideas, you know," said Conner to Archie.

"Tell me something I don't know. The Mulberries?

Which one?"

"Plato."

"Oh, the fuel pipeline, it wasn't much of an idea; they have short, small circumference rubber pipes now, that was just a wider longer pipe. Hey Presto."

"Yes, and the cheeky bastards have called it PLUTO, pipeline under the ocean, instead of PLATO, pipeline across the ocean."

"Instead of naming it after a great mind, they named it after an imaginary cartoon dog! Fucking brilliant."

"Is Pluto a dog?"

"I think so, or is he the tall dog that dresses as a man and stands upright but's really another stupid dog?"

"I thought he was Popeye's arch enemy?"

"No, that's Bluto!"

"Are you sure?"

"Yes, I'm sure; look, a ten-year-old boy could understand that."

"Well, go out and find me one because I can't make head or tail of it."

"You stole that line!"

"Who from?"

"The Marx Brothers."

"Karl Marx had nine brothers and sisters; what's that got to do with anything?"

"Not Karl, Groucho!"

"Oh right, he's the one who can't talk."

"No, you're doing this deliberately, aren't you?"

"Yes, Alan is teaching me humour. Alan style."

"It's good; I like it. Are you here all week?"

*

Saturday 9th October 1943 - Bletchley Park

On his return to Bletchley, Archie sought out Alan. He needed to understand precisely how the probability matrix worked in practice so he could evaluate the prospects of success and failure for individual elements of the D-Day plan.

Every single day, Conner's people decided which

decoded information to safely use. They worked out chances, odds, probabilities, and how many would die if we acted or failed to act on the decoded Enigma intelligence. They did that by working mathematically. Numbers, percentages and calculations come at the end of it.

Archie needed a means of evaluating different elements of D-Day planning to display to an audience what he could only express as his instinct. He knew what would work but needed an effective logical means of convincing others he was correct.

Archie needed Rebecca to do this for him; he understood it while Alan demonstrated it, then afterwards, it always eluded him. His mind worked in facts, words, and pictures; numbers had always been his weakest point. With Rebecca, it was effortless and instant; she'd developed exponentially beyond the strictly logical and emotionless girl she'd been. He knew she still kept that part of her in a box where she could use it if necessary.

Archie spent a lot of time talking with Alan and Rebecca that winter; he didn't learn any mathematical skills; he learned patience instead.

Chapter Six

March 1944 - Bletchley Park

It was early March 1944, roughly three months before the scheduled D-Day. Archie went for a short run with Alan, no more than a mile, more than enough for Archie and his heavily bandaged ankle.

Alan played along, knowing the run wasn't Archie's purpose, the conversation afterwards while resting on the bench was. The D-Day planning was going well, and Archie was content, with one exception, one important issue remained off limits.

"Alan, I want to talk about rockets," he said.

"No, you don't."

"Yes, I do; it's other people who don't want to."

"Point taken."

"So, I can talk, and you can listen."

"Yes."

"Everyone knows the Germans are developing bigger, faster, deadlier rockets than we are. You know, I'm talking about ones that can hit London and New York, available within maybe twelve months."

Alan stayed silent, so Archie carried on.

"I've been raising the subject for years, and they've always stonewalled me when I've suggested taking any action. Especially when I suggested targeting the scientists involved. Fucking hell, we killed Heydrich for less, and he was a more difficult target. The best way to stop a weapon is to kill the man making it. We've killed thousands of German civilians with area bombing, so it's not squeamishness. This is just a few boffins. No offence meant."

"None taken."

"Now, we're about to invade Northern France, a whole invasion fleet would make a great target, and I'm told to do nothing. I need to know why, no, that's probably wrong, I want to know, and that want feels like a need; it's difficult to explain. There's something they're not telling me, and it's eating away at me."

"I can't tell you what I know."

"I know that, Alan. Can you tell me what you thought about it before you knew?"

"Now, that is an interesting question; I could tell you what my opinion was in 1938; that's no secret.

"Which was?"

"The Germans were miles ahead of us in rocket research; that's recorded fact and hasn't changed. Furthermore, in scientific circles, there's a concept called the brain drain; the richer countries steal the best minds from the poor or even the less rich."

"So we can hardly steal a brain if we've killed its owner. There'll be no shortage of thieves when this war ends and no shortage of need for brains to fight the next one. It doesn't smell good, though." Archie thought for a moment, slightly annoyed he hadn't concluded that for himself.

"And that was your opinion, Alan, in 1938?"

"Yes, my own uninformed opinion."

"Alan, this is a complete stab in the dark. I'm guessing you've never changed your opinion on anything in your whole life."

"Oh goodness no, why on earth would I?"

"Thank you, Alan."

*

March 1944 – Bletchley Park

Rebecca sat in the crowded railway carriage, returning her to Bletchley from her parent's house. She'd managed to get a seat by the window, a young Lieutenant had stood up to give her his seat.

Her infrequent visits home were a trial; she performed the duty only from a sense of obligation. She struggled to find any subject for conversation; she couldn't talk about her work, the War or her hobby, another War.

She couldn't say where her propensity for warfare and violence originated; her childhood had been safe and peaceful. Her education was similarly uneventful, so when

SOE offered her work in France, she expected the same outcome.

Nothing ever happened to her.

Except the maelstrom of history that engulfed her since she'd first set her eyes on Archie Travers in the grounds of Bletchley Park, that was it, definitely.

She'd never felt a physical attraction to any boy or man, and she couldn't see Archie well from that distance. He was talking to Gubbins, who she knew as a formidable and highly rated man. Yet, the obviously younger man had appeared confident and relaxed, graceful gestures conveyed the passion he was expressing, and the frequent nods of agreement and consent from Gubbins confirmed that he shared that mood.

She'd felt something for the first time, a sharp intake of breath, the tiniest whisper of exhilaration, excitement, and butterflies in her stomach for a few seconds. A tingle in her groin that intrigued her. She knew she needed to return safely from France and find out who that man was, and she began to worry for the first time in her life.

Since then, she'd come to love him, and she loved him enough to want Una to make him happy in ways she couldn't. Her virginity and total lack of experience weren't what Archie needed, and Una was her best friend and more, a mentor, a sister, a role model even.

She'd grown better with people, all people, especially the two teams and friends from Bletchley.

It was strange how the other teams called Bletchley, BP, and Archie didn't. He called it Bletchley or Bletchley Park. His two teams did the same. Somehow, he still felt as if he were an outsider like he used Building Thirteen, it was the thirteenth building, and nobody else wanted that number.

"There are no Gods and no superstition in my building," he'd said.

She had friends, a new family, love, purpose, and status now, and it felt good; it felt fulfilling and worthy. Worthiness in hard times was a strong feeling. The trouble was, the awakening of her feelings made her want Archie even more, physically. She'd felt that longing and warm, inviting moisture for him; she'd seen Una's face and her post-coital satisfaction after one of their quickies no-one was supposed to notice.

In short, she needed to be fucked, but she needed to bury the ghosts of Gerolf and Gottlieb first; if not their bodies, burial implied some form of respect. She wanted Archie to feel for her, the sheer animal lust they had for her, and she wanted to let him, let him do whatever he wanted to her. Whatever he did for Una. Whatever she did for him.

The groin kicking and penis slicing definitely came from the unanswered incident in that alley in St. Nazaire. Rapists deserved death; that was simple. Violent sexual attack deserved death; attacking a child in that way deserved a painful, slow death with a modicum of torture thrown in. She was in a position to deliver that justice and had competent and similarly motivated friends, so she'd done that. She'd given Archie a lecture on handling the emotion that came with it; the lecture was easier to deliver than receive.

She'd never have Archie all to herself; it was a puzzle she couldn't solve.

The young Lieutenant, who'd given up his seat for her, was a handsome young man and well built. He was intelligent, articulate, polite and a gentleman if required. He'd watched Rebecca carefully for some time and positioned himself outside her compartment where he might catch her eye. He was single, well mostly, he'd give up those casual flings if he had someone like her to stay faithful for. She was everything he wanted in a girl, beauty and brains; he could tell she had class. She was so beautiful he stayed on the train two stops past his own because he couldn't leave the train without speaking to her properly.

The train slowed down to pull into Bletchley station, and she rose to her feet, so he had to make his move quickly. As she brushed past him, he decided to leave the train with her.

"Goodness, that's a long journey," he said, smiling warmly, walking next to her, "are you based locally? I'm at Abingdon. You wouldn't know where I can get a bus? A cup of tea perhaps, you could join me? Yes, that would be nice."

He stopped walking and turned to look at her.

Rebecca continued to walk on a few more paces silently, then turned around.

"Sorry, did you say something?" she said, gave him a puzzled look, then turned around and walked on towards the waiting car.

Must be lost? Fucking idiot!

*

Una was waiting in their staff car to collect her. Rebecca hurried inside, they embraced, and each had a tear in their eye.

"There's no rush. We've plenty of time. The roses are in the boot," Una said, then still drove far too fast to their building.

It was cloudy, cold and damp. The drizzle was thankfully light and wouldn't stop them from planting the bush; nothing would.

At Bletchley Park, Conner and Jimmy McKay walked towards Building Thirteen from the Mansion, Colin Gubbins walked between them, and no-one was sure this would work.

A few people gathered. Gubbins didn't like fuss, Archie dug the hole as they approached, and Rebecca and Una pushed the bush into place.

Gubbins looked on impassively as Rebecca said, "John Michael McVean Gubbins."

No-one knew what to do next. Gubbins had done so much for them; they couldn't let the death of his son pass without a memorial.

Michael was 22 years old when he was killed in action at Anzio in Italy on the 6th of February 1944. His parent unit was the 5th Battalion of the Cameron Highlanders, and everyone knew he was in Number 1 Special Force of the Special Operations Executive.

Archie felt bad enough sending friends to their death, Gubbins had sent his own men, including his own son, on a mission, and he'd died.

I will never have children, never; I'll only kill them too.

He broke the silence by clapping the dirt from his hands, then continued to clap as others joined in the impromptu applause.

All the men shook Gubbins' hand, as did Una and Rebecca, who both insisted he lower his face, so they could kiss him on the cheek. Archie knew he could see a tear in his eye as he shook his hand, and he knew why Gubbins walked away before people might see it.

Later, occasionally, with no one else around, the huts empty and unlit, Gubbins would go to that rose bush, sit on that bench and talk to his son.

*

Late March 1944 – England

As the planning for D-Day in France progressed, Archie's frustrations grew less. Ike assiduously weeded out the weak from the important positions. He sometimes moved them sideways, rarely out completely and always to where they could do no real damage. Brigadier Kesler was in charge of subsidiary procurement, supplies, not even weapons, just tins of bully beef. The strongest prevailed and remained, every man raising the performance of others by example. Archie had to work hard to keep pace with them and managed with help from his friends.

Separate planning took place for the invasions of Sicily and the Italian Mainland from North Africa, leaving Archie to concentrate on what he did best. Gathering knowledge, making the best use of it in Northern France and revenge.

He still spent nearly five days a week in meetings and then went to the Manor and Bletchley on the other two days, usually weekends. Una and Rebecca worried that he was working seven days a week, but he still couldn't see talking and thinking as real work, so it became their routine.

His health and strength improved; the tennis ball had

helped with his right wrist, and with the lack of pain in the foot, his mobility improved. Although he could run a little better, his pace remained stubbornly slow. He quietly took half a day when he tried an SOE obstacle course on a liaison visit to Jimmy McKay. He finished the course in twice his usual time, and he ached everywhere for days afterwards.

Four days later, when the aches had worn off, and he was satisfied he could bluff his way to an operational role on D-Day, Archie approached Asgeir in the Manor garden.

"I've decided I'm going to France with the team on D-Day."

"No, you're not," Asgeir replied and shouted at Lightfoot, who was practising his knife throwing on an archery target.

"James, over here, Archie's bet me he could still do that trick you taught him with the knife."

Lightfoot walked slowly over and took out his own knife, securing the leather strip to Archie's wrist.

Archie balanced his wrist and swung the knife at the right speed and trajectory below the open palm of his right hand. He flipped it up slowly and failed to grip the handle.

"Best of three?" Archie said casually.

"Okay," said Asgeir before Archie failed on his second try.

They smiled sympathetically.

"That's a beer you owe me, Boss," said Asgeir as James walked away back to his target, knowing Archie had lost something more than a bet.

"Don't make me do that in front of everyone, Archie. Your body has taken enough punishment for two lives. We need your brain now; that's enough. You still have a slight limp; you think we don't notice, but you've taught us what that one per cent is. We see it missing in you, and it's more than one per cent. Don't ask me again, don't make me say no. We all wish we'd stayed with you rather than go to Dieppe, but we didn't."

"I taught you too well, didn't I?"

"That's what Jimmy McKay said when I rang him to check what you'd been up to with him."

*

Later that night, Una lay next to Archie in their bed, it was midnight on Saturday, and Archie was fast asleep. He'd had an unusually busy week, and she and Rebecca had tried to take the load off him and hadn't succeeded. It was more of a mental than physical tiredness; she'd made a meal for him and insisted he have a whole glass of wine and relax. It worked rather too well, and he'd gone to bed early without her.

She'd stayed up and talked to Rebecca, mainly about Archie. That was a bit selfish of her, but she needed to share thoughts with her best friend to get them straight in her own head.

She felt an overwhelming need to be pregnant and give Archie a son. He hadn't asked for that; he didn't want that. It wasn't the right time, during the war or for Archie's age and temperament. He wasn't ready, she wasn't ready either, and none of that mattered.

It was instinctive; he was the fittest, she was the fittest, and their child would be the fittest. It needed to happen; she needed it to happen; the tribe, the nation, and the species needed it to happen.

When she was pregnant, nearly due, might be the time she could let Rebecca have Archie... once. She knew there was no such thing as once with Archie, perhaps one night or maybe a weekend at a push. She'd made that promise after Rebecca saved his life, and she meant to keep that pledge, but Archie was hers. She'd lend him to Rebecca, she was her best friend, and she loved her, so she deserved it, but not to keep. She'd find someone else for Rebecca; yes, that would do.

Their personal war needed some thought as well. She and Rebecca would do whatever Archie needed and wanted; it couldn't last forever, though. She'd left her home and family far behind and could never return; after the decisions she'd made, perhaps they'd have to do the same,

America maybe? She had no regrets about what she'd done to survive her own family. Maybe if they found or avenged Freddie's sister, it could stop, and the Animal certainly needed to die. He'd hurt her, and Archie would see him dead; that was a fact. Trouble always found them, though.

She concentrated on the present to try and settle herself before sleep would come. She had Archie, the best man, the best lover she could have; he'd kept her safe and always would; he had apparently unlimited money, they could live anywhere they chose. She had friends, real friends whose bonds would bind them forever. She'd gained so much in such a short space of time. She had more than she'd ever hoped for; she was happy, happy but not yet content.

She felt a small change inside her vagina and reached down to place a finger there. The familiar feeling of sticky fertile mucous touched her middle finger. Okay, then she thought, and her hand reached for Archie's cock, a slow encounter with her mouth and tongue should wake him up nicely; we can both sleep later.

*

Early April 1944 – Dawn - The Normandy Coast

Billy Perry flew over the Normandy coastline along what would be Sword Beach on D-Day. Relaxed now after several flights, his usual pilot, a survivor of the Battle of Britain, was excellent.

Billy had asked for one final flight over the beach defences. Sandbagged machine gun nests, mostly. Billy knew about sandbags and machine guns. He saw what he needed to, the pilot got the photographs he needed, and Billy relaxed fully, even as they flew at near wave height back home.

*

In the Great War, Billy had devised his own sandbag formation to give his team maximum cover and the maximum arc of fire. He could identify a blind spot and make sure he filled it with other gun crews alongside him. He got offered Corporal, but promotion meant a move, and he needed to stay where he was, with his mates. He started maintaining his own weapon and developed a real feel for it. He did a better job than his manual; other crews copied that too. He worked on other skills in his spare time and got a proper feel for his rifle and a pistol that came into his possession, a Luger.

Billy's machine gun never jammed, it was his lifesaver, and he took many lives with it. Billy Perry had killed a lot of people. Especially that last time, in the German offensive of late March 1918.

No one knew what was happening with the new German attack near Amiens.

They attacked his strong position as a feint, sacrificing men to Billy's gun, fifty at least to his alone, then bypassing it. There were Germans everywhere, all around him, infiltrating the British line. He'd found out later they were specially trained squads called Stormtroopers. He found out much earlier they'd surrounded his unit.

Luckily, and it was sheer luck, they had a good officer with them. He was a young lad early twenties, posh, and he'd still lasted two months which, sad to say, was longer than most. The good ones always copped it early. He'd organised them into new positions, a square like Waterloo, he'd said, and they waited.

Every man knew this was a fight to the death; Jerry would take no prisoners today, not after they'd stepped over hundreds of their mates to get there.

The next attack was brutal and determined, there were weaker spots in the makeshift square, but Jerry didn't spot them, and the attack only lasted twenty minutes.

They'd got closer, this time, close enough to see faces and eyes as they fell. They killed and wounded countless Jerrys, and many spent the next two days dying noisily as Billy and his oppos waited for the next attack.

Billy could have finished off plenty from his position. Each bullet he wasted on that mercy might be one that would save his life later, so he held his fire.

That sight and those sounds stayed with him always; it

appalled him, always, but none of that troubled him overmuch. He enjoyed it; that's what haunted him.

The next attack never came; Jerry had wisely decided to ignore that small pocket of men and look for an easier target. Fortunately, their advance failed elsewhere, and relief eventually came. Only then did Billy and others get proper care for their wounds. Billy lost a lot of blood from a shrapnel wound low on the left side of his back and was hospitalised. The officers allowed no one else to leave the line; the medics patched them up and left them there. Most of those fifty odd men made it back, but the officer didn't. One of his small wounds turned bad, and he died from poison in his blood. Lemuel Galliford was his name; he was from Bethnal Green, too; he should have stayed there.

Billy was lucky, his wound was an awkward slow healer, and his war was over. Billy hadn't put too much effort into a quick recovery. He'd had more than his share of fighting and enjoyed more than his share of luck. He was happy for one to run out but not the other. Besides, he knew the Americans were in the war now, and it would be over soon. Strangely, he'd always felt an element of guilt over his early departure from the front until he'd helped Archie and Conner.

He'd returned from the war, a somebody, with new skills and got a regular legal job in an Engineering firm.

He'd first seen his wife Mary when she was fourteen, before the war; she was eighteen when he first saw her afterwards. She was starting work in the canteen kitchen as a cleaner, her first job ever. God, she deserved better than that.

"Hello, William Perry," she said, remembering him after all those years; she was lovely with the sweetest smile.

Billy had spoken to her several times before he asked if she'd walk out with him. He didn't think for a second she'd say no, and she told him he'd have to ask her father first.

He'd borrowed a shirt and tie from a friend before he went around there; her father had said yes, and a year later, they were married. They'd kissed, but he'd never laid a finger on her until they were wed.

They'd been happy, bloody poor, living in one room in someone else's house and still happy.

*

May 1944 Maidstone, Kent

At the end of May 1944, Archie drove to Maidstone in Kent. D-Day was a few days away. The wait for the right tides and weather had begun. General George S Patton was heavily involved, of course. His involvement consisted of pretending he was involved, in charge of an imaginary army in Kent. There were fake army camps, fake vehicles, and fake radio transmissions. Several people claimed credit for the deception plan, but Archie knew Conner had included it in the report he'd written before the war had started in earnest. The Germans would see Patton publicly attending functions in Kent and believe the invasion would begin there.

Archie knew from reading decoded Enigma transmissions that it was working. The Germans knew Patton was the most effective Allied General and couldn't conceive that the Allies would sideline him, no matter what he'd done.

What he'd done was to hit two young American soldiers who had battle fatigue. They couldn't take any more, and doctors had removed them from the front line. George had slapped one and called him a coward; it had gone down badly in the American press.

Who knew the difference between needing a break and being a coward? Who needed a coward or unreliable man next to them in the heat of battle?

Each man had his own breaking point, Archie had heard that said, and he'd been privileged to pick only the best for his team. Joe Dempsey had angered him by not following an order, he hadn't been a coward, and Archie certainly wanted to slap him. The hesitation he'd shown cost him his life and perhaps others. In the German Army, you'd have been shot for less; who could blame George for his anger? His every decision killed good, brave men.

The absence of George on D-Day would probably kill men.

Unable to take an active role on D-Day, Archie went to see George for a day to commiserate. George opened a Fete that day and spoke to an audience at the local Women's Institute; the printed press took scores of pictures. BBC and Pathe news cameras were present. There were cakes, George was polite, and Archie tried to keep a low profile; it was all so trivial.

George was willingly doing the penance for his sins because he knew they'd need him once D-day was over. They'd need all the competent, experienced Generals they had for a head on fight with the Germans in France and their home borders. George said he'd work for anyone, under anyone, even lesser men, if he could only get back alongside his men.

Archie told him everything he'd heard in meetings and had made it clear there was a need to give him a role sooner rather than later.

"I've heard some of that; I hear you've been telling anyone that'll listen I'm needed now, for D-Day itself. Brad said he swore you were doctoring the intel to suit your argument."

"Doctoring? No, I may have emphasised some details more than others, that's all."

"Whatever, thank you, I owe you a few favours, you've saved lives, and you're trying to help me get mine back."

"You don't owe me anything, George."

George insisted Archie share a drink with him in the evening, Johnny Walker Black Label. It was disgusting, and Archie had to use ice and a bottle of Coca-Cola to even inhale the smell. Patton called him a pussy, but the drink loosened a few cobwebs in his mind, and an idea formed in his head before he fell asleep, drunk in his chair.

"Damn Limeys can't hold their drink," Patton said as two of his men carried Archie to his bed.

*

Many of those involved called D-Day the biggest

military operation of all time. Archie knew you couldn't judge it properly against what the Romans and Greeks had achieved centuries earlier. He hoped it would work and never need to be surpassed.

Very few people had authorisation to know the whole plan for that day. Even those few people didn't have the time and mental capacity to absorb all the detail involved. Archie knew the overall plan as well as any man. He'd cheated; when his brain was full, he'd used Una and Rebecca's as additional storage space. Between the three of them, they managed; only by focusing tightly on the landing day, the five beaches involved and who needed to be where and when. He'd also cheated by discussing some of it with Conner and Alan.

You could describe it as 10,000 inter-dependent small actions, all needing to happen precisely within 24 hours. Everything didn't have to work perfectly for success, but no one could tell in advance where that delicate line might fall. It was like Archie's mantra, a millionfold and written down rather than a single instrument of thought. He could never have organised all that; he could only do his small part.

Two such small actions were the Benouville and Ranville Bridges that provided a strategic crossing of the Caen canal, only a few miles from the British landing beach 'Sword'. It was crucial for the Allies to take these bridges and hold them intact to facilitate the capture of the strategically vital town of Caen on D-Day. At 0015 on the 6th of June, the glider-borne troops of the Ox and Bucks Light Infantry, Royal Engineers, and then men of the 7th Paras would capture those bridges. They had to hold them until relieved by the 1st Special Service Brigade, Lovat's Commandos. They would land at 0800 in the second wave at Sword Beach, Queen Section, between Lyon sur Mer and Ouistreham and planned to reach the bridges by 1300.

Archie saw Sword Beach as the easiest of the five landing beaches. The sandy landing area was extensive and flat, without cliffs but with countless man-made obstacles.

Belgian gates, Teller mines, ramps, hedgehogs, walls of barbed wire, minefields, dragon's teeth, then pill boxes, machine gun nests and concrete bunkers with 88mm guns.

Crisscrossed stakes with broad areas of barbed wire that would slow infantry down. Star-shaped metal obstacles that might delay a tank and thick reinforced concrete bollards that would stop one dead. Then, among all of that, anti-personnel and anti-tank mines.

Tanks would land first, and a man could find weaknesses in any defensive line if he knew what to look for. If you'd manned a machine gun and had a hundred men running at you, all intent on putting a bayonet in your gut, like Billy Perry had, you knew.

Archie's additional plan was to drop his men by submarine at the same time as the Paras landed. They'd already carried out three clandestine surveys of that beach, scouting and clearing a route through the mines. A narrow path leading them to a sheltered part of the dunes behind the beach, where they could wait and do two pieces of significant damage.

This time, they would land and stay until relieved. While there, they could target the dragon's teeth tank traps with deeply planted high explosives. Begley tested various combinations during his time with Hobart and was confident he could make a shaped charge destroy enough concrete and metal to allow a tank through. They planned to destroy two or three in the right places. Timed correctly, tanks could move from landing craft through the line of defence in one minute instead of five. A lot of men could die in four minutes on that beach.

Another part of the plan was inspired by Billy. He reckoned there was a weak spot in the line of pillboxes and heavy machine gun nests. A position where, if you took out one pair of nests, you'd create a thirty-yard blind spot where troops could advance without coming under fire. Two carefully planned explosions would create a couple of useful advantages for the first wave of troops ashore.

Archie had another idea he'd stolen from Caesar.

Archie and Billy put the plan to the men, no one queried it, and everyone wanted to do it.

"I'd rather do that six times than be at the front of any landing craft," said Asgeir, looking at his men, "if we do our jobs properly, and we will, we'll be fine."

Chapter Seven

6th June 1944 – D-Day – Normandy

Archie Travers Chosen Men had undertaken forty-seven silent landings like this one for reconnaissance work and had one more part to play on D-Day itself. They needed to be in danger again, one last time perhaps; once they survived that, they knew they'd hold their heads high forever. They'd help Lovat's men get ashore faster and fully intact. They'd reach the bridge, fresh and in numbers, the bridges would hold, and Caen could be taken. This was what Archie called Plan A, B, C, D, and E.

It was 0100 on the 6th of June 1944 when Asgeir's men crept ashore on Sword Beach. They weren't the first Allies on French soil that day, but they were among them. They gave each dinghy a slow, silent puncture so they'd lie flat and unseen until dawn. By then, the general mayhem would make their presence irrelevant as a clue to what lay ahead for the defending Germans.

Progress up the beach to the Dunes was slower than normal; Archie ordered all the Chosen Men to wear body armour. Every other man carried what he called a Tarrian and was really a modern day; Billy Perry designed replica of a Roman Legionaries shield, the Scutum. He'd told the men Smudger would have christened it the scrotum, and he retold Tarrian's story and the old meaning of his name. The metal was tough, lightweight steel with a thin vision slit, and they'd be essential later in the mission.

They'd cleared all the mines from a small strip of sand on two previous nighttime visits and hoped they'd done the job perfectly.

They placed smoke bombs on timers to either side of the sweet spot they were creating, and they silently sliced their way through the barbed wire.

The men reached their planned position under a high overhanging dune with plenty of grass dangling long above their heads. Begley's group went eastwards to the tank traps, which were blocking the road from the beach. Freddie's team went from the beach further into the dunes. Even in the dim light of the moon, they saw the two large open-air machine gun nests, as expected, unmanned at night.

In both locations, Chosen Men took up guarding positions on all sides while Begley and Freddie prepared their explosive work.

Begley already knew which three tank traps he needed to destroy and carefully shovelled and scooped as much sand as he could from their bases. Then he instinctively positioned his custom made explosives at the best angle to do the most damage and then set the timers, keeping one charge as a spare.

Freddie placed his two high explosive charges under the sandy wooden bases of the machine gun nests, next to the ammunition stored there. Then he ran and hid a detonator wire to the spot they'd left the Tarrians earlier. They'd lie in wait there until the nests were full of German vipers. Asgeir left last, taking mental pictures of the trench layouts and their approaches.

The devices in position and primed, the seven men with Freddie and four with Begley dug deeper into the sand, interlocking their Tarrians for protection. Bombing and shelling of the beach fortifications would start at 0400, a direct hit would finish them. Otherwise, they'd be safe.

"What odds did Archie give on a direct hit, sir?" Freddie whispered to Asgeir.

"One hundred thousand to one."

"And who told him that?"

"Alan Turing."

"And what is he again?"

"He's a bona fide genius, Freddie."

"And how clever is that then?"

"It's as clever as a hundred of you, Freddie."

"I should probably shut the fuck up and have a kip."

"Good plan. Shall I wake you when it starts?"

"That would be very kind of you, sir; I am known as a

deep sleeper; a cuppa would be nice an' all."

The Allied naval bombardment of the beach area started exactly on time. Alan was right. Stones and sand rattled their shelter, the ground shook under them, and they lost count of the deafening explosions, but they remained unscathed. Then they listened for movement in the nearby nests in the silence that followed.

Asgeir looked through the vision slit on his Tarrian, watching the ships in the distance, waiting for the landing craft to approach the beach. Right on cue, the two smoke bombs ignited by Begley's timers went off, streaming red smoke upwards and signalling the sweet spot on the beach below them.

The German machine gunners above them started shouting immediately, puzzled by what that smoke might mean. They had no further thinking time; their shouting was the moment Freddie twisted and pushed the small detonator in his hands. Both devices exploded instantly; that was the easy part.

In two groups of four, all eight Chosen Men sprang up quickly and moved into the tangled mess of sandbags, equipment and men, finishing them off with Thompsons where they lay.

"Shoot to kill, take no prisoners, that's an order," Archie had said and gave each of them that order in writing; they hadn't needed him to do that, but he'd done it anyway.

Inside the ruined nests, each group took up guarding positions against any reinforcements arriving. The Germans might not notice two silent positions amongst the general furore. They ought to be concentrating on firing at the men in front of them. Billy said if they were good, they'd notice, so they watched carefully.

In the other group, Begley's devices worked as planned, their noisy explosions masked by the overall bombardment. Concrete had partly shattered, and odd pieces of rusty metal poked up, but a tank track or base plate would crush them easily. They'd done their job; all they had to do was wait, they were safe, and Begley still had one charge left.

"Brad? Gabe? James?" he said.

"Yeah, let's do it," they said.

They discarded their Tarrians and crawled carefully east, along the line of the dunes, towards a thick concrete pillbox about twenty yards east of them. It contained a heavy calibre 88mm artillery gun, already seeking targets at sea. No German saw them crawl towards or on top of it; all their attention was seawards, the last thing they expected was someone on top of them already.

Gabe reached the pillbox first and boosted the others onto it with his huge cupped hands, then two of them dragged him up. On the flat bunker roof, James and Gabe stayed next to Begley while Brad guarded their rear. Begley set the timer for 30 seconds, took his device in both hands and lay flat on his stomach facing the sea and counted.

Five, six, seven.

As they'd practised, time after time, Gabe and James took an ankle each, then pushed and lowered Begley slowly to the front of the pillbox, above the large gaping, bigger than barrel sized slit.

Sixteen, seventeen, eighteen.

He balanced the bomb in his hands above the slit.

Twenty-two, twenty-three.

Another shell fired from the bunker beneath him; it shook him, almost taking the bomb from his hands.

And he lost count.

He gambled and threw the charge into the bunker, then Gabe and James jerked him immediately upwards; half a second later, the explosives went off, ruining the gun and the men manning it. Smoke and flame burst from the bunker opening, and he felt the heat blast up towards him, singeing the hair on top of his head.

"Shit! That was close," he said.

"Lucky for you, we can count better'n you can," Gabe drawled back at him.

"Let's get under cover before some limey lands and

starts shooting at us," said Brad.

Asgeir's group of men waited, hearing and seeing nothing approaching them. They had time for a closer look at the Germans they'd killed.

Firstly, they made doubly sure they were dead.

Secondly, what useable guns, grenades, and ammo did they have?

Thirdly, did they have any souvenirs they could take without excessive guilt? A watch or a knife were good, but a wedding ring wasn't.

One of them wasn't dead; Freddie finished him off silently with a knife. In that particular case, it was a mercy; the blast had blown his lower stomach and groin apart.

They found stick grenades they could use; the machine guns were useless after Freddie's explosive blast.

The Germans had no valuables worth taking; they looked no more than boys. Freddie thought they were a little older than him.

"Don't look at faces; turn them over, look at hands and guns; that's all you need to see," Asgeir ordered sharply, and they obeyed without question.

"No pity, not today; that's the order," he said. Archie had used those exact words to him.

They waited impatiently for sounds of landings on the beach behind them, then listened to the machine gun and rifle fire as men landed, ran and fell. A ten-minute exchange of fire and lives lasted longer in the mind, and Archie had prepared them for that too. He'd even made them practice patience, waiting alone in a dark room, silent or noisy or both, counting to six hundred. Asgeir still checked his watch six times before he finally heard the noise of the fighting on both sides changing tone as men advanced up the beach and were beside them rather than behind. He sent Freddie to their rear to signal troops safely forward to support them. No one could mistake Freddie for a Jerry.

"It's time to go inland and see what we can see," he said and took the lead as his men moved forward cautiously. As they approached a T-junction in the trench network, he put a hand up to stop them and listened long enough to hear German words spoken ahead of them. He signalled George Flowers to go to the right and indicated he'd go to the left, silently mouthing one, two, three, go.

He and George jumped out and fired into the two groups of Germans, killing them instantly. They both fired a few more rounds to make sure they were dead. They turned the bodies over, didn't look at their young faces or notice the white sheet they'd been preparing and walked on past them.

"Every man guarding a prisoner is one who isn't watching my back," Asgeir said.

They soon realised they were part of a wider flank of Allied troops advancing, and the beach and area of dunes had been successfully taken. From their elevated position and in the clear dawn light, they saw signs of order and groups of men forming into units by flags and officers.

"We go east now," Asgeir said, "let's make sure Begley hasn't blown himself up."

'So far, so good, not a scratch.'

*

They saw Begley and his men standing next to a line of tanks that were pushing through the ruined tank traps and past the silent pillbox. Every man in each group counted the numbers in the other and smiled inwardly.

"Second wave on shore now, sir," Begley shouted, pointing out men about twenty yards away.

"Oh Fucking Hell, Lovat's wearing that jumper his mum gave him for Christmas again," Freddie said, "don't tell him I said that; the bugger'll slit my throat. Hang on, I know that walk and that limp; that's Archie fucking Travers with him."

"Excuse me, does anyone know the way to Calais? I seem to be a bit lost," Archie said. He, too, had counted his men as he approached and saw the line of tanks moving on.

"Good God, Travers, how on earth did you get here?"

said Lovat, who slapped him on the back and shook his hand. "Must go, old chap; I've got a couple of bridges to visit."

"Archie," said Freddie, "you are a bad man."

"Sorry, there's no way they're having a D-Day without me on the beach. I was here when we were losing; I had to be here now we're winning."

"Do your girls know you're here?" Freddie asked.

"Yes."

"You told them!"

"Don't be daft, mate; they'll have worked it out by now and didn't manage to stop me, so they must have decided to let me do it. Right, let's go home; I've got more work for you."

*

They found out later that D Day had, overall, been a major success. The glider troops under Major John Howard had taken both bridges and, with the Paras, had held them until Lovat's men arrived, only two minutes behind schedule. Lovat lost a dozen men crossing the bridges that day. One of Howard's officers, Lieutenant Den Brotheridge, was the first Allied soldier killed by enemy action on D Day. The town of Caen, scheduled for capture on the 6th of June, didn't fall until the 18th of July 1944, 42 days and many lives later.

At least that was someone else's responsibility; Archie hadn't killed them, he'd done his part, and his men had survived.

*

The team was back in Newhaven at 1800 on the same day. Una, Rebecca and Billy were waiting for them on the quayside, which surprised no one. The men pushed Archie to the gangway first, wary of the reaction he'd get from them. He went towards them, determined not to limp and smiled.

"Thanks for not stopping me; Lovat told me you knew, and you could have; that's the last time. Honestly, I promise you."

"We know that because we won't let you do it again," said Una with a calm certainty she knew he wouldn't argue against.

This particular war was over for Archie, and this time, he did sleep on the journey to the cottage, his head in Una's lap and she stroking his hair.

*

7th June 1944 – Vichy – France

The order to attend a meeting with Heinrich Himmler in Berlin the next day shocked Dolf. The fact that it came on the 7th of June 1944, the day after the successful Allied landings in Normandy, was puzzling. There was no hint of threat involved and no arrest, so his false deportation figures couldn't be the issue.

Nevertheless, he made some private arrangements with Dickon for Annette's well-being and drove there on his own.

*

After D Day, when they'd returned to the cottage, Una confessed to Archie she'd been trying to get pregnant for six months, and nothing had happened. He had noticed she'd been leaping onto him even more during regular periods each month, always demanding he come inside her.

Subconsciously, he'd been trying not to get her pregnant. This was no time for children, and he wasn't ready for them. Although, when he'd seen how much she wanted to have his baby, he couldn't refuse. So he resolved to fuck her as much as possible during times of fertile mucus; she even did handstands after sex to ensure maximum sperm penetration.

It was beyond Archie, he could find no paternal instinct within himself, but If Una wanted something, anything, he wanted her to have it. He determined to get her pregnant.

*

Less than two weeks after D Day, Dolf found himself in Munich, Head of State Security in Bavaria. He was still technically in the SS and brought his own trusted former

Wehrmacht men from Vichy, as well as those men who had formed his SS personal guard and others, Oskar included.

The upper echelon in Germany still trusted Dolf and held him in high regard. He'd displayed the skills needed for controlling a hostile population. That didn't surprise him, but he hadn't expected he would need those qualities in Germany.

He shrewdly told Himmler the level of deportations from Vichy would fall with Oskar and his best men transferred to the front and other duties. Himmler didn't show the slightest interest other than agreeing with Dolf's suggestion that no incriminating paperwork should fall into Allied hands. Dolf sometimes marvelled at how events fell into place for him and had his men burn a vast number of papers containing his signature systematically and efficiently. All was overseen personally by Dolf and with a few documents retained for his personal use later if needed.

*

Friday 21st July 1944 – German / Swiss / Austrian border

Dolf stood at a roadblock in Lochau, a small town on the German-Austrian border, also close to the Swiss border. He watched his own SS men searching every vehicle and checking every occupant trying to leave Germany. He didn't want this duty, but, on this date, at this time, his life depended on it.

He felt no fear, though; if anything, he felt bored. He knew what he had to do; he knew his men had to see him doing it; he knew he'd do it.

The security role in Munich was easy, if not what he'd expected. His top priority was to control the flow of stolen property from Germany to Austria and Switzerland. Every greedy fool in Germany trusted him to handle it for them, Heinrich Himmler included. Although Senior Wehrmacht Officers and Aristocracy were not immune to greed. No matter how much wealth and privilege you had, you always wanted more, Dolf also suffered from that vice, but he was no man's pawn.

The previous day, the 20th of July 1944, there had been a spectacular, flawed and unsuccessful attempt to assassinate Adolf Hitler, with a bomb placed in his headquarters in the Wolfsschanze in Rastenburg, Eastern Prussia.

There was widespread confusion at first, and Himmler immediately gave Dolf the task of preventing the escape of any treacherous plotters fleeing south.

Dolf wasn't one of the plotters, but he had come uncomfortably close. Three weeks previously, Canaris had invited him to a personal meeting. He knew such a meeting was risky, but he felt a duty to attend as asked, alone and unseen, he hoped.

Canaris had started to tell him the plot details, and he'd refused even to listen.

"You know whose side I'm on," he'd said, "whoever wins, come and see me when you've won; you know who I work for now! My own men will shoot me, even if you win. Don't even tell me when it will happen.

"When you flee, Admiral, flee south; that's all I can say. I owe you that. I know you've helped me; I also know now how much you used me when I was in London. We are even."

Dolf expected the plot to fail. He already knew there had been a dozen other failed attempts; Claus Von Stauffenberg had been especially useless. He tried to kill for honour and had failed, of course, like the stupid Vichy French. If he'd been willing to die alongside Hitler, then he would have succeeded, but he tried to escape before the bomb exploded and blew up a table instead. That stupid Irish bauer Canaris had paid to shoot Churchill was willing to die to kill his prey, and he might have succeeded. Instead, the English had killed him and most of his family. Gubbins was definitely involved in that, and maybe Archie too.

Dolf knew about revenge. That café owner in Paris saw what revenge was; Churchill knew too. Canaris had thought the absence of Churchill might enable a settlement with England, and so did his aristocratic contacts. He was wrong; the English instinctively knew the difference between right and wrong and died for it.

To die with honour, you needed to be willing to give your entire existence, forever, for a worthy cause without the prospect of redemption. You could perhaps be a brainwashed primitive who believed in a non-existent God and expected a non-existent reward in a non-existent heaven. You could be a plain lunatic like van der Lubbe or mortally gullible, like the Divine Wind or the Jihadi. There were enough deranged madmen running loose in Germany; did they all have to be on Hitler's side? Surely we could have found one mad bastard, big or stupid enough to give their life?

Mein Kampf, my Struggle, my Jihad, my Crusade, my stupidity, perhaps only the truly evil could attract the most useful idiots? Dolf found a little comfort in that fact; it might help see him through this day.

So it was then that Dolf stood at a roadblock in a beautiful part of southern Germany under the glorious warmth of a bright blue sky, holding a list of names.

They'd only been there two hours and had already arrested two Generals, supposedly going on short holidays to Switzerland. Dolf's SS troops had executed their bodyguards on the spot, and the Generals were already on their way to Berlin, bound and gagged. Himmler's men would shoot them if they were lucky; they'd be tortured, tried and hung with chicken wire if they weren't. Family members would see no mercy either; his superiors had made that clear to Dolf.

"As it must be," he'd said when he received the order; his own cowardice made him sick sometimes.

As his men took the two Generals away, he still made a mental note of what he'd smuggled to Switzerland in their name and added it to his personal list. He'd give some to Himmler, of course, the founder of the feast, that would serve to further assure him of Dolf's continued loyalty.

"Oberst!" came the shout from Dickon.

His men had stopped a car and pointed their machine pistols at it threateningly.

Oh, shit, he thought as he saw an officer with his wife in the car next to him.

Oh, fuck no, he saw the two young children in the rear.

It was a Captain, and Dolf approached the vehicle, seeing the officer with his hand held towards his pistol.

"Dolf!" the man said to him in recognition and relaxed.

Dolf recognised him when closer, Dieter Von Klug, a contemporary of his at school and Military Academy, a family friend even, but not a close friend. A friend whose name was on his list, with a wife now, pretty and two children aged maybe two and three.

"Dolf, you remember me? It's Dieter."

"Yes, of course, I remember you, of course, calm down. I can sort this out, trust me, old friend," he smiled and nodded briefly at him.

Dolf turned away from the family and looked at his three closest men, with him since Calais and St. Nazaire and then at the dozen men of his fanatical personal guard.

He walked towards Dickon, keeping his back to the car and his friend.

"Is your Schmeisser well maintained, Dickon?" he asked.

"Yes, always, Oberst."

"Give it to me."

"What?"

"Trust me, this is for the best."

Dickon gave the gun to him. Dolf disengaged the safety catch and turned around smoothly and swiftly, giving no one a chance to move or a hint of his intent. He then sprayed the full magazine into the car, surely killing everyone inside.

He handed the weapon back to Dickon.

"The filthy cunt tried to bribe me to let him and his shit family go, Dolf said. "He thought my men would take money to betray the Fuhrer, search the car for any papers that might help us."

The car boot contained luggage, hastily packed children's clothes and toys. One bag contained a significant amount of Reichsmarks, with papers showing a bank withdrawal that day, together with gold and jewellery from a safety deposit box.

If the fool had left immediately instead of clearing his bank account first, he might have escaped sooner. If he hadn't stopped to clean out his safety deposit box, he'd have been in Switzerland hours before the roadblock was in place.

He'd been a greedy fool; he'd killed his family, not Dolf.

"Take the money and property, split it evenly among you, burn the bodies and throw the remains in the lake, the Swiss side; I don't want this shit contaminating the clean soil of the Fatherland."

When darkness fell, Dolf left his SS men in charge of the roadblocks; they'd seen what they needed to see, his loyalty to the Fuhrer. Their unquestioning loyalty to him was assured; Dolf and Annette were safer that night than they had been that morning.

Dickon drove him back to his quarters in Munich, where Annette was safe and waiting for him.

"Dickon?" Dolf said. "What am I?"

"I don't know, Oberst, I don't know, I am sorry."

"I am alive, Dickon, that's what I am, alive. A thousand will die this day and this night; the best we can do today is not die. A man who has murdered as I have today could not possibly have any involvement in a plot to assassinate the Fuhrer."

"And nor could any of his men," Dickon realised.

"No, have your family moved west as I told you?"

"Yes, they have."

"We must lose to the British or the Americans."

"Yes, we have the names you gave us."

"There will be money after the war when it's safe; the men and their families will survive."

"Yes, we know we can trust you."

"I must disappear, you know."

"And when you do, we'll no longer follow you. Until then, we'll stay."

Chapter Eight

Friday 21st July 1944 – London - England

That same day, the 21st of July 1944, a Friday, six weeks after D Day, Archie gave the whole team an extra day off. They needed it. They'd worked seven days a week building up to the Normandy landings and immediately afterwards.

Archie took Una and Rebecca to London before their weekend break; after D Day, the whole atmosphere in the country had changed, especially so in London. The sun shone brightly, and people were on the streets, smiling, less fearful somehow.

Archie took them for their scheduled check-up at his Doctor in Harley Street. He stayed outside, enjoying the warmth; they re-joined him an hour later, saying they were well and smiling broadly at him. They were up to something, he knew it, hatching a plot, ready to outnumber him; he knew what it was this time.

Archie drove them northwards out of London, Rebecca asked if she could visit the shop, which she'd put up for sale, and Una asked if she could visit the Cronins.

"Only for half an hour; I'll drop you at the door and pick you up from the door 30 minutes later exactly," he insisted.

"Okay, Mr Ultra-Cautious, I'll be fine; I have my sidearm with me, anyway."

He stopped the car right outside the Cronin's door, approaching the one-way street correctly. He wouldn't let her leave the car until she kissed him and said she loved him.

"I love you, thirty minutes exactly," she smiled at him.

He waited for Mrs Cronin to answer the door and watched the door close behind Una before he started for the shop.

The shop was still the shop, and business was good; Rebecca made small talk with the girls; she could do that now; they left after twenty minutes.

Archie got in his car, started the engine, and the biggest

explosion he'd ever heard erupted to the southwest. The ground shook, and tiles fell off nearby roofs.

"Una, the Cronin's," he screamed, "that's a fucking V1," and accelerated away from the back of the shop. He reached the main road where the traffic had stopped, blocking the road. He left the car on the pavement, the door open, the key in the ignition and ran, followed by Rebecca.

He couldn't even find the street, never mind the Cronin's house; he was frantic.

There were about thirty small terraced houses flattened; you could barely tell the difference between house and street, yard or garden.

"It's here," Rebecca shouted, pointing, "this is the street; that's the house."

Archie knew she was right, he didn't know how, but she knew. It was outside the edge of the central blast crater; there might be a chance. If they were quick.

"Dig here, throw there," she indicated when she stood on the correct spot, "this is the front room, right here."

They both started; the machinelike Rebecca took over her body, and they dug at the rubble with their bare hands.

Others joined in. They didn't know why. Two officers were digging, so they helped. No one watched, no one took photographs, no one talked. Ordinary English people followed their lead without question. Those who couldn't get near enough to dig and pull, moved the discarded debris pile further away to create a clear space for easier digging. Those close to him noticed the tears silently running down the Major's face and worked harder. Hands, fingers, and elbows scraped and were bloody, fingernails were broken, as well as hearts, and they carried on.

There might be a void; there has to be one, Archie thought, a cellar, Calais, ten more minutes. A thousand thoughts tried to fill his head; he only allowed one in. Is she alive? Is she alive?

Fire brigade men arrived and air raid wardens; they asked no questions, they joined in. They knew it was hopeless but dug and pulled regardless. As long as that Major dug, they'd dig with him.

They carried on like that for half an hour, moving tiles, beams then beds, more beams, ceiling then a sofa, an arm, a woman, grey haired.

Another body, an old man clutching something and another body under his, a female.

Una, motionless, lifeless, dusty, hardly a scratch on her. Mr Cronin had tried to shield her somehow.

Archie and Rebecca carefully freed her body from the mess and checked for a pulse repeatedly. Archie tried to breathe life into her dead lungs through the dead lips, and then he kissed her one last time.

Una Travers, his beautiful wife, who he'd promised would be safe forever, was dead.

"She has to go to Hertford," was all he said.

"I'll make the phone call," said Rebecca, "I'll be back in a minute."

An old lady, she looked about ninety, wearing a pinnie and a headscarf, brought him a flask of tea. It was strong, and he drank it from the plastic cup. Christ only knew how she'd made it across that debris. He smiled and said thank you.

The Harley Street ambulance was there within half an hour, and a stretcher gently took Una away.

Archie was still on his knees and became aware of the people watching him now, his hands and arms still bloody and scraped. He wiped his face, noticing his tears and bloody hands for the first time. Tears had streamed down his face but had stopped now; perhaps he had none left; he didn't know if you could run out of tears.

He stood up, shook his head to sharpen his wits and looked around, opening his eyes wide, then walked over to each person there.

"Thank you for helping, thank you for trying, thank you, thank you," he shook each hand and clapped each back.

Those people looked at that young man, young for a Major.

He had scars on his face, fresh blood dripping from his left palm and a bad limp that came from fighting for them, and they knew they hadn't done enough. He'd done more; he'd lost more than them.

They hadn't done enough; they'd never forget; they'd tell their children and never let them forget either. They were all wrong; they'd done their best, that was enough.

Mrs Ida Layton wished she'd been able to give him a biscuit with his tea. She had no biscuits in the house; she couldn't afford any.

Rebecca took his hand and led him, stumbling awkwardly, away from the scene and back to the car; she noticed he was limping badly.

"Did you twist your ankle?"

"No, it aches a bit, though."

"I'm taking you to Hevlyn."

"Okay."

*

Mrs Layton walked slowly back to her small terraced house, about a mile away from the Cronins and near where the Dempseys had lived. It took a long time, and that gave her time to think.

When she reached home, she went straight into the kitchen, shut the door behind her and washed the flask and cup. She dried them carefully and replaced them in a cupboard.

She went into her living room and collected her two cushions from the settee before returning to the kitchen and placing them on the floor.

She made sure the door was shut again and checked the window was closed.

She turned the gas on and left the oven door open before lying down next to it, her head comfortably on the cushions, and went to sleep.

She knew that young Major and that young dead girl hadn't killed the Dempseys.

She had.

She never woke up.

*

By the time Archie and Rebecca reached Hevlyn Mansions, Archie was in silent agony, barely conscious; a passerby and the concierge had to help him upstairs.

Archie could only speak through gritted teeth.

"Get Billy. Get Billy," was all she could make out.

She rang Billy at the Manor.

"Billy, it's Rebecca, Una's dead, a flying bomb in Holloway, it's Archie, it's his leg again, he's in agony."

"Listen carefully, and I'll be right down there."

After she'd hung up the phone, Rebecca rushed straight to the tin of coffee on the high kitchen shelf Archie never used and found the syrette of morphine, as Billy said.

She remembered his instructions and carefully slid the short needle under the skin of his thigh and squeezed gently.

He calmed down immediately and lost consciousness; she didn't know if she'd given him too much. Billy was explicit about using it all.

Archie had passed out on the floor, and she couldn't move him, so she began cleaning his cuts and grazes, ignoring her own. He'd badly reopened the wound on his left palm. She stripped him and cleaned him all over, carefully looking for more needle marks, as Billy had told her to and couldn't find any; she wasn't sure what they looked like anyway.

She covered him with a blanket and washed her own cuts, finding nothing too bad.

Archie woke after an hour. He was in no pain and appeared distant, absent, lost in thought, concentrating intensely. She managed to get him upright, in his bathrobe and onto the sofa with his leg on a stool.

Billy arrived an hour and a half after that, but Archie was still unresponsive.

Rebecca hugged Billy, and they both cried, Rebecca realised she hadn't cried for Una yet and let it all out. Billy was angry; he badly needed to kill someone; for Una, any German would do.

"Let's have a look at the boy then," he said finally.

Archie was still silent, so Billy looked into his eyes and scanned his arms and legs for needle marks. Rebecca felt less pain; now Billy could see nothing amiss.

"Archie," Billy said, "it's all right; I know you haven't had any morphine since last time; that's why this lot knocked you out. What's up? Why now?"

Archie blinked several times, like a man trying to clear something from his vision then he saw Billy.

"I've been blocking out the pain in the leg," he said, "and I blocked out the cause as well. My mind stopped working properly today, so I felt the pain and can't control it now. It took me this long to find where, but there's definitely a tiny piece of shrapnel in a blood vessel in my right ankle; I don't know its correct name. It needs to come out, or it'll move to my brain and paralyse or kill me. I've got about," he closed his eyes for a few seconds, "six hours; get an ambulance, please."

"Rebecca, I'm sorry," Archie said, "I should have given you a hug earlier; it's okay, I'll be fine; I can tell the doctors exactly where it is, come here; you need a hug."

She sat next to him and buried her face in his chest, sobbing.

"Let it all out," he said, "you'll stay beside me, I'll be on my feet in a week, then we'll kill some people who make rockets. Then maybe some of the people that wouldn't let me do it years ago."

"Oh, we'll kill somebody for this son, don't you worry, no rush, though, trouble finds you easy enough," said Billy, tears and rage fighting for supremacy in his thoughts and emotions.

*

Rebecca stayed with Archie in the operating theatre, refusing to let go of his hand even when she got in the way. Billy had his gun ready if needed, and a good poke in the chest from Rebecca settled the argument in her favour, anyway.

The surgeon, who looked not unlike a young Noel

Coward, sported a bow tie and white shirt under his gown.

"Right young man, my name is Doctor Peter Martin; I'm going to operate on your leg. What's this nonsense about you wanting to be awake?"

"I've had morphine, I might need a little more, but I'll tell you if I do. I need to be awake to direct you to the exact point where the fragment is."

"You'll no doubt be able to tell me, in your humble opinion, if the artery is damaged beyond repair and how I'm supposed to fix it?"

"You'll be able to do it."

"What?"

"You will. You can replace it with a section of another vein; you won't need to; the blood vessel will be okay if you go into the right spot. You can use a vein to repair an artery, can't you?"

"No, you can't, and how would you even conceive such a thought."

"My body told me."

"Oh, for heaven's sake, let's get on with it."

After the operation, with Archie having remained fully conscious throughout, the Doctor spoke to him again.

"Okay, young man, I must concede you took me to the precise position in the artery. It was delicate work; the stitching is tight and secure now. The artery will be as good as new, but I must insist you have seven days of complete bed rest. I'm going to require you to stay here. I don't want you too far away if anything goes amiss. Is that clear?"

"Okay, Doc and thanks. Remember the vein; it's important."

Rebecca stayed with him for the whole operation and the night afterwards. Once in his small private side room afforded to him by his rank, they stayed in silence for an hour, she held his hand, and he held hers. Rebecca broke the silence.

"You can cry if you want; I want to," she said.

"I don't know if I can; I'm too angry to cry. I need you to

stay, please."

"Of course, forever."

"Forever would be good, thank you."

*

Friday 28th July 1944 – London

Rebecca was still with him a week later when the Doctor discharged him, lightly bandaged and using Billy's stick.

Archie had refused all visitors, except Rebecca and Billy, for seven days, even Conner; no one else could see him until he was ready.

Archie spent that week talking to Rebecca about Una, their friend, sister, wife, and lover and then began to work out how they'd have justice for her death. The war was nearly over, but they could milk it for one more advantage; they had a strategy, plan, and purpose he felt might keep him sane. It had to keep him sane, he had to appear sane, or the plan would never work.

They talked about boxes in minds; Archie needed to understand how Rebecca used hers; he explained how he'd closed himself off from his pain and blocked out the sensation too. Somehow he hadn't done it properly.

Rebecca talked him into planting a rose bush for Una, telling him other people had lost Una too, and they all needed to grieve, something to see and remember.

Archie returned to Bletchley Park with Rebecca, who stuck closely to him, not holding his hand but joined to him by a piece of invisible string, no more than a foot long. She knew he might break apart any second and needed her to catch him. She'd found a new purpose too.

He met Conner first.

"Sorry, I couldn't face seeing anyone before. Are we still best friends?"

"Yes, of course we are."

"Are you okay?" Archie asked, seeing Alan from the corner of his eye.

"Yes, privately, things are still good."

"Good."

The ceremony went as well as such an occasion could. The sun shone, and it didn't rain; Rebecca planted the rose bush for him.

Alan played an Irish Lament he had composed himself.

Archie looked the right look, said the right words, dried the right tears, accepted the hugs offered and gave some back. He was the consummate liar; he was normal, he was sane, he would allow the Army to continue using him, and he would use the army for his own purpose.

Freddie took Billy and Begley aside afterwards.

"He's dead, isn't he? He's as dead as I've ever seen him; that's not him. What can we do, Billy?"

"We wait and watch, then help him when he needs it, mate," Billy replied.

The same conversation happened twenty times in both teams; they'd watch over that boy forever. No one said a word to Archie or Rebecca; they'd seen how reliant on her he was, and they knew she was strong enough to help him and maybe more in time.

*

The ceremony over, Rebecca took Archie to the cottage, and they stood in the garden breathing. His hands were in his pockets; she held the crook of his arm.

"There's something I haven't dared tell you, Archie."

"I know Una was pregnant," he said, "I was waiting for her to tell me; I could sense it, taste it, I can't explain it. We'd been trying. She had, for a long time, but I wasn't, then when I started trying… "

"You always know, don't you? You feel what others can't?"

"Sometimes, yes, sometimes, no. There's more, this morning before I woke, a dream she was in my mind, trying to reach me. She was confused and alone and needed to find me, then she was gone."

Archie stopped talking and took a deep breath; he meant it to be life-affirming. It wasn't.

"The leg, if I'd kept blocking the pain for half a day more, the blood clot would have killed me."

He took his hands out of his pockets and held Rebecca's hand, intertwining their fingers and squeezing tightly.

"It was a boy," he said.

He breathed in again, even deeper, searching vainly for life.

"My wife… and my son… died so I could live. Fate chose them to die and me to live; how does a man live with that knowledge?"

*

Billy Perry stood by himself in the workshop of the Manor and boiled the kettle, tea for one.

He felt like he'd lost more than a daughter.

He loved his daughter Grace, but the loss of Una was more. Grace's fiancé was a good lad, and if Grace died, he'd cry for Grace, not him. He'd cry for his kin, not for any others, and yet, today, he was crying for Una, for Archie, for Rebecca, and for his guilt for loving his Una more than his Grace.

He could still feel the rage he'd felt the first time he'd met Una. He asked if they'd laid a finger on her; she knew what he meant and said no, only a couple of slaps.

Billy had only been with one woman in his whole life; his wife Mary had died while giving birth to Grace, eclampsia, a blood pressure problem he didn't understand. He understood if he'd been able to afford a better doctor, then she'd have lived; they'd have spotted it earlier. He didn't know there was such a thing as a better doctor.

Billy hadn't killed the doctor, he'd considered it, but Mary wouldn't have wanted that; she was the gentlest soul he ever knew. Mind you, that wasn't saying a lot, considering the company he kept as a young man.

Billy had needed Archie and Una to have children, for Una to survive the childbirth, and for the three of them to have what he hadn't with his Mary. That hadn't happened. Rebecca told him Una had been pregnant too, and he badly needed to kill someone for it; the Animal might do; yes, that thing needs to die, he thought.

*

Tuesday 1st August 1944 – Hevlyn Mansions

Archie sat quietly with Rebecca in the flat at Hevlyn. He'd tried to go back to work at Ike's headquarters the previous day. A Lieutenant, who'd never left his desk during the war, told him his role was no longer needed. D-day had happened, and he would receive notice of reassignment in due course. He said the decision had been taken weeks ago, and he didn't know why he hadn't been told, nor was anyone currently available to speak to Archie.

Rebecca was partly glad about that because she'd known he wasn't ready to resume duties, even if he could put his full weight on the ankle now. The real Archie might have considered shooting someone for such a slight; that day, he walked out calmly, eyes down, not even looking where he was going. It had broken her heart to see that. His heart wasn't merely broken; it was dead. He was a blind man sleepwalking aimlessly through his life.

As they sat there, a dispatch rider knocked on the door and delivered a telegram to him.

'To my dear friend Archie,

I regret deeply that I was unable to attend the memorial ceremony for your beautiful wife. Words cannot express the shock and sorrow I felt upon hearing the news of her tragic death.

I also sincerely regret that you're unable to continue in your role, and I hope to have the opportunity to explain this to you in person.

I hope I may remain your friend until we meet again.

While you're waiting, the President himself has asked to meet with you, and a formal invitation will follow this message.

Your friend

Dwight David Eisenhower.'

"This was waiting for you when we got back," said Rebecca handing him a letter on Downing Street stationery. It was from Churchill, saying much the same as if they'd come from the same author.

It moved Archie; it was her due, perhaps less than her due. As much as two mortal men could say, anyway.

*

Friday 4th August 1944 – Washington

Archie's mood remained precariously low, but he functioned well enough for Rebecca to take him to the United States. General Harlan Winters met him personally at the steps of the plane.

Harlan had a tear in his eye too, when he embraced Archie and Rebecca before driving them directly to the White House, where he took them straight into the Oval Office.

Hopkins stood next to the President, who, after apologising for being unable to stand, presented him and Rebecca with the United States Congressional Medal of Honour.

It was unexpected, and as Archie looked at Roosevelt and Hopkins, he could see two men who were giving their health and their lives for their country. He'd only given the lives of others; he still had his life and felt the guilt of a fraud.

As he took a step back, the President said, "No, please, there is one more; this is for your wife, Una. I know the price you paid; I know the chance you had and didn't take because you needed to help another old man much like myself. You could have been safe."

"Thank you, Sir; I promise you she'll wear it one day."

"In heaven by your side?"

"Perhaps," he said, not wishing to cause offence.

*

Winters insisted on them staying in the same hotel as him and booked two rooms for them.

They ate an excellent dinner with him, and he acted like the world's guiltiest man trying to atone for a mortal sin. Harlan could see the more he talked indiscreetly about the war's progress, the more alive Archie seemed. So he told him much more than he should have. There was no safer person to tell and no one who needed to know the truth more.

The truth about rockets, the truth about their connection to the Manhattan Project, nuclear war, the race to reach space and even the moon. The truth about the Establishment in England and the United States.

So Harlan told him and was glad he had. He apologised for having to leave early the next morning, returning southwest, then finally said he owed Archie several favours, and he need only ask.

As he said that, Archie felt words forming in his head as if he'd heard or read them before but couldn't remember when.

"There are times when I feel a dozen knives at my back ready to strike, that's what… England feels like to me now. There may come a time when I won't be such a welcome guest here, and I might need that favour, thank you. It's been an honour to help a man such as you and a country such as yours. We'll speak again; let's hope it's not at the gates of Hell."

"Those gates hold no fear for me, son, nor should they for you."

They parted and wouldn't see each other again.

Rebecca and Archie went back to their room; without words, they'd checked into two rooms and only gone to one of them. Neither had slept alone since he'd left the hospital after Una's death, and sleep was all they'd done or would do.

They lay in the bed, naked and close.

"I love you, Rebecca, and I need your help again," Archie said.

"Anything," she said.

"Tonight, when I spoke of knives at my back."

"Of course, you must feel that way; it's natural for a man like you."

"No, it's not that, it's… when I said England, I was going to say Rome. I still want to."

"I'll have to think about that. Can I ask you some questions? I'll know if you're lying or if you can't tell what

the truth is."
"Please."

Chapter Nine

Tuesday 8th August 1944 - Wallingford

Archie and Rebecca returned immediately from the United States, and Rebecca sensed a small spark she could fan to make a flame in Archie.

She forced him to do something, anything. She made him drive them along the length of Watling Street between Bletchley and Wallingford.

They walked outside his old school and went to the Grammar he never got to. They visited the church where he'd been brainwashed into worshipping and went inside. He automatically dipped his fingertips in the small quarter sphere of holy water on the wall and crossed himself. He missed a step when he realised what he'd done.

"Vampires," he said, "can't be too careful."

"I brought my gun," she told him, patting her hip.

"I bet you forgot the silver bullets, though."

"Yes, dammit, I did. I'm ready for zombies, though."

"A reasonable precaution in premises of this nature."

The unique perfume of the false Gods assaulted his nostrils and senses; candle fire, wax and stale holy water polluted his mind with memories. The confessional booth caught his eye, the same red velvet curtains behind which he'd confessed the sin of being human and found forgiveness by reciting some meaningless words several times. The primitive naïve savagery of his youth embarrassed and enraged him.

'What a fucking waste of time, of potential, of innocence. Fuck all of that; I'm somebody now, somebody else. I am not Teddy Austin. I am Archie Travers; now he'd have a fucking tale to tell in that booth.'

He thought about why Rebecca had made him do this and why he'd agreed when he hadn't wanted to. He'd progressed since he'd left this small town and that smaller life behind. He liked what he was now, infinitely better than what he'd been then.

She hadn't meant it to be a nostalgic trip down memory lane; she wanted him to think more about what he'd gained rather than what he'd lost. That would help, not today, maybe tomorrow.

At four in the afternoon, they were hungry, and Archie took Rebecca to a fish and chip shop in the High Street he thought would be open. They shared fish and chips from a newspaper while sitting on the low wall outside the Oddfellows Arms Public House.

He'd had his first ever pint of beer there, Ludlow Ale, flat and dark, the desired effect without the taste. His friend Simon, his only friend, was with him and chickened out of going in and demanding his first man's drink. Archie sneaked out with a small bottle. He thought it was disgusting, which was true, but he drank it all because he didn't want to let his friend Archie down.

Today, they needed something to wash down the grease, and after wiping their hands and lips with Rebecca's handkerchief, they went inside the pub. Major Archie Travers asked the elderly barmaid for two half pints of Ludlow, and not a soul recognised who or what he was.

He drank his beer quickly and asked Rebecca if they could leave. She left half her glass and followed him out.

The barmaid was Mrs Seabury, Simon's mum.

He'd lost count of those he'd killed; he couldn't measure the vengeance he'd delivered; he couldn't look at the face of one old woman. He'd done so much but had undone nothing.

Dead was still dead.

At the end of a long day, confused and reflective rather than cathartic, he drove, then parked a short distance from his old home and waited.

He waited until a single decker bus drew up nearby, and his father and two brothers got out.

"That's them," he said.

"Fucking Hell," Rebecca said, "stay here, don't move."

She left the car and followed the three men nearly to

their front door; she stopped them and engaged in a conversation. They smiled and nodded, then pointed and spoke as if they were giving her directions. Rebecca appeared to thank them, she returned to the car, and the men went into the house.

Rebecca told Archie she'd drive now and ushered him out of the driver's seat, apparently intending to drive off immediately.

As he sat next to her, he saw she was tearful, tears falling without crying or wailing, the worst kind.

"I'm sorry, I'm sorry," she said.

"What for, what?"

"I'm sorry, I love you, I'll do anything for you, but… that's not your father… or your brothers. They don't look like you, not at all; that's the easy part. They don't sound like you either; they don't feel like you. You know I can sense when you're near like I saw you with Gubbins and knew you from fifty yards away. You know I can smell and taste you; you know I can."

"I know, I know that. So they're different; that could be natural."

"No!" she shouted, angry, surprising Archie. "That's the last thing it is," she lowered her head onto the steering wheel and sobbed. She was fully crying now and could barely speak.

It had taken a few minutes before her tears and nose had dried enough, then finally, she turned her head towards him and spoke.

"They smell like the people we kill."

Rebecca opened the car door and vomited onto the pavement, collapsing. Archie rushed round to her, lifted her, cradling her body and put her back in the passenger seat.

"I'm sorry, I'm sorry," she repeatedly said, "I'm supposed to be looking after you; I'm sorry. I'm supposed to be helping you, not making it worse."

"It's okay, it's okay, tell me what you saw," he said, as calm as he'd ever been in his life.

"I asked for directions. Then I looked into their eyes and saw nothing, no emotion, no loss; they hadn't lost a son or brother. They smiled and showed me where to go; they felt nothing; they're not even related to each other, Archie!"

"I'll kill them."

"No, we can't start again; we can't kill them all."

"Yes, we can; I need to find out who I am first, then I'll kill them. We only need a plan."

*

Archie drove, and when they reached the cottage, he carried Rebecca inside, set her down on the sofa and lit the fire. It wasn't cold, and she was still shivering as if from fright. He made two mugs of tea and wrapped her in a blanket.

"I'm sorry; I'm supposed to be helping you, not making it worse," she repeated.

Archie turned her face upwards to look into her eyes.

"No, Rebecca, you've helped more than I ever thought possible; you always do. I was meant to go there with you today," he said, then paused, finding he couldn't hold her gaze and looked at the fire instead.

"I hated my family every single day of my life. My whole life, I thought there was something wrong with me. Now I know it was them; they smelt wrong, they always smelt wrong, and it made me sick. I couldn't tell anyone all of it, not even Una."

He paused again, this time for five full minutes, and Rebecca waited for him to say more.

"It first happened when I was about five, maybe younger. I dreamed about my mother; she was naked, and I was standing on her, using her as a doormat and wiping my dirty shoes on her…, and it excited me. Then I had dreams about my father, brothers, and sisters; I was torturing them, things no five-year-old could possibly know, and that excited me too. They were my slaves in the dream. In the daytime, I could usually forget the dreams; I felt bad about them. I thought there was something wrong with me, but each night, I wanted to have the dreams, I enjoyed them. How could I tell that to anyone, ever?"

Rebecca remained silent, still waiting for more.

"That's why I can't look at the victims."

"That's why I can feel the pleasure of inflicting their pain."

"That's why I dreamed of being someone else."

"That's why I needed to be someone else."

Rebecca put her tea down, then took his from his hand and placed it carefully on the floor. Archie put his head on her lap and slept while she stroked his hair and planned how she would kill his family for him.

'That's why Gaius Julius Caesar had ruthlessly pursued and then crucified the Turkish pirates who had kidnapped him as a young man.'

'That's why all wrongs must be righted.'

*

Monday 14th August 1944 – Bletchley Park

Archie and Rebecca used the whole team to work on gathering information on the Austin family history. It took several days of travelling and phone calls, misusing their military status to secure access. They searched birth, death, and adoption records. Then they searched the local hospital, church, christening, and school records and concluded Archibald Travers Austin had never been born. His family had been born in Scotland, their antecedence was traceable, and they hadn't produced a son called Archibald. In fact, it looked distinctly like there were two separate Austin families, one still in Scotland, Aberdeen and one in England.

The team didn't understand why they were doing this and still did it without question. Things happened to Archie, important things, and they poured their energy into helping him in whatever way they could.

Rebecca was bereft at what she'd revealed to him. He'd lost the woman who had defined his life by being his lover and wife, he'd lost their unborn child, and now he'd lost a whole family and his identity.

She sensed his lack of shock at her discovery, as though events and feelings made sense now but left more confusion in their wake. Archie had lost his purpose and himself; she had to help him find both; she just didn't know how.

She'd always known he wasn't ordinary. Unknown events had taken Archie a million miles from who he was. Then he'd spent his life, instinctively and painstakingly dragging himself, bit by bit, towards who he should have been.

She thought about boxes, compartments, folders and notes, processes and organisation, mathematics, physics and cosmology and decided to retrace the steps that had taken him to where he was now.

Working day and night with barely any sleep, she re-read the work he'd done on D Day, their report on the threat from the Japanese, but nothing came.

The intelligence threat assessment Conner had written from Archie's thoughts on the German advance through Holland, Belgium, and France, still nothing.

Then she read the translation of 'Achtung-Panzer!' by Generalleutnant Heinz Guderian, and she saw something, an echo of another book she'd read some of at school; Caesar's Gallic Wars.

She read an English translation and heard Archie's voice in the ideas and Latin diction of the stories. She knew an early ghostwriter had written it as a political statement on behalf of Caesar; she also saw where some of Archie's qualities originated. He'd read that book, she knew that, so what! Did his voice mimic the book, or did the book mimic his voice?

She read more about Julius Caesar, voraciously now, faster than she'd known she could, seeing Archie's qualities everywhere she sought them. Perhaps, *because* she sought them.

Then finally, she read the History of Julius Caesar by Jacob Abbot. On page 132, she found an engraving of Julius as a young man; the engraving was from the Borgian era,

1503. She'd seen dozens of representations of Caesar in numerous books, all stylised as an emperor, dictator or conqueror. This engraving, from the wrong place and wrong time, purported to show Caesar as a young man aged only twenty, speaking to fellow students at an exclusive gathering of the sons of the great. The poise she saw in Caesar was exactly as Archie had shown when talking to Gubbins that first time she'd ever set eyes on him. The engraving gave her the same enticing thrill she'd experienced then. The representation of Caesar's face was finely detailed, and she had no doubt whatsoever that the engraving was Archie Travers, as she'd always seen him.

She could only guess what that meant and couldn't imagine how she could tell him without him thinking she'd lost her marbles. As surely as she had boxes in her mind where she could place and hide things, she had other boxes that showed things no one else could see. She saw two men born worlds and times apart, undeniably linked across space and time.

You could read a book and imagine yourself as the hero, but you couldn't give yourself his face! She knew Julius Caesar's bloodline had died with him; everyone knew that. Caesar must surely have had some illegitimate issue, but that was untraceable.

Archie could be a distant descendant of the great man; a Roman Catholic upbringing and a penchant for Latin and Roman history had drawn him to Caesar. How on earth would he then manage to appear in the middle of England as part of that unholy family?

She spoke to Doc Ward; he knew of the existence of nucleic acids and the theory they were unique to each individual. Any technology that might discern that for certain was decades away.

That theory linked to Archie's reasoning behind collecting blood and tissue samples from his teams. That, too, was only a dream, not a reality.

All that research only left Rebecca with a link to a possible ancestor nearly two thousand years ago, some traits, a likeness and nothing else.

Only his false parents could possibly provide any answer to the mystery.

*

Tuesday 15th August 1944 – Wallingford

Archie and Rebecca waited impatiently in their car in Wallingford; it was getting darker, about nine in the evening. They'd driven past his family home much earlier, seeing signs of occupation, movement, and dim light. They'd waited outside the town and talked through the plan repeatedly.

They hadn't involved any other member of the team, they'd taken time away, and no one questioned any time they spent together. They'd consciously excluded Billy, Freddie, and the others; their plan was cold blooded murder. Kidnap and torture followed by death, they could see no other way to get any information.

Although his family had never physically abused him as Rebecca had dreaded, they'd clearly kidnapped him as a baby. She knew she'd have murdered the whole family herself for that fact alone, but they were keeping him for something or someone.

Archie found other puzzles he'd half seen and half sensed within his family that had pained him. That lack of belonging, that God, little memories that didn't fit. Archie felt a tremendous sense of relief that they hadn't been his real family. He never could have told anyone the truth of his childhood dreams, no one else, no other man, not even Conner. Rebecca had lifted that burden from him, and he loved her for it. That helped at first, but when he felt the absence of his real parents, whoever they were, it began to hurt him afresh.

He began to question why they'd chosen him, selected him, why him? What had he done? Now he knew they weren't family themselves; why had they stayed in place? He'd been reported missing in Calais; perhaps they were waiting in case he came back. Trouble did seem to find him; he wasn't going to be a victim, though; he was going to deliver the tenth plague on that whole family. There would be no Angel of Death, only the echo of the Thompson gun, the slash of a German knife and perhaps the clash of a Mauser.

At precisely 2200, Archie used a sledgehammer to smash the lock on the front door of his former home. Rebecca flung herself in first, silenced Luger in her right hand, ready to shoot the first brother or sister she saw. She stopped her trigger finger as it began its first squeeze, pulling the trigger only a fraction less than she needed to fire.

Confusion filled her as it did Archie behind her.

Two old men, neither less than seventy years old, one stood on a ladder, one crouched before them, painting the walls and ceiling of the hallway.

Archie's family had left the property a week ago, the same day Rebecca spoke to them. The men were decorating the property so it could be re-let as soon as possible.

His family had stripped the house entirely; there were no personal items left, only the furniture and curtains remained, the rent had included that.

Archie and Rebecca, as Military Intelligence in pursuit of fifth columnists, their guns still in their hands, pressed the dotards hard for anything the family might have left.

One of the men took them to his bag, where he showed them a beheaded teddy bear. His family had left it, posed, the head alongside the seated body in a bedroom; Archie knew which one.

"I thought I could fix it and give it to one of my granddaughters," said the old man.

"It's mine," said Archie, "I mean, I need it as evidence."

"Of course, sir."

The other man led Rebecca to a drawer in a bedside cabinet, old newspapers left to line the drawer, some still jammed inside. A few pages of a flattened and folded newspaper, crisp and yellowed with age. The Scotsman newspaper detailing the gruesome murder of an Italian couple in France. Their hometown had connections with Aberdeen; hence the paper's less than parochial interest in a foreign crime. There had been a murder, unsolved, and a child, Alessandro, had gone missing and was presumed dead. The family was called D'Annunzio, wealthy, it said.

*

On the late night drive back to Bletchley, Rebecca found the courage to tell Archie about the research she'd done and what she'd found. The connection she'd made between him and Julius Caesar didn't seem to surprise him. He asked factual questions about the book and the engraving, then said he'd look at it when they got back.

They went straight to their bed in the cottage, and Rebecca lay silent next to Archie. He was asleep; he had a broken, no, a murdered teddy bear and a name. He had even less than when he smashed that door down. He had no real answers, only more questions. She felt an animal urge to give him what he needed, her body as well as her soul. It made her chest ache, strain, as if ready to burst apart, but she couldn't give herself to him, not yet, and she knew he wouldn't take her if offered, not yet.

The waiting was agony for both of them, and each would bear it silently for the other.

*

Gaius Julius Caesar rode his horse, Tres Respice, North to South along Watling Street. This was the beginning of his triumphal journey back to Rome. The entire British mainland was his, not Rome's, his. The relatively poor booty wasn't the issue; he had the land and its people. Their former leaders, who they jokingly referred to as kings, were in cages to the rear of the huge caravan and army that followed him. He might not even bring the prisoners back to Rome; they were poor specimens to parade in front of Rome's finest. Little more than savages, less than Roman, less than human. No Vercingetorix here. Their purpose was to cow the population, to display their final defeat, and to show their young men that Rome and the Roman army were their future. They could join him and be part of his army that ruled the world or be part of his world under his heel. Better led by better men and better Gods, these people had potential.

All of Rome would bend to him now.

Caesar's horse stumbled slightly, one leg giving way on a loose stone; he had to jump clear nimbly to avoid being crushed.

He woke when he hit the ground, he'd rolled from his low bed onto the soft carpet of his tent, and he suffered no harm. The conquest had only begun, victory was at least two years away, and there was some harm in that. Thinking too far ahead could lead to a fall today or tomorrow. He would return to sleep and think only of that next single day.

*

"Archie, Archie, are you okay?" Rebecca said as she knelt next to him, beside the bed, stroking his forehead and calming herself at the same time.

"You were talking in your sleep, mumbling; I couldn't make out any words; it wasn't English. Then you fell out of bed."

He laughed.

"I dreamt I was Caesar, and he fell off his horse, fucking stupid really and before you say anything, hardly surprising since we'd talked about him and we'd just come down Watling Street. I've dreamt of him before, talking to him, giving him advice, reporting to him from other Generals."

"There's more, tell me," she insisted.

"He'd conquered Britain when he never did; of course, he was dreaming as well."

"Not that."

"What then?"

"The horse, how did you fall off? Tell me exactly."

"It stumbled, the right front leg gave way, and it was going down for certain. I knew I couldn't stay on and correct the fall, so I let go of the reins, took both feet out of the stirrups, relaxed and took the fall. I rolled like a hedgehog away from the horse like I'd been trained to. Like I'd done a dozen times before… "

"You've never ridden a horse, have you?"

"No."

"And?"

"And sometimes I dream I'm Caesar; at times it's one of his Generals or a Legionary, sometimes a personal slave, he's always there."

"And when you gave him reports from other Generals, were they verbal?"

"No, they were letters."

"Were they in English?"

"No, of course not, they were in Latin, they were… in code, sometimes in code, in times of conflict, even ordinary ones, so no one would know which was important or routine."

"And what is he telling you to do now?"

"He needs advice from Pompey or Crassus, and he doesn't know where they are, if he's killed them, or if they've killed him."

They were wide awake now, so she took him downstairs, put the kettle on and fetched the book with the engraving.

"Okay, that looks like me, and I suppose the pose is one I've made in front of the team. Look at the rest of the book; there's other pictures, busts and the like. That one there, that's nothing like me. What is it, one out of ten?"

"That is you, and that was your dream, wasn't it?"

"Well, yes, of course, but people dream; they just do. It's called self-actualisation; I used to dream of being a cowboy, but it doesn't make me General fucking Custer. I dream I can fly, but I don't jump off a building when I'm awake. I've put a lot of effort into not believing in God; I'm not going to start believing in spirits instead. There's science, and there's nature and nothing else. I'm not Caesar; look at me; I can manage a dozen men, not whole armies. I'm no Eisenhower, no Patton, shit, I'm not even a Montgomery. My real name may well be Alessandro

Spaghettio; how does that help me now?"

"Oh, for fuck's sake, you're impossible sometimes."

"And you want me to be impossible all the time instead? Ouch!" he said as she playfully slapped his face, and they both burst out laughing.

"Sorry," she said and went to kiss it better, then instead of the gentle peck on the cheek she planned, she kissed his lips, forcing her tongue urgently between them. He responded with equal force, and they kissed deeply and passionately; it took her breath away, and she reached for his groin.

"No, not yet," he said.

"You're right," she said.

"Yes. I love you, you know that. It's too soon for both of us."

She kissed him again, slowly, deeply and passionately, longer than the first time and finished with two smaller pecks on his lips.

"No harm in practising?" she said.

He carried her back upstairs, and they slept.

*

Wednesday 16th August 1944 – Glasgow

Rebecca maintained her relentless pace and drove Archie to Glasgow and the offices of the Scotsman newspaper, where their status gave them immediate access to the archives. The custodian, Mr Brown, found the relevant copy for them dated the 6th of October 1920. They read that edition from beginning to end to see if anything else in the news was relevant and found nothing. Brown remembered the story but knew no more details. The article said the family had connections to Aberdeen and was attributed to an unnamed staff reporter; he told them that could mean anything. Anyway, there would be such a turnover in staff after more than 20 years. Brown was a friendly sort, and he was happy to show them around the building. He told them the history of the paper and let them see old staff records, which they looked at, searching for any clue, a name, a sacking, a death, anything. They found nothing.

*

Thursday, 17th August 1944 – Aberdeen

They drove to Aberdeen and spent two days searching for anything that might hold the name they were looking for. They found no trace of any D'Annunzios, very few Italian connections at all and found nothing around that date in local papers.

They did trace the real Austin family, as named and aged, but they had no clue that anyone was using their name. They couldn't understand how anyone could misuse their names; surely the Government would notice that sort of thing?

The tenuous link to Aberdeen was there, but why and what it was, remained a mystery.

*

Saturday 19th August 1944 – Bletchley Park

They returned to Bletchley only slightly less confused than when they'd left and decided to continue their other war. The threat of their personal war felt worse, but they didn't share their fear with any of the others. What was the link between a malice now and a kidnapped child more than twenty years before? How many wars were they fighting?

Archie then used all his remaining influence arranging to be informed of any unidentified bodies found in England, Wales and Scotland and waited.

"Trouble finds you," Rebecca said.

*

Thursday 24th August 1944 – Carlisle

A body discovered in a Tarn near Carlisle came to his attention only days later. The body was naked and had been weighted down to keep it under the water, with lead weights and chains around the ankles. A method he'd used himself. That should have been enough to ensure it was never discovered, but the chain had tangled on the steeple of a church!

The village of old Talkin had been submerged in the

Tarn for centuries. A dry winter and summer in 1944 had meant the head of the body had rippled below the surface of the water, and an angler had seen it.

The body was that of a woman, the same age and size as his 'mother', drowned, lungs full of water before death.

He knew it was his mother, someone he should have loved, who should have loved him. Someone who had been evil beyond anything he could have imagined and who, in turn, had been killed by something more evil than that.

Archie went straight to the Tarn with Rebecca and tried to imagine what had happened there. Tried to feel whatever it was.

Sheep wandered around, keeping the grass closely cropped. It was warm and dry, not a cloud in the sky. He sat down on a small wooden jetty next to the still window of water, felt the chill of death on his face and thought. Rebecca held his hand, and music came into his head. He tried to envisage his soul at peace and couldn't. The stifling choking death by asphyxiation haunted the place and hurt him. Even though he cared nothing for the bitch now, he had once, she'd fed and clothed him. Whoever it was, hadn't only concealed the body here, they'd killed her here, punished her here, tortured her here for failure. A failure, beyond blame, unavoidable and unforgiven.

The music he heard was Jascha Heifetz.

Archie knew you hid bodies in the best spot near where you killed them. You wouldn't kill five people and drive around the country visiting five lakes; there had to be more bodies in that Tarn.

He arranged for a team of Navy divers to undertake a secret training exercise in the Tarn. They found the Church and other smaller buildings; the village was tiny, no more than a hamlet, easily searched with huge waterproof lights. They found no trace of any other bodies.

The realisation there were no other bodies was another puzzle. The family had become separated, they'd remained in place together for years after he'd left, and all disappeared the day he returned.

The family must have separated themselves somehow, evading pursuit by Archie surely. Then another deadly threat had pursued and found them.

He knew it would be a miracle if he found any other members of his family still alive, and the war still prevented any meaningful examination of Italian or French records. Another dead end to match the witnesses.

*

Monday 28th August 1944 – The Cottage

Archie felt as though someone hated Archie Travers and Archie Austin but hadn't linked the two of them until his family had seen Rebecca in Wallingford. That made no sense to him either; why kidnap and keep him, let him leave and go to London, then ignore him?

"I have a name at least," he said to Rebecca as they lay together in bed, "Alessandro D'Annunzio. Is that me? I feel a need to have been English. I feel English. I want to be English. Italian wouldn't be too bad; I could have been French. Sorry, Rebecca."

She pinched him under the covers, and he kissed her to make up for the insult. This time, his kiss turned into a deep and passionate one, and he finished it by kissing her lips and both eyelids.

"You can insult my nationality any time you like if that's how you make up for it," she said.

He was glad he'd kissed her; she deserved to be kissed. To be kissed by him and no other, Una would know that, wouldn't she?

Trouble continued to find him.

Chapter Ten

Thursday 31st August 1944 – Bletchley Park

Following his return from Aberdeen and the disappointment of the Tarn, Archie's spirits sank.

The war was going well, as far as Archie knew, as far as he cared.

Work was routine and boring; Archie only got up each morning to enjoy the presence of Rebecca. Not for the first time, Churchill's black dog had bitten him, and the rabid cancer of depression ate at him. True purpose still eluded him after the cul-de-sac of Wallingford. He had vague plans, but he could only put them in place when the war in Europe finally ended.

He sat outside Building Thirteen because it was drizzling slightly, enough to deter interruptions. He was tired of questions everyone thought were vital, but he didn't, and the effort of pretence drained all the patience he thought he'd learned. It was mid-morning, so he hoped to be left alone with his bitter thoughts and Una's rose bush. Sometimes, the disgust he felt for his self-pity snapped him out of it, and he thought he'd give it a try; it wouldn't be difficult. He thought of Una and letting her memory down, then stood up immediately to confront the day.

He saw the girl approaching him from the direction of the Mansion to his right.

He'd seen her once, in the main canteen; she looked eighteen and wore a private's uniform. The same frame as Una and Rebecca, a slim face, mousey straight hair, full lips and a pair of blue eyes that stood out across a crowded room. She carried herself well as she walked, and she had dimples, too; he could see them now she was close and smiling at him.

'Oh, bollocks, not now, I don't need this, not now, maybe never.'

"Major Travers, my name is Aria Lescott; I need to be in

your team."

"And what's your real name?"

"It is Lescott, legally by Deed Poll; my family name is Leshchyov originally, my full name is Ariadna."

"Were you born in Russia?"

"Yes, in the upper Volga, we were farmers. We left in 1932 and came here in 1933."

"1932?"

"Yes, why?"

"You weren't allowed to travel; you were supposed to stay there and starve to death."

"Like millions did, yes. My father and mother were very determined people. We sold our horses to pay for travelling, and we left before the ban was fully enforced."

"And I'm impressed. Were your family wealthy?"

"Stalin thought so; we didn't; we were called Kulaks, anyway. We weren't allowed to keep our farm; it was to be shared, whether we liked it or not."

"One of three escaping out of three million is certainly the sort of person I need. Why do you want to join my team?"

"I speak and read Russian, so I translate words; some would be content with that, but I'm not. I need to be in a team that kills people; everyone knows your team kills people. I need to help kill Germans in this war, then Stalin in the next one."

"Okay, that's very perceptive, and I like forward thinking people; there's something you haven't told me, though."

Archie enjoyed the verbal jousting, and Aria was extremely sharp. She was annoyed at the question; she had something to say but wasn't ready to say it.

"I'm going to marry George Flowers."

"Oh, sorry, I didn't know you were seeing one another."

"We aren't, but I've seen him, and he's mine; I have to make sure no one else takes him first. He's free, your Rebecca told me so, and he needs me."

"You'd better come in and meet the team then," he said,

half joking.

"I've already met the team; Rebecca and Mary showed me, and then they made me ask you myself. They told me you'd get the truth from me."

"Yes, I can see that."

"Please don't tell George yet. I have to catch him myself."

"There's no point arguing, is there?"

She laughed.

"Ha, they both said you would say that too."

*

Friday 1st September 1944

Archie wasn't sure what to feel for George; he was a big boy and could take care of himself. At least, he was until Aria spoke to him for the first time.

"Blimey Boss, who is she?" George said to Archie when he accidentally steered him towards her in the canteen at dinner time the next day, "Is she with anyone?"

"I've no idea; she only joined the team yesterday."

"She is gorgeous," he said, and they went to sit at her table.

Archie exchanged pleasantries and pretended to introduce George casually.

"Oh look, there's Rebecca; I'd better go and sit with her," Archie said.

*

"Never stood a fucking chance," he said to Rebecca, "I'm not sure they even noticed me leave. Don't ever do that to me, please."

"Fuck off, you're mine now," she said and lightly scratched the back of his hand with the nails Una had made her grow. He smiled; she hoped she'd said the right words. She had; he didn't even notice, and that showed how right the words were.

Archie stopped talking and ate, thinking deeply, back to his trip to Moscow with Churchill on the 12th of August 1942, before the raid on Dieppe and the massacre at the cottage.

Rebecca watched him think and waited; she was doing a lot of that lately.

He took some facts and feelings from his memory and drew each one into a box he created in his mind. He shuffled the facts around the box, placing them in order, where they started to make a story and a puzzle.

*

"You will not be my bodyguard," Churchill had told him, "because I shall not need one in such friendly company. Therefore, you will be armed with nothing but your wits. Stay close and alert."

Archie smiled, "shall I tell you when Stalin is lying?"

"No need; his lips will move, and I shall see it. Now, remember, on your best behaviour, young man."

Churchill's company were a mixed bunch, posh, upper-crust, noble, high ranking and ordinary, like Archie. None of them spoke to Archie much, other than Russell Lescott, who was officially Churchill's driver and was a constant unused presence like Archie. He spoke with a London accent when he did talk, which was mostly to Archie. Archie could tell he wasn't from London but chose not to press the matter.

Russell seemed watchful, too sharp for a driver. Archie supposed Churchill would need a sharp one, specially trained. He'd wondered if Russell was another discreet bodyguard and saw it clearly now, kicking himself for not noticing sooner.

Russell was a native Russian speaker, specifically to monitor what else was said in the background and inform Churchill quietly later. There were two translators with Churchill already who appeared competent. Nothing would be missed or mistaken, he was sure. Unless it was the two translators, he was watching and watching both of them.

Who was watching who, though? Churchill must have been in on it, but who else? Why had Archie been there? He'd done almost nothing while there. Unless he was there to do any dirty work necessary, he could make a broken neck look like a fall down some stairs.

*

"Rebecca, did you notice anything remotely false about Aria?" Archie asked, having finished eating now.

"No, nothing at all; I decided not to kill her when I realised the devilishly handsome man from Building Thirteen meant George, not you."

"So what else do you know about her, her family?"

"She has none, her mother died of pneumonia shortly after they arrived here, and her father died in a car accident two years ago."

"What was her father's name?"

"Russell, formerly Ruslan, according to her file."

"Oh shit."

"If you're worried about her, ask Gubbins; he gave her the job here. She's clean as a whistle; that's just been cleaned."

"I know that. It's just that trouble's found me again."

"Us," she corrected him.

"We have a purpose."

*

Monday 4th September 1944 – Bletchley Park – The Mansion

Archie saw Gubbins in his office in the Mansion.

"I could have her transferred?" Gubbins said.

"No, you don't understand. She's in my team, madly in love with one of my men, and he with her. He's spent the weekend teaching her how to shoot; she's learning for a reason, but she doesn't know it yet. She's one of mine now, sir. People don't leave my team, they may get killed, but they don't leave."

"Okay, Archie, her father was SOE, and it wasn't a car accident. Someone poisoned him, very obviously, in fact, a warning, one that said; we don't fear you. God, I was trying to help the girl; this is a big place now. I didn't think she'd meet you."

"The pair of them remind me of when I first met Una. It was meant to happen; she was meant to meet me."

"And you think you were meant to do something about it."

"That's the way it usually works."

"Right, listen, you're persona non grata on the liaison front now. You work for me, you follow orders, you don't kill anyone, is that clear?"

"Yes, sir."

"And no unfortunate accidents in your proximity, either."

"Yes, sir."

"Right, I'll tell you what's what; sit down, man. You've probably worked out Russell was there checking both translators; we suspected one was wrong, but we didn't know which. We had to use an SOE man; we didn't know who else to trust. You were there in case of a fight. Russell heard enough in Moscow to damn both of them, so we kept them in post, under close surveillance to see who else we could snare. The buggers were trained to detect surveillance, walking round blocks, doubling back on themselves. They both disappeared on the tube going home on the night of the 19th of October, two months after we raided Dieppe. We found Russell dead the next morning, poisoned at his own desk by a cup of his own tea.

"We got precisely nowhere with our investigation. We did it all ourselves; I can't have the police and MI knowing we can't protect our own. We couldn't even pinpoint the exact poison, something related to a Mongolian snake, hardly a common ingredient."

"There's a hint of Russia in there?"

"Probably. What grinds at me is that some bastard walked into my HQ, poisoned the right man with the right tea and walked out."

"Was there a leak on Dieppe?"

"Yes, there bloody was."

"Any clues on that?"

"Nothing, MI investigated that Daily Telegraph crossword puzzle idiot, Leonard Dawe. He had 'French port' as a clue and 'Dieppe' as the answer, the bloody day before the operation. Coincidence, they concluded. He did the same around the time of D Day, no less than eight times, you know."

"I heard some of it."

"All the clues and solutions were pure coincidence!"

"Nothing happens without a cause. I don't believe in coincidence."

"You wouldn't. There's a whole storm of excrement that tracks you around Europe."

"I can't argue with that, sir."

"The fact is, my people in the area were ready to disrupt any German reinforcements moving to Dieppe on the day; there were none to disrupt; they were already there."

Archie thought in the silence for a couple of minutes; Gubbins let him think.

"Why kill him at all?" Archie said eventually, "I know it sent a message, but he'd already talked; they must have worked it out when we conducted surveillance on both translators."

"And both translators disappeared on the tube the same evening, not a trace since."

"Dead?" said Archie.

"Could be."

"I would; they were a liability, no longer needed, these chaps are at least as ruthless as me, and I'd do it. Who needs two more poofs in Moscow?"

"They were homosexuals?"

"Sorry, I thought you'd know. They both fancied me, I can tell. It happens to me. I might ask Alan if he knows them from University."

"Archie, do nothing that jeopardises his work or him; none of us know anything about him at all, and make sure it stays that way."

"Don't worry, I'd kill anyone who tried to hurt him."

"Well, try not to, man."

"We're both of us gone in twelve months, aren't we?"

"Yes. The bastards tried to do it last January," Gubbins

said, "wanted to shut us down, only Churchill stopped them. Told them he needed to hear more than the sum of their fears. That's why they're not too keen on you either, Archie."

"Let's do what we can while we can… there must have been something Ruslan saw or heard that he wasn't supposed to. Something he didn't even notice himself, something they couldn't risk him working out later. It would have to be something here, though, not there, they'd know he was never going back to Russia, and he can't hurt anyone there; it has to be something here."

"And if it's here, we have to do something about it."

"Can I read the report and see any investigating papers, then have a long think about it?"

"Yes, of course; I'll get them to you tomorrow."

"You told Aria he'd been murdered then?"

"Yes, I did; I made sure Anna looked after her while she was at school, then sorted out a job for her here. She asked me straight out, and I couldn't lie to her about that. She's sharp as a tack anyway."

"You're an honest man, sir, a good man, all the risks we take, all the lies we tell, all we do, and you're still an honest man."

"And I know now why she sought you out soon after; she needs revenge as much as we do."

"Let's save her some trouble then. Are you content for me to deal with this for the time being, and I'll let you know what I find before I act."

"Yes, please, try to avoid treason and murdering any of the Royal Family."

"You didn't mention the Government, sir."

"I think that ship may have sailed."

"I promise I won't let her take any risks, sir."

"Good, we all feel guilt for those we've killed, you know. And keep your gloves *on* this time!"

*

Tuesday 5th September 1944 – Bletchley Park – Building Thirteen

The next day Archie sat with Rebecca in the private room in Building Thirteen and went through the reports twice, beginning to end. As Rebecca watched him intently, she was both calm and excited. No sign of black care in him; he was riding fast enough, he was alive again, and she was beside him.

The reports on Russell's death and subsequent SOE investigation were detailed, thorough and very thin on actual evidence and clues.

They knew full details of everyone who'd signed into SOE Headquarters in Baker Street that day, sixty-seven of them. They knew from colleagues he'd had a cup of his tea at three pm with no ill effects. The time of death was between seven and ten pm, probably nearer seven. He wouldn't have worked any later than eight.

Most people worked nine to five, so they could only rule out a few as not being present after three o'clock.

Of the fifty-two left, forty-eight were SOE, one was a visitor to Jimmy McKay from the Ministry of Works. He was an escorted visitor, "spent the whole time with me, never even went to the toilet, never left my sight," Jimmy said.

The other three were workmen installing extra phone lines; they'd been the primary target of the investigation even though it was a reputable company with Government contracts. Their best investigators had rigorously interviewed them before they released them. They re-interviewed them all six months later; all were still doing the same jobs, living in the same places; it had to be a dead end.

None of the SOE people had seen anything or anyone remotely unusual, only three apparently blameless workmen.

*

Wednesday 6th September 1944 - 0730 – London

Archie and Rebecca drove to Baker Street, parking opposite the SOE building.

Archie stood across the street staring at the wide

building, six stories including the attic space, then walked around the block twice and through alleyways he could access. The view reminded him of Calais and the buildings he and Spud had ferreted through.

"Rebecca, how many ways can you see into that building?"

"Thirty-two."

She'd already counted the windows that showed at the front of the tall terraced building.

"Assuming the same number at the back, that's sixty-four."

"Any others?"

"Basements and attics, that's another four at least. The street behind is a rabbit warren."

"We've only looked at one door! Let's go and see Jimmy."

*

Archie, Jimmy, and Rebecca spent an hour moving old desks and rubbish away from the walls of the cellar, jumped up and down on the floor, and Archie kicked the wall with his feet. They found only brick and concrete.

"I can get a proper team in here with tools to search," Jimmy said.

"Let's check the attic first," Archie said.

The dozen attic rooms were fully occupied with desks and personnel. There was a small triangular loft space above those rooms running the length of the building. At first, they couldn't find any access points, then they finally found a small inspection hatch in a toilet at the top of a stairwell.

Archie undid the latch, and the lid fell down on hinges leaving a hole about two feet square.

"No one could get through that," Jimmy said.

"That latch is designed to be shut from the inside and the outside; look at it," said Rebecca starting to take her clothes off.

"No," said Archie indignantly.

"Oh, shut up and get me a torch."

Rebecca went in head first, boosted by Archie. Ten minutes later, Rebecca's head appeared at the hatch.

"Jimmy, you have to leave the room," she said.

"Why?"

"Because I caught my bloody knickers on some wood, and they've ripped off."

"Oh, right."

Archie helped Rebecca out; she'd come back head first somehow on the return trip.

For a second, he held her, almost naked and upside down, then flipped her the right way up and began to help her dress. She looked at him mischievously.

"Stop that right now," he said.

"What?"

*

"Jimmy, get back in here."

Jimmy came back in with a glass of water for her; she sat down on the closed toilet seat, drank deeply, caught her breath and said.

"It's wider once you're in, leads next door, there's a wooden floor in the tunnel, and it opens up into a small room. I think there's a false wall that leads into the building next door. I didn't disturb anything, there's wires leading from this building to tape recording and radio equipment. Someone's bugging SOE HQ, Jimmy," she said, "and there are blue overalls hanging on the wall."

"Bugger," said Jimmy.

"You still wouldn't get a grown man through that hole," Archie said. "It would have to be a girl or a child or...."

"An Animal," said Rebecca.

"Bloody hell, that's it," Jimmy spat the words out in anger, "how could I be so stupid? They killed Russell because he saw something or someone he shouldn't have. That bastard Newell from the Ministry kept me in my office so I wouldn't see a face I knew. I saw him at Holloway Police Station in the background, skinny as a rake, and you don't forget that face. It was the Animal."

"We need a secure line to Gubbins right now, not in this

building," said Archie.

They conducted inquiries next door that afternoon, discreetly dressed as plainclothes policemen; Billy, Freddie and Begley joined them from Bletchley. They didn't want to tip off the owners of the equipment, and they didn't want anyone to know of any compromise of SOE.

It looked like the offices next door were clean and uninvolved. However, there was a small office in the loft which had remained unused and apparently unlet.

The office was empty and ordinary; the false wall was a skilful piece of work.

"No!" Begley shouted at Archie as he approached the wall. "Something smells wrong; this is too easy. Rebecca, did you touch anything inside?"

"No. Definitely not."

"How did the equipment look? Was it new?"

"No, it was old and dusty."

Begley knelt next to the wall, listened carefully and sniffed.

"Almonds, Nobel 808. We need bomb disposal, and we'll need to evacuate the buildings, too. Someone expected us to find this hidden door."

*

"So why no tripwire in the toilet then?" Jimmy asked as they stood outside, a safe distance away.

"You'd only kill one small one that way; you'd get more in the office space," Begley said, "that's what we'd do."

"Christ, you can't think you were targeted, Archie?" Jimmy said.

"I don't know, it feels personal; the discreet plan is out the window anyway, now the UXO boys are here."

"The unexploded ordnance in the roof's a good line; I've sent men to detain my friend from the Ministry...."

"Down!" Archie shouted.

The roof blew off both buildings, small pieces of tiling flew into the air, scattering around, a small fire started, and at least one UXO man was in pieces.

'I hope he was single; please let him be single.'

"Find out who he was for me, Jimmy, please," Archie asked.

"Sir!" shouted a young motorcycle courier to Jimmy and handed him a note.

"Damn it," he said as he read it, "Newell is asleep at his desk in the Ministry with blood coming out of his nose."

"They're always one step ahead of us; each clue is another trap; they're laughing at us. I'm not putting up with that," Archie said, angry.

"What are you going to do?" asked Jimmy.

"Don't ask."

"Don't kill anybody, then."

"Speak to Gubbins for me; tell him I'm taking one glove off, only one; he'll understand."

*

That evening Archie's team kidnapped all three telephone engineers and took them to a familiar warehouse in the East End. One of them somehow told the wrong person they were working in SOE the day the Animal killed Russell. Archie was going to find out which one.

No one was to lay a finger on them, but scaring them until they soiled themselves was a good substitute.

Seeing them for the first time, Archie knew which one he wanted, Derek Spicer, whose heart had skipped a beat when he saw Freddie then relaxed. He thought Freddie was someone else, someone he feared and who looked like Freddie.

Archie saw him alone; he sat him in a chair and sat opposite him like he'd done before, wearing his full Major's uniform. Then he took his jacket off and rolled his sleeves up like they did in the films.

Derek was a skinny, short, middle-aged chancer, too old for active service even if he hadn't been in a reserved occupation.

"What does he call himself now?" he asked, "the man who looks like the older brother of my young friend."

"I don't know what you mean, sonny boy," Spicer said,

falsely assuming this was only another interview by SOE.

"I'm worse than him, you know, he's got a bad name, but he's an amateur. I can have you shot for treason tomorrow morning for the work you did in Baker Street; it'll be in the papers too. Your wife and kids are ruined; they won't get your pension, won't get fuck all. I could shoot you now, and no one would ever know or give a monkey's, you stupid old cunt."

Archie paused.

"When you saw him, I'd just killed a dozen coppers who were with him, he had a limp where one of my lads knifed him in the leg, and he'd damaged his left hand escaping."

He paused again.

"The little bastard was scared shitless when you saw him, scared of me that was, and he was still too scary for you, though, wasn't he?"

Archie put on the leather gloves he'd punched a Bishop to death with.

"Smell that," he said, holding the gloves to Spicer's nose, "that's the last cunt I beat to death."

"Fuck off," Spicer said less than a second before Archie broke his nose. A short arm jab Billy taught him.

"This is the deal, you talk in the next," Archie checked his watch, "five minutes, and I get you a job in Scotland and a new name for you and your family. This could be you," he said, passing him a new set of papers with his photograph already on them.

"Christ," the old man said.

"You see, he can only threaten you; I can help you too," Archie said, "I'm a busy man, by the way; please don't inconvenience me by making me get a new picture of you to match your new face."

"I ain't seen him since, don't want to, never even spoke to him; he was there, though. I got a set of company overalls for him; that's all. Needed for a job, a robbery, that's all I know."

"If you didn't speak to him, who did you speak to?"

"Bryson, John Bryson, left the company after the war

started, worked for the army. He said it was communications, surveillance, spying, and he had money. He was always a bullshit merchant, mind you. I used to see Bryson now and again. I probably mentioned we was working in Baker Street again, I told him, and he was working for the Government, so there was no harm done."

"A friend of mine is dead; that's harm enough," said Archie as he compounded the fracture of Spicer's nose.

The other two men both confirmed Bryson as a former colleague, who was dodgy, but they'd not seen him since the war started.

Archie kept the three men in the warehouse under armed guard. The whole team was in London by now.

They went straight to Bryson's home and took him, his wife and their children back to the warehouse. Archie simultaneously arranged for SOE to take the wives and children of the three engineers into protective custody. They'd go to the Isle of Man eventually; he'd keep them in Hertford for now.

"Know this," Archie said to the detained men, "If you leave my protection, you're as good as dead, and so are your families. What happens from here depends on Mr Bryson."

"Get the families out of my sight, keep them separately, to be safe. Use what guards you need; Gubbins will help with numbers, Asgeir, you make sure no harm comes to them from inside or out," he told the team, "Bryson is mine."

Bryson talked, Archie told him what happened that day, and he knew he was next; he knew enough to get himself killed. He provided the technical expertise to tap telephone lines and install listening devices for Military Intelligence. They paid him well, and the premises looked official.

Bryson was a gambler, short of stake money, and when an officer offered him extra duties for extra cash, he'd agreed eagerly. He'd seen him only occasionally in his building and had never known his name. That officer had left the unit, and he still called him *the Major* now. He contacted him when he needed extra work done, he followed orders as he saw it. He said he was a uniformed Major when he first saw him but wore a suit now and gave a good description. Getting safe and secure access to MI personnel records to discreetly identify him would be a problem, though.

Bryson also gave him a new name for the Animal. Mr Auld.

Chapter Eleven

Thursday 7th September 1944 - London

Archie liked this particular lead. If Clive Newell, a senior civil servant from the Ministry of Works, was expendable, so were Spicer and Bryson, perhaps the other two just for knowing Bryson. A Major might be needed, so this clue might last long enough to unravel part of the Gordian knot confronting him. Someone was wondering what had happened, and that might flush them out.

The Animal was fair game now; he was no longer a bent copper's henchman; he was a spy and treasonous killer of a good man in SOE.

*

Friday 8th September 1944 - London – East End

Billy Perry sat with the Frazer family in The Blind Beggar Public House in Whitechapel. He'd been there countless times but felt uncomfortable today. It wasn't fear; he had his pistol plus two knives and was harder than any man there. He'd killed more men than all the other patrons combined. This wasn't who he was now; he was better than this and glad of it.

He'd put the word out on the Animal long ago and heard nothing.

This time, he had a new name, Mr Nicholas Auld, someone had a sick sense of humour. He was working with bent Army people, spies probably; he described the Major to the Frasers, and their ears pricked up.

"You know him then?" said Billy.

Maurice looked at his two brothers, who nodded.

"We don't know his name; we have done some work for him in the past, he pays well, and he contacts us; we don't contact him."

"My friends can pay more than he can."

"Yes, we know that, Billy Perry, we are businessmen, you know, it's not the money; we know you're sound enough. We done his work for him gladly, we took his money, but he's posh and a queer. As you know, we don't hold with queers. As a rule, we'd slice any posh queer that came through them front doors."

Billy pulled a folded newspaper from his coat pocket and put it on the table.

"There's some good stories in this paper; you'll enjoy reading it later."

Maurice accepted the paper; it contained £500 in notes.

"Thank you, Billy, that's very kind of you, Francis; get us all another pint; we'll tell Billy some stories while he sups it."

Billy was awed by the Frazer family. They all knew the exact line between good and bad and ignored it. Yet were bound by selective unspoken rules of behaviour. They'd do any crime for a suitable reward and sometimes because they felt like it. Taking the side of a posh queer against an East End mate, especially Billy Perry, was beyond any logic they possessed.

Billy made it plain he wanted no harm done to the Major or the Animal. Their harm was Billy's to do; they understood that logic easily too.

*

Saturday 9th September 1944 – Windsor

Nicholas Auld relaxed in a comfortable chair in his small terraced house in Windsor. Previous owners had named it Clyve Cottage, it was a small old house, but it was his; he owned it.

His former employer, Inspector Tennent, had paid for it, but he didn't live long enough to know that. The Animal knew where Tennent kept his stash; anyone else who knew was conveniently dead; it belonged to him now.

Tennent had planned well, always, but not as well as that Archie bastard, he thought. I'll steer well away from him unless I ever get a small army.

He'd escaped from Archie and Freddie easily; he kept a spare key to the handcuffs on him; an Animal could plan too.

Having scouted the cottage location well in advance,

he'd gone straight to the layby they'd stopped in that night. Tennent's spare car was there, keys in the ignition and extra equipment ready in its boot.

He had difficulty walking and driving with the stab wound to his leg, and his first stop was in Holloway. Dodgy Doc Frank would fix nearly anything for a price. Doc cleaned, stitched and bandaged the thigh; before the Animal strangled him and took anything worthwhile before he left. It would look like a robbery, which it was.

He never went back to Holloway, ever.

The stash, cash, valuables, and weapons were in a safe house in Merton, South London, and he recuperated there for ten days before the unexpected caller rang his doorbell. Only one man, middle-aged and overweight, definitely not a copper. The man looked at the window where the Animal watched, peeking through the neat lace curtains, pointed firmly at him, then the door. The Animal obeyed; he recognised a new master when he saw one.

He became Mr Auld and moved out of London.

*

The first killing was his most difficult, involving too many risks, all of them taken by Mr Auld purely to make his new owner's point. He recognised it as a test and complied without question.

He'd never squeeze through that tiny hatch now; he'd put on weight with good living since then. His master's planning was impressive; two years' worth, in and out without a hitch. Poisoning was an unsatisfying killing, though.

The subsequent murders were merely routine but face to face and enjoyable. The two posh interpreter queers were a special treat. The mugs had delivered themselves to the secluded rendezvous point, confident of flight and reward. Mr Auld had relished killing them and the acts he'd made them perform before they died. Yes, he felt that had been his best ever; using the metal garrotte on the pretty boy had made the animal come in his pants.

That had convinced his new master of his continuing

usefulness, and he would survive. Nonetheless, he'd have to remain alert and make plans for when he became expendable.

He'd done a couple of recreational killings for himself, in his spare time, at his own risk. Two young girls, one blonde, one dark-haired, whose pitiless suffering he could savour, now his previous targets were off limits to him.

His home was a mansion compared with his childhood home; he kept it and the small garden neat and tidy, and he even exchanged pleasantries with his neighbours. He was older now and better fed; he started to fill out in his face and frame, he grew a moustache and let his hair grow longer.

He was as happy as he could remember, fulfilled, and sated for the moment, but the people he feared wouldn't forget him forever. The Animal knew the rules for survival of the fittest; his new employer might well have his own army one day; for now, he was Mr Auld and was content.

*

Sunday 10th September 1944 – Bletchley Park – The Mansion

Archie briefed Gubbins and Jimmy at 0800, early Sunday morning; none had managed much sleep.

"Well, congratulations on not killing anyone," Gubbins said.

"Apart from the bomb disposal man," Archie said.

"Yes, Captain Reynolds, wife and two, I'm afraid, he knew the risks and took them."

"If you can get me his details, we'll do something for his family, sir."

Gubbins nodded.

"Jimmy, you sort out the access to MI records discreetly. You have a contact I know," Gubbins said, "and you, Archie, do you wait and see what flushes out?"

"I don't think they'll come heavy handed like the cottage, but I can't take the risk. They've sent us two messages now; they might take a step back or send a message to Bletchley or the Manor."

"I've already doubled the guard, good men; I've handpicked them," Gubbins said, "and Lovat will send some too."

"There's something still nagging at me. At Abbotsinch, when we dropped Bohr off with the Alloys people. There was a round-faced man with curly hair and a big nose, more like a snout. I don't know who he was, MI6, we thought at the time. In Moscow in 42, there was a man like that, hovering in the background, never spoke, stood next to Beria. Couldn't be the same man, the one here was a good ten years older, looked like, I can't describe it properly, looked like a circus clown without the makeup."

"He had the nose and lips without the colour."

"That's him; you know him?"

"No, only saw him once at a meeting, Whitehall; he looked like a bag man in the background, left at the same time as me. The press were there, so Winston stopped for the obligatory photo, he scooted off pronto. Could be MI6; looked untrustworthy enough anyway, worse than Special Branch, you know."

"I can't imagine that."

"You will in time, old boy, don't worry. So, hear this, the war's won; it's only a matter of time; you're half gone already, they don't need you anymore. In twelve months, they won't need me either; let's see if we can't dispense some justice for Ruslan while we can; he was one of mine."

"Which paper?" asked Jimmy.

"Oh right, the Times, I think," Gubbins said.

"I'll check that too."

*

Monday 11th September 1944 – Bletchley Park

Archie waited for Billy's inquiries to bear fruit and for Jimmy to secure access to MI records; neither would use official channels, so it would take time.

He and Rebecca took George Flowers and Aria into the private room and spoke to them.

They spoke first.

"We're engaged, and you're to be best man," Aria told

him, as she'd told George.

"Please, Boss, it worked for Asgeir and Briony," George said.

"Okay, I'll do it; there's one condition."

"Anything," Aria said, and George nodded.

"I'll tell you later."

"Okay," Aria said. He could see she'd recognised the trap he'd set for her. A predator could see a trap coming.

"Aria, tell me everything about how you came to England."

"I will; I apologise, George; there are some pieces I haven't told you yet. There are things I remember well for myself, but there are also things my father told me. After my mother had died, he told me more about how bad things were. He told me there were things that should never be forgotten and should be passed from generation to generation. We should never forget what the communists took from us nor what the English gave us when they took us in."

Aria spent nearly three hours telling them the whole story. Archie only spoke to ask for specific names and descriptions of people, which he wrote down. The story beggared belief, the horror understated in places by Aria as simple facts; she'd been eight years old.

George held her hand; he, too, had fled a country he thought was bad, but his story was less than hers.

Archie nearly cried as he listened, and Rebecca held his hand now and then under the table.

Her account of how they'd bribed their way past the local communist party officials to secure their escape struck Archie the most. One such man was called Peezditovich, Mikael, who had bought Ruslan's horses for an unfair price, then signed a bill of sale and travel authorisation for them. In life, children remember best the moments that made them feel secure or insecure; Aria had a remarkable mind for a young girl.

She described him to Archie, round faced and fat, then the next question pushed itself into his mind, and he asked if he had children.

"Yes, he had two sons. One son, Grigory, was always with him. The other, Lazar, his firstborn, died young. Grigory looked very like his father. I never saw the older brother."

"Are you sure he was fat?"

"Yes, they both were. That's why I remember them so well; everyone else was skinny."

"Think back. Is there anything else you can recall, knowing what you know now, not just what you knew then?"

"Yes, you're right, they weren't fat; they just weren't as skinny as everyone else. They must have eaten better than others. They lived in a large house, they called it party headquarters, but only they lived in it. They bought and sold many things. They bought people's belongings for less than they were worth, then sold them food for what little money they gave them. They weren't really communists; they were rich people pretending to be communists. People called them the 'Ruriks'."

"The Ruriks ruled before the Romanovs," Rebecca said. "They were still wealthy during the Romanov's time but not as powerful. Many left Russia, and some came to England."

Archie could see Aria's adult mind revising her childhood thoughts.

"There's more, isn't there?" He asked.

"Yes, there is; I'm sorry, George, I know it now. When my father was meeting them, Grigory looked at me and said he would take me as well as the horses, then offered him more money. I thought he meant he would take me as his daughter to the big house, and that didn't seem so bad at the time. My father spat at his feet, and today, I know now what Grigory really wanted."

George put his arm around her and squeezed her hand even tighter. Archie saw himself and Una.

"That's enough for today."

"No, I can carry on."

"No, honestly, that's enough, George; you and Aria, take tomorrow off, be together, and that's an order."

When they'd gone, Rebecca hugged him and kissed him repeatedly on the top of his head.

"I really need to fucking kill someone," he said.

*

Wednesday 13th September 1944

Two days later, Jimmy sent a courier to Archie with a photograph, time, date and location, the clown's face enlarged, without too much loss of definition.

It was the man he'd seen at Abbotsinch, the resemblance to the man he'd seen in Moscow remained. They could be brothers, though both were heavyset now."

"They certainly hadn't suffered in a famine," Rebecca said, "that's it, isn't it!"

He sent for Aria, who was working in the main body of Building Thirteen. She stepped into the private room apprehensively.

"Have a look at this photograph," Archie asked.

"That's him, that's Mikael with his long nose and big rubbery lips; we used to call him the clown and run away. He was like Baba Yaga to us; you call it something else, the Bogeyman."

"This picture is about one year old. I think it's the older brother Lazar."

"It could be… where is he now?"

"I'm not sure, but I think he killed your father. I'm going to find him, then kill him and anyone with him."

"Good, I knew you killed people; I'll help?"

"No, you can't," he said.

"Yes, you can," Rebecca said, "but only when I say so."

"And there's no point arguing," Aria smiled at him.

*

Thursday 14th September 1944 – London

Owen Benedict Tudor was angry, frustrated at his own hubris. He'd made a mistake settling his younger brother's old score. A brother was a brother, though. He was the only true family he had left, and he still needed him.

He wished he'd arranged a subtle accident for Ruslan. He'd wanted to test his new pet, and it pleased him to show Gubbins and Travers they weren't safe. They faced a greater foe than those simpleton amateurs in Special Branch and the Establishment. Churchill would know too. Who did he think he was? One more half noble, half son in charge of a fading empire and still in thrall to the false kings and queens from Northern Europe he tugged his forelock to.

Tudor was truly noble; he'd been the ruler of a real empire, he'd ruled half the civilised world while the British savages were still wearing blue war paint. His father Mikael had told him the family history; their line went back to Roman times. He knew it; he'd seen it in his childhood dreams and more clearly with each passing day.

He'd known Travers was Austin. He'd left those worthless peasants in place as his 'family' in case Austin returned home, and they might have proved useful. Then that Rochford bitch had seen through them; they knew it, he knew it; they had to die.

Travers still didn't know who he was, even though he'd given him enough clues when he was Austin. He was a big disappointment with his frailties, his petty causes, and his friendships, but he had to make sure Travers knew who he truly was to suffer the full humiliation of his defeat.

Von Rundstedt, also from a noble line with links to Russia and England, was just as vulnerable now; his greed and lust weakened him as before. However, he still couldn't risk the two of them joining forces against him. He'd proved difficult to kill; the Gauls were still a weak nation; they had wine and not much else. Tudor had used the best of them on the German, and they'd failed. The foolish, half noble whore, Judith Cunningham, he'd personally trained and sent, managed to fail and escape but only after alerting Crassus to his existence. Von Rundstedt surely knew now who he and Travers really were. He'd had to kill Judith for that knowledge and failure, which was a regret. He'd spent time breaking her to his will, she was very strong, and that made the breaking more satisfying. Circumstances and lack of time had now forced him to use one already broken by others; she was beautiful and young, as he liked, and he owned her. Her previous owners had broken her so long ago she knew nothing else.

He did like those fleeting moments when the eyes of a victim knew what they'd lost. Nevertheless, he'd settle for the absolute submission she gave him.

He was Gnaeus Pompeius Magnus, Pompey the Great; he knew it, he would rule again, and that fact would break Gaius Julius Caesar.

*

Thursday 14th September 1944 – Moscow

Grigory Peezditovich had worked without mercy to secure his position in Stalin's secret police, the NKVD. He was one of Lavrentiy Beria's key men. Beria was the head of the NKVD and second only to Stalin in influence.

He knew he'd displeased his brother for allowing Leshchyov to see him in Moscow. He couldn't raise any alarm at the time, it would raise too many questions among his peers, and he couldn't kill one of Churchill's men. Stalin needed Churchill and the Americans against the Germans. Old Ruslan was dead now; that was all that mattered to him. He knew the man would have kept the bill of sale and authorisation for travel his father had signed. Nor could he forgive the peasant for spitting at his feet.

That could be dangerous for his position after the war ended; corruption itself attracted no blame, being caught was frowned upon. His comrades and rivals might not kill him for it, but he'd be less powerful than he planned and needed to be.

He wished his father had chosen him to send to England instead of his brother; Lazar had a luxurious life there while he had to graft for everything in Mother Russia. He sometimes thought his brother was mad, talking of having lived before, but they still needed each other, as their father had told them endlessly before he died.

Their father raised them to be what they were, bullies, entitled to anything they could get, wherever they found it.

Lazar had his adopted family, wealth, and education in England.

His family was old and noble; they still had connections across the world, blood ties, and some still had the easy life. Not Grigory; he'd worked and sweated for everything he'd gained. He wanted more, and he deserved it. He loved his brother, though; who else was there for him?

*

Saturday 16th September 1944 – The Manor

Archie sat and watched George Flowers teaching Aria how to shoot; Archie had loaned her the rifle Billy had obtained and converted for Una's smaller frame.

Recounting her journey to Archie brought back many memories to Aria. She was eight when they left Russia and nine when they arrived in England. She'd left two brothers behind, they were to work the land and join their father later, but no news ever reached them, letters remained unanswered. She felt sure they were dead.

A strange feature of her childhood memories was the small insignificant things she could still see. Like catching a caterpillar in a jar, putting holes in the lid, letting it breathe, and next day finding it gone and replaced by an earwig. She could remember the field, the sunshine that day, the friends with her, everything.

She could remember that earwig, but she couldn't remember her brothers' faces.

She needed a family of her own; she'd been alone too long. She had plenty of offers from young men, boys, and office clerks. She knew she was beautiful; boys and men had told her that often enough. She waited patiently for a real man.

She'd seen George in the canteen and near Building Thirteen; he was handsome and strong, definitely not a clerk.

She pointed him out to a colleague who knew his name

and reputation.

"They kill people in Building Thirteen, you know; he's a real ladies' man as well and a terrible flirt."

"Not anymore, he isn't," Aria had said with conviction.

*

Sunday 17th September 1944 – The Manor

George Flowers was content to be a private, a member of a team with his brother. Special duties attracted extra pay, and Archie gave generous bonuses to his team. He and Henry sent money back to their father, and he'd used it to set up another market stall, doubling the family income. When the war ended, he and George would set up a third stall further afield; that was the height of his ambition.

Until he met Aria.

That small plan was no longer enough. She was intelligent and beautiful, she had a way of standing and walking, of holding herself, and she had class that belied her eighteen years. She told him he was better than that, a shop at least, a big one or maybe several shops. She told him: he believed her and he'd do it.

Their shared past as refugees welcomed into England bound them.

Aria was a virgin, as were most eighteen-year-old girls in 1944; George asked her to marry him within a week of meeting her.

"I don't know why you waited so long," she said.

They had kissed, then a little more, and George said he would wait until he married her before they slept together.

"Don't be silly, girls have told me how good you are, and you must start teaching me now," she told him, so he did.

*

Monday 18th September 1944 - The Manor

Asgeir spoke to Archie about Operation Market Garden, a massive ground and airborne advance into the Netherlands, which had started the previous day. He was annoyed at the team's lack of involvement in what was obviously a large scale if top secret project.

"I asked about it yesterday, and they told me I didn't need to know; I told them I didn't need to fucking care. They won't even tell me what the overall plan is. The stupid bastards didn't even tell Conner about it; he's actually angry! I've never seen him like that.

'They let him do all that, make all those choices, which Ultra intelligence to use and which not to use. Every fucking day. How many needed to die so you can save others. What to lose, so we win in the end. Nothing in writing, no credit at all when he gets it right, and that's all the time. Then when something goes wrong, when it's a wide collective blame, suddenly, it's all down to him, all his fault.'

"He won't talk about it, says he can't. It must be really fucking bad. They must have had no intel requirement. I can tell you they've rushed it, and the wrong man's in charge. I've got plans for the next ten days anyway, don't worry. It might be a convenient distraction, whatever happens, success or failure.

*

Wednesday 20th September 1944 – London

Two days later, Jimmy found a name for the Major who'd recruited Bryson. He was a Captain; they weren't sure he was even that. He'd fabricated his service record on his application; he was posh and came from a noble family, so no one checked, and they rushed through his assignment. He claimed to have known everybody and done everything, so they took him on.

When his superiors discovered that deception, he disappeared, and they hushed up the scandal. Military Intelligence didn't like to look stupid.

They had a name, Charles De Montford; he'd never existed. At least they had a good photograph, a verified height and the colour of his eyes; brown.

"Fucking brilliant," Archie said, "we're looking for two needles now, and we're not even sure where the haystack is."

"He was always talking about nightclubs in Soho, trawling for girls."

"Or boys. He also sounds like the kind who leaves without paying his bills."

"Let's give it a go tonight," Jimmy said.

"No," said Billy, "the lads on those doors won't talk to no-one remotely official; people who don't pay get a good seeing to if they're lucky, a nice float down the river sometimes. These boys are hard as nails; I'll get the Frazers to ask; these places all pay them each week, a sort of fire insurance policy."

*

Sunday 24th September 1944 – Bletchley Park

The Frazers came back to Billy with several different names; most places had barred him. A mixture of money owed and paying unwelcome attention to the male clientele. One club had a very old address of his where they'd taken him to see what property they might repossess to settle his account; not enough, so they'd given him half a hiding. Another had heard he was active in Kensington with a new name and plenty of money, always cash.

The address for him was in Holloway, empty now and bomb damaged. How that place produced the likes of the Dempseys and the Animal was beyond Archie.

They did find a club in Kensington, 'The Greek,' gentlemen only, very exclusive for those of an elegant persuasion, not a brothel, only a meeting place. The manager there did recognise the photograph and was keen to avoid confrontation, so he agreed that his silence and cooperation were proper.

"We need to follow him home from the club. He sounds like he's going to be surveillance aware, so that might not work; then we've cocked up our only lead," said Jimmy tentatively.

"We have to meet him in the club and then let him take someone back to his address," said Rebecca

"Fucking great idea," said Archie.

"We could ask Conner?" she said.

"No, never," he kicked her under the table.

"Oh, sorry."

Jimmy blushed.

"Not a word Jimmy."

"None," Jimmy replied.

"I'll do it," Archie said after some thought. "I seem to have an attractive arse."

Chapter Twelve

Monday 25th September 1944 - Kensington

Archie Travers had never felt more uncomfortable in his life, ever.

He'd told himself he felt no fear of or hate for homosexuals, and that was true. Thirty of them surrounding him was an entirely different experience. He attracted numerous glances and tried not to return them while still searching the room for the face he wanted. He sat at the bar on a stool drinking a glass of red wine that wasn't quite Gall in *The Greek*, a gentlemen's club.

Three men separately offered to buy him a drink, but he politely refused. Two men approached him, saying they'd both suck his cock at the same time. When he declined, one of them offered to lick his arsehole while the other sucked him off. He'd only been there fifteen minutes!

"You seem to be lost, young man?" said a voice from behind him.

"Pardon?" Archie said, turning around and seeing an older gentleman aged about forty. Although not wearing a uniform, he was unmistakably an army man and very well spoken.

"You obviously don't belong here at all. Now, why would a strong, handsome young man like yourself come here if not for the usual purpose? You're not a policeman; you look far too intelligent. You're not one of those queer bashers, are you? You do have violence in you, but you don't wish to hit me; I can see that."

"I'm waiting for a friend, if you don't mind."

"Who is your friend? I might know him."

"I doubt it."

"Does he have a name, though?"

"Several; he's not exactly reliable. Hence, my having to wait."

"I do know a man with several names; most people here use two names; I use two, of course. However, several does narrow down the field. A man like that would be unlikely to always pay his bills."

"That does sound like him."

"Pretends to be what he is not, apart from the obvious?"

"I think that's a major problem for him."

"Ah yes, you can see what I saw then, that's good; I do know where you may find him, but you must tell me why you really want him. My name is Bertie; at least it is here, and you are?"

"Teddy."

"As in the bear, yes, I like that. Yes, I'm afraid I do know the cad you speak of. We had a brief meeting, his place, not mine; my wife just wouldn't understand, you know. He was very attractive, and such is my weakness; he also helped himself to a few notes from my wallet while I was in his toilet. Strange that; he lived in a very elegant place and clearly had money but couldn't resist temptation. Still, who am I to talk?"

"Can you tell me where he is and what names he uses?"

"I'm not sure you want to know. I made some inquiries among my acquaintances with a view to a small measure of retribution for the theft and found he has some powerful friends. More precisely, one extremely powerful friend who exerts power over many. My private hobby is my own business, and I am not unique. Privacy has to be purchased on occasion when one has been indiscreet. The price may sometimes be money; other times, it may be information, silence or even alliance. Now, it may be that I don't possess what you seek."

"You do; you have the name and the address."

"Do I possess the courage to give it to you, Archie Travers?"

"I could beat it out of you," Archie said, ignoring the fact that Bertie knew who he was.

"You have that within you, and worse, I'm told, not for me, I hope."

"I could use someone with fewer scruples."

"Oh, you could, but you won't."

"I could expose you too."

"You won't."

"Why not?"

Bertie took a deep breath and held it, letting it out.

"Because the war is nearly over, and after some careful thought and consideration of how little soul I still have, I am going to help you. We'll take the booth in that corner and talk."

*

"The man you really seek is Owen Benedict Tudor," Bertie continued after they sat down. "Viscount De Montford of Surrey, hence the misuse of that name by Charles Parrish, your handsome and elegant prey. Parrish is no danger to you, a frontman, a charmer, talks a good game, looks classy, entitled, wholly without substance.

"Tudor has the title, none of the charm, only the ruthlessness. Tudor is the master; nominally, he works for MI6, but he works for himself, that's not unusual in the chamber of charlatans around us. Superficially, he has no ambition, although the title of Dictator in Perpetuity would suit him well.

"There are others who work for him, some without knowing, others are directly under his control, and some are in his thrall; those are the dangerous ones.

"Some have titles; some of them are half German anyway and foolishly have loose tongues; you would call them spies, they themselves would not.

"Some are subject to coercion, blackmail or have other expensive tastes and needs.

"Some have naïve left wing views, children who never grew up, idealists.

"Some are what you would call the Establishment, a vain Illuminati, an orgy of self-interest, convinced of their entitlement to power and status.

"Some have the urge to force themselves on children, some on adults. Your minor crusade against that brought you to notice. I'm afraid you only secured a small victory against a few petty henchmen. Forgive me; I don't seek to belittle what you did, it was worthy, but you cannot conquer the cancer of idolatry and the corruption of power without first conquering the whole world.

"Myself, I have a minor title which I won't state here. I married because I believed it might cure me of my ills. It didn't, and my weakness snared me into silence when I should speak, and the guilt for the crimes you know of is partly mine. There, it's done, I have confessed. Bless me, Father, for I have sinned," Bertie concluded.

"Why are you telling me this, all of this, now, here, why? I'm no priest," said Archie.

"Oh goodness, that's a big question, young man; now that I look you in the eye, I see the potential to best Mr Tudor, perhaps even to protect me from my due. You're not what I was led to believe by others; you are more than that.

"It felt good to say it, and I watched you as I spoke, saw the anger and know you've killed for lesser reasons. So I know now that had I not told you willingly, you would indeed have coerced it out of me, whatever it took. You would not have enjoyed it, as some would, but you would have done it if necessary. I'm rather fond of my good looks; I'd like to keep them... and my cock too."

"I'd like you to give me all the names now, please, don't worry, I'll remember them; you won't have to write them down and well... "

"People in my position often suffer unexpected and fatal accidents, I know. I shall be careful; that's normal for me."

Bertie hadn't been ready to give Archie his full name and antecedence yet. He knew he would find out when he needed to.

He hadn't told him about his niece, his sister's daughter, Judith Cunningham, who'd disappeared recently. He knew she'd gone to France as an agent and spent nearly a month there; that wasn't the issue.

He was aware she'd returned safely; she'd phoned him seeking advice. After that, she'd disappeared; she worked for Tudor, she was in his thrall; that was the issue.

*

Monday 25th September 1944 Holloway

Gubbins agreed to the plan, and Archie took selected Chosen Men straight to Parrish's current home that same night, bursting through the door, shattered by a small shaped charge. Give no chance to prepare, no chance to reflect, no chance to think, attack.

He was in bed, drunk, with a naked man and a girl. They subdued all three easily and took them away. Archie unleashed his fury on the rooms of his flat, lifting carpets and floorboards, overturned beds and mattresses, ripping them apart.

The mayhem disguised a thorough search of every inch of the flat, divided into grids in advance, for the whole team to search without exception; they missed nothing.

Demon Ford, as Billy christened him, gave him some ill-advised abuse on their prospects of success against his master. Billy sliced one of his ears off and left it, bloody, on the ruined bed.

"Let's see how your mates like that message! You think you work for an evil cunt?" said Billy grasping his throat and thrusting his knife blade none too gently up his nostril.

"I can outcunt anything your cunt can do," he spat in his face and head-butted him, smashing his beautiful nose into several pieces.

They drove to a fresh site in Hounslow, never used before and unknown outside the team.

"Is outcunt even a word Billy?" Archie asked.

"I don't believe it's in the Oxford English Dictionary in the Manor's library at present; it should be. It's like cuntery."

"Country?"

"No cunt err ree, the act of being a cunt."

"Cuntishness being too clumsy an expression."

"Absolutely. There's also a subtle and important difference, for example, between a big cunt and a cunt and a half. A big cunt may just be a normal cunt who's unusually tall or overweight, whereas your cunt and a half will be fifty per cent more of a cunt than your normal cunt."

"And one particular cunt will be more inclined towards polite conversation."

"He will do, with my bayonet up his arsehole, fucking hell I enjoyed that, Archie, excuse my language, Ma'am," he said to Rebecca.

Rebecca was almost in tears with laughter at that point and could barely talk.

"Rebecca says you can finish him off later if she can have the Animal," said Archie.

"Oh no, there's a queue to kill that cunt, and I'm at the front; I remember when… well, I remember what that cunt did and would have done."

They all thought of Una's first encounter with the Animal and an orderly queue formed in their minds.

*

Gnaeus Pompeius Magnus, Pompey the Great, Owen Benedict Tudor was twenty years old when he'd first discovered a rival presence, Gaius of the Julii, in the 20th Century with him and nearby.

He was shocked; he'd thought he was the only one; fate chose him because he was the fittest. He knew he was the firstborn and took heart from that. His vanity was boundless; the Parcae: Nona, Decima, and Morta, were giving him Gaius as a prize.

He was in Nice that summer, in the family villa, enjoying the warmth and comfort that came from vast wealth. Gaius had been easy to find, signposted for him even. The Fates had brought Tudor to England and then to France in order to deliver his mortal enemy, Gaius, to him.

His new family had taken him to a theatre, and there on the stage, he'd seen his rival's father and mother perform. The mother's lineage and features were unmistakable, but only to him. Only a man with his detailed knowledge of history could see it and feel it.

To find where they lived and where their child slept

was a simple task.

He'd easily bluffed his way into their hotel room. The maid acting as babysitter didn't suspect anything, even when he'd raped her; she was already dead, her skull smashed from behind with a small virga. He'd then lain in wait in their dark hotel room, subdued and silenced the father and mother by holding a knife to the baby's throat. He made the mother tie the father's hands, then tied up the mother himself. On their knees, bound and gagged, he'd slain them in a fitting manner, Roman style.

Neither parent said a word, knowing a single word, a shout, a cry for help might save one of them, but would certainly kill their son. Gaius would never know that. Pompey would deny him any comfort that knowledge might bring him.

He considered fucking the mother too; she was quite beautiful even in death, then the sound of movement in the hotel corridor alarmed him, and he left by the fire escape with the child and a few possessions. Pompey was never a brave man.

He had no interest in the provenance of the child, only the child itself. He hadn't killed human beings before in this life; it was as easy as he expected.

He controlled Gaius now, and he could destroy him as he saw fit. He could kill him easily. He also had the chance for vengeance. Gaius, the child, must know who he really was to know the full suffering of his defeat and the depth of his fall.

Pompey's new family hadn't questioned his actions; they were ruthless and powerful too. They'd humoured him in this respect, which offended him. He'd killed them for the latter when the time was right; he'd still needed them in Nice.

They were distant relatives of his own dynasty; those blood ties and family resemblances had held over centuries after their rightful place had been usurped by lesser beings. A series of unfortunate accidents and illnesses had left him as the sole heir to their wealth, power and title. They hadn't been as ruthless as he.

The Rurik's would return and rule all of Europe, Russia included, and then eventually, the world. He knew it; that was his destiny.

That night, after his first murders, he dreamed of searching, flying and searching for something, someone, and could find nothing. Was Crassus there too?

*

Tuesday 26th September 1944 – Hounslow

The two who'd shared Demon Fords bed knew nothing about him, apart from where they'd met him, a public house that might merit scrutiny later. Detaining them securely for weeks or months would do more good than harm, so that happened. What mattered was keeping Owen Tudor on the defensive, reacting, not acting.

Five more minutes of Billy staring at him silently, fingering a blade, was sufficient to extract the complete truth from John Joseph Malahide, originally from Blackpool. He gave a detailed statement in writing in front of witnesses attesting to the crimes he'd committed, as directed by Tudor.

No court would ever hear that testimony. There could be no trial for Tudor, no police involvement, no Jury or Judge, none who might owe him fealty. There would be justice; it would be summary and swift.

They'd keep Malahide alive and secure for a while, and that was his real name.

*

Wednesday 27th September 1944 – Holloway

Shocked by the speed of the reckless attack on him, Tudor went personally to Malahide's address to see the mess. He made certain his MI6 stooges protected him thoroughly. They were worthless fools to a man, but he didn't need men who were too capable or who thought too much about what they were doing.

He entered the property and looked at the bloody ear lying on the shredded sheets.

Fucking typical, my stupid pawns left a fucking teddy

bear as a warning, he leaves the bloody flesh of one of my key men. This isn't good, and it's downright evil for my men to see this weakness.

He looked around him to see if any aspect of the room remained intact. They'd been utterly thorough, even checking behind pictures on walls; he paused to straighten one above the fireplace.

"Shit!" a small explosion went off behind the framed picture, Tudor had shown fear, and his men had seen it. Only a firework, no more, but he'd shown fear.

He remembered Dyrrhachium: where Pompey had Caesar at his mercy and was too cautious, expecting a trap typical of Gaius. Pompey held back and lost his advantage. Was this runt of a boy waking up? Was he leading him into a trap?

Tudor had read Plutarch's work, Caesar had taunted him in his grave.

"Today, the victory had been the enemy's, had there been anyone among them to gain it."

He had to be reckless now; he would lose face if his men doubted him for one second. He had to take risks, or they'd see him as weak. He had to be bold.

*

Thursday 28th September 1944 – England

Archie's next step would be closer to home for Tudor.

A full squadron of Mosquito fighter-bombers overflew his family seat, De Montford Hall in Surrey, the next night on a training mission. They dropped no bombs, of course, but locals heard and saw a huge number of separate explosions; some new Nazi bomb was the rumour. Decrypted intercepts backed up that story. Archie had powerful friends too. Begley, for a start, he could make an explosion look like a bomb, several bombs, in fact. Alan and Conner could produce any intelligence they chose to.

*

Friday 29th September 1944 – London

The following morning, at his headquarters in London, Tudor was still only in the planning stages of his reckless blitzkrieg against Travers when he learned of the destruction of his family home. Burnt to the ground by new German incendiary bombs.

Intelligence sources were aware of the intended attack and chose to take no action for fear of compromising those sources. A ploy Tudor himself had employed occasionally.

He couldn't believe what he was hearing; his opponents were timid small people he could cow with their foolish standards and ethics.

This was open barbaric hatred, without quarter and relentless, they were two steps ahead of him now, and his men knew that.

He gathered his closest, most trusted men around him and went on the attack.

He reluctantly accepted the challenge offered and outright battle, the history, and the future; neither gave him any choice; it was the battle of Pharsalus again.

Caesar couldn't hope to field more than twenty men, Pompey had one hundred and armoured cars, Morris CS9s at his disposal, superior numbers, and resources, and he would choose the high ground for the battle. Their so-called Manor was a house with a few Tommy guns held by Plebeians. He'd destroy it that very day; it was a viper's nest of spies and thieves, no-one liked Travers, and the victor invariably wrote the history. Most would be pleased to be rid of that annoying upstart.

His convoy of men set off from his base in North London; they'd gone no further than one hundred yards when the first armoured car exploded. One armoured car with a neat hole in it and three dead men burned alive inside.

Begley loved the Panzerfaust, the German equivalent of a bazooka. Asgeir then drove them at high speed to the Manor; their car could outrun the trucks easily.

"Come on, we can see what we're up against; we must do this now and without mercy," Tudor shouted, exhorting his men. He re-joined Mr Auld in the rear of his staff car and told his driver to push on.

Mr Auld checked his weapon again. He was looking forward to this.

*

An hour and a half later, Asgeir and Begley reached the Manor.

"One armoured car down, there's only about a hundred men, trucks, a staff car and two more armoured cars left," Asgeir said to Archie.

Archie looked carefully at the fourteen men, including Billy and Rebecca, who stood in the Manor garden with him.

"No problem, I almost feel sorry for the bastards," he said.

Rebecca looked up at him, one hand in the crook of his elbow, the other holding her Thompson. He was the man people would die for, and he had death in his eyes as never before. This was who he was, whatever the name.

"I've got time for another surprise," Begley shouted as he ran across the garden and climbed the small fence.

"Positions, everybody," Archie yelled; everyone moved immediately; they knew exactly what they were doing and why. Why was important; a man would try harder when he knew what the fight was about.

*

Mr Auld, the Animal, sat impassively next to his master. He'd undertaken this journey before; he liked the odds even better this time. He still had doubt, Tudor was the best he'd seen close up, but Travers was good and lucky.

They drove hastily, reaching the Manor within three hours of setting off and took up positions north of it, ignoring the main driveway and front door.

The thin wire fence was good enough to keep curious children out. Tudor's men took apart a whole section of it in two minutes and entered the empty grassy practice field next to the Manor's garden.

Tudor's men, well equipped with heavy and light machine guns, took up infantry positions behind the remaining two armoured cars and set up mortars in two empty lorries.

Suddenly, two handheld incendiary devices flew over their heads into two of the lorries, setting them ablaze and blocking any retreat. Archie had made Begley practice his throwing for hours before he agreed to let him do it.

Begley moved back into the woods he'd crept from, returning to the cluster of Lewis Guns he'd left camouflaged there. Four Tarrians, painted by Rebecca, matched the trees perfectly.

Tudor remained unfazed and continued his march forward.

"Sir," said the officer to his left, "outside the fence."

There were twenty men in Lovat's commando dress fifty yards to their left, all with weapons ready. To their right, slightly closer, were twenty SOE personnel led by Jimmy McKay.

Ahead they could see more movement from the Manor, Archie's men.

"We still have them outnumbered, they're still fifth column, and we'll still take them," he shouted, and his men took one more step forward.

"There's something else, sir," said the officer, "this," and stabbed Tudor between his shoulder blades.

Another officer turned and stabbed him from the front, and another knife came into him from the left.

Tudor's men stopped, shocked and unsure. They hadn't fired a shot in anger and couldn't make sense of what was happening.

Their former leader dropped to his knees and knew what had happened; again.

Damn the Gods, it's the 29th of September; I know the real date on which I was born and on which they killed me centuries ago, but I forgot the Julian calendar. They use the Julian calendar, not the Republican calendar; this is the true anniversary of my assassination by my own treacherous men. That bastard Caesar even decides what fucking date it is. I am cheated, tricked again. I will come again. I will come again.

He thought of his brother and breathed his last as the blood flowed from his wounds.

Tudor's men didn't know what to do; they were a mixture of British, Free French, and Norwegian. Each of their officers, Captains Sylvester de Vivenemaine, a titled British Gentleman, Achille de Breve, a Frenchman and Magnus Sevensson, a Norwegian, had stabbed their General in turn.

The Animal sensed what was happening.

"Come on, they're just traitors too; we have to go for the house now, come on, come on," he screamed. He knew they couldn't win and needed some mayhem to have any chance of escape. Then, as he raised his pistol to shoot at the officers, a small crossbow dart penetrated his smart suit, and he fell, asleep before he hit the grass.

Billy had been tempted to kill him straight off but had no pity in him that day.

Confused and seeing their inevitable defeat all around them, all Tudor's men surrendered as soon as their officers told them to. There were some less than innocent souls among them; some had followed the wrong man's orders and sometimes his threats.

Sylvester 'Bertie' de Vivenemaine breathed the long sigh of an eased soul. He hadn't had to use his own men to fire on the others, and the two officers had followed his lead as he'd asked them to. This had been their chance too.

Bertie's phone call to Tudor was a risk, but Archie had gauged it perfectly. Telling Tudor he'd seen Travers in the Greek asking about the Major was enough to display his loyalty to his master. His false promise that he'd already primed his men to assist immediately ensured Tudor would use them at the short notice, which Archie had correctly guessed there would be.

Messrs Turing and Duncan had gathered detailed, Ultra Secret intelligence reports based on intercepted German Enigma transmissions over several months. They showed conclusively that Tudor was a Russian-born spy, a sleeper all his life and guilty of the most serious treason; no one would ever know they'd fabricated them that same afternoon.

A firing squad later executed four of Tudor's army men who had committed the gravest and most gratuitous murders. The rest were dispersed to various front line units. Most would not survive the war, the real war.

The civilians, Malahide and Bryson, died on a gibbet for treason in the Tower of London; only a noose and well deserved broken neck would ensure their continued silence.

One man, Mr Auld, who never existed anyway, disappeared without a trace again.

The other civilians were released with small compensation for the disruption to their lives, accompanied by the most serious warnings about the Official Secrets Act they were made to sign. Archie set a small sum aside for Bryson's family.

*

Friday 29th September 1944 Vichy

Dolf von Rundstedt felt emotion, a sense of loss; he'd gone into a room to find something, then when he got there, couldn't remember what. He left the room and came back in. That didn't work; he stopped worrying and went back to sit at his desk. He needed to check that report and sign it, but when he sat down and saw his signature on the papers, he realised he'd already done it.

Feelings like this would usually make him insecure, yet this made him feel safer. He left his office to check Annette was safe anyway.

*

Friday 29th September 1944 - The Cottage

Archie felt elation but dared not show it; he couldn't allow hubris to become his nemesis, as well as Tudor's. He'd won; killed none of his men and as few enemy men as possible. They were fools who followed the wrong lead; maybe he had done this before?

A plan other than complete violence had worked. He'd set people free and punished the guilty, he'd set a trap, and his prey had taken his bait; perhaps he *was* Caesar?

He and Rebecca went away when it was all done or for others to do. He found himself mortally, morally tired, trouble would find him soon, but for today it was over, and like God, he needed a day of rest.

That night he rested his head on Rebecca's breasts, and she held him rather than the other way around; he thought of Una and felt guilt for feeling rest and warmth without her. For a few short hours, there were no knives at his back and no-one to kill.

*

Saturday 30th September 1944 – Hertford

The next day, after a good lie in and a full breakfast, Archie went with Rebecca to Hertford. Only then did he recall that he hadn't starved himself nor committed any self-harm this time. He was growing, becoming stronger and softer at the same time; wisdom and experience tempered his youth. He was better today than he had been yesterday; that was a worthy purpose.

He still had names on his list, but he'd cut the head from a spy network that would know fear and know where it came from. Exactly who Tudor was, and had been, wasn't clear to him, and he didn't exactly care.

In Hertford, they went to the small building where they'd caged the Animal, well apart from the others. Billy was waiting for them.

"It's not good," said Billy.

"What's he done?"

"He's talked, and we ain't laid a finger on him."

"Alice?"

"Yes, he loved telling us that. She was Tudor's favourite toy. Delivered to him each weekend, but nobody knew where from, and they ain't gonna deliver her to a dead man, whose house we've blown to fuck."

"This is going to take some working out. How's Freddie?"

"He ain't too bad; the boy's done some more growing up."

"Who else is here now?"
"Aria with George, Freddie with Begley."
"Okay, we're all here; let's fucking kill the cunt."
"Who and how?" said Billy.
"I've got a good idea," Rebecca said.

Chapter Thirteen

Saturday 30th September 1944 - Hertford

Aria Lescott handed the army issue water bottle to the Animal. She'd securely tied him to the chair Billy had screwed with brackets to the metal floor of the disused, soundproof freezer. She'd roped his ankles, knees, elbows and hands to the chair. Billy had already stripped him naked and broken both his ankles crudely with a house brick; he knew how to stop a man from running.

No-one else was there.

The Animal held the bottle in his right hand, he was already thirsty, and she casually slit the rope holding his right wrist with Rebecca's razor sharp knife. He could use that bottle to drink if he wished; the bottle would only just reach his mouth; he had no chance of escape, but he could drink.

"I've poisoned the water," she told him, "only rat poison, so it'll be slow. You'll bleed to death from within. It's no less than you deserve for killing my father.

"You can choose to quench your thirst or die of it; neither will be a good death. I leave it to you."

He tried to spit at her, but his mouth and cracked lips were too dry. She left the room, sealing the heavy bolts behind her, letting him know there could be no escape or aid.

*

A week later, she returned and went into the freezer alone; the stench was strong; he'd shat and pissed himself. Strange how a thirsty man could piss himself, she thought. She knew he'd died of thirst, agonisingly, hallucinating and slowly. The water bottle lay at his feet, any spillage having evaporated. She kicked it gently, and more came out, so she knew he hadn't drunk any; it was only water, not poison. He'd killed himself; he had more life in his hands and chose death, he deserved it, and Aria smiled.

It was Rebecca's idea, and everyone had agreed to it.

Aria had insisted on doing the deed, and they'd all shared in the retribution.

Aria had a family again.

*

Archie should have felt better now Tudor was gone and the Animal dead, yet something was still missing. Elements of the plot eluded him, not only Alice but more than that, deeper mysteries. While he'd watched Bertie, through his binoculars, stabbing Tudor, there was a sense of déjà vu that lingered still. A sense of loss, then a distant sense of different menace, the brother Grigory probably. Yes, his brother, he'd know who'd done this, although any retaliation against Archie would be too difficult for him. That was worth thinking about; he might need to die. He wondered if Tudor had children, his bastards could threaten Archie or those bound to him.

As Rebecca snuggled comfortably closer to him in bed, his thoughts drifted towards his real family. Was there a link?

All reason left his mind as the darkness of betrayal and melancholy brought another night to him. It brought the night but neither real sleep nor rest. His whole life was a lie, his entire world. He'd never been who he thought he was. Nor had he been with who he thought he had.

His name hadn't been his, his purpose hadn't been his, his joy hadn't been his, nor had his pain. It was a sham; it meant nothing; he was nothing. Nearly twenty years, the vast majority of his short life, wasted, stolen, meaningless, half an existence gone, disappeared. The lowest, meanest of men had more, an animal even; ignorance was preferable to that knowledge.

No, he asserted within his mind. He had knowledge now; knowledge was power; today was his first day of life. He'd design and decide his own life, fuck everything else, fuck everyone else, fuck the world and the universe.

Except for Rebecca, just Rebecca, nothing else, one small step closer, that's all, but not yet. They'd be one person soon, one body; they were already one mind. The crippling absence of Una would cast a shadow over them forever, friend, sister, wife and lover, but they could sustain each other enough to survive. They would survive because they were the fittest, with no self-proclaimed worth, no entitlement. Nature and science defined them, nothing else. They would endure together, and he'd chosen others for the same destiny. This was life, this was meaning, this was the Cosmos. Who he was barely mattered; Caesar, Archie, Teddy, someone else, he was here, and he'd endure.

If only Una could share this, that was his purpose, to exist and bring Una back; science would do that, he knew it; he would make science do it. He'd do it and disregard the consequences. Convention meant nothing, standards meant nothing, ethics nothing, three people; that would be the whole cosmos, nothing else.

That was it, he realised, God or gods meant nothing, nature meant nothing, science meant nothing, three people meant something. He and two small females meant everything in this universe. If you didn't like that, find your own fucking universe, this one... is mine!

The warmth of Rebecca at his side brought sleep to him at last.

*

Monday 30th October 1944 – Bletchley Park

More than a month after Tudor's death, Gubbins asked Archie to meet him in the private room of Building Thirteen.

"Sorry we've not spoken sooner, Archie, the enforced search of Tudor's buildings took some time, and we stood on many toes. Winston backed me, Force Majeure and all that. Your source, 'Bertie', was good."

"And we can help him?"

"The top brass ordered me to hand over every scrap of information uncovered, which, of course, I did... slowly and not before cataloguing every scrap."

"Oh!"

"However, you know me, better at the action than the

paperwork," Gubbins smiled widely at Archie, who realised that was the first time he'd seen him smile properly.

"A couple of items were 'overlooked'. One is your friend 'Bertie's' file; Tudor was remarkably well organised."

"The other?" said Archie taking the files from Gubbins and opening one.

"A loose-tongued Lord of your acquaintance, a somewhat sanctimonious individual… "

Archie spluttered a spontaneous, coughing laugh looking at some photographs.

"Not averse to a measure of hypocrisy."

"Fucking Hell."

"He hopes they do."

"Is that a dog lead he's on? Oh, for fuck's sake," said Archie putting the photographs back in the folder, unwilling to see more and handed it back to Gubbins.

"No, it's yours to keep; after everything that bastard said about you behind your back, you deserve it. Do what you like with it, don't get caught, though, and if you do, I'll say you stole it and dare them to call me a liar."

*
Thursday 2nd November 1944 - The Manor

Archie and Bertie met at the Manor in early November.

"You'd never killed before Tudor?" Archie said.

"No, that's right, it was surprisingly easy."

"Don't worry, he was a good target, and you saved the lives of some good men on both sides."

"I also saved some complete bastards. There have been a few resignations lately, people changing jobs and some unaffected."

"And you'll be one of them, not the bastards, someone who made some mistakes and made up for them, believe me, I know." He handed him his file.

"I haven't even opened it; best not to; it's yours."

"Thank you."

"Just a thought, do you know anything about who might have supplied Tudor with his 'entertainment.'

"No, that was hush hush, so I don't have a name, but I do know of someone else who uses the same provider. He is utterly untouchable, though."

"We'll see about that."

*

Saturday 4th November 1944 – London

Bertie proved a most reliable source, Archie didn't tell him, but he'd given him the name of the same loose-tongued lord whose shame Archie held in a folder in a safe in Hevlyn Mansions. Personal contact with him was a big problem; he was either in a palace, country estate or military base.

However, it took only two days of full surveillance before they saw the Lord leave his exclusive private residence and enter a car that awaited him at the rear entrance. It was an expensive chauffeured Bentley, driven by a smartly dressed and ill-favoured man who looked like what Archie could only describe as a weasel in human form.

The weasel drove to a substantial mansion in Knightsbridge, the Lord entered the building, and the car left, returning after two hours to collect him.

*

Monday 13th November - Knightsbridge

It took seven days for Archie's best researchers to pin down who owned and rented the building. Who really owned the company that owned the company who paid the rent. These people knew how to stay hidden; they could afford the deception easily. What they couldn't afford was for the truth to come out.

Landed gentry, as usual, the Frazers with better manners. Robber Barons, who remained, thieves.

Archie's most careful, most discreet men spent the same seven days in clandestine activity, posing as cleaners, bin men, delivery men, and telephone installers.

They gathered sufficient evidence to raid the property and prosecute anyone they found there or involved. They didn't intend to do that; they only wanted to find Alice;

anything else was secondary. Archie still felt bound to the promise he'd made to Gubbins and would avoid bloodshed. If he possibly could.

*

Monday 4th of December 1944 – Knightsbridge

Finally, on Monday, 4th December 1944, they saw Alice arriving at the address by car, which dropped her off a few yards past the driveway. The driver went on his way, not checking if she went inside, but she did, clearly willingly.

The driver returned six hours later, to the minute, and she kissed his cheek before they drove off.

Her driver was surveillance aware and shrewdly doubled back a couple of times. Archie had radio communications, three cars and a motorbike following them. They kept up, tracking the car to an address in West London, a small but good looking detached house too.

Alice entered the house, linking arms with the driver and laughing. This wasn't going to plan, it was lucky Freddie wasn't there tonight, but he had to be when they went inside.

*

Tuesday 5th December 1944 – Bletchley Park

"Forget everything else; I want to know everything about that house and the people in it. I want it all in twenty-four hours," Archie said, and no-one questioned him.

*

Thursday 7th December 1944 – West London

The house was owned by Alice Yoeticius, she'd bought it the previous year, and Archie sat outside the next night. Alice and her driver were the sole occupants.

Her driver was an Albanian immigrant called Anatoly 'Tony' Yoeticius; he'd been in England for twenty-five of his thirty years. Tony had a British Passport and was a draft dodger who'd somehow been granted exemption from service on the basis of being employed as a steeplejack.

A truck full of Chosen Men sat nearby, and they planned

to smash their way into the front and back doors simultaneously. Archie planned to have three in the front door and three in the rear. They'd use sledgehammers, both doors, same time. Billy, Archie, and Freddie in the front, Begley, George and Henry in the back.

They burst through the flimsy wooden doors and rushed inside. In less than five seconds, Billy had Tony pinned to the living room floor. George and Henry held Alice down as she screamed, spat and bit at them... trying to help Tony.

"Begley, check the rest of the house, make sure there's nobody else around; hang on, I'll come with you just in case. Nobody does anything until I say so!" Archie shouted.

There was no-one and nothing of interest upstairs; they checked the kitchen and its cellar door, unbolted it, turned on the electric light and descended the stairs... into Hell itself.

Archie went first and vomited; there was a child's corpse in the corner, still clothed, the head was almost shrunken to the bone, wrapped in a transparent heavy-duty plastic body bag.

"That's David; he was bad," said a girl child's soft voice from his right.

"Fucking hell," said Begley, "what are we doin' here boss? Who are we rescuing? From who?"

"You don't eat if you're not good. David wouldn't be good, no matter how hard she hit him," the girl said, "can Daisy come out now?"

They heard a single shot from upstairs, and Archie leapt back up, twisting his ankle slightly, but he didn't slow down.

In the living room, Tony lay dead; a single bullet from Freddie's still smoking Webley had blown his brains from his head onto the floor. Alice was screaming at Freddie, Billy was telling him gently to calm down, and it was all George and Henry could do to keep her pinned to the floor.

"He shouldn't have said that, he shouldn't have said that," Freddie was saying to himself and Billy.

"Easy, son, easy," said Billy.

"You stupid bastard," Alice screamed, "you simple fucker, I'll fucking kill you. Nicky was right; he told me you was looking for me. He told me how fucking stupid you was. You've fucking ruined everything now; we was doin' fine, you little piece of rat shit."

They all turned to look towards Archie, then beyond him, seeing the two girls, aged about six and three, bedraggled, bruised, dirty and skinny, each holding one of Begley's hands.

Archie could hear more Chosen Men coming in the front and rear doors.

He looked at Freddie, who looked at the two girls; Freddie looked at Archie.

"Sorry, Boss," said Freddie and blew his sister's brains out.

Billy tried to stop him, Archie tried to stop him, George and Henry would have tried too, but Freddie was far too slick for them all. He put the still hot barrel of his pistol into his mouth and pulled the trigger.

After the third loud bang, there was a short silence, then Archie's team cleared up the mess as they'd become accustomed to doing. They disposed of the bodies, invented stories, and another small house would be damaged by fire. Billy and Mary would find somewhere for the children, Conner would help.

Later, Archie looked at the now empty room and the blood on the floor.

'That's it then, I've killed the lot, every last fucking man who came to France with me, everyone who called me comrade. Lieutenant Duncan, Conner was always going to survive, but it was my job, it became my job to keep them alive, and I killed the fucking lot of them. Then even those I came to know, Joe, Ben, Siggy, Spud, Spud most of all and too many others to think about.'

Old words came into his head.

'Listen, if you've got anything to say, say it now, cos when we leave that door, we never talk about it again.'

Archie tossed the lit match on the floor, left and closed the door behind him. He saw it more clearly now, with hindsight, even in Calais, even Teddy had needed boxes.

*

Archie had insisted on breaking the bad news to Marion Hill personally. He didn't tell her the whole truth; no one would ever do that. Killed in action during a secret operation was a good enough lie, one she wanted to hear. Nothing had happened between them yet, but it would have, and now it wouldn't. That was his fault.

*

Thursday 14th December 1944 – Zurich

It was a long time since Conner first mentioned it, but before Christmas in 1944, after the successful invasion of Vichy France, they were to finally meet his Guardian, Alex De Cyrene, in Zurich.

Archie had put his search for his real roots on hold until the end of the war in Europe. There was a rose bush for Freddie outside Building Thirteen and space for him in a freezer. He needed to do something.

Alex was never able to come to England or America to meet Archie sooner, which struck Archie as strange since the man had seemingly limitless resources and matching connections. The man was avoiding him, only meeting him on his home territory and on his own terms.

He declined to meet Rebecca, though, and that annoyed Archie, prejudicing him further against the Swiss Banker. The slightest disrespect for Rebecca was a capital offence in the court of Archie Travers's mind; he'd come to rely almost entirely on her presence.

She said she didn't mind, but it was a poor lie which she knew he would recognise. He brought her with them nonetheless for the journey and sightseeing in Switzerland. She came with him to Alex's Bank and planned to wait in the foyer outside his office.

"Monsieur De Cyrene will see you now," said the attractive, well-groomed secretary in perfect English.

"No, he won't because I'm not coming in without

Rebecca," said Archie. He hadn't mentioned this to Conner or Rebecca.

"I'll go in and tell him, shall I?" Conner said.

"Yes, please," said Archie

"It's alright," Rebecca said.

"No, it's not. The man has to learn his place, and it's not above you."

"Oh fuck, there's no point arguing, is there?" she smiled at him, enjoying the mischief.

"None at all."

Archie sat outside while Conner went in alone, waiting with her adamantly and embarrassingly for Rebecca. Rebecca contemplated her embarrassment and decided it was good, human, normal, and an emotion.

She watched Archie sitting impassively and knew he was deep in thought. She'd seen that distant look before.

He was creating and deleting boxes in his mind, feeling doubt pressing in on him. He wanted to meet Alex, the intriguing, mysterious and all-knowing Alex. Only on his own terms, though. He'd moved beyond the restrictive terms of other people.

Nevertheless, he had doubts; they pressed into his mind, and he considered them in turn before deciding not to yield to them.

Further doubts pressed into him, and he easily did the same again.

Then his doubts increased in number and speed, and he saw the same doubts repeatedly. He stopped considering them and deleted them as soon as they appeared, but they still flowed towards him, so he deleted them and moved towards them, deleting them as he went.

Somehow, he sensed he was no longer defensive. He was attacking the doubts, not fending them off. Exhilarated by his success, he hunted the doubts and their source, suddenly realising he was outside of his own mind. Somewhere else, no… someone else's mind, the source of his doubts.

There was a struggle; the other mind was strong,

unaccustomed to challenge and perhaps too strong for Archie. He didn't think he could win, but he still refused to yield, the mind could only force him to yield if his willpower ceased to exist, and it never would. It became a test of patience and time. Archie placed his willpower at the head of the confrontation and left it there. The rest of his being took a step backwards, relaxed and waited, observing the battle from a safe distance, unperturbed by the maelstrom of sparks and shooting stars he could see.

And then he dreamt again; Gaius Julius Caesar spoke to him.

"Do you require my aid? It is yours to ask for and use as you see fit."

Rebecca spoke to him.

"Don't even ask; it's yours, you know that."

Una spoke, but no words came, yet he felt her presence. That same instant, he took the help offered and pushed headlong into the mind where Una was; trapped, hidden, alone and needing him.

The mind collapsed, yielded, the lights stuttered, went out and ceased to exist.

"Monsieur De Cyrene will see you now," a voice said.

"What did you do?" Rebecca said, "I helped, I think. When you asked."

"I had a dream, and you were in it."

"I know. I was there, remember, don't even ask; it's yours."

The meeting was brief; Alex agreed to everything Archie asked, not coerced, only following new instructions. Alex wasn't the mind.

At the end of the meeting, Alex said, "Please send me further instructions as you see fit; we don't have to meet again. There's nothing else I can teach you."

They left.

"What the hell did you do to him?" said Conner

"Nothing?" Archie said.

"I have known that man all my life. He's never been less than convinced of his own rectitude and superiority. He's been pleasant and sincere, of course, but always in control, in command."

"He looked like that to me."

"No, he's never been more deferential in his life; he was in awe of you and feared Rebecca almost as much."

"I don't know what I did, there was a fight, and I won, with help. Would you mind if I spoke to Alan about it alone, please?"

"Anything. So what did you make of Alex, then?"

"Rebecca?" said Archie.

"He's not Swiss or Italian," she said. "He's a mixture of Greek, Roman and something else I can't pin down."

"Could be Gaul," Archie said.

"France?" said Conner.

"No, Gaul," Rebecca said.

*

Tuesday 19th December 1944 – Bletchley Park

Archie Travers sat with Alan Turing on a bench outside the Mansion at Bletchley Park. They hadn't spoken for months; Archie had spent a lot of time thinking about Archie. That wasn't the best perspective from which to see things clearly, so he sought out Alan. The war nearly over, Alan seemed more relaxed than usual though still uncertain, distracted, about his own future, Archie suspected. When you'd given most of your adult life exclusively to one cause, what did you do when that stopped?

"Sorry about Market Garden," Archie said, "I didn't hear the full story until recently."

"Well, if the stupid bastards had told us what they were doing, then we could have passed the intelligence on more urgently and to the right people. They had all the intelligence and didn't act on it properly."

"And they wouldn't have landed on top of a Panzer Division. The bastards would have carried on anyway, a fool can't admit he was wrong, and another fool can't tell him."

"They won't even discuss the problems with us now;

they're too busy!"

"Too busy looking for a scapegoat."

"Secrecy isn't all it's cracked up to be," Alan said.

"There will come a time when there is no place for secrets."

"We may be dead by then."

"Abso fucking lutely."

"What."

"Sorry, it's one of Patton's."

"I may use it; Eu fucking reka has a good ring to it."

"I like it; you can have it free, well not entirely free; I need your advice on boxes in minds, in a thinking machine and a brain."

"Oh, this is good; you have something there, definitely."

They talked for an hour, and at the end of it, Archie had a clue.

"It's a straightforward concept," Alan said, "sounds and light are detected through the ears and eyes, the brain turns them into words and pictures; who's to say there might not be more."

"Like a mind that was half brain and half machine."

"Possibly. Think of radio waves flying through the air, invisible and meaningless; they arrive in a very basic machine, a radio, which sorts the information and speaks the words. A human brain may be a billion times more powerful than a radio; can we not do what the simple radio does? Could we learn to do it as you said?"

"Or could we connect a radio to a brain and cut out evolution?"

"That's why I love you, Archie."

"Sorry?"

"Platonically, of course, old boy. When we talk about thinking machines, I start from the mathematics of it; you start from the utility and the humanity. We meet in the middle, and it works; it inspires me. Tommy could build it for us with the right tools."

"Tommy, who?"

"Oh, sorry, I can't tell you who he is."

"Or that he works in the noisy hut with all the clanking, and they wear brown coats."

"Certainly not."

"And it'll take a hundred years and be the size of a small country."

Alan laughed.

"One final thought, does the name D'Annunzio mean anything to you at all?"

"He wrote a novel in 1889 called Il Piacere, the Pleasure, about a man who loves two women at the same time, if that's why you ask? I haven't read it, I'm afraid."

"Sorry, who?"

"Oh, that wasn't why you asked, was it? Perhaps it should have been. You do that sometimes you know, you ask the wrong question but get the right answer. It could be sheer luck, could be genius or plain old destiny. Gabriele D'Annunzio died in 1938, aged 74, Italian poet, journalist, playwright, soldier and politician associated with the Decadent movement. Bizarrely, some of his ideas are said to have influenced Mussolini."

"Sounds like a complete wanker."

"Well, being a wanker and a genius are not mutually exclusive. The practical application of intelligence, as you call it, is by no means as common as genius. I prefer your genius."

"I am not a genius."

"True genius seeks to defend us from itself."

"Who said that, then?"

"Well, I just did, obviously. It was written by Ralph Waldo Emerson. There's more, 'true genius will not impoverish, but will liberate, and add new senses,' think about that for a moment."

"So I may have new senses then?"

"Or better-developed senses, senses that transmit as well as receive; Conner knew you were alive even when he'd seen you die; Rebecca knows where you are without looking."

"That's just being a female."

"Does she scare you?"

"Yes."

"Do all females scare you?"

"No."

"It's not just her being a female then."

"Okay, so was D'Annunzio a wanker or not."

"Oh, God, yes! The pinnacle of his military career was to fly 700 miles to drop leaflets on Vienna. That would have worked jolly well against the Third Reich and the tide of Nazism."

"Alan, when the war ends, stay close, please."

"My pleasure. No, wait, you need to know this too; Il Piacere can also be translated as 'The Child of Pleasure,' I'm sorry about that; Conner and I have no secrets now."

*

That night, Rebecca and Archie went to bed early, put the light off, hugged and talked in the darkness.

"It could be my imagination or some part of my mind that always remembers what I've read," Archie said, "I've dreamt before, and it seemed real at the time. This was different, there was a voice in my head, and it was Caesar speaking. People dream, and people hear voices in their heads."

"Yes, and they put them away because they're fucking bonkers; you're not bonkers."

"Yes, yes, I know, and if the voice tells you to do something bad, you're bonkers. If you hear a God, and he tells you to be good, they make you the fucking Pope and put you in charge of millions."

"And I heard you asking for, no, I didn't hear you asking, I felt you needing help. Then I thought what I thought, and for a second or two, I felt like I was inside your head, like you dragged me in. I didn't hear Caesar, and I didn't feel Una, but I felt her absence inside you; I suppose I do have the same absence in me."

"Sometimes, I have to concentrate hard before I know who I am. Teddy, Archie, Caesar, Alessandro, whoever. Am I an actor losing myself in a part? A liar believing his own lie?"

"No, you don't lie to yourself; you question yourself and sometimes aren't sure what the answer is. You can act, and you can lie, but not to me, and you're not doing it now. You and I are linked somehow; I know that."

"Una's there somewhere; I know her body's in a freezer, but her mind is still there somewhere. The mind we fought with wasn't Alex; he was a functionary, a slave. We fought a master who had nothing to do with Caesar or anybody else. There was no emotion, no humanity, just a mind. Huge and powerful, yet in the face of the challenge we made, or the way we made it, it felt shock when we found where it was, though."

"Did you notice the smell?"

"No."

"And it didn't smell like the people we kill."

"It didn't smell of anything."

"No, it smelt old, ancient even."

"And it's not there now, not at all; I've tried to reach out a hundred times and nothing."

"No, it came into your mind, trying to control you, and you fought it off and followed it back to where it came from along the road it made into you. It took the road away, and it's not there now. It's frightened of you."

"Yeah, right, so we've concluded there's some establishment plot against me because I kill abusers. Some high ranking ennobled spies are helping Germany and the Russians. They're part of the establishment and protected somehow. Now there's some fucking gigantic entity that's frightened of me and lives in Switzerland with a banker. It'll be a space alien from the planet Arsehole, I'll be Fuck Rogers, and you can be Dale Hardon."

"You need to take this more seriously," she admonished him, then leant her face towards and across him with a conciliatory kiss. As they expected, the kiss turned into a passionate open-mouthed and deeply shared pleasure, then stopped.

"Besides, it's exciting, isn't it?" she said.

"Well, it's not boring, that's for sure."

"Who's Fuck Rogers? And that Dale Hardon sounds interesting too."

"They're fictional characters, only slightly more unlikely than you and me."

"What are we doing tomorrow, then?"

"Waiting."

"What for?"

"The War to end."

"So we can start another one?"

"Exactly."

Chapter Fourteen

Tuesday 8th May 1945 – Bletchley Park

On Tuesday, the 8th of May 1945, the announcement officially came; Germany had surrendered to the Allies.

In Bletchley Park, people ran out of huts and buildings, laughing, dancing and waving small flags. That scene was repeated across Britain and Europe, in some places at least. Many in Germany saw no difference yet. In the Far East, none saw any difference.

Asgeir watched the wilder celebrations and remained seated. He watched George and Aria hugging each other silently next to the rose bushes. They'd married too, another quiet ceremony at the local Register Office and could finally relax, perhaps.

This day was long in coming; Asgeir knew some would forget the war the very day it ended, never look back, never talk of it. Some would talk non-stop, perhaps those who talked most would have done the least, but the world shouldn't forget those years or repeat them.

Asgeir celebrated by sitting next to Briony on what had become known as Archie's seat, next to the rose bushes and Smudger's tree, still little more than a sapling. He held her hand; they didn't talk, and both thought about the number of times they'd seen Archie on this seat, sometimes alone, sometimes with Rebecca, but without his Una.

He'd never seen such a strong man so broken. He knew he and a dozen others would give their lives if Archie could have his Una back. Archie had saved their lives, cared for them so well, and they would always owe him. He saved so many, but not his wife and his unborn child.

Rebecca and Archie were inseparable, but madness and darkness consumed them. They had unfinished business, unfinished vengeance. Now this war was over, he didn't know where they'd find their purpose. In each other, he hoped; Briony told him they were in love, but Rebecca was still a virgin. Something held them back from consummation. How did women always know these things?

Where were they now? They were behind a desk in Southern Belgium, Detention Centre Five in Noville, interviewing Prisoners of War connected to war crimes. He knew the top brass had sidelined Archie since D Day. Then he sidelined himself further after Una's death; what a waste of two great minds behind desks armed with typewriters. He couldn't understand why they'd agreed to do it; it was demeaning, they deserved better. Unless it was one final act of vengeance against the Nazis who'd killed Una, that made sense. He could hardly shoot them all personally, not even Archie… well, maybe both of them… that was an interesting thought.

Asgeir had a purpose, a country to return to and a family to show his wife. Briony agreed to go to Norway with him. They weren't sure how they would cope with safety after so much danger. They knew being together would be enough.

Asgeir thought of those men he'd killed while leading the team and looked at the rose bushes. So few in the vast scheme of war, among millions who'd died. The recce missions were less dangerous than earlier missions, one in ten military casualties was an accident, and they'd had none. It was training, practice, exercise, and diet that one per cent. Archie Travers had kept that number low.

No celebrations for Asgeir then, only relief that he and Briony were together, alive. Many paid the ultimate price in this war; some, like Archie and Rebecca, would continue to pay a price for as long as they lived.

Then, he looked at Aria and George; they'd stopped hugging. He could see Aria shaking her head and half read her lips, saying, "It's not over, not yet."

*

Wednesday the 9th of May 1945, Noville, Belgium.

Archie knew the war in Europe had ended; celebrations for what would later be known as VE Day, Victory in

Europe, had started. Archie Travers's private war certainly wasn't over, the Americans still needed a victory against Japan, and he now knew how that would end.

Archie and Rebecca had been in France, Belgium and Germany for three solid months. They were setting up teams to sift newly established Allied Prisoner of War camps for Germans suspected of having breached the rules of war and war crimes. The dark irony of their self-righteous involvement in that process wasn't lost on them. They certainly knew a liar when they saw and heard one.

*

Wednesday 11th April 1945 – Buchenwald Concentration Camp

Only a few weeks earlier, on Wednesday, 11th April 1945, Rebecca and Archie had entered Buchenwald Concentration Camp in Germany with the advancing US forces. General Patton ensured Archie and Rebecca were welcome alongside the US 6th Armoured Division. They'd seen other, smaller camps recently and all the Top Secret intelligence and photographs long ago. It was still a horrifying assault on their senses and stomachs. They concentrated on their purpose, placing their humanity in a box.

They had to find two particular German guards before anyone else killed them.

Archie's role in prosecuting war crimes gave him immediate access to the main offices and camp records together with a group of investigators. He'd pleaded with the American officers to gather any remaining guards in the yard outside the offices and not to shoot them summarily, no field justice this time, whatever they saw.

Camp guards were a good source of intelligence and evidence against those higher up the German chain of command who had the means to flee now but could face trial later. All sins must be paid for.

Archie checked the paper records inside while Rebecca checked the faces outside. Her need to find Gerolf and Gottlieb consumed her; the closer it came, the more obsessive and desperate it was.

Rebecca checked the faces frantically, becoming visibly agitated. Six GIs watched her back while she lifted faces and examined features, trying to clearly recall faces.

The high number of female guards disturbed Rebecca. She'd killed, tortured even, easily when she had to, but this was different. She didn't need to look at the female faces; her eyes were drawn to them nonetheless. They looked normal; one was small and pretty, vaguely reminding her of Una.

She saw fear; she expected that, afraid to smile and afraid to frown, wondering which was more likely to get them shot.

Rebecca sank to her knees and vomited, the stench suddenly overwhelming her.

She sensed a female hand on her shoulder, and a female American voice spoke.

"Here, rinse your mouth out," the voice said, handing her a canteen of water, "this is the worst I can even imagine."

Rebecca rinsed her mouth three times and calmed herself.

"Thanks, I just have a need to kill them all," said Rebecca.

"Well, it would make a good photograph," the American said, showing her camera to Rebecca, "it might have unpleasant consequences later."

"Yes," said Rebecca, standing now and seeing Archie coming out of the camp offices slowly, forcing himself not to run. He was angry, but only Rebecca would notice that.

As the American started to take photographs, Rebecca carefully and methodically took in the full scene around her for the first time.

The site was huge and must have contained tens of thousands; there were hundreds of faces looking at them through wire fences, filthy and emaciated, some still standing, impassively, silently, waiting. They were the 'healthy' ones; others lay dead, singly or in piles, some lay awkwardly, uncomfortably where they were, immobile. They hadn't begun to look inside the huts.

Archie reached Rebecca.

"They're gone a month ago, AWOL with an officer; it looks like, fuck knows where they are," he said.

Archie noticed the photographer, an attractive woman mid-thirties. A war correspondent, a typical parasite, at least she was at the sharp end. No, he corrected himself silently; there needs to be a record of this; we can't forget this was done. Words alone can't describe this crime.

Archie looked at the photographer for perhaps one second longer than he should have then began to notice the female German guards gathered alongside the male ones. Then he looked full circle languorously around him, taking in all the Hellish panorama, burning the image indelibly into his mind.

"Gerolf Klein und Gottlieb Adalbert. Wo sind sie?" Archie said quietly in a measured tone, Conner's calmest voice. He waited ten seconds, then shot one of the male guards in the head with his pistol.

He looked at the small crowd of German faces before him; one of the females said something Rebecca didn't catch and spat at him.

Archie grabbed her by the top of her hair and pulled her face back. Then when she screamed in pain and protest, he placed the barrel of his Webley pistol downwards into her mouth and pulled the trigger. Her head and neck exploded, and he let her limp body fall to the earth.

"Wer ist der nachste?" he said even more quietly, this time, his face still impassive, emotionless.

The prisoners remained quiet, then even that short fearful silence was shattered by a single gunshot from deeper inside the camp.

Archie smashed the body of his Webley into the face of the small, pretty one, breaking her nose and smashing her teeth.

"Gerolf Klein und Gottlieb Adalbert. Wo sind sie?" he

quietly asked again.

Another single shot rang out from nearby this time, and one Jewish inmate began clapping weakly from his spot behind the fence. He looked like the effort might finish him off; only his rags caught on the barbed wire held him upright. Others joined in.

"Ich weiss," said a German female, about twenty-five, not as attractive as the blonde whose face had formerly been so, but pleasant looking.

Archie kicked her to the ground, then grabbed her long hair and pulled her after him toward the offices.

A short burst of machinegun fire came from further away, three seconds, no more.

A young GI Lieutenant approached him; he was frogmarching an SS officer towards the group. He stopped next to Archie and asked him what to do with the officer.

"Whatever the hell you fucking like, son," said Archie.

The Lieutenant drew his pistol and shot the officer in the head. Some of the blood sprayed onto the back of Archie's left hand; he looked at it, turned it over and checked his palm closely. He wiped the back of his hand on the female guard's uniform and walked on.

Rebecca watched the photographer watching Archie, not raising her camera once.

"Jesus Christ, I heard he was dangerous as well as good looking," the photographer said.

"Oh, him, he's a little subdued today, and you have no idea how dangerous he is," Rebecca said.

"Don't worry, Rebecca Rochford, I know you'd kill me if I looked at him again," the American said.

"I might kill you anyway; he looked at you too long," Rebecca said without a trace of emotion.

"Please don't," she said smiling, "I'm a close friend of Roland Penrose. He's probably seen my tits; most men seem to have."

"Sorry, who are you?"

"My name's Lee Miller; I work for Vogue and Life."

"Never heard of it," said Rebecca and walked off to see

Archie.

Lee Miller was the topless model in the photograph Archie had found on Corp's kitbag when he was Teddy. Archie didn't recognise her.

*

Archie and Rebecca drove away from Buchenwald four hours later; that was all they could stand.

"We don't have to see that again," said Archie as he drove, "I wanted to kill every last one of them and thinking we'd lost those two bastards pushed me over the edge."

"We had to kill some of them in front of the Jews; others need to answer questions or face trial," said Rebecca.

"I got lucky with that female guard, lucky she worked in the offices and knew what went on, fiddling the books, access to money and gold, then the forged documents. We have their recent photographs too. They've gone southeast, where the officer lives. We'll catch up with them, and she'll be a good witness for other things as well; she knows she's dead if she isn't. We'll bring her back to Belgium and keep her there. She has an interesting story to tell, and Dolf Von Rundstedt features heavily."

Archie paused, thinking hard, reluctant to give voice to his thoughts.

"We should have done something, though, years ago," he said.

"What could we have done?"

"I don't know, anything, something, even if we knew it wouldn't work, we should have done something."

"I'm sorry I said their God was a cunt."

"What was he then? He watched it all and did even less than we did."

"Why did that photographer think you'd seen her tits?"

"Who? What photographer?"

"The one with the tits, you idiot."

"I have no idea."

*

Thursday 10th May 1944 – Noville, Belgium

In Belgium, the British and American Forces they

worked with showed a real enthusiasm for the task. Everyone knew the reality of the death camps now; it beggared belief. They needed a new vocabulary to describe it. A crime so bad it had no name; according to Churchill, Geno Caedere, it took a combination of Latin and Greek words to describe it, the killing of an entire race, genocide, and holocaust.

Archie's sins felt so venial in comparison. He still had no intention of being held accountable for them, whatever category they fitted into, whoever might seek to judge him.

As soon as news arrived of the German surrender, Rebecca asked for time alone. He expected that, and he still asked if she needed him there, too. She said not, so he pressed her no further and watched her go. Rebecca had to deliver her vengeance personally, suitably and proportionate to the crime.

Archie's intelligence contacts, bribes paid, favours done, and rewards offered secured Gerolf and Gottlieb's location for the British. Those fools had fled southeast with their ill-gotten gains, using the identities of three Czech Jews they'd murdered years before. Unfortunately for them, the first Russian troops they encountered were more interested in robbing them of their possessions than helping them as refugees.

Much as Archie disliked him, he'd bribed his Russian Army equivalent to capture, not kill, Gerolf and Gottlieb if they were encountered. He'd known, better than any, where the Russian lines were. The Russians knew the price of a life too, and he was willing to pay, however much it cost him.

*

Rebecca took their car and spent several days alone in the Western end of Germany, fully controlled by American forces.

She visited the small rural village of Prum quietly at midday on a Sunday. As she'd expected, two families returned from church. The village was of no military importance and remained largely unscathed by the war.

She already knew where the wives and families of Gerolf and Gottlieb lived.

She took her camera and other equipment, including her silenced Luger, from the boot of the car and gained entry to the first house.

She relayed the bad news to the family on behalf of the Allies, did what she had to do quickly and effectively, then left.

She repeated her evil deception at the second house and drove off smartly, only removing the wig and fake uniform when she was back in Belgium. Gerolf and Gottlieb were going to suffer; this was only the start.

*

Wednesday 16th May 1945 – Eastern Germany – Russian occupied territory

Major Archie Travers had travelled across Germany with a truck and five GIs to collect two German Prisoners from the hastily constructed POW camp behind Soviet lines in Eastern Germany. The camp held suspected war criminals, mainly SS personnel, but also civilians and anyone suspected of *terrorism*. The scene of numerous summary executions, the camp held anyone the Russians took exception to, and they could do whatever they liked to them while they starved them to death.

The conditions were appalling, nearly as bad as the concentration camps Archie had seen briefly. Russian records of prisoners held were dreadful; God knows how they'd got the correct details for the pair he was after. He hoped they had.

He entered the wooden building that held the office and doubled as the Lieutenant's quarters. It was shabby and unkempt, a half-empty bottle of vodka was on his desk, and he gestured to it.

"No, thank you," Archie said, "do you speak English? I can speak German if you need to?"

"No, not German; my English is good, is it not?"

"Yes, excellent, thank you."

Archie saw he was overweight, forty going on fifty

years old. He could smell alcohol on his breath, though the man showed no signs of drunkenness. He looked like he was accustomed to volume. There were two open trunks in the office, looted trinkets, jewellery, bottles and even some candlesticks of Jewish origin. Archie recognised it as booty; he couldn't fault that shared sin; he could use it to his own advantage, though.

The GI behind him placed the crate of twelve bottles of French Wine on the floor and left when Archie indicated. Some business needed privacy and discretion even in this small Russian corner of Hell.

"A gift from the British Army," he said when they were alone.

The Russian rose from his relaxed position and walked over to inspect the wine more carefully, studying the labels. As he did so, Archie caught sight of a young girl's shape in another room behind the Russian.

The papers Archie presented were perfect and official; the two men had killed British POWs after Dunkirk and faced a trial for their crimes. He placed them on the table, but the Russian officer cared nothing about the paperwork or the prisoners. The case of vintage French Wine he'd produced was enough to secure the release.

The shape in the other room approached the half-open door behind the Russian officer. Archie saw the frightened eyes of a young German girl. Those eyes pleaded with him, begged for his help. Her lips formed the German words bitte, bitte, then the English word, please. Her dishevelled hair and clothing told her story. The lines on her forehead, as she winced in pain, moved towards him as her eyes met his and reached out to clutch at the soul he didn't have.

That wouldn't work; he had no soul, he didn't save the world; that was someone else, another life.

'Not now, not here. She's German, there's nothing I can do, her father's probably in the SS, she deserves it, it's not my fucking war. I've got five men, I'm as good as in Russia, he's killing thousands in this camp, he's not going to fear me, I have no power here. This man could kill me and my men

without a thought, on a whim. People are disappearing all the time in occupied Germany.'

However, the picture that formed in his mind was something he'd never seen in real life. He saw Una in a warehouse with three men, tied to a chair, wearing only a thin nightdress, cold, dripping wet and waiting for torture, rape, and murder.

"The girl?" he said; his mouth moved before his brain could stop it.

"It is mine," the officer told him.

"Yours?"

"It is here by choice."

"Choice?"

"Yes, it had a choice; me or one hundred of my men; it chose me. A virgin too, tight as a noose around an SS man's neck," he laughed.

"How much? My men are bored and have a long journey back; I can give them a present."

"What present do I get?"

Archie fished in his pocket and produced a few valuable items he'd acquired and kept for barter; rings, a bracelet, a necklace and a couple of solid Gold coins. He placed them on the table casually; he'd done this often recently, the way things worked in occupied Germany.

"Which would you like?"

"All of it, it's very tight, you know."

"Okay."

"And one more thing, English."

"What?"

"You have to go in there and fuck it right now, I've fucked it a few minutes ago, so it'll still be wet."

"I'm not exactly in the mood."

"And I have to watch."

Trouble finds me again, thought Archie, the girl's as good as dead. When he's done with her, he'll still give her to a hundred of his men. One of those men would end up killing her, and the next man would fuck her corpse regardless.

Archie entered the back room, ignoring the Russian now standing near the doorway to get a good view.

The girl knew what was coming and backed away from him, frightened and sick looking. When she reached the filthy mattress on the floor, she lay back on it and lifted her skirt to her waist.

Archie lowered his body on top of hers, reaching for the back of her head and hair, pulling it tightly and jerking her hair up towards his.

"Shut up, don't say a word, and you'll get out of here alive," he whispered in German into her ear as he fumbled with his flies.

She lay passively beneath him. He reached down to her vagina, which was dry and spat heavily onto his fingers to achieve any kind of opening.

"Don't worry, I washed the dirty bastard out of me," she whispered in German to him. "Go slow, he fucked me dry, so I am sore, and there is blood."

Archie hadn't had intercourse since Una's death, and part of him needed it badly. The thought of Una and his current situation wasn't conducive to any lust, and no erection came. Ivan, the bastard, laughing loudly in the doorway, didn't help either.

He worked his fingers into her, hoping for something to happen. Some animal instinct, he knew it was there; he'd felt it since childhood, aged five. Where the fuck was it when he needed it?

Gradually, as he massaged the g spot inside her vagina, he felt her push down against his fingers, and some new and more natural moisture appeared. Then he felt her left hand reach down towards his cock and stroke it firmly.

"Come on, you have to do it, do it or he may kill us both; I have seen it here. You must fuck me, Englishman."

Archie put his now erect cock inside her; she was tight and now wet.

"Slowly," she said, "it hurts, but you have to do it."

Her face contorted in pain as he fucked her carefully.

"Come quickly. He'll see if you don't."

211

Archie wanted to come and be done with it; the slow strokes wouldn't do it, so he had to speed up, making her scream and push at him. He came, after thirty seconds of hard strokes, she had tears in her eyes.

"Slap me," she whispered, "slap me," she spat in his face, and he slapped her.

When he raised himself from her body, he noticed the fresh blood on his cock and emerging from her.

Ivan laughed.

"You fuck like a Serbian bastard, Englishman," Ivan said, slapping Archie on the back; he'd come closer for a better look, masturbating his semi soft cock. Archie pulled up his trousers and did up his flies while the girl pushed her skirt down and reached for a blanket to cover herself.

They left the Russian's quarters, and once outside, he saw and recognised the two animals he'd come for. Both had untended broken noses and old festering cuts on their faces and hands. The Russians were beating them to death as well as starving them; for a moment, he wasn't sure a relatively quick end was bad enough for them.

He was glad he'd brought a truck and guards. He couldn't stand the smell or sight of those two. He asked his men to give them some rations only because he wanted them alive.

The GIs he'd used as guards and drivers knew what was happening. There were numerous unofficial field trials for prisoners. They'd ceased now, officially. Archie had paid them enough US dollars and favours to buy their silence and restraint.

There were no summary executions of concentration camp guards like there had been no rape of German women by Allied troops. Giving someone a bar of chocolate after two of your mates had held her down while you took turns to fuck her wasn't rape, was it?

War was bad, victory was even worse for the losers and what the fuck had he just done?

As they left the office, she spoke quietly to him in perfect English.

"Thank you for your assistance Major; I speak excellent English and Russian; I was an interpreter until a few weeks ago. My uniform would have been my death warrant; the civilian clothes only got me raped; it would have got worse."

The German girl continued to talk to him in the truck's cab, only in German, so the GI driver wouldn't understand.

She was from the small town of Cottbus near the Polish-German border. When the Russians came, the women knew exactly what to expect and tried to hide or flee westwards. For three days after the surrender, the Russians did whatever they wanted. When caught, she'd told them she was 15 and a virgin, but they hadn't cared. She was attractive, well-proportioned with large breasts for a young girl, so an officer saved her for himself.

"The stupid pig believed I was a virgin; the last tight hole that bastard fucked was his own daughter's arsehole. His wife's hole must be like a bucket. He showed me pictures of his family, can you believe it? I pretended to come for him; it was my only chance to survive. You could make me come, Englishman. I can't go back to the East; I'll stay with you. You would treat me well; I'll fuck some of your men if you ask me and if they're nice to me."

"No, no, you don't have to fuck anybody; you're free."

"Free? You fucking stupid Englishman, no one is free in Germany. Did you not enjoy me? I know you enjoyed me. You came a lot; I can still feel your juice inside me."

'Oh, for fuck's sake, what have I got myself into now?'

*

Saturday 19th May 1945 – near Noville, Belgium

Once in Belgium, Archie made the truck take a small detour to his interrogation unit and made a decision. He spoke to one of his Lieutenants and handed her over.

"What's your name?" he asked.

"Magda Kirschau."

"Magda, you work for me as an interpreter; okay, this man will look after you."

He drew the Lieutenant aside.

"Keep her here, clean her up, get her some clothes, use my account. Give her a good meal, get her a proper identity card, get her a proper medical. Use her on routine stuff at first, her English is excellent, and she knows Russian as well. Everyone is to treat her with the utmost respect; no one is to fuck her, no one is to even think about fucking her. Any man who lays a hand on her shoulder will be on a charge; in fact, nobody even looks at her funny."

"Sir?"

"Do I make myself clear?"

"Yes, sir."

Magda smiled.

*

Sunday 20th May 1945 - 0100 – near Noville

It was a long journey back to Belgium and then to the isolated barn Archie now controlled and where Rebecca awaited him. Archie hadn't slept or washed, although he'd managed to eat, which pleased him, that remained a step forward for him.

Archie's GIs manhandled Gerolf and Gottlieb into the building, bound and gagged, then strung them up by the arms from the rafters.

Archie paid them their bonus, and they left; they wouldn't see one moment of the imminent *'interrogation'* by British Intelligence.

Rebecca entered the barn wearing the same clothes she'd worn when she first encountered Gerolf and Gottlieb years before.

Archie told Rebecca he would stay or leave, whatever she wanted. She said she needed him to stay; he remained without question, but he didn't want to see her do it. She needed him with her, so he needed to be there for her. He'd do it for her if she asked; he'd not let his fury rise that far since Buchenwald, but he knew she'd do it herself; she had to.

Rebecca looked up at the two men, their ankles tied and dangling, a tantalising six inches from the ground.

"Do you remember me?" Rebecca asked them in perfect

German.

They looked puzzled.

"St. Nazaire."

They shook their heads.

"An alleyway; you thought it would be fun to rape me, you couldn't manage it, you fucked my mouth and then pissed on me."

They remembered.

"Good, do you recognise these people?" she said, showing them the photographs of their wives and children, standing to attention and fearful in front of the camera. She held the photographs inches from their faces, and both sets of eyes opened wide.

"They're dead," she said in a forceful monotone, devoid of all emotion and shocking Archie.

"I killed them last week; I considered having them gang raped and tortured. The children looked so innocent, and it wasn't your wives' fault, so I shot them cleanly and quickly."

She left the photographs of their dead families below their feet, then calmly took her razor sharp knife from its scabbard.

They looked at her knife, wriggled, kicked and began to whine.

"Yes, that was me too, north of St. Nazaire," she said, then sliced the trousers roughly from the two dangling Germans. She couldn't get the trousers over their bare tied feet, which was a pleasing irony. Then, she slowly and deliberately held and severed the balls and cock from each of them. Billy Perry had kept that blade razor sharp for her. They screamed and squirmed; that would only make them bleed to death sooner.

Their blood poured at first, then steadily dripped down, obscuring the images of their dead families.

The last images either Gerolf or Gottlieb saw were the pictures of their dead families, knowing they had killed them, their actions had killed them. They were responsible. Rebecca wasn't sure if two such men would care that much, but it was too good a card to have and not play it.

They died agonisingly, painfully and fittingly; it would go in a box soon enough and stay there forever.

She hadn't killed their families, of course, she'd taken their photographs after telling them their husbands and fathers were dead, but they'd never know that.

Archie felt relief when she told him that later, she'd needed a shocked look on his face for those two bastards to see if it came to it. He'd still have loved her if she had done it; the choice was hers.

He took her to a standpipe and trough outside the barn and washed her hands thoroughly, took the old clothes from her and made her wash, naked and in front of him. He dried her with a towel and replaced the old clothes with a fresh uniform. He then placed her old clothes in a pile next to the barn door, covering them with petrol and emptied the rest of that can and another one around the wooden barn.

He thought for a few seconds, then took a bag containing his old private's uniform and placed it next to her clothing by the barn.

Then he rinsed the petrol from his hands, dried them and put Rebecca in their car.

He walked back towards the barn, sniffing his hands to check they were clean before tossing a lit book of matches at the old clothes and the old debts they represented.

The dry wooden barn lit up with petrol fuelled flame, spreading rapidly but not mercifully. Not before Gerolf and Gottlieb could taste and choke on the smoke, felt the heat and burning of their flesh, felt the pain of hell that was their due.

Archie had watched Rebecca throughout. She wasn't angry; she was calm, there was no emotion either way. This wasn't an act of violence; it was an act of redemption, justice dispensed, sins punished, and he loved her more than ever.

"I'm taking you home now."

"Yes, please."

*

Wednesday 23rd May 1945 – Calais

The journey to England and Hevlyn Mansions took over two days in the chaos of traffic and Channel crossing. They managed to secure some separate temporary overnight quarters in Calais, where they washed, fed and slept a little.

Early the next morning, Archie took Rebecca to the old jetty and showed her where he'd leapt onto the deck of the Gulzar. He couldn't make that jump now.

Then he took her to the Bakers who'd given him bread, cheese and wine. Some buildings had been rebuilt, and he couldn't locate the right street, let alone the Bakers. Rebecca asked some locals, and eventually, she had an address nearby. It was a small flat on the top floor of a drab new block in the town centre.

The door was answered by a suspicious look from the mother, whom he'd seen only briefly years previously. She then jumped at him, hugging and kissing him while shouting at her two daughters to follow suit.

When calm, she invited them in, explaining her husband and son were now working in a larger bakery. They were employees and had to make poor quality bread. They'd been lucky; they were alive. The Germans had needed bread, too, so they'd always had an income.

The mother gave them coffee with cream though she and her daughters didn't join them. They declined her kind offer of food.

Now the war was over, they hoped to find better work and save enough to restart their own business.

Archie looked at the small flat and cheap furnishings, working out their chances of success. He reminded the mother he'd never paid for his food before and wanted to do so now. She wouldn't hear of it.

Perhaps I don't hate the French so much, he thought.

After explaining they had to leave and catch their boat, he used their toilet before leaving and wished them well.

"How much did you leave?" Rebecca asked him after they'd left.

"Every penny I had on me. I'll send more when we get home. Remember the address, please."

She took his hand, tickling his palm with her finger, and they walked to their car.

"I love you, Archie Travers."

*

Thursday 24th May 1945 – Hevlyn Mansions

Rebecca withdrew into herself more as the journey went on and was less talkative. He knew the signs; he'd seen and felt them before.

He told her about the German girl; she only listened and nodded, no more than that. He needed her to say he'd done the right thing, but she didn't. They'd spent so much time and effort searching for those two bastards they were both strangely rudderless. That purpose had always been there for them from the first moment they'd met.

As soon as they reached the flat, Archie checked if Conner was at home; he was elsewhere as usual now.

Once in his flat, he let Rebecca sit in his thinking chair and made tea for her and him as the flat warmed up.

She sat in his lap while they drank their tea. He stroked her hair and neck gently for several minutes, then went to run a bath for her. She remained silently in his chair until he returned and led her by the hand into the bathroom. He'd already taken his clothes off and wore only his gown. She still said nothing as he took her clothes off and moved her towards, then lifted her into the bath and started to sponge wash her back with warm soapy water. He moved to clean her elsewhere, everywhere, with his hands and the sponge. She didn't say a word and lay back with her eyes closed and sighed with enjoyment.

Rebecca had known the pleasant feeling of internal moisture before; only Archie had ever induced that in her. This was much more than that, and she asked him to join her in the bath. They both knew they were approaching their Rubicon, intended to cross, and there would be no going back.

"We should both wash the sin away today," she said and began to sponge him clean too. She'd washed Archie before; this time, she paid particular attention to his cock. She'd seen his erection before and had never touched it, she wasn't surprised to see it was erect, but it became bigger and harder in her hands.

"I think I'm clean enough now," he said, getting out of the bath and taking her hand with him. He dried her with a fresh towel all over, then she dried him.

She turned to face him, naked and held both his hands in hers, standing on tiptoes to place a kiss on the lips, and he lowered his head to receive it.

"There's something you don't know, and I have to tell you," she said, reaching up to peck his lips again, maintaining eye contact the whole time.

"I've never felt sexually attracted to any man in my life, not until I met you," she reached upwards for an open-mouthed kiss with a flick of a tongue on his.

"It's only ever been you," another open mouthed tongue reached deeper for his.

"Until St. Nazaire was in its box, I couldn't; now I can let go," another longer, deeper kiss.

"Una helped me become a woman, told me how, what to do, what to expect… "

A profound, urgent and almost painful kiss, teeth clashed.

"… from you, how to please you and how you would please me," another breathless kiss repeated again and again.

"I asked for this, and Una told me, promised me, my first time could be with you," she saw a tear in the corner of his eye, and she kissed it away.

"That's not enough anymore; I want all of you forever, just you," she said, "it can only ever be you."

Archie picked her up and carried her to their bed, placing her gently on it and laying her on her back while he kissed, stroked and caressed her all over her body. He pulled himself up alongside her, looking her in the eyes and placing his erection at the entrance of her wet lips, but not entering her yet. He moistened his middle finger with her tongue and began to play gently with her clitoris. Using her own moisture as well, he drew small gentle circles around it and over it, making her shiver with each flick. Then, after a few more gentle flicks, he made the touching more rhythmic and harder until she began to gasp and approach orgasm. She panted, shivered and gasped with each touch, kissing him deeply.

"Don't stop, don't stop, don't ever stop," she said.

Then at the start of her orgasm that she couldn't stop or interrupt, he gently slid himself into her. He felt her moisture and a little blood on her muscles gripping him tightly as he continued to thrust in and out of her. Her first ever orgasm merged seamlessly with her second, and she looked into his eyes and demanded he come inside her.

"For all time," he said to her, knowing for certain now she possessed exactly the same scent and taste as Una.

"For all time," she replied.

*

He thought of Una, and it broke his heart.

Chapter Fifteen

Monday 18th June 1945 - Germany

The war in Europe had been over for a month when Archie's intelligence sources notified him of the detention of some German Rocket Scientists, including Werner Von Braun. They were in the North West of Germany, an area under the joint control of British and American forces.

Archie needed to act immediately, so he and Rebecca drove straight north from Belgium to Langwedel near Bremen. The fraudulent orders he carried authorised Von Braun to be given directly into his custody to face trial for war crimes. His V1 and V2 rockets had intentionally targeted civilians in London and the South Coast. One of his rockets had killed Una, and Von Braun was going to die for it.

Archie and Rebecca arrived at their destination very early in the morning. The place was teeming with American Personnel, ambulances, buses, cars and guards everywhere, only Americans, not a Tommy in sight.

Damn, if only I hadn't taught them so well, they might have messed up, he thought as he introduced himself to the Captain in charge. His spirits lifted when he heard Von Braun was still on site, having a complex break on an arm plastered back into place. Von Braun had refused to leave Germany without all of his family, and they were being brought to join him.

He asked if he could speak to him.

"Sorry, Major Travers, my orders are that US Army personnel only are allowed on site."

Archie produced his United States Army Military Identity card, signed by Eisenhower himself and showed his US passport for good measure.

When the man still hesitated, he showed him his United States Army Medal of Honour in its original case and presented privately to him by President Roosevelt only weeks before he died. Archie had thought of everything.

Nearly.

"Look, sir, you can go in alone, and I'll have to disarm you first."

"Okay," Archie agreed, "I could always strangle the fucker if I wanted to, you know?"

"That's why I'll be armed and watching you while you're in there."

"I can break a neck in two seconds."

"I'm an excellent shot with a pistol."

That was alright; Archie's mantra had already moved him on to Plan C. He went into the large empty room, which held only Von Braun in a wheelchair and two disinterested but well-armed and beefy Military Policemen.

He casually approached Von Braun, pulled up a chair and sat next to him smiling, then spoke in well practised German.

"Hello, Von Cunt; my name is Major Archie Travers of British Military Intelligence. You're reputedly the big brain behind all the rocketry technology."

Von Braun nodded, slightly confused; his handlers had told him to say nothing to anyone; no one should know who he was.

"All those rockets were the product of genius and all that. So I'm sure the Americans have offered you amnesty and citizenship. The same for all your colleagues and all your families and their friends and maybe even your fucking dogs and cats. I can understand why they would do that. I can even understand why you would do what you did in the war, fuck me, I've done some bad stuff, no, some downright fucking evil stuff, as it happens.

"It's just that one of your rockets killed my wife last July in London. She was sitting quietly in a peaceful civilian house, and she was pregnant with our first child when she died. Her name was Una, she was beautiful, and I loved her. I still do."

Von Braun turned white as a sheet and nearly shat himself; Archie thought he'd pissed his pants and a wet patch near his groin confirmed that.

"Now I know we did the same to your cities, and if you'd won the war, you'd kill Bomber Harris, and me for that matter, so it's only fair.

"Your problem is you deserve to die, I'd like to kill you, and they've taken my guns away. Now I'm fairly sure I could snap your neck before they could shoot me, but I don't deserve to die, not here anyway, and that isn't part of the plan.

"So, I've decided to let you know I'm not going to kill you today, and it'll probably be too difficult to kill you in America. You'll have great security, so I probably won't even try.

"However, you need to know something. One day, years from now, when you're out having dinner with your wife or going to church or shopping, the man next to you might be me, and he might kill you. A man has to be prepared to face the consequences of his actions. I am, and I welcome anyone who thinks they're good enough to make me do that."

Archie nodded, smiled and left, much to the relief of the American Officer watching him.

"I'm afraid Herr Von Braun Trousers needs another pair; you'll smell it from here in a minute or two."

Archie collected his weapon and let Rebecca drive him away, then two armed guards stopped them at the exit checkpoint.

"Fuck it, I never touched the bastard!" he said.

"Are you Major Travers, Archibald Travers Austin or whatever?" the GI guard asked.

"Yes, that does sound like me?"

He hadn't used that particular version of his name for years, since Calais, and it intrigued him.

"There's an urgent message for you; it's been trying to catch you up for days. You can use this phone to ring this number."

Archie stepped into the Guards' watch-house, relieved he didn't have to shoot his way out, which would have been difficult to explain.

He rang the number and eventually spoke to General Curtis Harcourt, who explained he was in charge of a Unit tracking down high-level Nazis trying to flee to Switzerland. He had a prisoner, an SS General, demanding to see an Archie Travers Austin.

"I knew your name and your involvement in the same line of work as me on the British side, so I figured it must be you. Guess he got the name wrong. He's Rodolf Von Rundstedt, and he swears blind he saved your life."

"Sorry, where exactly are you? I'll be there as soon as I can. Tell him I'm coming, and don't shoot him, please; he might be useful to me, to the British, I mean."

*

Thursday 21st June 1945 - Germany

It took nearly three days to reach the United States Army Intelligence Base in Sontofen in the south of Germany, stopping in Belgium to collect anything they might need. He tried to work out what Dolf wanted apart from his life.

Archie and Rebecca relaxed as they approached such a breathtakingly beautiful place. The scenery was stunning, high snow-capped mountains, even in summer, lakes and rich green meadows, a million miles from war and seemingly untouched by it.

"Good place for a holiday," he said, "we should come here, yes we'll go to Switzerland after this, fuck everything else. I think I may be approaching the end of my military career after Von Braun, a holiday in the United States may not be an option either. You deserve a holiday. It's a pity… well, it's a pity, that's all."

Harcourt was ready, waiting for them and kept them in the garden of his quarters rather than bringing them in. Something was up, and Archie could guess what. This was unofficial, and some bargaining would take place.

"You know this Dolf then?" Harcourt asked.

"Yes, I do, he did save my life, but I saved his, so we're one apiece. I don't think I owe him too much."

"The situation is, Travers, he is one evil sonofabitch; the French want him for resistance fighters tortured and shot in St. Nazaire, one female strangled personally by him. There's a dead policeman and a café owner and his family in Paris, raped and murdered. There're five hundred dead hostages from one town as a reprisal, and that's when he was Wehrmacht; there's more and worse from his time in Vichy with the SS. The Russians want him, too, although he was never anywhere near the East. On top of all that, there's pressure from senior Germans who are, shall we say, 'cooperating with US forces,' and that's down to his family connections."

"What are you offering, and what do you need?"

"Well, first, let me tell you straight, I was in North Africa, and those Vichy bastards killed plenty of good men, so I wouldn't piss in their face if they were ablaze. Neither of us would give the Russians the cowshit off our shoes. Now, you know George Patton, and we came through the Ardennes together to get here."

"You want Peiper?"

Joachim Peiper was SS Standartenfuhrer in charge of the 1st SS Panzer Division's attack on American lines during the Battle of the Bulge. His men were responsible for the massacre of American prisoners at Malmedy, and the Americans wanted revenge; Archie could understand that.

"Damn right, we do, for Malmedy."

"You know there's not much of a case against him; he was verifiably miles away at the time."

"There's not much against him *yet*, is what you mean. We need a senior officer to be prosecuted for that, and Peiper's one of Hitler's finest."

"Straight swap?"

"You get my drift."

"Let me and Lieutenant Rochford speak to Von Rundstedt first, and we'll see what arrangement I can suggest."

"Fine by me. He's cuffed and chained in my quarters.

You need to know; when we caught him, he was on his way back to Germany from Switzerland, genuine Swiss Passport and all. Beats the Hell outta me; he was off and free and came back, won't say a word about it."

Archie had Dolf brought outside, and they sat at a table in the garden in warm summer sunshine. Archie undid the leg irons and handcuffs and asked Harcourt for a bottle of wine and three glasses.

Dolf rubbed his arms and stretched his legs, the drab prisoner clothing he wore couldn't mask his class and poise, and Archie smiled at that. Dolf still had something he aspired to, real class, not feigned.

"So, Archie, you've done well, a Major; you were a lot less when we first met. I could see that darkness in your eyes even then. It's been good for you. It wasn't easy to keep track of your exploits; I acquired a good source of intelligence; sadly, that source is of no further use to me in my current circumstances."

"That source was in England?"

"Of course, don't press me on that; we haven't begun the barter yet; you still know the price of a life, I assume?"

"Yes, I saved your life; you saved mine; we're even."

"Perhaps, perhaps not, you took my rifle and my watch… my mother gave me that watch; it had value beyond the price."

Archie took it off and gave it straight to him.

"I apologise, Dolf; I was in dire need."

"Thank you, you used the rifle, I know it; how many did you get in Calais?"

"Between thirty and fifty, it's difficult to tell in the heat of the moment who I killed, wounded or even missed. I had it maintained by the best man in England."

"Your Billy Perry?"

"Yes. Your source was good then?"

"The best. You used the Mauser well; that's what matters. It was a thing of great beauty; I had it made to kill; that was its purpose; you may keep it; you earned it. I had another one, not so good but good enough to see you and your friends run out of the fort towards the old jetty. We shot the first man out, then I made sure we held fire when I saw it was you. We were in the Phaire, the lighthouse; you would have known that."

"Fucking Hell, you did, didn't you? No one else could have seen that or known it!" Archie shook his head, closed his eyes and then opened them extra wide and stared at him.

"So you see, Archie, you do owe me a life."

"Fucking hell," he said, then sipped his wine while he thought. "I do, at least one, no... more than that two other good men, the best of men, both of them."

"Conner?"

"Yes, he's still alive; the other died on the Krebs."

"The Krebs! I fucking knew that was you, only later, though, when it was all too late. You cracked the code, didn't you? I can see that now. You didn't use it all, though, or we'd have noticed. You only used some of it; you let your own people die so you could win in the end. That took patience and resolution; you English know about patience, you know how to queue, to wait your turn, even at Dunkirk. No wonder we lost; we ran headlong into Russia when we should have waited.

"You know, Archie. When Patton was in Kent pretending he was planning your D Day. I asked if you were with him. When they said yes, I told them the invasion would definitely be Calais, and you'd want to go back there. Calais, Calais."

Dolf went silent and seemed absent, thinking deeply, thinking back, reasoning or realising something for the first time.

"Yes, it was... the lighthouse; I never saw it until now; in Calais, they call it Le Phaire, the Pharos in Alexandria in Caesar's time. Calais was Alexandria; we had already burned the books this time. I burned the books, you know, this time, I threw them on, I laughed... that was wrong, a greater crime than the people. I killed knowledge."

Archie stared at Dolf, oblivious to Rebecca, the situation

and the present day. No, it couldn't be; it was his imagination, they were dreams, fantasised conversations with great people, Caesar even, but his voice told a different story.

Archie was talking to himself or maybe more, and he spoke aloud.

"The Library of Alexandria, the greatest collection of knowledge the world has ever known, burned, destroyed, lost forever, forgotten, slowing the progress of all mankind for centuries. All of it gone, Eratosthenes the Librarian dead, and all his knowledge with him. With two sticks and the light of the sun at midday, he calculated the circumference of the Earth almost exactly. The circumference, mind you, he knew it was round, not flat. He knew the earth went around the sun; he knew the stars were other suns, not lights in some imaginary ceiling. He'd read the work of Aristarchus of Samos. He knew there were other Earths going around those suns; he knew there were no Gods, only science, and I should have… Caesar should have stopped it. Somehow."

"You like books though, Archie," said Dolf, "you know the value of knowledge, you liked the Library in London, you read a lot. Did I see you there? You read too much… did you know I helped to translate Guderian's book 'Achtung Panzer' into English as part of my studies? You read it, and I fucking wrote it for you; I see it now, I see it now. All the time, I thought I was doing it for myself, but it was for you. I see it now."

Why the fuck is he using those words? What does he see now? Archie thought as he spoke.

"Yes, I did read it in English; the German would have been too much for me to fully understand it, to clearly see what he'd do."

"You were there too," Dolf said, barely audible, nodding. "Alexandria, you must have been Caesar himself… I was with Pompey Magnus for some of the time, I think. I was always with the fucking loser; I should have stayed with Caesar even when he outgrew me. That's why I played so hard to win this time... you were Caesar himself; that's why he had to hurt you."

"Who?"

"Was I one of the three? Was I the third? Was I? I still have his thirst. I must have been Crassus, it's the only thing that fits, and it doesn't make any sense. It cannot happen. We read the same books, felt the same history and shaped our lives to fit into our fantasy."

Dolf shook his head now as if telling himself how stupid he'd been.

"Who had to hurt me?" Archie asked again.

"Pompey, of course, Gnaeus Pompeius Magnus, Owen Tudor, that was you, yes? Canaris told me, and he has a brother in Moscow, Grigory; he'll pursue both of us when he can. Why do you think the Russians want me? It's not only the gold and diamonds they think I have. He must have revenge on you and me for his brother, or maybe he'll become Pompey now? He will not only seek us. He will also seek all those who are bound to us. That is the way of it."

"No, I wasn't Caesar," Archie said, "I couldn't have been; I remember talking to him, trying to save the books, the knowledge. I think I dreamt it, dreamt it so well; it seemed real; I couldn't have been there. I'm Archie Travers Austin."

"No, you're not," Rebecca said quietly and gently, not even looking up. "You already know that's not who you are."

"Who knows what you are?" said Dolf, "but you did read that book, and I did write it; we both know that as a fact. Why did we meet for a few minutes five years ago, and yet we sit at this table now, we should both be dead, and here we are, me for you and you for me."

Rebecca looked up, staring at them, open-mouthed, feeling she knew some of what this meant. She'd heard the story of Calais and marvelled at the effort, endurance, and fortune that brought Archie and Conner to safety.

'Everything that becomes or changes must do so owing to some cause; for nothing can come to be without a cause.'

Timaeus of Locri said those words in 36 BC if he ever

existed if Plato hadn't invented him. If Plato hadn't only written those words so she could read them two thousand years later and begin to understand what the fuck was going on in 1945 AD. Meaningful coincidence? She'd think about that later.

To know Dolf held Archie's life in his hands and saved it was more than she could describe. If Archie didn't save him, she would; this man had earned another life whatever he'd done.

Dolf sipped at his wine, concerned it would go to his head.

"I wonder, Archie, if I might have some decent food, please, I'm unaccustomed to hardship now, and the American rations are poor fare. I feel a bit lightheaded."

Rebecca said she'd get some.

"Anything fresh, please, anything not from a can," he asked.

"She's your lover now, yes?" he said after she'd gone, "and she was in St. Nazaire too? She was Maria Secondigny?"

Archie nodded.

"I couldn't be sure, but Maria disappeared from the Hotel at the same time as the agent escaped. Did you find Gerolf and Gottlieb? I know what they did to Maria and others? I knew you were seeking them, and that could be the only reason."

"Yes, Rebecca killed them a few weeks ago."

"Good, good, I am glad it was by her hand; that was… correct."

Dolf paused, then said, "Your wife, I'm sorry; I'll say no more; I'll give you the source of my information no matter what you decide to do. Sometimes it's good to give someone something you don't have to. Like you gave me my life in Calais."

Rebecca brought a plate of bread, fruit, and cheese.

"Thank you, Rebecca. It is a pleasure to meet you, I have never met a Schildmaid before, so it is a privilege. To lose a war to people such as you is a dishonour I can bear."

"Dolf, you should eat," Archie said, "I will tell you every bad deed I have ever done, then you will talk and tell me the truth of the charges against you. Then we will decide what to do. I still possess some power, it is severely limited by time, and I must use it wisely and for the absolute best."

'Why the fuck am I talking like that?'

Archie told Dolf all of his history as he'd told Rebecca and Una; he deserved that.

Then, when Dolf had eaten, he'd been starving but had eaten unhurriedly with dignity despite his perilous position, he spoke.

He didn't deny any accusations; he explained the circumstances within which he'd undertaken the acts and admitted a good deal more than the Allies knew about him. He still had contacts in England from Canaris. However, any attempt to use or blackmail them would ensure his death rather than save him. Archie was his only chance.

Archie took it all in, denying then admitting to himself that had he been Dolf, he'd have done much the same. Dolf had lived in a different Universe from Archie, yet they'd lived much the same life in many ways. There was also a change in Dolf, a sadness that hadn't been there before.

"So you returned to Germany to find Annette. You had everything you ever wanted and risked it for one young girl?"

"There could be no more honourable reason. She was safe when I left her, and now she isn't."

"No, there couldn't. I'd give the whole Universe for the one thing I don't have."

"Who can fathom the mind of a man in love?"

"I need to think," Archie said while standing up, "they want to swap Peiper for you," and walked away across the garden.

"Peiper for me, now that is an honour; he's worth ten of me," he said to Rebecca. "You know, before today, I had known him for less than twenty minutes. Now I feel as though I've known him all my life."

"You see him every day in the mirror."

"Perhaps, but he's become more, and I've become less; he's won, and I've lost; I have nothing; he still has you and good friends. I have nothing… unless I can find Annette again."

Archie had to think hard and long about Jochen. He'd interviewed him six times, at length and found out all he needed in the first half hour. Jochen said he'd not been present at the Malmedy massacre, and if his men had done wrong, then he would assume responsibility as their commanding officer. He should face punishment, not them.

Archie knew there were times when you didn't, couldn't, take prisoners; he knew plenty of Allied troops hadn't during D Day. He'd ordered the Chosen Men not to. There were lines not to cross that he placed on himself, like with Dolf. Who could say where that line was for one man on one day and another man on another day?

Archie sensed Jochen was a hard man who did what he needed to because he needed to, not out of malice and somehow, he liked him. During one conversation, Archie told him he expected the establishment to cast him aside and forget him after the war and when his usefulness had ended. Jochen told Archie if he'd been German, they'd never forget him, he'd never buy a beer again in any part of Germany; he laughed.

In the end, it was an easy decision. Dolf stood no chance with the French or Russians; whatever they sought from him, Jochen would at least have a fair public trial from the Americans. Archie had already found an American officer who'd testify Peiper captured him and treated him appropriately as a prisoner of war. Archie could still ensure Jochen had a competent defence lawyer when tried.

He knew beyond reason he had to help Dolf and returned to the table to tell him he'd agree to the swap immediately.

After collecting Dolf's belongings, including his car and dressing him as a free man, Archie and Rebecca drove him to the point on the French Border where he'd arranged to meet Annette. That was days ago now, and she wasn't at the Guesthouse where she'd stayed. The proprietor was evasive and, under duress from Archie, admitted that Frenchmen had taken her to France as a collaborator and had beaten her badly when they found her.

Dolf was raging and wanted to go straight to France and hunt for her.

"No," said Archie, "the French hate you… and me, and they're not keen on the English half of Rebecca either; we'll start another war. They won't kill her; they'll shave her head and spit on her, she'll survive, and we'll find her. I'll bribe the best possible people to find her, it'll take time, but we'll find her. I promise you, I mean it. We'll find her for you; only I can know how much it means to you."

"Okay, okay, okay," Dolf repeated, regaining his composure, "It's my fault; that's what hurts, she's not safe, and it's my fault."

"Right, let's get you back to Switzerland; I have the start of a good plan."

*

Friday 22nd June 1945 – Switzerland

The journey to Switzerland was uneventful and pleasant despite Dolf's restless melancholy, and they entered Switzerland with consummate ease. Dolf saw Rebecca and Archie had civilian clothing and luggage in their car. They transferred it to Dolf's car for the journey and held their own genuine Swiss passports, having lived there for years, apparently. Archie knew how to plan; they already had the full confidence and cooperation of a highly reputable Swiss Bank.

Archie was as good as Caesar; Dolf had no doubts now.

They booked into the best hotel in Zurich, as recommended by Conner, the Dolder Grand. They sat on the open terrace of the restaurant and ordered dinner.

Dolf looked more like his usual self and calmly said to Archie.

"We need to barter again. First, I need to give you something that you weren't going to take. Then I need to ask a favour. I suspect only you can do for me."

"Carry on."

"I have my own contacts in France who may find Annette for me; all it takes is money. I have resources in Switzerland but not enough disposable currency.

"I need a way to convert my assets into legitimate disposable funds; I also need a new identity. The French and Russians are aware of my current details, and I need a new one, preferably an American one; Europe is no longer a safe place for me.

"I'll give you thirty per cent of my assets in exchange for their conversion into disposable assets and an American identity – a fully legitimate one, please; I believe you have that ability."

"There are two of us and one of you; fifty per cent seems fairer."

"You still know the price of a life, and I like you, a new identity within four weeks, and you may have half."

"Agreed, and for fairness, I'll provide you with details of my contacts in France who may help you in your search for Annette."

*

Saturday 23rd June 1945 – Galgenen - Switzerland

The following day they drove to Galgenen, south of Zurich, in Dolf's car. Dolf drove, it wasn't far, and Archie kept a close watch on him; he wasn't sure why. Dolf could have run off during the night and didn't; he might be waiting for the new passport, though Archie still needed to play his cards carefully and in the correct order.

Dolf turned right off the main road near a small hamlet and went up a slight incline, a narrow track through thick conifers. The track ended with a medium sized chalet in a sunny clearing, well shielded from the road by trees.

"My retirement home," he said and stopped at the front entrance.

Chapter Sixteen

Saturday 23rd June 1945 – Galgenen - Austria

The chalet wasn't large; it looked like no more than two bedrooms to Archie; the ground floor was open plan, well furnished with large thick leather Chesterfield style sofas. Dark wood panelling and beams framing white walls Gave the interior a spacious old feel, even in a newly constructed building.

Dolf approached one wall panel and reached to the top of it, feeling for something which he clicked, making the panel swing open to reveal a small stairwell leading down.

"Archie, you may wish to go down first; there are weapons hidden behind the locked door. Rebecca, you may take your gun out behind me; I won't take offence."

They did as he invited them to and went down the narrow, well-lit stairs. The stairwell widened at the bottom, and a huge metal vault door led underneath the chalet.

Archie followed Dolf's complicated instructions on the two combination locks that unsealed the vault door and swung it open inwards. The bulkhead lights of an extensive cellar came on automatically, flickering into life by ones and twos.

The cellar was half the size of the chalet with a low ceiling and contained boxes of gold bars, some loose and still managing to glint in the lights, dusty as they were.

"Bloody hell," said Archie.

"Indeed," said Dolf.

"What else is here?" Rebecca asked.

"Here, there is only gold, silver and precious gems. No necklaces, no marking on the gold bars, no rings, no evidence of its provenance, nothing... traceable."

"How did you get all this, I mean so much, one man? You must be hiding it for others," Archie said.

"Or from others, only three people know of this place, and we are here. The men who acquired this wealth are all either dead or face execution for war crimes; the men who built this chalet are all dead."

"How dirty is this gold?"

"As dirty as the war that spawned it."

Archie and Rebecca were silent, contemplating their options; Dolf continued to explain.

"There are two other sites in Switzerland; both contain much traceable jewellery and artwork with some gold bars thrown in for authenticity. They're less secure than this, and the authorities will uncover them eventually. In fact, you might wish to do so, officially; it would reflect well on a man who did that; you could be that man."

"I like your thinking, Dolf; you know how to plan; you had this property built two years ago?"

"Three."

"And the people who think their plunder is safe in two other locations would naturally assume the Allies had recovered all of it. They'd know nothing about what was missing."

"Exactly so."

"If there were any discrepancies in the items recovered, they would assume the Allies had taken some for themselves, especially the untraceable stuff," Rebecca added.

"We're still thieves, though?" Archie mused.

"We are thieves who steal from other thieves," Dolf said, "many have profited from this war entirely without risk. Your country is bankrupt and will be in debt to American capitalists for a hundred years. You've profited from war, Archie, but you risked everything for that... look at what you've lost... a wife and a child... who has lost more? Tell me, what did you spend your profit on?"

"My men, the best weapons and equipment for them, increased salaries, pensions, doctors, funerals, black market food, and drink."

"And a dress shop in Holloway," said Rebecca.

"There are groups of people, Archie, influential people. I was once in that group by family name; I have left that group now and cannot go back. I am inconvenient. They still need me a little; they need what I've concealed for them. You're not in that group or any of them; in England, you call it the Establishment, but you'll never be in that. They tolerate you during war because they need you, and they can use you. In peace, you're also inconvenient, even more so than me, and they'll throw you away. If you're lucky, they'll ignore you. You told Von Braun to watch his back; you'll be watching your own, my friend."

"There's a phone upstairs?"

"Yes, of course."

"Let's have a cup of tea and start this now."

"Tea? We don't have tea; we have coffee, black."

"Coffee will be fine, my friend."

*

That evening, they finished their hotel meals hurriedly; the food was excellent, although its consumption was functional rather than pleasurable. They needed to replace the energy they'd expended that day and build up reserves for what lay ahead. The waiter collected the plates from their table, and they thanked him by nodding silently.

"I apologise, Archie and Rebecca," Dolf said, "for my mood over dinner; I can't relax in the absence of Annette. I know, having escaped once, I can't help her if I am captured again. It doesn't make me feel any better."

"We all miss others," Archie said, "let's go on the balcony and talk privately."

A slight chill in the fading sunlight ensured no guests sat near them. They sat at the table farthest from the restaurant doors, setting down their wine glasses.

Dolf spoke first.

"I'll tell you what I know, or at least what I think I know about Grigory. He calls himself Grigory Ivanovich Gagarin now, and that name is closer to his real ancestry. He is of the Rurik dynasty, I believe, a formerly noble house in Russia, rulers at one stage and that, in itself, is remarkable enough.

"How the fuck do you find all this stuff out?" said

Rebecca.

"I have sources in England and Russia, although there are fewer now than at the start of the war. We had access to a few secrets but mostly gossip, relationships, weaknesses and strengths. My godfather was Admiral Wilhelm Franz Canaris, chief of the Abwehr."

"A remarkably useful source; for a time anyway," said Archie.

"Yes indeed. The Nazis executed him in Flossenburg Concentration Camp; they hanged him on a meat hook, naked, only days before the war ended. He deserved better; a uniform and a bullet, at the least. I tried to help as I could; they should have used him to sue for peace with the British while we fought the Russians in the East. He was in contact with the English throughout the war, after all.

"The Gestapo came for me in Munich too, you know, after the bombing at the Wolfsschanze, for questioning, they said. There wasn't a shred of evidence they could have used against me, but that wouldn't have stopped them. My SS guards refused to let them even enter the building. There was a short struggle and some gunfire; my men were very ruthless and had seen what I'd done on the Swiss border. They were willing to die for me… my loyalty, as ever, was without question. Himmler told Gestapo Muller to call off his men, and I was clean again. Those men and boys would have died for me; they saved my life four times, maybe more; there is a debt now I must repay. Whatever debts they owe, whatever crimes they've committed, in who cares what name, I must repay that debt."

"Sorry, Dolf, please go on," Rebecca said.

"Many of the Ruriks left Russia and settled in England, Germany and Italy. They had money and good blood, so they married well and acquired new land and titles. Some claim Italian, Roman ancestry and links to the Vatican.

"Tudor was born Lazar Peezditovich but also used the name Gagarin. His father was known as a fantasist, thought himself a great man and raised Lazar to share that trait. He fancied himself a king or emperor when in fact, his one strength was to masquerade as a communist while hiding his own wealth and stealing all he could from the Kulaks. At the same time, he sent Lazar to England to ensure his safety and that of his lineage. As you know, Lazar became Tudor and prospered."

Dolf paused for a moment, took a sip of wine and then continued.

"The younger son, Grigory, remained in Russia and rose to become one of the few closest aides to Stalin. He is perhaps one step below him; it's possible he's one of maybe ten who could succeed Stalin in the next decade or so. He's ruthless and has immense power; he will use any means to rise to the highest level. He was with Beria's secret police for a while, proving his commitment to the party. He still prefers to leave the dirty work to his inferiors; that may be his weakness. He was never a brave man. It's known that Grigory has often thought his brother and father to be decadent and dreamers prone to self deception. While such may be true, Grigory has delusions of grandeur and is prone to flattery, surrounding himself with sycophants and those under his thrall. Part of Tudor's charade was to provide intelligence to his brother in Moscow before and during the war. He must, therefore, avenge him and strike at you or, more likely, both of us to avoid losing face."

Dolf paused again for longer this time.

"Now, my friend Archie. I can tell you only what I know from these sources. Some of this is fact, yes. What can I say about mysticism, reincarnations, dreams, fantasies, wishes, meaningful coincidence, acausal synchronicity, perhaps fate or simple good fortune? I can say nothing of such with any certainty at all. This I can say, and I know it. He'll be too strong for us in the future; he may come for us at any time, but he will come. In ten years, though, he may come for our countries as well. We have to take him now while he's weaker and still angry."

"The trap will have to be the best ever then; he'll be expecting it," Archie said.

"It's easy," Dolf said. "We don't have to believe it, he does, and he'll want to."

*

Monday 2nd July 1945 – Moscow

A week later, Grigory Gagarin received a handwritten letter by special diplomatic courier from the British Embassy in Moscow.

Archie's SOE identification had gained him entry to see the British Charge D'Affaires in Zurich. He still needed to use Churchill's letter to persuade him to allow the use of his diplomatic bag for that purpose.

'Whatever this man does, he does in my name. Winston Spencer Churchill.'

Grigory sniffed his letter tentatively, then asked one of his secretaries to come in, not his favourite, a plain, old one. He handed her the letter and asked her to go into his private toilet, shut the door, then open the envelope.

She returned, saying, "It's only a letter, tovarisch."

"Sniff the paper," he said, repeating himself when she hesitated, "sniff the fucking paper, suka… good, now lick the paper and stand there for five minutes."

I shall have her killed for that, he thought after she laid the letter on his desk and left. It was in perfect Russian script and language.

Gnaeus Pompeius Magnus, Consul of the Roman Republic,
We write to you as old friends and colleagues.

We regret the death of your brother greatly; he was rash and chose to attack us. His defeat was a simple matter, and we know of his delusion that he was Pompeius.

We recognise you as the sole inheritor of the great mind and come to you with a proposal for a second true Triumvirate, confident that you have the ability to make it so.

We propose a meeting in neutral Switzerland as would be fitting, but as a token of goodwill, we agree to meet in a neutral place of your choosing.

The petty squabbling by our inferiors on spheres of influence is foolish. We three know the spoils of war should go to the fittest.

We, therefore, propose that the second True Triumvirate divides the world into three zones. England, the Americas and the Anzac countries for the Julii. The rest of Western Europe and Africa shall go to Crassus, you shall have the remainder of the world, including the Arabian countries, the Indies, and Japan. Although we favour the annihilation of the population of the latter.

You will be aware of our access to the known and secret weapons of Germany, England and America. We have a short time within which to accept the hand of fate that offers us a unique opportunity to realise the power that is our due.

As a further token of our goodwill towards our esteemed colleague, we have obtained for you the girl you know as Ariadne Leshchyov. She is older and will not disappoint you; she remains intact and should have been yours many years ago. She has written this letter, and we will deliver her to you when we meet.

Yours in eternity
Gaius Julius Caesar and Marcus Licinius Crassus
Consuls of the Roman Republic'

Grigory felt elation, he knew he was better than his decadent brother, and this was his proof. It increased his ability to succeed Stalin within ten years, but this prize was great and immediate; therefore, he would enjoy it longer. Yes, he would enjoy Ariadna, too, the thought excited him, and he felt an erection growing.

He pressed the button on his intercom and asked for the youngest prettiest secretary, Raisa, to come into his office.

He grabbed her hair as soon as he shut the door behind her, dragging her roughly into his toilet.

"Na kalenu, suka," he said and fucked her mouth until he came, smearing his semen on her face with his cock as he did so.

Fucking peasants, he hated them almost as much as the Communist Party. He knew he came from a regal heritage; they'd ruled until 1598 when the Romanov upstarts succeeded them. The Romanovs were a weak-willed and weak blooded line; they deserved their fate. Their demise pleased his family, who saw communism as an opportunity to profit and rise again. Grigory had done it.

Grigory wasn't stupid, though, he wouldn't meet them in Switzerland, but he had to give them enough rope. He would meet them in Austria, Holzschlag, an isolated place near the Czech, German border. He could easily bring enough good party men with him to deal with any threat and still have a division at his disposal in nearby Czechoslovakia.

He didn't expect the negotiations would take too long.

*

Friday 6th July 1945 – Munich

Archie sent for the whole operational team, plus Mary Murphy and Aria, the morning after the dinner with Dolf. They flew into Munich, Dolf still had the civilian contacts to get things done post haste there, and Archie's legitimate status secured the right papers.

His team was extremely well armed for a country where the war had officially ended. They could explain that by citing continuing incidents within the civilian population and pockets of resistance by fanatics, usually former SS men who had nothing to lose. Well-armed English troops arriving didn't look out of place in any way.

Dolf had explained the 'Werwolf' plan to Archie and Rebecca. The Nazis intended them to act as a loosely organised underground resistance to the Allies before and after Germany's inevitable defeat.

'Der Wehrwolf' was a German novel about a peasant called Harm Wulf whose family were killed by soldiers of an invading army. He organised a resistance group that hunted the invaders down, killing them without pity. In the end, the peasants come to realise they enjoyed the killing as much as the soldiers they fought.

"Sound like anyone we know?" Rebecca had said to Archie.

"So, do you think we could use any of them?" Dolf asked.

"Yes, we certainly could," Archie had mumbled, lost in thought.

Archie welcomed each man and woman off the Dakota transport aircraft. He needed to use them one last time, just one last time, he promised himself and hoped it wasn't a lie.

He took Mary Murphy aside.

"Archie, I'm happy to be here, but what do you need me for?" she said.

"Mary, you are here specifically to stop Aria from doing anything reckless and dangerous," he said.

"Couldn't Rebecca do tha... oh, sorry Archie, that's possibly the most stupid thing I've ever said or even thought."

"Correct, and thank you, Mary," he smiled.

Archie gathered the team on the tarmac next to the Dakota.

"Listen up everybody, Rebecca, stay here with Dolf and brief the team; I'm off to see George Patton. Dolf's in charge."

"Okay," she said with only a slight hesitation.

"You can't put me in charge; that's crazy," Dolf said.

"Since when have we been sane?" Archie replied and left.

"There's no point arguing, Dolf," Rebecca concluded.

The team looked bemused, and Billy walked up to Dolf, looking him up and down but with a measure of respect.

"You must be this Dolf then?" he said.

"Yes, you must be Billy, his father?"

"Are you a good man, Dolf?" Billy asked.

"Fucking hell. No! I'm an evil bastard."

"Honest and evil, I like that in a man. I'll follow you. Let's kill some fucking Russians."

The whole team knew this operation followed from all they'd seen and heard about the murder of Aria's father, an SOE man. Then the bomb at SOE and the subsequent attack on the Manor by a rogue MI6 man with proven Russian connections.

Who knew how many other deaths that spy was responsible for, thousands perhaps? They knew they'd only partly answered that crime. If this meant taking on some of the people behind that, they were content and eager to do it.

"The best way to avoid revenge is to go first," Billy had said on the plane, "we can sit and wait for trouble; this ain't the time for that."

*

Saturday 7th July 1945 – Munich

"Couldn't be better," said Dolf when he saw Grigory's proposal, "he has to be close enough to his army so they can take care of him, but he doesn't want too many Russian witnesses for his power grab. He'll bring only his own men if he can, the cover story, at least half true, will be that he's coming for me and my gold. He might try and capture us to find out where the gold is, but I don't think so. He's coming to kill us, that's all. He needs to be Pompey more than he needs the money, he needs Caesar and Crassus to be dead, and he needs revenge for his brother."

"And he's rushing because he wants Aria," said Rebecca.

"If he can. It's always been the same; men only want money and power because they get more sex. Caesar fathered many bastards, you know," added Dolf.

"I may be one of them. What's your bloodline like?" said Archie.

"Pure, of course… pure bastard," laughed Dolf.

*

Sunday 8th July 1945 – Austria

Dolf then made his own way to Northern Austria, using the genuinely issued British Army identity papers Archie had given him.

Two turnings off the main road, he found the road he

needed, a small stone and shingle track well away from the main road near Habernau. The area was heavily wooded and mountainous; tall, strong pines gave excellent cover all year. He left his car in the turning space for forestry vehicles at the end of the single track road. He watched and listened for thirty minutes, then walked along the footpath that went further into the forest, no more than one footstep wide. After one mile, he stopped and checked around him; he was lucky so far; he was the one man alive who could walk that path unopposed.

After ensuring he was alone, he stepped aside from the path, careful to bend but not break any foliage; he began to climb the slope. There was no track to follow other than to ascend. After half a mile, he reached the line of the small animal trail that led further upwards, towards, but not to the summit. He stopped every so often and looked around, showing his face clearly to anyone watching him, he hoped. Who could know what they would think of him now?

"Halt!" came the shout from behind him. He'd seen nothing. He'd trained the men well, and they were already the best.

He smiled and raised his hands.

"That sounds like young Matthias?" he said.

"It is, Oberst."

"And Otto."

"Friedrich too."

The familiar voices came from the undergrowth. He still couldn't see anyone.

"We had to make sure you weren't followed," Matthias said, stepping out from behind a tree.

"Good, good and how are you?"

"We are bored, Oberst, but with full bellies, thanks to you."

"Perhaps, you can get me some coffee then; I gave you the best, you know."

Dolf hadn't liked these boys and men when he'd first encountered them; he hadn't trusted them. He was ashamed of that now; they were what Germany had made them, as was he.

*

"Where's he gone then?" said Billy to Rebecca.
"He won't say, he'll be back, and he's on our side."
"Ours or his own?"
"It's the same thing, I think."

*

Major Oskar Alber sat in his private quarters, the best his unit and present purpose could provide for him. He had his bed, a wooden pallet with a straw mattress, a table, and a chair. His privacy relied on a blanket draped across a rope that hung from one corner of the cave he called home.

He was content, he had his purpose, a noble one, and he had patience. Not all his men had shared his goal, but the best of them had. It was an inevitable fact; the black uniform gave no quarter and received none; he'd always known that. Others found out later, with a bullet in the head following surrender. He shared the guilt of that crime; he'd told his men to feign submission before attacking their softer American and English opponents.

Every man in his group of fifty had suffered a relative murdered by Allied bombs on their unprotected homes. A home destroyed, a parent, a sister or a child killed by bombing. How many the Russians had raped and killed, he couldn't even guess. Some Americans and English had done the same, although he knew they weren't as bad as the Russians. As the Wehrmacht weren't as bad as the SS.

Oskar took pride in his deeds; if you were going to be bad, you might as well be the worst. The Russians were Untermensch; they were lower than men, they were animals, and he would put them down, insects to be trodden underfoot without thought.

When he struck, he would strike east. He planned to take his revenge later when it would be better. When the allies were less cautious, it would be easier and more deadly and then, after time, however long it took, the Fourth Reich. Oskar Alber and his men were not defeated yet.

Dolf had equipped them well with the best weapons and ammunition, vehicles, fuel, and generators. The tunnels were carefully built and finished a full year before the war ended. The slave labourers that had built them were long dead. They even had one Koenig Panzer in another cave, with ammunition and fuel. One Koenig would take out ten Shermans, more if they weren't expecting it. It would be a glorious way to die.

Von Rundstedt had played his part; he hadn't been ready for suicide, such was his nature, decadent. He felt no ill towards him. He knew Dolf had to flee; he was a dead man, whoever caught him. Oskar had nowhere better to go to, and only a poor family, father, and mother left in Germany; he had his men and no other purpose. Von Rundstedt had promised to provide for his parents, and he kept his promises, always.

Dolf had ensured his small group had two years' supply of food and other provisions.

"Be patient," he'd said, "you'll be more effective."

He'd provided books for the men, a whole library, and films. That didn't occur to Oskar, and the men had needed them badly. The old films raised their spirits each night, the same ones, again and again; they'd only been there for three months. 'Die Dreigroscheneper' was still their favourite. Oskar saw himself as Mackie Messer, even he enjoyed it.

There was a bond between his men that would never be broken unless by death. There was nobility and heroism in that; that was Oskar's purpose.

In surprise, he automatically saluted Dolf when he entered from behind the curtain. Dolf returned the salute and said…

"No, Oskar, you're the officer now, not me. I've forfeited that right; these are your men now; they belong to you. You'll decide their fate."

*
Sunday 8th July 1945 – Moscow

Grigory took the greatest risk of his life by speaking to

Stalin personally about his proposal.

He explained what he might gain, the Nazi hoards that Stalin already knew about, and the real reason the Russians wanted Dolf when he was a prisoner of the Americans.

Stalin was aware of Travers and the murder of his foremost agent in England. He suspected Travers's involvement in the discovery of his spy network in the Manhatten project. Travers had no clue about his spy network in Germany; he was one man with some intuition and luck; he had no network and few friends; he was nobody.

Grigory wanted vengeance for his brother; Stalin understood that, and Grigory was greedy; he understood that too. There was a risk, and Grigory was taking it. If it failed, he could blame, disown or shoot him. Stalin put his own man with him to ensure propriety was observed and that the results of any greed found their way to him.

He also agreed to provide a full division on the Czech border, but not beyond it, except on his direct orders.

He also gave him one hundred German prisoners of war, those in better condition, which meant still alive and no more. Their fresh corpses would explain any Russian army presence, following an escape intent on terrorism, Werwolfs.

Chapter Seventeen

Wednesday 18th July 1945 – Austria - Holzchlag – Hochficht Ski Cafe

On the morning of Wednesday the 18th of July 1945, sixteen Chosen Men and women, all wearing armour, took up positions in the front of the empty Hochficht ski café near the tiny hamlet of Holzschlag in Austria. It was a large rectangular, one storey building with a thick sloping flat roof over tall, twenty-foot windows and massive wooden beams. Its rear sat tightly against the mountain behind it. The main cafe area was wide and long, running the building's full length, as did the counter and bar to the rear.

They took up six good lines of fire, by thick oaken pillars, through doors and windows, facing a hundred yards of open space for parking outside. The six Bren Guns they'd brought would provide a healthy rate and angle of fire. Billy Perry picked the spots and directed the men to them, organising dark wooden benches and tables for cover.

Archie climbed a small maintenance ladder to the left side of the cafe and sat, squeezed, high in the rafters. He carefully sorted out a good sniping position for later by smashing the tile cladding that ran between the roof and the wall of the front. From his high position, he saw Dolf entering the main café floor from the eastern side of the building, followed by about fifty men. They were dressed head to toe in American camouflage gear with GI rifles over their shoulders. They looked like men who'd come a long way on foot; some carried heavy bags over their shoulders, some brought larger bags, one between two.

Billy watched them too; they didn't say a word, looked around, occupied positions allocated to them by their commander and waited, as poised and alert as any man Billy had ever seen.

Dolf spoke softly to the commander and laughed.

"Billy Perry, he says you've taken all the best positions," the officer nodded at Billy but didn't smile or speak, "it's a compliment."

Billy nodded back; to his eyes, all these men looked familiar. They looked like those he'd seen in the sights of his machine gun in the first War, they looked like men already dead, and they all looked German.

Nobody said a word when each of the camouflaged GIs discarded their outer clothing to steadily reveal their black and silver braided SS uniforms, all in excellent condition. All were clean shaven, in their best, ready for inspection, not even a dirty fingernail as far as Billy could see.

They opened their bags to show their helmets and real armaments, Mauser rifles, MP40 Schmeissers and brand new MG42 machine guns, even deadlier than the 34. A few of them had a lighter version of the Sturmgewehr 44 Assault Rifle; Billy hadn't even heard of that. This Dolf made sure his men had the best like Archie had.

Billy waited; this was always the worst part, time to think, better to be busy.

Billy looked at his other Mary, Mary Murphy, making sure she was at the rear with Aria.

His first Mary's death had broken him apart; what on earth was he to do with the baby and earn a living at the same time. One of the porters in the hospital offered to have the girl adopted for him, legitimate he promised and offered him money. Billy broke his cheekbone with one good punch.

His old boss Nat Cairney came up with a surprising proposition, offering him new employment to suit his new abilities. The money was suspiciously good, and Nat promised he'd have Grace looked after by his youngest daughter whenever Billy was busy. Nat wasn't an honest man, but he kept his promises. Billy kept some of them for him as well, promises made to enemies as well as friends. After the hundreds of lives he'd taken in the trenches, a threat, slap, punch or the occasional knifing was effortless.

So Billy did what Nat asked of him, and Grace was safe

and happy. Nat sorted Billy out with the Savoy job when Billy asked to retire from the sharp end of his work. Nat always looked after his mates.

So Billy became a runner again, quietly, calmly and profitably, and Grace became an angel like his Mary.

Mary Murphy was part Angel, part Rebecca, and part Una. Billy wished he was twenty years younger and a different Billy; he might have done something with that knowledge and those feelings.

*

Grigory Gagarin sat in his staff car on the Czech-Austrian border a few miles from his destination. He had a full division of men allocated to him, with armoured support. Stalin ordered him to leave the armour and ninety per cent of his men behind the Czech border; he wasn't ready for another war, not yet.

Grigory already knew the identity of the man Stalin had assigned to spy on him, Sergei Rogotov, one of his own plants in Stalin's team. That presented him with no immediate problems, but they'd still have to play it carefully. They knew someone else would also be watching Rogotov; that was Stalin's way.

Arslav Voloshin watched Comrades Gagarin and Rogotov disobey their orders and decided not to follow them. They were taking four tanks with them, captured German Tigers, still with their original markings, and four hundred men in trucks. This was no meeting of friends, nor was it strength in the event of an ambush; it was nothing less than an attack. He could see Gagarin was cunning, and he might seek an alliance with him later. If his attack succeeded, he'd have something to report or to ally with; if it failed, he had a good tale to tell already. Voloshin waited and watched.

Grigory arranged for a Yakolev light aircraft to reconnoitre the area for several days, and he had scouts planted in the woods. All they reported were two ordinary trucks and less than twenty men. He'd ensure he was too big for any trap they were trying to lay. No bases or concentrations of troops were anywhere nearby. His four tanks would overcome any possible resistance and provide a good scapegoat if necessary. Werwolf activity justified pursuit and murder.

The men he'd chosen to bring with him were enough.

*

When Archie saw and heard the first vehicle approaching from a distance, he took Dolf and Aria, wearing Una's armour and stood in the gravel car park of the ski cafe.

They were in the middle of densely wooded mountain slopes; fir trees surrounded them apart from two long high ski runs that converged on the large cafe and its parking area. It was empty. At this time of year, there was no snow and no reason to be there.

There were about twenty separate ways into the area, roads, tracks, paths and forestry clearings. No place for a trap at all. The cafe was built against the side of a mountain with no rear exit; now that looked like a trap for Archie and Dolf, they hoped Gagarin agreed.

It was only barely inside Austria, a few miles from Germany and the same from Czechoslovakia, an area where borders, physical and mental, became confused.

"Are you sure this will work?" Dolf asked.

"No. We have to make him think he can trap us. So the only way is to set no traps for him."

In truth, Archie had many plans, none worth the name; he was making it up as he went. Armed men were in place, his men wearing their armour, and the man who thought he was Pompey had to die; it was simple.

A Russian staff car drew up the main road from the east, their right, followed by a pair of trucks. The Russian trucks parked at the far end of the gravel a hundred yards from them. The car came fifty yards closer and then stopped. No one got out.

"He's making sure it's us; he knows the rules of parley," said Dolf, "take your hat off so he can see you properly."

"Shall I get my tits out for the bastard?" Aria said.

"No. Well, not yet… shit!"

The car reversed at flat out speed, the two trucks unloaded their men, about forty of them, and they took cover; ten other trucks pulled into view, parked, and their men leapt out.

"I think he saw me properly," said Archie, grabbing Aria's hand and heading for cover.

They heard the distant crump of mortars firing.

"He's certainly falling for it," said Dolf as they ran to the cafe.

Archie handed Aria to Mary and ordered them to the rear, behind a Tarrian.

The mortars took a few minutes to find their range, but the specially designed roof of the building could hold a heavy layer of snow for months and withstand avalanches. They did no damage other than two windows cracked by stones flung up by the explosions.

Then, as the mortars were still falling on the car park, the Russian infantry ran headlong straight at the café.

Billy Perry had seen that before, long ago. The Bren Guns did their job well enough; in truth, they weren't needed. The accuracy and rate of fire of the short staccato bursts from the MG42s cut them down as they ran and finished them off as they lay bleeding. The Bren guns enhanced the already murderous rate of fire by fifty per cent. There were no blind spots, no lucky runners, and no cover other than a dead man's body.

He doesn't know what he's doing, he thought; they're not his men, Jesus, they're not even men. Whatever they were, about a hundred and fifty of them lay scattered, lifeless in the car park. German Mausers tracked across the killing ground, looking for any sign of movement and when they saw it, ensuring it stopped, dead.

Billy had taken a few out with his rifle, concentrating on single men behind the melee. They might be officers, or maybe a Commissar ensuring his cannon fodder knew their place.

"Der alte Mann ist sehr gut," said one older German.

"Jah, hast du die schildmaid se?"
"Sie weiss, das seine Waffe."
"und ein messer."
"Mackie Messer."

"They say you're good, old man," said a young man, impossibly blond and handsome, tall and athletic.

"I know what he said, and so does she," said Billy indicating Rebecca, who nodded at him.

"Ich habe immer noch das messer," she said and tapped her belt.

The Germans nearby all laughed. She did still have that knife.

"Achtung Panzer!"

The shout from Oskar broke the reverie.

They all heard the rumbling of engines and the clanking of tracks.

"One of ours, Billy, a Tiger, I think. Filthy Russian scum," said Oskar.

"Everybody down, let them get close enough," Oskar shouted as two of the Germans pulled Panzerfausts from a bag, taking up positions on the extreme right and left of the cafe area. Most other Germans were already moving back to better cover.

The first tank came into view from the far right end of the car park; it was an old model Tiger. It advanced ponderously towards the café, men tightly packed behind it as they crouched and moved cautiously forward over the bodies of their former comrades. The individual meant nothing; the state and the party were everything.

At precisely fifty metres distance from the cafe, two Panzerfaust projectiles launched from the right and left. Both shots pierced the weaker side armour of the Tiger. Those shots killed at least one of the three men inside then the whole tank exploded in a broken sphere of bright flame. The notoriously leaky fuel system of the Tiger Tank helped the Germans this time.

Two MG42s remained in place and fired at the Russians leaving the shelter of the flaming tank, dying in a volley of bullets instead. Another twenty or so gone.

*

Grigory looked at the scene in front of him carefully, but not well, from his position behind his car and two large pine trees. He couldn't see well enough to direct the fight effectively. He knew he had more men and tanks, so what more did he need to see. He'd send them in fast, all at once, a blitzkrieg, he thought.

He called over his two commanders.

"I want all the tanks at once, keep a safe distance and pound the building. Get all the men, including the mortar men and scouts, behind the tanks, then move in close; no one is to get away alive, no one. Do you understand?"

His two commanders understood very well. He didn't know what he was doing, and they knew if they disobeyed, they were dead, and two others would take their place.

*

Archie was now crouched on a rafter well above the cafe floor; he'd hammered a good sized hole through which to aim his Mauser. Dolf was acting as Spud, this time, scanning the scene through his binoculars, searching for Grigory, Pompey; he'd know when he saw him.

Above the melee of bodies, smoke, flame and blood forming in front of him, Archie could see the staff car parked far behind the action.

"He'll be in the trees, behind the car somewhere; he'll be in civilian clothes in case he needs to run, I know it," said Dolf.

"I can see him, but there's…."

His silence showed he'd found a target, and he calmly centred on it. The mantra began; firm position for the barrel, push the barrel down, still firm, butt to the shoulder, cheek in the rest. Firm and comfortable, take aim, deep breath, let it go slowly, deep breath and hold it, this time, aiming, aiming for the biggest part of the target, torso, squeeze, shit, got him. Breathe again.

"He's down but moving; there's a leg to the left of the tree behind the car," Dolf shouted above the noise of battle and approaching tanks.

*

The three other Tiger tanks pulled into view and drew up three abreast at the far end of the car park, beginning to fire sluggishly and inaccurately at the cafe.

"They're staying well out of range," Billy said. "We'll have to…" One high explosive shell hit the front of the building, scattering SS and Chosen Men alike. Another single shell thudded into a pillar, armour piercing, not explosive; it did no damage. Another went overhead, and another smashed into the middle of their number but didn't explode. The badly trained Russians couldn't tell the difference between armour piercing and high explosive shells. Too many to count still lay on the floor of the cafe.

*

Archie looked at a grey trouser leg and shoe; the rest of the person was unseen behind two trees. He finished his mantra and fired; his view was good enough to see a spurt of blood from a broken shin. He almost felt the pain himself.

"You got him, quickly, downstairs," said Dolf.

*

More explosions rocked the building, and the aim was still terrible. The Russians were using badly trained men in an unfamiliar tank.

"Get back, get back, behind the bar, into the kitchen, there's a cellar. Mary, get Aria back," Archie shouted.

George was still firing a Bren gun. Archie shouted again, then, even as the words left his mouth, he watched the young blond man taking off his helmet and most of his kit. He strapped a satchel charge to his back, picked up two stick grenades, one in each hand, then positioned himself ten paces behind one large window. Most of the glass was already missing, and two others took up positions to its right and left, aiming their Schmeissers at the frame.

The man took up a starting position, like an athlete about to do a high jump, swinging his arms and legs backwards and forwards.

He looked towards Billy and said, "I'll see you in hell, Billy Perry," and smiled. "Now!" he shouted.

The two machine guns ripped the rest of the window frame and glass away. He bounded towards it, leaping head first through it and somersaulting on the ground outside before bouncing seamlessly upwards into an instant sprint.

Then two others with fresh full clips in their guns jumped through the window after him, running alongside him, continuing to fire to either side, trying to keep Russian heads low.

The man leapt over dead Russian bodies and was at the first tank in less than ten seconds for the seventy-five yards distance.

Billy watched, fascinated, as the man leapt up to grab the barrel of the Tiger's 88mm gun and ram a stick grenade down it before leaping off to his left towards his next target.

The barrel of the first tank blew out smoke which signalled a small internal explosion; no real damage to the vehicle but the gun barrel would never fire again.

The man paid no attention to the smoke behind him, taking three long strides towards the next tank, where he tried to repeat his act. He leapt onto the second gun barrel for only a moment before a spray of machine gun bullets from behind the tank ripped into his legs. He used that moment, his last, to stuff his other stick grenade into the tank's gun barrel. Then he fell onto the gravel in a crumpled, ungainly heap that bore no relation to the grace, poise, and beauty he'd possessed in life.

The two other Germans avenged him by concentrating their final bursts on those who'd killed him, then they fell quickly too.

"Bloody hell," said Billy, "I don't suppose there's one more like that in the world, never mind this caff."

"Fucking Hell, Billy," said Rebecca, grabbing his arm and pulling him back.

The one remaining fully working tank continued firing

slowly at the café front. The two others kept firing their heavy machine guns at the café.

"Back, back behind the counter and into the kitchens," Archie shouted again.

"We have to rush them, take them on," said Oskar.

"No, we all stay inside here, no one else outside, in the back now!"

Even Oskar quailed at the force of the order from Archie and signalled his men back.

"We'll die later if we hide. We shall be more shamed, that's all," Oskar said, but he went back with his men.

"Who did we lose?" asked Archie

"Brad and Baldr, sorry, Archie," said Billy

"And Mickey, sorry, Boss," said Doc and went straight to see to the wounds of the Germans.

Archie counted at least ten in black, silver and now red on the floor. How many was he going to kill this time? After their war was over, they were still fighting his. This better be worth it. This better work!

He heard the drone of approaching aircraft coming from the west.

"Come on, get down," Archie said.

"This better be the cavalry," said Dolf

"And not the 7th," said Billy.

*

A full squadron of twelve P47 Mustang Fighter Bombers flew over the site, and Archie could hear some ill-advised gunfire directed upwards by the Russians.

He stayed at the rear of the cafe, ready to duck but watched them return in three waves of four, firing rockets at all four tanks, regardless of their state. The next three waves machine gunned the line of trucks jammed fast in the thin road between the trees, and another final three waves emptied their machine guns into whatever remained.

Archie shouted as he'd never done before, rapidly snapping out the words with all the command he could muster.

"Okay, everyone out now. Dolf, get your men to sit down outside and lower their weapons; they can keep them, but keep them lowered, please, Oskar. We can all get out of this. Asgeir, finish off anything still alive out there; the Chosen should do it; these others have done enough. Finish off any Russian wounded without exception, my direct order, Nulla vita data. Sine Missione. Billy, you make sure we don't kill one another."

"Oskar, no more, no more," Dolf shouted, then added a softer, "please."

Archie went out to the front of the building.

"James, Dolf, with me, we need to hunt someone. Rebecca, stay here with Mary and Aria; that's a direct order, promise me."

"Yes," she said and followed him anyway as soon as he turned his back.

Asgeir led his remaining men outside.

"From a distance, don't look at the faces; you know the drill, it was them or us, and it's not us. Not today."

*

As Archie looked in search of Grigory, Billy walked towards the spot where he saw the young blond lad die.

He looked down at his ruined legs; at least he'd bled to death almost immediately; there was fresh blood everywhere. Billy had never touched a dead German; he picked him up carefully, regardless of the mess, and carried him back to where the SS men had arranged themselves neatly in three rows. He laid the body down, arranging the limbs as best he could. Oskar came beside Billy and dressed the young man in his uniform jacket.

"He would wish to wear it," he said. "His name was Matthias Frey; he was the younger brother of Konrad Frey, who won two gold medals for gymnastics in 1936. Matthias was only twelve then. He was better than his brother, some said; we'll never know."

"Well, I've never seen better than I saw today," said Billy

"He sets an example for others to follow," Oskar said.

"There's been enough today; look around us, man."
"No, there must be room for one more small sacrifice."

*

Archie, Dolf, and James jogged, single minded and cautiously towards where he'd last seen the bloody leg. Hundreds of bodies lay around them, those who'd run recklessly, headlong towards the café, behind the Tigers, in the trees, bodies torn apart by thick shards of pine tree rather than gunfire. Archie saw a line of shattered and burning trucks leading down the pale gravel track to his right and the east. All torn apart by the P47s, like the photographs he'd seen of the Germans fleeing the Falaise pocket in Normandy. Like the trucks of his own company, he'd seen ambushed on the way to Calais a hundred years and another lifetime ago.

'Don't even think about it; that was someone else, not me.'

They reached a bloody patch of earth and pine needles where they expected it to be, and James led Archie and Dolf onwards watchfully.

"He's making a trail with both feet and both hands," said James, "I don't think he's armed; he might have a pistol in his pocket or a rifle over his shoulder."

"He's running like a hen before a fox; he was ever an ignavus," said Dolf, and they moved on into the forest.

"He's not moving fast; we can afford to be slow and careful," said James, "and he is alone."

"No man worth the name would flee with that worm," Dolf added with the vehemence of a man who had once admired his ancestor.

While they moved on, an uneasy standoff took place between the SS men, the Chosen Men and a large number of American troops. American troops who'd arrived in too timely and organised a manner to be a coincidence. The Americans held off at some distance, about fifty yards, no one advanced, and no one drew back a single step.

Asgeir went forward to the GIs and walked confidently towards the man he knew was General George Patton.

"Good morning, sir," he said in a tone he hoped would make Archie proud. "As you can see, we've encountered some unexpected enemy terrorist activity; the fighting has been fierce and without quarter. A truce holds now, and when Major Travers returns, we hope to achieve a settlement which will be… honourable to all and can end this…."

Asgeir choked on the last few words, his mouth suddenly aware of how dry it was.

"Get this man some water, somebody," Patton shouted, "Jeez, there's been a hell of a fight here, son."

"Twenty minutes, sir," said Asgeir, "that's all it was, twenty minutes, by all the old Gods; I hope it's over now."

The remaining Chosen Men stood between the two groups of Americans and Germans. As time passed, men on both sides relaxed, sitting down on their haunches, smoking and drinking water. Billy sat down with the Germans, conversing in pigeon German and English.

Billy noticed, for all the superficial relaxation, those SS men at the front kept their weapons close to hand and watched. After a while, they swapped places with those behind them, had a drink of water and a smoke before taking another step back. They then checked their weapons before returning to the front rank, weapons close.

He'd never seen anything so impressive in his life; there were a few older men there; most were only in their early twenties and must have been teenagers when the war started.

He had no doubt each of these men would take down half a dozen Americans before they fell, and he wasn't sure which side he would take if any shooting started. Jesus Christ, these boys were good at what they did.

He saw Begley; the insane fool had found some bottles of beer in the basement of the café bar. He was carrying a crate around with Henry Flowers, dishing them out, starting with the Germans!

This is definitely not an ordinary day, he thought as he

accepted a bottle; it was icy cold and strong, Staropramen Lezak, the label said. He'd never tasted better, never would.

Mary Murphy walked towards him; Aria was safe with George now. He offered her some of his beer, and she accepted it without wiping its top.

*

James led Archie and Dolf through the trees following Grigory, a footstep here, a broken twig there, a smear or drop of blood.

"He always runs in the end, always," said Dolf, "he runs, and he loses. Caesar never ran; he made fools of his enemies and killed them later, remember the pirates? He killed every one of them and even made them ask for more ransom when they undervalued him."

"He's slowing down, stopping and staggering; we're close, be careful," James whispered.

James raised one hand to halt them, then signalled Archie to go straight on and Dolf to go left. James went right, and they crept forward to the smallest of clearings in the thickly grouped pines.

Pompey sat limply, facing them, back up against a tree, with blood still leaking freshly from a shoulder wound above the heart. A leg wound also showed at the bottom of his left trouser leg. He was weaponless but held something small between the index finger and thumb of his right hand.

"You'll not take me alive," he said weakly between shallow breaths.

"We never wanted to, you daft cunt," said Archie pointing his Mauser at him from the waist. Dolf stood to his left with a Schmeisser and James to his right with a Thompson; all three stood ready with weapons aimed at the man before them.

"I will return, I will have my time again, I will seek you, for all time," he spat towards them, and the phlegm barely left his mouth, stuck to his lower lip and hung swinging slightly from his chins. He pushed a small glass capsule into his mouth and bit into it. His face contorted, one last breath rasped from his lips, and his head sagged down onto his fat chin and breast, the life draining out of him instantly.

"No, don't touch him; wait, listen, think, close your eyes," Dolf said insistently, "feel it."

"Nothing," said Archie after about thirty seconds, "you?"

"Nothing."

"James?"

"What?" said James.

"What did you feel?"

"... I felt the man's spirit leave his body, it reached for me... my spirit refused it... and it was gone."

"It was too easy," Dolf said.

"That! That was too easy? There're a few hundred fucking bodies back there."

"A few hundred is not a big number Archie; six million is a big number. You were always too good for him, but he was better than this; this piece of dung never led an army, never would. There's something we've missed."

Rebecca came from the trees behind them.

"I felt nothing," she said.

"You followed me?" said Archie.

"Of course I did, you idiot."

Chapter Eighteen

Wednesday 18th July 1945 – Austria - Holzschlag – Ski Café

Half an hour later, Archie and Dolf left the woodland carrying Grigory's body between them and dumped it next to the other dead Russians.

Aria walked over to where he was; George still watching her back, she spat on the corpse.

"That's him," she said.

Rebecca gave the corpse a quick and fierce kick in the balls.

"One last time," she said.

Archie smiled.

"That's my girl," he said.

Some of the Germans smiled and snickered at that too.

"A pity she's not German," one said, and some laughed.

Archie and Dolf walked towards the Americans and Patton.

"Major Travers, how the hell are you?" asked General George Patton.

"Never better, sir," said Archie.

"The intelligence on residual German activity in this area was correct then."

"Many dressed in Russian uniforms and using their equipment too. We'll need to dispose of the bodies and damaged equipment to ensure no misunderstandings among allies. There's an ideal spot nearby, and you've brought some recovery vehicles."

"And some in full uniform, too, SS?"

"I've never seen better men in action; I'd take every last one of them in my team tomorrow, so would you."

"I know that. Just don't let any of my boys hear you say it. You haven't seen any GI equipment around, have you?"

"Yes, my men borrowed it, thank you, it's in what's left of the cafe. These German gentlemen here have been outside radio contact for several weeks and had no idea whatsoever the war was over; I imagine they'd quite like to surrender, sir."

"Their commander wishes to speak to you, General," said Dolf, "I am already Major Travers's prisoner."

Oskar put his pistol back in the holster, clipped the button firmly and walked towards General Patton open handed.

"General Patton," he said and saluted, non-Nazi style; Patton returned the American salute.

"I find it an unexpected pleasure to meet you; Montgomery or Bradley would be less honourable. Yielding to you, the best is not the fate of mean men. My men and I have committed harsh acts that you would call crimes; who can say they have not. My name is Major Oskar Alber; I am the commander of these men; all they have done has been because I have ordered it. The guilt is mine and mine alone. If I surrender to you, will you give me your word that only I will face punishment for those crimes? My life is yours and mine to give you."

"I can't lie to you, Major; there will be punishment; I give you my word as an officer that none will face the death penalty."

"How long will they serve?"

"No longer than two years."

"Your word?"

"Yes."

"You give me your word as one who's lived before?"

Patton hesitated for a second, "I do."

"It's done; my life is yours; one moment, please."

Oskar returned to his men and looked at them, all standing now.

"It is over; we have fought one last glorious fight against those we despise. We shall surrender now. We shall wait a while before we return home, but when we do, we shall be free, and you shall know we have done the right thing today; the war is over. My last order to you is to lay down your arms."

His men watched him and thought for some seconds,

then began to drop and place their weapons slowly onto the ground. A full ten minutes followed of hidden Lugers and knives dropping, crunching onto the gravel; some even spat out suicide pills and crunched them underfoot.

One man dropped to the ground; he'd crushed his glass pill between his teeth, but no others followed his example.

"Good, good," Oskar said, "it has been my honour to lead you."

As he was speaking, he'd casually undone the holster clip holding his Luger in place; he took the gun, raised it to his right temple and squeezed the trigger.

Archie knew what Oskar had done during the war and still felt a lump in his throat at what he'd done for his men. Honour was found in the unlikeliest places; there were men in England he'd rate lower than Oskar for that single moment. Oskar, a psychopath, accepted responsibility for his actions and saved the lives of his men.

Dolf did have a tear in his eye.

"Even Oskar had one small piece of his soul left, some small capacity for love and honour, even Oskar at the last."

"Deus ex machina?" asked Archie.

"Not so, Archie, no less unlikely than our story itself."

"Good enough for Aristotle, though."

"Did we meet him too?"

"Before our time."

"Are you certain?"

"No."

"Oskar's final cause?"

"His nemesis, peace was not to be his time," said Archie. Patton shouted.

"No one lays a finger on these men, is that understood? These men have saved allied lives this day; there must be some honour left in this goddamn war."

Dolf approached Patton.

"General, would you allow me to introduce you to Otto Kruge, a good friend of mine. He saved my life in France and Germany. He'll direct you and your men to a place, an excavation, where this whole mess may be hidden, and a small explosion contrived to hide it forever. Otto will show you the location of a new Koenig Panzer, yours to keep. Begley put that beer down; I understand you know how to make explosions. Could you help General Patton if you have the time."

George Flowers took Aria aside and held her hands.

"It's over," he said, "we can go home now and begin to live; we'll have children and peace and be together forever."

"Yes, for now, you know if he needs us again, we must go."

"I know that too; we all know that, but we'll have children first."

"You're right, George. Can you see any place nearby where we can start trying?"

As the SS men moved forward in surrender, Archie watched them brushing the dust and dirt from each other's uniforms. He spoke to Patton.

"George, I know the need to kill better than most men; these men had one last killing left in them that had to come out. I provided some worthy targets for them, and they did it. Their war's over now. Good luck to them."

"And you?"

"No chance; there's spies, cowards, and scum aplenty where I live, and vengeance will be delivered unto them."

"Sir," came a shout from behind Archie, one of Patton's officers walked from the direction of the line of destroyed trucks. "There's two trucks in the convoy with about a hundred dead Krauts in them. Each one has a bullet in the head, been dead for about a day."

"Shit damn it, those bastard Russians are even worse than I thought," said Patton.

"Can we manage some decent burials for them and the other Germans, George?"

"We can, Archie. Yes, we can."
*
Monday 23rd July 1945 – Moscow
Joseph Vissarionovich Stalin sat in his office in Moscow,

the Kremlin, reading comrade Voloshin's report. Grigory had gone into Austria with troops and tanks, more than he'd agreed. None returned; they'd disappeared without trace apart from distant sounds of a short battle. The man he'd sent to watch Grigory was gone too; Voloshin had stayed at the Czech border and heard sounds miles distant.

Travers and Von Rundstedt fought Grigory and won, he'd remember those names, but they weren't worth his vengeance; he had better and bigger targets for that.

Grigory was a faithful ally at times, and he'd ensure he took care of his bastard by his secretary when it was born. He might take care of the secretary, Raisa, too, Grigory knew a good looking woman when he saw one, and he would have trained her well.

*

Wednesday 25th July 1945 – Zurich

A week after the Holzschlag incident, Archie collected Dolf's passport from the United States Embassy in Zurich. Inside the passport was an envelope with a one-word note Archie knew was a coded message from General Harlan Winters; he was to ring his private number from a public payphone.

He did so in a hotel across the street from the Embassy.

"Hello, Archie?" Winters answered.

"Yes, sir."

"Don't talk; listen, this passport is the last favour I can do for you. There's some free advice that comes with it, you can never return to the United States, and you watch your back, Archie, wherever you are. Sorry, and good luck, my friend."

He put the phone down.

Archie rang him back immediately; the line wasn't engaged, the phone wasn't ringing, it ceased to exist.

*

Wednesday 1st August 1945 – Zurich

They spent seven more days in Switzerland until Archie and Dolf were fully satisfied the chalet was empty, and the resources safely banked and disposable. Alex's Bank was efficient, and their fees were high yet fair for such a delicate, discreet, highly illegal and very familiar task.

Archie and Dolf left detailed instructions for investing their resources and its continued use as a trust fund for relatives of fallen comrades and pensions. They arranged the discreet demolition of Dolf's Chalet.

They left Dolf at the airport in Zurich, where he would fly to New York via Lisbon. Many Germans sought new names and lives after the war ended, but none would fly to New York, the Lion's Den so brazenly. Dolf was confident he was prepared for whatever lay ahead of him, except for the absence of Annette.

"I don't think we shall meet again, my friends," Dolf said.

"I have a feeling we may," Archie replied, "there's a link between us; we were meant to meet in Calais and were meant to meet again."

"I can't feel it," Dolf said, his brow frowning with thoughts. "If we do, it's far off. We are what we are; we cannot be others. We read some books and dreamed some dreams. For some moments, I had to be Crassus and you, Gaius; that moment has passed. If it's needed, you'll find me, or I'll find you; I'm certain of that. I wish I had Annette with me; I need her badly."

Rebecca reached up and kissed Dolf on his cheek.

"Sorry, I nearly forgot the name of my source in England," Dolf whispered a few words in Archie's ear.

"Shit!" said Archie smiling.

"Not shit! Here, I've written everything out for you," Dolf smiled and handed him an envelope.

"One final question, Archie, it always puzzled me, and Canaris too. We knew it could only have been you; it made us respect and fear you, both were wise choices. Kline, how did you know he was one of ours?"

"Klein, he was a nobody, a trooper?"

"Not Gerolf. Viktor, Viktor Kline, your teacher, how did you know he was Abwehr, my first contact in England? Even his family didn't know."

Archie looked at Dolf, his brow furrowed; he took a deep breath, looked at Rebecca and exhaled.

"I didn't; I didn't like his face, that's all. Was he related to Gerolf?"

"Yes, distantly, we checked later, but you couldn't have known that not so soon after St Nazaire."

"No, I couldn't, could I? Sometimes, I ask the wrong question and get the right answer."

*

Wednesday 1st August 1945 – Sontofen

Archie and Rebecca arrived at Sontofen the same day, having reverted to uniform after the Swiss border, using Dolf's car. They went directly to Harcourt's office.

"What the hell have you done, Travers? Peiper's here, but the British want him back."

"No, they don't; I'll sort it."

"You'd better; there's a warrant out for your arrest, now get outta here before I recognise you."

"Can I have a few minutes with Peiper?"

"No, you cannot."

"Keep the car," he shouted to Harcourt as they transferred their gear to their official one. He did salute them as they left.

*

Friday 3rd August 1945 – Noville

On their return to Southern Belgium and their unit, General Henry Paceworth awaited them. Two Red Caps, who they knew well, half-heartedly frogmarched them in to see him.

It was Archie's office, and Paceworth sat behind his desk.

"Stand," he said.

Archie and Rebecca promptly sat down.

"You've been relieved of your command, Travers, pending an inquiry into your conduct. You will both remain here in custody until…"

"I don't think so. Do you, Rebecca?"

"No, absolutely not."

"Let me tell you what's going to happen, and don't speak until I've finished," Archie said in his now perfect Conner impression.

*

Saturday 18th August 1945 – Hevlyn Mansions

Two weeks later, Mr Archie Travers sat in his flat in Hevlyn Mansions, Victoria, London, with his lover and best friend, Miss Rebecca Rochford.

They'd been medically discharged from service the previous day; ankle injuries had been endemic and sometimes useful in his team.

Archie arranged for both of his teams to be demobbed with immediate effect; there were no more beaches to scout, and no more risk was needed. There was no more intelligence to analyse, only lives to resume and lead.

Archie and Rebecca ensured individual team members received their enhanced salary for the rest of their lives from a reputable trust fund in the City of London. Each received a substantial lump sum to do with as they pleased. Somehow Archie knew none of them would sit and do nothing with their lives. If they did, they'd earned it; they were free to choose.

Lightfoot and Gabe would go home soon, as would Braydon and Roebuck. Lightfoot was marrying Madeleine Wood from the Bletchley Park team so she could go to the United States with him. Archie hadn't noticed anything about it but was happy for them; Lightfoot's knife trick had saved his life once.

Months ago, Archie had correctly assured the New Zealanders and Americans the war against Japan would end by mid-August. Atomic Bombs would secure that peace at an enormous price in human life. You shouldn't start a fight you can't win. If you show no mercy, that's what you get back.

Archie had already spoken personally to Billy and told him to have a rest and a comfortable life for six months at least. He asked him to stand ready his skills were still required, and there was work to do if they wished. Begley's unique skills might be needed too, and Archie urged him to remain outside his family business.

They'd held the best ever party at the Manor and planned reunions each year, same time, same place for as long as they wanted.

Conner resigned his commission and went on an extended holiday with a good friend; he'd be back in three weeks. Conner and Archie decided to retain the flats in Hevlyn; Archie arranged to buy his from Conner, although the transaction was largely irrelevant.

Archie had greatly upset the Establishment in England, and he was unwelcome in the United States after his encounter with Von Braun.

The death of his prisoner, Rodolf Von Rundstedt, while attempting to escape, had been less easily explained. Dolf had fallen from rocks while attempting an escape on some unidentified Alp neither could clearly recall later. Neither of them had ankles worth the name, so they could hardly chase him. They'd shot at him, and he plunged to his doom in the icy waters of a high lake, never to resurface. A bit too Conan Doyle to ring entirely true, but it was eventually accepted as fact, and all official slurs on Archie's character were withdrawn.

Archie knew what General Paceworth was as soon as he looked at him. He was Feckle. Providing him with details of Dolf's two other stashes in Switzerland, promising him full credit for their discovery, secured backdated secret orders authorising everything Archie and Rebecca had done with Dolf.

Archie had made quick visits to both locations, only to take photographs and collect the inventories. Archie had suspicions about the ultimate destination of the items and collected evidence for blackmail later if needed.

He also had a written statement from Dolf detailing the astonishingly powerful source in England that Admiral Wilhelm Canaris had used during the war. That made a useful bargaining tool, although Archie wasn't completely sure how to use it as an insurance policy against him or any of his people suffering unfortunate accidents.

Archie had sown some seeds about the inventories in Paceworth's mind he knew would be repeated and probably find the right ears eventually.

The inventories, photographs, and papers were secure in a Swiss Bank vault with specific instructions in the event of his death. Archie, Rebecca, and his friends were as safe as they'd ever been. Archie was content but without any complacency.

*

Sunday 19th August 1945 – Grasmere – the Lake District - England

The next day Archie took Rebecca to the Lake District for a week. It wasn't warm, it was cold and damp, but he wanted her to share everything he'd shared with Una. They stayed at the same Swan Hotel in Grasmere; they talked, laughed, talked more, ate, drank, relaxed and shared stories, planning a future together. A quiet, peaceful, idyllic future without killing and maybe children, but not yet.

Rebecca was an enthusiastic pupil in bed, and Una had shared great detail when tutoring her on feminine wiles. Archie lost himself in the simple act of giving pleasure to her. She was a different person from the girl he'd first met, but Una still occupied much of their minds.

They felt a sense of betrayal to Una for each moment enjoyed without her because of her absence; her presence would make this union impossible. Their lovemaking became more intense and urgent, even more frequent than with Una. They fucked everywhere and did everything he had with Una. It was gentler and longer, then quicker and rougher. Rebecca became more insatiable than Una, catching up on lost time, and they never grew tired of each other.

*

Thursday 30th August 1945 – Nice - France

Once Archie was sure all his remaining Chosen Men and women were safe and cared for, and he and Rebecca were temporarily sated, he decided to visit France and Italy. They'd try to find out who he really was.

He felt a strange reluctance in him; he'd taken considerable trouble to become Archie Travers and was fond of him. He knew his real birth was one more piece of trouble that would find him eventually. He wasn't Caesar; that had been a dream.

So it was, on the 30th of August 1945, Archie and Rebecca went to seek out the trouble, whatever form it took.

They travelled to Nice first to search local records for the murder and disappearance of the people who might be his real family.

Their pose as British Police investigating a link to a crime in England impressed the Surete, and they allocated a keen junior officer, Jean Trepel, to assist them. The junior officer was aged twenty-nine and had recently been discharged from the Free French Navy, where he'd served with the Marine Commandos First Battalion.

"You were at Dieppe?" Archie said without thinking.

"And Sword Beach," the man replied, "as were you, Major Travers."

"I wish I'd been there earlier."

"Your men made the landings easier for us."

"The anti-tank encuvee and the Casino were difficult enough for one day."

"Yes, we lost many good men, one in four, but you lost more in Calais and later."

"Maybe, I lost count long ago."

"I'll never lose count. When I returned to France, all my family were gone, killed by the Nazis as resistance fighters, men, women, and children. De Gaulle himself gave me this work. I'll learn to be a detective and hunt down those who did it."

"The war has to end sometime?" Archie said.

"You know that's not true," replied Jean. Archie looked at the man; he knew it wasn't true. "Or why would you be here?"

"This is another war."

"So is mine. Don't worry, I'll still help you. You fought more bravely in France than many Frenchmen but no more bravely than some French women," he said, nodding respectfully to Rebecca, "and I will find the name of the man who betrayed you in St. Nazaire, Madame."

*

Monday 3rd September 1945 – Nice

They finally had official access to the old files, allowed to read them and make notes. Trepel had already re-interviewed anyone still alive who could possibly know anything, and the mystery remained.

Rebecca read the file to Archie. His potential parents were Anastagio 'Gio' D'Annunzio and Alessandra D'Annunzio, born Abandonato.

"The baby boy was called Alessandro D'Annunzio.

"They were actors, performing in Nice, a production of … you have got to be fucking joking… Caesar and Cleopatra by George Bernard Shaw at the Theatre De Verdure."

"They were from the village of Sant'Alessandro in Northern Italy, near the Swiss border."

"The baby had accompanied the mother as she was still nursing him. When the officers found the bodies, the baby, its clothing and other items were missing."

"Wait, go back. How could two Italians perform an English play in France that makes no sense?"

"There's a poster here," she said, unfolding it, "it was in English, French and Italian, three nights, a different language each night. Nice attracts wealthy Italians and English in the summer; it's an affluent, exclusive audience. Here we are; most cast members did one or two versions, your father and mother were fluent in three languages. It was part of a larger cultural festival.

"Many potential witnesses or culprits left Nice when the festival finished.

"The play was adapted, translated, produced and directed by Gabriel Pascal, who claimed to be a friend of George Bernard Shaw."

"Pascal had many witnesses to his whereabouts at the time of the murders. He wasn't what he appeared to be. He was certainly not a native French or English speaker and couldn't possibly have translated the play himself as he claimed."

The photographs of the two bodies were graphic and gruesome. Their passports and photographs were still there, though, and Rebecca said she could see a likeness, but Archie couldn't. Trepel said he, too, could see the likeness; a stranger could see that sort of thing more clearly. A long knife had killed both victims, the wounds delivered from above, through the left collarbone of a kneeling victim, into the heart, a brutally quick death.

"It was a Gladius, a Roman short sword," Archie said, "an execution."

They'd been killed in their room in the Hotel Nice Beau Rivage.

"Oh, fucking hell, no. There was a third body, a maid, who was acting as a babysitter. Her skull was smashed by a blunt object, she was naked and…" Rebecca paused, reading but not talking. "Your mother was fully clothed, she was fully clothed… wait, wait, listen," she said, "another child, an older brother, name and age not known, was left at home in their village."

There were no witnesses, no motive other than kidnap, no noise, no suspects, and no clues. They went to the Hotel and Theatre personally, but the war years were so disruptive no one knew anything of that previous time, years ago.

*

Wednesday 5th September 1945 – Nice

Before he left Nice, Archie and Rebecca spoke one last time with Jean.

"I have one more detail, one name, nothing more. An English family with your royal name, Tudor, were staying in Nice at the time of the murders. They were above suspicion, of course, and they did leave Nice early the day after the killings."

"Thank you, Jean. It's a name I've heard before; their line has died out, I hear."

"That's a pity."

"No, it's another puzzle."

"Can you forgive those who killed your parents, Major Travers?"

"Never," he admitted, not even acknowledging that Jean knew why he was looking at this long forgotten crime.

"So you cannot ask more of me than you ask of yourself."

"I can tell you, you won't find what you seek," Archie said.

"I shall still seek it," Jean replied.

*

Monday 10th September 1945 – Lasnigo village - Italy

It took days to track down which village was Sant'Alessandro; several places had the same name. It was the name of a small Catholic church outside Lasnigo village, a few houses near the Swiss border. They reached the village five days after leaving Nice.

The church was the obvious place to start; they'd have local records of births, deaths, baptisms, and funerals. The young priest Father Sarti, aged about 25, made them welcome. He spoke English, German, and French, an intelligent, handsome and well-built young man. Priesthood seemed a strange calling for him, although he exuded an air of gentle calm and patience which soothed even Archie.

They found the baptism records for Alessandro and for a brother Constantin, 18 months older.

"No, there are no D'Annunzios or Abandonatos in the village," Father Sarti said, "I know; everyone comes to this Church every Sunday. I'll take you to Father Aloisio, he's retired now, but he'll remember the mother and father.

"May we use your car? The Church only has an old car, and we have no petrol; I usually walk. Nowhere is too far, but Father Aloisio has a cottage high on a hill."

Archie felt apprehensive at meeting a Father Aloisio in

an isolated cottage; he guessed Rebecca felt the same. They found the old man tending his neat vegetable garden haltingly and stiffly. He had the same gentle feel about him as Sarti. He welcomed them into his small, sparsely furnished home.

"Please, you must have some wine," he said, "I have few visitors. You're lucky I have some left," he said, pouring two small glasses of red for Archie and Rebecca. The man's voice had a calming effect on Archie, it reminded him of when he'd first met Billy at the Savoy and he'd told him how to behave.

Neither Archie nor Rebecca appreciated red wine, but they drank it to avoid offence and in deference to their host.

"You want to know about your parents," he said, sitting down, "yes, I've been waiting for you, are you, Constantin? I hope you're Alessandro; I have prayed so much for your return every day.

"Let me look at you, here, kneel next to me; my eyes are not so good… you must be Alessandro, you must be; you could be your father before me. I've prayed for you every day."

Tears flowed from Archie and Rebecca, Archie buried his head in the Father's lap, and the old priest stroked his hair.

"Yes, your brother favoured your mother in her looks; you're the image of your father."

Father Aloisio remembered the D'Annunzios well; he'd married them, they were born in Lasnigo from local families, neither had siblings, and their parents were long dead. They were talented actors and singers even in childhood but had no fame or wealth; their roles in Nice were their big chance to be noticed. They'd taken Alessandro with them as he was still being fed from the breast, but Constantin, aged less than two, remained here with a local family.

The deaths and theft of the child were an evil beyond any explanation.

Archie composed himself and dried his eyes with the handkerchief Rebecca had given him for Spud a lifetime ago.

"Father, where is Constantin now?"

"I don't know, my son; he was adopted by a Swiss gentleman, a good, wealthy man who was childless, a good Catholic too. Alexandre De Cyrene."

"Constantin… my brother is in England, and he's already my friend; he's safe. Alex raised him as well as any man could. Father, do you know anything about my lineage?"

"No, my son, there are no noble bloodlines in Lasnigo, only the old tale that no one believes; it may please you, but it's not true. Julius Caesar fathered a bastard by his favourite mistress and made her flee from Rome before he was killed. She came here, of course, and lived in secret, as she did in countless villages across Italy. One day, he will return, and Rome will rule the world again."

"An old wive's tale, we call them in England."

"Do you know who took you, my son?"

"I know some of it; I know some of those who hid me."

"Did they… no, I won't ask those questions here, my son."

"They didn't use me, Father, and they cannot answer any questions now. They're all dead."

"Is there anything you need to confess, Alessandro?"

"No."

"Let me look in your eyes," the old priest said and studied Archie's eyes as closely as anyone ever had, even Una.

"I can see no trace of sin in your eyes," Father Aloisio said after a full five minutes. "Nothing that requires penance. Not one sin. It is said that vengeance is the Lord's, are we not also told to do the Lord's work for him?"

They spoke a little longer with the old priest, and he reflected on the parents, their habits, and personalities, telling what he could remember; there were no other sources of that information.

"And this is your wife with you?" he asked.

"No, we are one forever, but… I had a wife and lost her in the war."

"You will see her again."

"I hope so."

"You will." The old priest said with conviction, then excused himself as he needed to have his afternoon nap. "It will not be in heaven, though, and that is a puzzle for me," he added as he shuffled to his bedroom.

When they reached the Church again, Archie had thought of more questions for the younger priest.

"Father, you and your colleague speak English in a particular way. Did you both learn in the same place?"

"We both went to the same college in England, Blairs, which is near to your Aberdeen."

"Yes, I thought I heard a trace of an accent; thank you."

"Alessandro, Mr Travers, you know your full name at baptism now."

"Yes."

"Alessandro Augusto Di Julio D'Annunzio. It means *Defender of man, born in the Month of August to the Julii.*"

"It's a name that tells me a tale I may not wish to hear."

"And do you know who you are now?"

"No, but I know more today than yesterday."

"As do I, and I must tell you what I know now. Father Aloisi is the kindest, gentlest soul I have ever known. He can see sin in any man; he is never wrong."

"Until today," said Archie.

Rebecca put her hand in the crook of Archie's arm and moved closer to him.

"No, Alessandro, he is never wrong, never. I have been told he met Pacelli himself decades ago before he became Pontif. Pacelli could not hold his gaze. One of the Savoy family passed through Lasnigo ten years ago and attended mass; he ran out from the front pew when he saw Aloisi. I saw that. I know it. He is never wrong."

"Until today."

"I can only tell you what I know, Alessandro; it's for you

to find the meaning of it."

*

Archie drove the car about a mile from the Church and parked on a wide piece of road that looked down onto Lasnigo.

"Am I mad, Rebecca?" he asked.

"No."

"Are Sarti and Aloisi mad then?"

"...No," she said after some hesitation.

"What am I missing then?"

"It's perfectly simple; Aloisi senses sin like I sense you."

"I'm with you so far."

"Sin can be atoned for, yes?"

"I can imagine that."

"You atoned for your sins before you committed them, so they don't show; you're probably still in credit, so to speak."

"That's why I love you, Rebecca. You make perfect sense of anything."

"Thank you. Or it could be you killed a bunch of cunts who deserved to die anyway."

*

Monday 17th September 1945 - Lasnigo – Italy

A week later, Father Sarti woke early, as was his habit, but the noise outside his old and weather worn church was unusual.

A group of workmen were unloading a truck and preparing to carry out long-needed repairs on his building. He hadn't arranged for any such work; there was no money for that.

As the leader of the men told him it had all been paid for already, another truck pulled up with a new car on it.

At the same time, another truck pulled up at Father Aloisio's cottage to carry out repairs, not before unloading six cases of the best red wine in Italy. A Cabernet Sauvignon from Tebuta San Guido not released publicly yet. The vineyard owner swore it would become the best.

Father Aloisio would enjoy it for many years; three

cases of twelve bottles would arrive every month.

Chapter Nineteen

Thursday 20th September 1945 - The Cottage

Archie arranged to meet Conner at the Cottage as soon as he arrived back in England. It was a cold evening, and the fire was roaring to warm up the house for the first time since the previous spring.

Rebecca made three mugs of tea.

Conner was intrigued and waited for Archie to speak. Archie was nervous and didn't know quite where to start.

"Just fucking tell him," Rebecca said.

"You know who you are now, then?" Conner asked.

"I know who we both are," Archie said.

Telling Conner what he knew of their birth was one of the best moments of Archie's life, third only to meeting Rebecca and then Una.

They embraced for longer and more closely than they'd ever dared before. They both cried, as did the watching Rebecca.

"That would explain the bond that was always more than friendship but less than sexual," Conner said.

"A bloody good job we never fucked each other," Archie said.

"Can I say something?" asked Rebecca.

"Yes, of course," Conner said.

"I love you both even more," she said.

"We have questions for Alex, though," said Archie, "not that he's likely to answer them."

"Why were our parents killed," Conner said, "why were you taken and kept? How mad was Tudor? How did he find you, choose you to hate? Why was I trained as I was for what I did."

"We can tell no one else, not yet, not until we know why," Archie said, "not until we understand it."

"Agreed, we were best friends and still are," said Conner.

Archie embraced Conner again, crying again. Una

wasn't there to see this.

*

Wednesday 26th September 1945 – Italy

On the way to see Alex in Zurich, Conner and Archie visited the graves of their parents with Rebecca. It was a simple act, not of remembrance; rather, it was of absence, and it only fuelled their curiosity further. All they had were two copies of passport photographs.

"No news of Annette?" Conner asked.

"Nothing from my sources, and Dolf would have let me know somehow."

*

Thursday 27th September 1945 - Zurich

They were in Zurich the next day and drove to Alex's bank.

"He's not there," Archie said as they climbed the steps leading to it.

"What? Where is he then?" asked Conner.

"He's not anywhere."

Mr Basile, one of Alex's many assistants, met them at the door.

"I am sorry, there has been a terrible tragedy; Mr De Cyrene is dead, a heart attack, this morning at his home."

No one believed a word of it.

They stayed for the funeral and received reassurance that their assets were safe. Alex had also bequeathed all his considerable assets very specifically, equally split between Conner, Archie, Rebecca and… Una. Alex continued to confound them, even from the grave.

Alex certainly wasn't around anymore; there was nothing they could do about that. The mystery remained, but it was certain now that someone other than Alex was making sure they could ask him no questions.

Archie withdrew into himself a hundred times, reaching out for the presence he'd felt briefly, and nothing appeared.

Archie and Rebecca stayed in Zurich for a few days, feeling nothing, then journeyed to Rome to see what he might feel there.

Archie still felt nothing; there was a door, a doorway, a path he'd seen once, and now it was gone.

They visited the famous sites in Rome, and still, nothing came to him. So, on their last night, they chose to stay in the best room in the best hotel and have the best meal they could find. They drank too much and slept too deeply.

He could hear Rebecca stirring in the night next to him, having a dream, an argument, a nightmare, talking and mumbling; she was upset and tearful in her sleep.

He decided to wake her rather than let her feel bad, even in sleep.

She woke and thrashed around with her arms, hitting him hard, hurting him.

"Oh, sorry," she said, confused, "where are we? When is it? I love you more than anything that exists."

"I know that I feel the same."

"But one instant's thought of Una destroys me, shames me," she continued.

"I know, I know," he said, hugging her, "She deserves life, and I would give all I have for one more minute in her arms, one last moment with her. Can you forgive me for that and stay with me?"

"Of course, that's not it; it's not over; I feel it now, can't you?"

"I can feel you, that's all. I can feel you a bit more if you want?" he said, kissing her tears away.

"No, listen, it's important; I have to tell you before I forget it again. All the time we've been here, I've concentrated on helping you feel something. When I drank too much, I lost control and drifted deeper into my own mind.

"Listen, Pompey came back, you know it, you felt it. You felt Crassus; you can still feel him. I can't feel him; I can feel you feeling him. Does that make any sense at all? You can feel Alessandro, you can feel the Julii, I know it. I know it because I can still feel the absence of emotion in me, the disassociation from my surroundings, the aloof nature I felt was my right, my birthright. I felt the certainty of power, the superiority of my ancestry. The power those thoughts gave me, the power to rule.

"I can feel myself giving it all up for you and placing myself in your complete control, your thrall, your willing thrall. Not sought, not taken, given freely to you and you alone."

Her voice had changed, almost the same; the intonation was different, like a person no longer speaking their native tongue. Archie turned on the light by the bed. Rebecca had closed her eyes, the eyelashes impossibly long as they always were, the eyes moving wildly, seen even through the closed lids.

"I was Cleopatra Philopator," she said, "absolute ruler of Egypt, the reincarnation of the Goddess Isis. I forsook all of that for you, a man, the greatest man who ever lived but still a man. I forsake all of that again now as I speak to you. I would forsake it all a hundred times if I could give you that one minute with your lover as you seek it. After your death, I took others, but I would not be the subordinate of any man until I saw you and would never be to another until I saw you again.

"I dreamt it once as a child and never told another until now. I never knew what it meant; I dreamt it again, here in Rome."

"A dream, another dream put in your mind by a place and time, still a dream," he said.

She ignored him and carried on talking.

"I wonder who Una was?"

*

As that conversation took place, a memory searched for information from the recent past.

Rebecca Rochford had characteristics not yet fully considered. That knowledge signified danger yet couldn't be fully understood or explained.

The information came as it always did. Yes, Una could indeed be Unitas, the bastard daughter of Marcus Tullius Cicero, an implacable opponent of Julius.

Julius had become aware of her when she was aged only 15, yet beautiful and beguiling despite her innocence, and he decided to despoil her to spite Cicero in his self-righteous pomposity. However, when he first laid eyes on her closely, inhaled her fragrance and spoke to her, he'd been so instantly struck by her beauty and wit that he kept her as his mistress.

He took no other until his death on the 15th of March, 44 BC.

Unitas died the day after Julius did, still bearing his boy child, an act of wanton revenge by his enemies; neither she nor the child could be allowed to survive.

No one could know; another child, a girl, had already been born in secret and kept safe.

The knowledge existed; the events had been witnessed two thousand years ago.

*

Rebecca demanded she be allowed to make love to him like never before. When she was done, she collapsed on top of him, sweaty, breathless and fulfilled; she stayed on top of him, he remained inside her and slept. She'd been rough with him.

*

In the following months, rudderless, they reflected on the knowledge, suspicions and questions they had, and it distracted them from their intended purpose.

They went on long holidays in the sun, Portugal, a small peace-loving country that had, like Britain, punched above its weight for centuries in exploration. The people were hugely friendly; they sat on empty beaches and stayed in a private villa. Rebecca tried to teach him how to swim. Nevertheless, he still sank relentlessly. He considered buying a house there, a vineyard maybe.

Something always drew him to England. To Bletchley, the Manor, the Cottage, the freezer in Hertford, the Doctors in Harley Street and the Scientists he now employed full time. To the bunker he was excavating in Scotland, the two in Austria only Dolf knew about. He even had his own rocket scientist.

To those rose bushes, to those ghosts that haunted him still, to those ghosts he'd not yet made. If we can find those who ruined Freddie's sister, maybe that'll be vengeance enough, he thought, but he knew it could never be that easy; trouble finds me; it always does.

Archie had a new mantra and still knew how to plan far, far ahead.

*

July 1946 – Dachau - Germany

Archie and Rebecca went to Dachau towards the end of July 1946 to visit Jochen Peiper. He was held there under sentence of death following his conviction for the Malmedy massacre. Archie had originally intended to apologise for swapping him for Dolf and to organise an escape attempt.

He was surprised to see Jochen so relaxed, and he explained he had a good friend in the United States. A friend organising his well-being and appeal against the sentence. His benefactor was anonymous, of course, but Archie knew all his names well.

The war had seen things done wrong by all sides. Archie had done plenty wrong; he'd cast and recast his moral chains so often he could no longer tell his limits, one day from the next.

He could tell that Jochen being tried and found guilty by paper pushers who'd never seen action was wrong and hoped he'd be spared execution. The war has to end sometime, doesn't it? Maybe his would, too; it couldn't go on forever, could it?

*

Tuesday 24th December 1946 – The Manor

Five months later, Archie sat at his desk in his sealed and private room in the extension he had purpose built at the rear of the Manor. It was midday on Christmas Eve, 1946.

He'd bought the Manor House from the Government and refurbished it to his precise specifications. Not lavishly, only functional for his and Rebecca's needs;

Conner was a frequent visitor.

He'd also bought the cottage, for him and Rebecca alone, the Manor for reunions and visitors. The cottage would be private and clean; no more dirty work there. He'd held a reunion in the autumn; everyone had been there. It was as good a time as he'd enjoyed since Una's death, but her absence still cast a cloud over him.

Archie had invested his assets wisely, and crude work was beginning on extending and giving life. Decades of work lay ahead; money was available if only science could catch up.

He'd postponed his actions time and again, but the search for Alice's abusers would resume soon. The initial euphoria of his life and wealth wasn't lasting. Death and savage revenge were ready, waiting patiently for those who deserved it, and he was born to deliver it. A rocket scientist working in the United States had to feel loss and then die, as did a member of the British Royal Family, who had treacherously retained his German roots and sympathies during the war.

He stood up and walked to the wall where he displayed the impressive painting Dolf sent him as a Christmas present.

'Vercingetorix throws down his arms at the feet of Julius Caesar' by Lionel Royer.

He wasn't an admirer of art, but to receive that painting from a man such as Dolf pleased him; he could even see a slight resemblance. Royer had never seen Caesar; of course, any likeness meant nothing, yet it amused him and Rebecca too.

Rebecca was doing last minute shopping for Christmas and would be back soon; for once, he'd let her go somewhere alone because he knew she was collecting his surprise present. Conner and Alan would join them on Christmas Day, a private moment when they could relax and care nothing for convention.

Archie had 'obtained' a copy of the film Caesar and Cleopatra by George Bernard Shaw and directed by George

Pascal; they'd watch that tonight and think together. He'd moved the thinking chair to the Manor.

Tudor was mad, but Archie and Dolf weren't; they'd trapped Grigory because he was crazy and reckless; it was over. He couldn't explain why or how Tudor chose to steal him, but there were lots of things he couldn't explain; that's why he needed so many good friends. Archie Travers, Alessandro, whatever was a man, no more than that; there was nature and science, knowledge and strength, nothing else.

He'd had luck, good and bad; he'd been in the right place at the right time, nothing else.

His mind worked in unusual ways sometimes; he had read, dreamed and imagined, nothing else.

Maybe his senses were better than some people, most even nothing else.

He'd felt no danger since the encounter with Grigory, no hint of a threat, no dreams, no voices, just freedom and safety. He'd never felt better; he was at his best. He should have been content.

'Your best is no use to anyone; your worst is what makes you useful. Idiot.'

He wasn't content.

There was still an anger inside Archie that spoiled his mood. Rebecca would erase the mood when she returned, but it still nagged at him that morning.

He'd finally managed to acquire a full inventory of the items the British Team had recovered from Dolf's stashes in Switzerland. The inventory held by the Foreign and Commonwealth Office showed only about a quarter of what he knew was there. It wasn't the theft that bothered him; the self-righteous hypocrisy of the thieves infuriated him. The sheer number of people involved, their status in society, and that they were already wealthy irked him intensely. These people routinely passed judgement on others while accepting no judgement on themselves, no accountability for their actions. A few of them might have to suffer, maybe more than a few.

Archie had delivered summary justice many times, and it was justice nonetheless. A few bystanders had suffered too, not maliciously so, no more than inconvenient accidents, he felt.

He'd tried to put the past in a box, his War Box, he called it. New things kept appearing, and each time they did, he had to open the old box to store the new. The old stale facts leapt into his mind, and it took time and real effort to force them back in.

Today he'd found out that John Winant, the former United States Ambassador to Britain, had separated from his wife, was deeply in debt, writing his memoirs and suffering from depression by all accounts. Another good man thrown away. He'd sort the money problems out after Christmas; it wouldn't take much, perhaps a job to go with the funding, that shouldn't insult the man.

The poisonous grudges and slights poured out of the War Box into his mind during breakfast as he read his letters and the newspapers.

Winston Churchill, no longer Prime Minister, cast aside before the war was even over by small, self-serving men.

Major Colin McVean Gubbins, the War Office could find no suitable position for him after the war and the Special Operations Executive was shut down by the same small men. He was now managing director of a carpet company!

Brigadier Claude Nicholson dead in a Prisoner of War Camp, perhaps even by his own hand.

President Franklyn Delano Roosevelt dead after a massive stroke on April 12th, 1945, barely days before the victory in Europe was achieved.

Harry Hopkins was finally beaten by his cancer and dead by January 29th, 1946, aged only 55, a few short months after the war ended.

The Americans had refused Archie permission to attend the funeral, which hurt badly. That was another cheap trick, but he'd visit the grave and Roosevelt's when he made his planned clandestine visit through Mexico the next year.

General George 'Old Blood and Guts' Patton suffered a car accident on the 8th of December 1945, hours before he was due to fly home. Yeah right. He died on December 21st, 1945 and was buried at the US Military Cemetery in Hamm, Luxembourg, with his men.

Archie and Rebecca attended the funeral, among thousands, the last time they'd ever worn their uniforms. They stood at the rear, avoiding the movie cameras, photographers, and senior staff. Archie's Medal of Honour attracted some interest from the enlisted men they stood with, and they swapped a few stories and handshakes. When the cemetery was nearly empty, Archie approached the grave, still not entirely filled with earth, and he meant to throw his medal in and cover it with two good handfuls of earth.

"No!" Rebecca shouted as she saw him, "Una will want to see that."

He placed the medal in his pocket and walked away hand in hand with Rebecca.

He'd written a letter to Patton's widow, nothing much, just his condolences. A few weeks later, she sent him one of George's old pistols, which he'd wanted Archie to have. She explained it wasn't one of the fancy expensive ones he carried for effect; it was one he'd fired in anger in the first war.

Add that list to the list of undeserving survivors, Stalin, alive and well, responsible for more murders than Hitler. Emperor Hirohito, alive and still a fucking Emperor. Caesar would have dragged the snivelling coward, like a dog, naked on a leash through the crowded, baying, spitting streets of Rome.

His list was no recipe for a peaceful retirement in a man such as Archie Travers, a man who knew the meaning of vengeance.

Ike had done well, Archie conceded to himself, he no longer needed Archie, that was okay, he'd stood on toes with Von Braun, and he accepted responsibility for that and the consequences.

Whole countries had been given to Stalin, for fuck's sake, Poland. We started the war for Poland and then gave it, lock, stock and fucking barrel to Stalin.

Then came the French; he knew now who had betrayed Rebecca's team to the Germans. He was second on his list, an aspiring junior Minister in the new French Government.

Archie was going to end a few lives, and nothing would be attributable to him or his; he'd learned a few more tricks since the war, keeping your hands visibly clean. He had limitless resources; what use power if you don't use it?

'And thine eye shall not pity; but life shall go for life, eye for eye, tooth for tooth, hand for hand, foot for foot.'

The Bible was a fairy story; there were still some good lines worth stealing in it.

'A man should know his own worth but not be content with it.'

Yes, he was still somebody, somebody to fear, and then he spoke aloud to himself.

"It has to stop, surely. Dolf has stopped, Jochen has stopped, I cannot... kill... the whole... world. I'm tearing myself apart and the few people I love with me. No... I will stop. Then, I'll devote my life to making things live; I'll make Rebecca happy. I'll buy an island and let Conner and Alan live on it. I'll use my resources to discover a way to make life from death. I'll make Una again from her cells and tissue; she may never know me, she may never know herself, but I will make her live again.

"Science will succeed in doing that, and I'll come back, and I know beyond all doubt, Una, and I will love again. We'll both read what I've written, and we'll love each other again.

"What if trouble finds me? It always finds me, always."

*

He felt something in his mind, in the hairs on the back of his neck. Rebecca was home, he left the room and went to the door, the car wasn't there, why had he felt her if... she was gone, he knew it, she was gone.

He looked at the clock; she was late back. She was

never late. Panic seized his gut, and he phoned Conner.

"Conner, it's Archie, Rebecca's gone, she's gone."

"Calm down, calm down, I'll…" The phone went dead.

"Shit!" Archie ran to the private room, pulling the single lever that secured the four separate bolts on the metal door behind him.

At his desk, he phoned Conner again; his own line was dead now. The lights went out; he flipped the switch on the battery powered emergency lights and opened his gun cabinet, his sniper rifle, and three Thompsons. He took two Thompsons, sat at his desk and began checking the mechanisms and the loading safeties off.

The secure private room had no windows and was armour and lead plated. A tank would break in eventually. He'd also installed an escape hatch below his desk, and a small tunnel led to the workshop. A second alternative exit led further into the wood behind the old practice field.

He sat at the desk; he needed to plan; he had time.

The emergency lights went out; no, that can't happen, they run off batteries, he told himself. The heavy steel door clicked and opened just enough to let in a chink of daylight. No, that can't happen. A tiny spark shone from the daylight, and he reached for his guns.

Nothing happened; he couldn't move, he couldn't breathe, no, he could breathe, but only shallow breaths. He could feel a tingling, like pins and needles and his vision was impaired by some sparkling phosphorescence in front of his eyes.

The shape of a man appeared in the doorway; in the gloom, Archie could see no detail, but the man had no weapon on show.

'Cocky? Good, that gives me a chance.'

"Hello, Teddy."

'What? Teddy?'

"It is your due that this is undertaken in… person."

'That voice is familiar, and there's a smell, aftershave?'

"There is a regret that this must happen."

'Oh shit, it must be God.'

"No, Teddy, we are not God… though in time, we may become as one."

'I didn't fucking say anything; I can't move anything.'

Archie started his mantra.

"No time for that, Teddy."

'It's Mr Heywood, my old Latin Teacher. What the…?'

The door opened wider, and in the increasing light from outside, the face of the figure showed a sincere, genuine smile. The voice, he now recognised as Mr Heywood's, was firm, soft, gentle, protective and empathetic. It entranced and calmed him.

"No time, Teddy… but there is some pity; let that comfort you and know that you succeeded in your task. This world will never know what you did for it; if it did, it would pity you, but that cannot stay this hand. You cannot be allowed to continue your war. You cannot be allowed to become who you might be, not now."

The hand raised, another tiny spark flew and… Archibald Travers 'Teddy' Austin, Alessandro Augusto Di Julio D'Annunzio, was no more. The body that sat transfixed in that chair would never draw breath again, no Mad Mike to shield him from fate, this time, no big cunt to stand behind.

No blood.

No wounds.

No unnaturally tangled mess of arms and legs.

His arms were still firmly in place on the sides of the chair, and his eyes were still open. His face still showed that elegant, raffish, knowing and honest smile he aspired to.

On the wall behind him, the painting showed Caesar seated in the same position as Archie, imperious, stately, lordly. Archie might have liked that irony.

*

Sunday 31st July 1966 – London

Billy Perry lay at peace in his final minutes on the 31st of July 1966.

His daughter Grace and her husband, David, a good

honest man, had seen him with his grandchildren that afternoon in the Marie Curie Cancer Hospice in Barnet.

The previous day he'd watched England against West Germany in the World Cup Final on television. George and Henry Flowers had watched it with him; they could have had tickets but chose to watch it with him. They were the best of men; he'd seen them both play for the Orient after the war. With a fair chance and no war, they'd have been good enough for West Ham. George remained with Aria, and Henry had married a girl from the Bletchley team as well, Lizzy Quinn, and had the war not happened, they'd never have met. They were successful businessmen now.

To see England beat the Germans with three Hammers playing was the pinnacle of his life, well, nearly. The real pinnacle had been as the friend and comrade of Archie Travers and his like.

He'd not seen him, Rebecca or Conner for what… twenty years, Una for longer. They'd gone, disappeared, all three in less than a day, Christmas Eve 1946. They were dead; he knew that then; he felt their absence before he knew they'd gone.

Mary Murphy was still well and hadn't married again. Molly was a fine woman now, married with children of her own, still living in the house Archie had given them and next door too. They still acted as caretakers for the Manor and the Cottage; Archie's trust fund had been explicit.

For a while, they'd all believed they'd come back; they couldn't conceive of anything powerful enough to take on those three and win. He felt their absence in the same way as Una's; they were dead, had to be.

Asgeir returned to Norway with Briony, and he became a member of the Norwegian Parliament, the Storting. He was ever a friend to the English, and he fiercely sought out any corruption, waste or disloyalty. He kept his war name on his return; he'd earned that name in blood.

Gabe and Lightfoot returned to America. Gabe became a backwoodsman again and never left those woods except to return to Bletchley for reunions. He talked more now.

Lightfoot had taken Madeleine Wood to the United States as his GI bride and had happily settled outside Dallas. Their son was on the shortlist for a NASA flight but hadn't made it yet.

Harlan Winters contacted Billy after Archie's disappearance and tried his best to find any of them. Even with his connections, he could find no trace of any of them anywhere. He found a Swiss company with a trust fund and specific instructions on who to look after and how, but nothing more than that. The police showed no interest at all; Rebecca's parents were distraught, she'd still seen them infrequently. Archie and Conner had no family they ever spoke of. The police said they were wealthy adults and could have gone anywhere. The truth was Billy was only an old Sergeant and could pull no strings.

Very early one morning, Billy received a telephone call from Dolf, who apologised for not keeping in touch; he was in hiding too. He'd known of Archie's disappearance and feared whoever could do that. He wished Billy good luck and long life and hadn't contacted him again.

Billy felt most for Alan, he was nobody after the war, and he couldn't complain about the loss of a male partner, not then, not even in 66. He'd come to a few of the reunions. Billy would never believe he'd topped himself, eating a poisoned apple, for fuck's sake. He'd put money on Special Branch being involved, the crooked bastards.

Archie would have stopped that. He'd have killed anyone who meant Alan any harm; he'd have known what to do.

Roebuck and Brayden returned to New Zealand and bought a Vineyard in Marlborough. They returned to England for each reunion even after Archie disappeared, and they'd taken two girls, Marjorie and Josephine, with them as their wives and lived there happily. There was something about the nucleus of that team that always brought them back together, something that couldn't bear the separation.

A reunion was paid for every year, and everyone still

made time to come. So many lives had been thrown away during the war, and many more when it ended. No one knew who Archie was. Churchill hadn't been forgotten yet, but who remembered who Gubbins was now, Harry Hopkins, Winant?

Something was still going on, though. He'd been diagnosed with cancer a year earlier, and the next day a private hospital had approached him to offer expert treatment and care.

He knew the money came in every month somehow. He was well provided for, but the speed and nature of the help he and his family received after his diagnosis could only be Archie's doing. Only Archie could plan for something happening twenty years after he died.

*

Billy would never forget hearing Bobby Darin singing *'Mack the Knife'* back in 1959. It was the same tune he'd heard Archie whistle and hum many a time more than fifteen years before that. Maybe the song was about Archie? Maybe Archie wrote it?

Even stranger than that, he'd first heard the song on a jukebox in the *Blind Beggar*. He was there for Nat Cairney's funeral, a proper East End affair, black horses and carriage, the full Monty. Billy sat next to Eileen, Nat's daughter, who'd been as good as a mum to Grace.

He heard some old drunk shouting.

"That's it, that's the tune; he was whistling it when I saw him walking away, a soldier, I tell you. The coppers never listened to me, I told them, the bastards."

"Who's that idiot?" said Billy, about to chin the fool for disrespecting Nat.

"Ignore him, Billy," Eileen said as two others showed him the door, "he's not worth it. That's Percy Baker, Norah's brother. You remember the old brass who got knifed during the war. He swears he saw who did it, and the coppers ignored him. You should know him; he was a porter in the hospital where Grace was born."

"Yes, I remember him. The bastard offered me money

for Grace."

"He did a lot of that, Billy. Norah helped him an'all. They said the kiddies would go to good homes, but they sold them on for a tidy profit to some Children's Home in Holloway, I think. He always was a wrong un."

"Yes, he was, wasn't he. Well, I must be going, Eileen; I told Grace I'd look after the grandkids."

Billy hugged Eileen and shook a few hands, none of them clean; on the way out, he still didn't belong there anymore.

A week later, Percy Baker was found with his throat slit in an alleyway near Leman Street Police Station. Billy did it, for old times' sake.

Archie Travers made things happen, always did, and couldn't help it. Even after he was dead.

*

Still, seventy-six was a damn good age, though, for a man who'd seen two wars, three, if you counted the private one. By God, he'd done some stuff.

As he drifted off from consciousness, Billy knew what was coming and thought he'd give up that World Cup yesterday for a few more minutes with his long departed friends. Yes, he would do that for the chance to say a proper goodbye to Archie. To tell him he'd been the son he never had or to hear him say he'd been the father Archie never had... he almost prayed.

'Nah. Fuck you; if I see you or any other fucking God, there'll be harsh words between us, and you wouldn't like that, I can fucking tell you. Yeah, you need to watch out for me, mate, I'm still somebody, and I ain't frightened of you. Yeah, you come and have a go if you think you're up to it. Archie Travers taught me a thing or two. Veni huc et tempta si te satis durum censes.'

The End

The Saga continues in the Presence of Hope Trilogy

Reviews

I'm an independent author who conceives, writes, rewrites, edits, proofreads and publishes his own work. The approval of discerning readers is, therefore, greatly appreciated. If you've enjoyed this novel and wish to leave a review, then please do so on Amazon.co.uk or Amazon.com.

For further information, see the author's website.

RichardAMcDonaldAuthor.com

Or contact the author at

Richard@RichardAMcDonaldAuthor.com

Other titles by Richard A. McDonald are available on Amazon in paperback and Kindle formats.

Printed in Great Britain
by Amazon